BOYS OF WINTER

SHERIDAN ANNE

Sheridan Anne
Dynasty: Boys of Winter #1

Copyright © 2021 Sheridan Anne
All rights reserved
First Published in 2021
Anne, Sheridan
Dynasty: Boys of Winter #1

This book is a work of fiction. Names, characters, places, and incidents are products of the author's imagination. Any resemblance to actual events or persons, living or dead, is entirely coincidental.

No part of this book may be reproduced, stored in a retrieval system or transmitted in any form or by any means, without prior permission in writing of the publisher, nor be otherwise circulated in any form of the binding or cover other than in which it is published, and without a similar condition, including this condition, being imposed on the subsequent purchaser.

Cover Design: Covers by Aura
Photographer: Valua Vitaly
Editing: Heather Fox
Proofreading: Noemi Vallone & Danielle Stansbury
Editing & Formatting: Sheridan Anne

DYNASTY

*To my children who are currently being assholes,
Please, please, please stop fighting over the one little blanket. There are fifty more in the cupboard. Also, I love you.*

1

The sharp sting of a man's hand slapping down across my leather-clad ass stops me in the middle of the darkened alleyway. A wicked smile instantly spreads across my face. This is exactly what I've been waiting for, exactly what I've been craving.

A thrill pulses deep inside of me, steadily growing and rising to the surface as I run my thumb over the gold-coated brass knuckles that rest comfortably over my fingers. Above each of my knuckles, the chunky metal is masked as four beautifully wicked rings, allowing me to get away with murder. It's my best kept secret and yet my worst.

My thumb skims over the black gemstone and circles the skull that sits just above my first knuckle, knowing damn well that this pretty skull is going to be engraved into this fucker's face for the next week and a half.

The adrenaline burns within me like a scorching fire, ready to fuck up everything in its path. I can't wait.

I spin on my heel, my black thigh-high boots making the task harder than it needs to be, but after a few years of practice in these bad boys, I have it down to a fine art.

I take in the man who stands before me, looking at me like his next non-consensual meal. I slowly run my tongue over my deep plum lips, watching how he tracks my every little movement. "Hey baby," he says, positioning himself right in front of me and putting on a show for his drunk friends. One even going as far as to rub his hands together like the pervy creep that he is.

I wonder what they would do if they knew I was only seventeen. Some might pull away in horror, while others would get off on it.

My show-stopping grin splits across my face, and I watch as he becomes suspicious. His eyes narrow, and he hesitates for just a moment. Guys like this don't expect a woman to play along; they live off their fear. He wants me to run. He wants me panicked and fretting because a chick who doesn't fight back is one hell of an easy target, and this guy, he's fucking with the wrong girl. I've never been an easy target and I'm sure as hell not about to start.

I'm not the girl who runs; I'm the one who hangs around to see how many heads I can make roll. I'm the girl who seeks it out. I'm *that* bitch. The one who guys like this need to watch out for.

I reach out and run my fingers from his shoulder across his chest as his eyes widen a fraction. Right about now, he's assuming this will be the easiest conquest of his life. "Hey to you too," I murmur in a purr, my eyes becoming hooded, letting him know that he can have whatever the fuck he wants ... at least that's what I'll let him think.

His hand falls to my exposed waist, pulling me in hard against his sweaty body, making me want to gag. I knew I shouldn't have worn a cropped tank tonight, but I couldn't resist. Leather, latex, chokers, and cropped shirts are my jam, add a deep plum lipstick and a high pony, and I'm down for anything. "What's a pretty girl like you doing out so late in a place like this?"

"Oh, you know girls like me," I say with a sickeningly flirty laugh as I walk my fingers up his chest, his eyes becoming more and more hooded by the second, his sleazy friends watching on with deep interest. I quickly glance their way, throwing a seductive smile at each of them, counting them as I go. "We're always down for a little bit of trouble."

Five altogether. This is going to be interesting.

My comment has his four friends moving in with excited smiles. Every single one of them assumes that they've hit the lottery and are about to get their dicks wet, but they've got another thing coming. I'm itching to feel flesh beneath my fist, and these fuckers just became my next high.

"What do you say?" One dickhead says, coming right up behind me and squishing me between himself and the guy who still holds my waist. He grinds his dick against the leather of my pants making me want to hurl. "Wanna go for a ride? I bet a girl like you could handle five guys. I swear, we'll take it easy on you, but sometimes I just can't help myself—I like it rough."

"Mmmm," I moan, tilting my head back toward him, my eyes flashing up to his with interest. "Sounds like fun. You know, I've never taken on five guys at once, but I guess there's always a first for everything."

A sick excitement flashes in his eyes, but before he gets a chance to say another word, my elbow slams back into his stomach. I twist in his arms, before bringing my knee up into his balls. He's down on the ground before the others have even flinched into action.

The first guy, who thought it was a smart move to put his hands on my ass, reaches for me, but I spin back around with my brass knuckles flying straight for his face. My fist connects with his nose, and the familiar crunch of bones breaking beneath my force is enough to send a jolt of electricity pulsing through me. Fuck, I love that.

Blood spurts from his nose, and despite the darkness of the night sky, I'm still able to see the blood pooling in his hands. "You fucking bitch," he spits, backing up and collapsing against a wall as he groans in pain, but I'm not done with him yet—not even close.

I only got a small taste of his bones breaking. I need more. So much more.

I go for his ribs.

My fist slams against his ribs, and he instantly doubles over in pain, his friend calling for him to man the fuck up and fight back, but there's no way. Even before his broken nose, he wouldn't have been able to handle me.

He crumbles to the ground, his hands flying out to catch his fall, and before he gets a chance to move them, I crush them beneath my boot, listening to the sweet, poetic sound of his little finger snapping like a twig. He cries out in pain and I grin down at him. "Maybe next time you'll think twice before grabbing my ass, or any other girls' for that matter. Ever heard of a thing called consent?"

He groans, tears springing from his eyes.

"Yeah, that's what I thought," I laugh, turning to look back at the other asshole who remains on the ground behind me. "Dickheads like you are always down for a bit of action, but it's not so much fun when the shoe is on the other foot, is it?"

I laugh to myself, that familiar need to beat the shit out of someone finally easing within me. I should be good for another few weeks now. I've got other vices that I can rely on until then.

As I move to leave, the three men left standing all glance around nervously. They aren't sure what to do, but when they come for me, I hold my ground, more than ready for a little more action.

"What are you waiting for boys?" I say, holding my hands out in invitation. "Dinner and dessert? Now that's a real treat."

What can I say? Some girls like to rebel with tattoos, drugs, and alcohol. Beating the ever-loving shit out of predators like this is my vice; and I wouldn't change it for anything.

They move faster, coming at me with determination to make me pay for fucking up their friends. My heart races in the best kind of way, making me feel more alive than ever as I run my tongue over my plum lips, welcoming the excitement.

They come at me like a triangle, one at either side and one from the front.

I grin wide, my fingers gliding over my brass knuckles once again. I didn't know what to expect from moving to Ravenwood Heights, but I can't deny that it has its perks.

The guy in front reaches me first and I don't hesitate. I duck under his arm as it comes flying at my face and instantly kick out, my booted toes colliding with his crowned jewels. He goes down like a sack of shit, groaning in agony, but before I can rejoice, my arms are grabbed from behind me.

Instead of fretting, I use it to my advantage. I lean back against him, bringing my foot up in another wild kick, and slamming it under the third guy's chin. He falls back instantly, and as the guy tightens his grip on my arms, I slam my stiletto heel down on his foot.

He instantly releases me, and I spin around, my arm flying toward his face just as I had with the handsy guy. My brass knuckles crack against his eye socket, and as he falls, I get in nice and close, grinning when I see the perfect outline of the skull that sits just below his eye. It's like priceless art, perfect in every way.

I look down at my brass knuckles like a proud momma bear. After wiping off the blood, I kiss the very top of the skull, and as I walk out of the alleyway, my laugh bounces off every wall, echoing like a deviant taunt behind me.

I finally reach the dimly lit street at the other end of the alley and find my matte black Ducati waiting ever so patiently. I flick my long ponytail over my shoulder and grab my helmet before fixing it over my head.

As I throw my leg over the Ducati, I feel my leather pants tightening against my ass, and I look back down the alley to find the five guys groaning and slowly getting up. I can't help but laugh again. I didn't know I was capable of taking on five guys at once. I guess we learn something new about ourselves all the time.

Before they have a chance to recover, my thigh-high boot kicks the stand, and I straighten my bike. Hitting the ignition, I feel the familiar rumble of its proud engine beneath me.

Get out of here, Winter. This isn't the place you want to be caught hanging around longer than necessary.

I'll never get enough of it. I won this bike in a bet last year, and it's the best thing I ever did. My Ducati is my best friend. As long as I have it, it gives me the choice to always be free, and while I'm stuck in the system for another two months, that tiny bit of freedom I get from my bike is absolutely everything to me. Besides, it's sleek and sexy as fuck, so what girl in her right mind wouldn't love it?

As the men get to their feet, I flip down the visor of my helmet and lean forward to grip the handlebars. My hand twists on the throttle, and like lighting, my Ducati flies down the street, leaving nothing but a mess and one hell of a good lesson in my wake.

My Ducati roars through the streets of Ravenwood Heights, racing past the massive glass buildings of the city. I see my reflection as I fly past each building, distorted and edgy, making a smile play on my lips. Call me an egotistical asshole, but there's nothing better than seeing myself on my bike. The curve of my ass in nothing but leather as I lean forward and grip the handlebars with my thigh-high boots that warn fuckers not to mess with me. The way my cropped tank flies around in the wind, showing off my toned stomach, and my black helmet with a crippling design of a skull across the side. I love it. I love everything about who I am, except for one big thing.

I'm one of the many foster kids wishing they were anywhere but where they are.

I've jumped around from home to home since I was born. It's funny how easily you can be rehomed when you're an innocent child with nothing but cute curls, big rosy cheeks, and a smile that could win the heart of any foster parent. But once you hit those dreaded teen years and find yourself in more trouble than anyone has the right to be, you're pushed away over and over again, you're forgotten, and hated. I can't even count how many homes and schools I've been in. But what I do know is that this is my last.

I'll be eighteen in two months, and then I'll be free. I'll be out of the system and able to build a life for myself. Though I don't really know what's going to happen because, in order to make something of myself, I need to graduate school, and I can guarantee these bastards I'm living with now will kick me out the second their checks stop. After that, it's going to be nearly impossible to enroll in another school with my record.

This has to be my last school. I have to make it work … somehow.

I came to this shithole of a town three days ago, and tomorrow, I'll be starting at Ravenwood Heights Academy. Years ago, the thought of starting at a new school was daunting as all hell, but now, it's more like a normal Monday morning.

I don't know how I managed to get enrolled in this place. Some serious strings must have been pulled. This school is for rich kids, and the last time I was enrolled at a place like this, they had some bullshit community service program where they took in less fortunate students. I'm sure this is going to be the same deal, which means that from the very beginning, I'm going to get their pitying stares and snide comments.

I can't wait. It's going to be a blast … not.

Though, I can't say it's any different from any other school I've been to. I've always been the 'poor foster girl' or the 'troubled girl' who needs to be kept away. Everywhere I go, it's always the same. There's no point trying to clear my name because, for the most part, it's true. Other kids' parents are scared of me. They don't want me hanging out with their precious babies, they don't want me getting cozy with their sons, they just want me away, but fuck them. I'm not here to impress other people; I'm here to make it through school and get the hell out.

It's getting late and instead of heading straight back to my eighteenth home from hell, I make a detour. Taking the long way means I'll avoid the inevitable bullshit from Irene and Kurt. They hate me, but I don't care. I hate them too. They're assholes. It's as though we have a silent agreement between us. I stay out of their way, and they get to cash a check at the end of the month. It's only two months anyway, which only goes to show how desperate they are for cash. If Kurt wasn't so dependent on alcohol and Irene stepped away from the slot machines, they probably wouldn't be in this position. In fact, I don't even know how they got themselves in this position. Surely there must be a red flag against their names.

I can't believe it's already been three days living with them. It's going to be hard, but I've been through worse.

The Ducati finally takes me out of the city and deeper into Ravenwood Heights. I ease up on the throttle and bring the roaring engine to a soft hum. There are homes all around, and I don't exactly want to spend my night behind bars because of a noise complaint. These rich people can be assholes, and they won't hesitate to try and teach me a lesson about disturbing their peace. Kids like me who can't afford to fight the legal system make perfect targets, and those rich assholes get off on it.

I take a look around, trying to get used to my new surroundings when a black SUV creeps up behind me. I glance in my mirrors before discreetly looking back over my shoulder, realizing it's an Escalade—and a fucking sexy one at that. I'm a car girl. Not many chicks are, but when cars, bikes, boats, and anything with a motor is a form of escape that could take me away from all the bullshit, I tend to fall hard and fast. Hence why I love my bike like it was my firstborn child.

Not wanting to become roadkill, I move over to the side to let the Escalade pass, and as it does, I can't help but roam my eyes over it. The windows are darkly tinted, so dark that I'm positive it's not legal, but there's something about this SUV that makes it impossible to look away. A shiver passes over my skin, and something screams at me that the people inside this car are watching me closely. I can't see shit, but I feel their heavy stares piercing into me like the sharpest knives right through my soul.

The Escalade passes in front of me, and I keep up with it, sitting on its tail and following it through the streets. I know I shouldn't. The crawling feeling over my skin is a big sign telling me to fuck right off and get my ass home. But I can't.

I ride along with it, taking every corner, every straight. We pull up at a set of lights, and just like when it passed me, I feel their stares again.

The light turns green and I follow the Escalade around one more corner until it's pulling into a cemetery. My brows furrow. Who the fuck pulls into a cemetery at this time of night? I creep behind it slowly while putting some distance between us. I watch as it drives through the cemetery, and as I creep forward around the corner, I finally see it.

It's a fucking party.

Cars are lining the streets, people hovering, laughter, squeals, drinks as the rich kids of Ravenwood Heights waste their night away.

A grin stretches across my face. This is the most morbid kind of party I've ever seen. Hanging out in a cemetery and getting wicked wasted is morbid as fuck, but it's totally my kind of scene. I creep forward just a bit more but play it smart. I don't know these people, and after the feeling I got from the people in that car, maybe this isn't the place I should be hanging out tonight.

I bring my Ducati to a stop, easing into the shadow cast by a massive stone angel on top of a tomb. I cut my light and sit back to watch, knowing that I can't be seen.

The Escalade drives over the curb and forces its way through the partiers, and I can't help but wonder who the hell it is. I watch a second later as the car comes to a stop, and the crowd is instantly drawn closer, as though the people inside are celebrities.

All four doors open, and as four guys step out of the car, my heart races faster than it had while facing down those five guys in the alley. With the darkness of night covering the cemetery, it's almost impossible to make out any of their features, but it's clear as day that these guys mean something around here.

The driver closes his door behind him, and as girls flock to him, he looks my way, his stare piercing into mine, but that's not possible. There's no way he'd be able to see me in the shadows, yet somehow, he does, and for some reason, I'm drawn to him like a moth to a flame.

I suck in a sharp breath as one by one, the other three guys join him and all look my way, their stares making it impossible to breathe.

Who the hell are these guys?

Trouble. That's who they are.

Not wanting to get myself caught up in this bullshit before I've even started school, I turn my bike around. It's not until I'm halfway down the street that I turn my lights back on, and I can finally breathe again.

I don't know what the hell that was, but damn it, I'm intrigued. I need to know who those guys are and I won't let anything stand in my way.

I didn't think it was possible but Ravenwood Heights just got interesting.

2

A scowl stretches across my face as I pull into the driveway of Irene and Kurt's shitty two-bedroom home. I open the dodgy fence that keeps the yappy dog contained and cringe at the high-pitched squeak that tears through the quiet neighborhood.

I dart across the front lawn and have to skip to the door before the dog starts nipping at my ankles. Don't get me wrong, I'm definitely a dog person. Most of the time, I can't get enough of them, but there's just something about this one that has me squirming to get away. I don't know. Maybe it's the way it seems to constantly watch me, or how it jumps up at my bedroom window all night, its nails scratching against the glass.

I fish through my bra for the key that Irene had reluctantly given me, and as I open the door, I instantly groan, finding both Irene and Kurt sitting in the living room. It's well after 11:30 at night, and for a moment, I wonder if they were sitting up to wait for me but quickly realize they hadn't given me one thought since I walked out first thing this morning.

My stomach grumbles and I walk through to the kitchen to find nothing waiting on the table for me. I let out a sigh and turn to the fridge. Maybe they'd put dinner away, but as I scan through the shelves, I find nothing. "What do you think you're doing?" Irene snaps, suddenly standing right behind me in the kitchen. "You don't see me going through your belongings, so why the hell are you going through my fridge?"

I turn around to meet her horrid stare. "I'm hungry," I grumble, slightly confused. "I haven't eaten since lunch."

"Well, that's your problem, not mine," she throws right back at me. "The deal is that I give you a roof to live under. You're already using my water and my electricity. You're not taking my food too."

The fuck?

I gape at her for a minute. Is she for real?

Surely feeding the foster kid is just common sense, right? Don't get me wrong, I haven't exactly looked into the contracts between the state and the foster parents, but surely there's a section that states 'the child must not die of starvation.' What do they think the check they get at the end of the month is for? It's not just to cover their inconvenience. It's not just something to help feed their alcohol and gambling addictions.

Fuck me.

I give her a blank stare, tempted to ignore her and grab a packet of crackers and retreat to my room when Kurt's voice rings through the house. "What are you waiting for? She told you to get, now go. Get out of my kitchen. It's off-limits to you."

You've got to be kidding. Not in the mood to start shit tonight, I move past Irene, shoulder charging her as I go and listening to her over-the-top dramatic howling behind me. I retreat to my room, making sure to close the door behind me and lock it before double-checking that the lock actually works. I've been in homes before where the lock is just for show, and the majority of the time, it's because there are dickhead men who like to sneak in at night.

I've been lucky that I haven't been in a position to have a man force himself on me, but it's not uncommon with some of the other girls I've met in similar situations. It's part of the reason I've learned to fight.

Out of the eighteen homes I've been in, only two of them had foster parents who actually gave a shit about me. Karleigh was a great foster mom, and I was with her between the ages of nine to thirteen. She saw something in me that I never saw in myself and was able to help me put aside the anger. Instead of getting in fights at school, she enrolled me in martial arts. That went well for a while—until I started beating the shit out of the other students as a way to let the anger out. I was kicked out after six months of training, but I took away a lot of skills that have always stayed with me.

Karleigh got me one of those heavy boxing bags that the MMA dudes train with after that. She hung it in the backyard, and regardless of the weather, I was out there pummeling my fists into it until they bled.

Good times.

I flip off my light and drop down onto the side of my bed, the moonlight from my window enough to guide me so that I'm not fumbling around in the dark.

This is complete bullshit. I knew when I heard that someone was taking me in for the next two months, it was going to be a disaster. Who wants a kid like me for two months? Every single conversation I have with them tells me they're only in it for the cash. Fuck, I hope some other poor kid doesn't get stuck with them after I do. I'm just thankful that it's only two months.

My stomach grumbles and my hand falls over it.

I can't do this.

I have school tomorrow, and I can't show up there after not eating for that long. I have to feed myself, but how? I can wait up until those assholes have gone to bed, or I can go and beg at a store. I have three dollars shoved down my bra, certainly not enough to get something for tonight and do breakfast and lunch tomorrow.

A frustrated sigh comes tearing out of me, and as I start reaching for the zip to kick off my thigh-high boots, an idea hits me like a wrecking ball—the cemetery party. There's bound to be food lying around there, not to mention drinks to help me forget that I'm in a shitty situation. There were a shitload of people, most of them probably with deep pockets, plus those guys.

Hmm ... intriguing.

A grin tears across my face as I feel my left tit to make sure my Ducati key is right where I left it. I cross the room before looking back at the door. No shadows are coming from under it and the house is silent.

I push up my window and slip straight through it before pushing the dog away as the fucker jumps up against my boots and scratches the shit out of them. I groan, sending up a silent prayer that my boots are alright. Just the thought of what I'd have to do to replace these boots will give me nightmares.

I close the window behind me.

After hurrying out the shitty gate, I throw my leg over my Ducati and hit the ignition before revving the shit out of my engine, the whole bike vibrating as the sound threatens to deafen me. I don't doubt the whole neighborhood is waking up, but most of all, I hope it infuriates the dickheads living inside of this house.

Hitting the accelerator, I take off like a rocket, leaving a thick black line across the broken concrete of their driveway. I head straight back to the cemetery and within the space of ten minutes, I'm looking around at everything that's going on, taking in my surroundings.

The black Escalade is no longer parked in the center of the party but has been moved to block the street so nobody can get in or out. I laugh at their pathetic attempts, as with my bike, I have absolutely no problem slipping past it.

The party doesn't just take up the cemetery but has spilled out across the street. Music blasts from a set of speakers that are propped on top of a tomb and is practically shaking the ground, more than enough to wake the dead who reside below.

I take a deep breath and look around. This is definitely my kind of party. I should have just hung around before. Though one thing is for sure, after finding something to eat and seeing what other goodies I can take for myself, it's going to be late before I get home to bed, and with school first thing in the morning, it's going to be interesting.

People linger everywhere and I can already feel their curious stares. I bring the bike to a stop right up on the curb, but unlike the Escalade earlier, I keep it respectful and park my bike off to the side, away from any of the graves.

A wave of nerves comes shooting through me as I spare a thought for the four guys who had captured my attention before. They're obviously still here, but I have absolutely no idea which guys they are. It was too dark to tell, and being at a distance, it was impossible.

I shake off the nerves. I may be the new chick, but I won't let that stop me. I slip off my bike, being sure to put the stand down and set the alarm. Boys have a habit of touching things that they can't have, and my Ducati has always been one of them. It wouldn't be the first time, not even the second or third, that my alarm has gone off during a party. Luckily, the alarm is usually enough to scare them away so I've never had to worry.

There are people everywhere, and being the weird chick on a bike who's been driving around town for the past few days, all eyes are on me.

I zone them out. After all, it's nothing different than what I've already experienced a million times before.

Lingering stares from the guys turn into desire, and I block them all out as I walk through the party. All the people here are dressed in designer clothes, lounging over the graves, and using their tombstones as coffee tables. I'd dare say that this party was meant for the rich kids who live on the other side of the city.

I certainly don't belong here, but then why the hell would I skip an opportunity like this? Hell, just digging in one guy's pocket could buy gas for my Ducati for the next month.

I get straight to work.

I start making my way through the busiest part of the crowd, constantly bumping into people and swiping what cash I can from open handbags. I laugh to myself. These people are clueless, but what's more, is that people like this wouldn't even notice if a bit of cash went missing. God, I'd love to live with that luxury. People like me are constantly counting our coins, making sure we have enough just to get by.

I do a full circle before realizing that while there's plenty of tables dedicated to mixing drinks, there's not one damn table that can feed me.

I groan and make my way around for a second circle. I bump and move against people, feeling like I have the world at my fingertips.

My shoulder barges past a guy, but before I have the chance to dip my fingers into his back pocket, the guy spins around, his hand curling around my wrist and holding it between us. My head snaps up and I meet his dark stormy eyes.

He holds me close, his stare unwavering, and in an instant, chills begin sweeping over my body. I can't help but wonder if this was the driver of the Escalade who had knocked the breath out of me from his stare alone.

I swallow hard, the seconds seeming to tick by as he holds me, or maybe it just feels like forever. Everything else zones out as all I can focus on are his eyes. I couldn't even say what his hair looks like, only that long black strands are falling into his eyes, and judging by the way I have to tilt my head to meet his ferocious stare, I'd dare say that this guy is as tall as they come.

It's impossible to tell what he's thinking, but something tells me that he can read my mind as though the words are written across my forehead like a tattoo.

At least thirty seconds pass, each of us stuck in the moment before he finally releases my wrist and turns away. I stumble back a step, staring at his broad shoulders as he dismisses me in an instant. His friends stand with him, but I'm spellbound, stuck gaping at him breathlessly until someone tumbles into me and forces me to react. The last thing I want to do is eat dirt in front of the rich kids that I'll no doubt see in school tomorrow.

My stumble pulls me out of it, and without a backward glance, I make my way over to the edge of the party to where people are more scattered and the noise isn't so loud. I drop down into the grass, parking my ass beside an old tombstone, and take a second to breathe.

Who the hell was that guy? Surely it's the same guy from the

Escalade—or at least one of them.

I can't resist reaching over and brushing my hand over the moss-covered stone to read what it says. Janet Moustaff died in 1978 from drowning and was only 37 years old. I let out a sigh. "Well, Janet," I murmur as I pull out the stack of cash that I'd managed to collect over the last half an hour. "I hope you don't mind me sitting with you, but to be honest, it doesn't look like anyone has in a while. Who the hell is supposed to be looking after this place anyway? They're doing a shitty job of keeping it clean."

Having said that, I glance over at the tombstone beside hers and wipe my hand over it before squinting as I struggle to read what it says, but as I do, my heart breaks. John Moustaff died 1981 from a lonely heart. He was only 42.

I finish cleaning off their tombstones and look back at Janet's. "Well, at least you have each other," I tell her, knowing that even in death, she has so much more than me. I let out a sigh and get back to counting the cash.

"Talking to the dead?" a deep voice asks from behind me.

My eyes widen, and I shove the cash inside my bra before spinning around and looking up at the guy who is slowly approaching me, hands raised as if to tell me that he means no harm.

I get to my feet and face him as he approaches. "Who are you?" I ask, my eyes narrowed as my fingers run over the top of my brass knuckles, making sure they're firmly in place.

The guy nods his head in greeting, and the closer he comes, the easier it is to make out his dirty blonde hair and deep hazel eyes. "The name's Knox," he grumbles as he pulls out a cigarette. "But I think the better question is, who the hell are you? I haven't seen you around before."

"Does it really matter who I am?"

He scoffs. "Well after you so effortlessly lifted a hundred-dollar bill from my back pocket, yeah, I think I'll make it my business to get to know you."

Ahh, fuck.

My eyes widen and I start shaking my head. "I … I didn't—"

"Chill out," he laughs. "Keep the cash. I don't need it. I guess I'm just more interested in how you were able to lift it so easily. I've been watching you, you know," he tells me, lighting his cigarette. "You've nearly hit every fucker at this party. Did you clean up well?"

I narrow my eyes, wondering if I can trust him, but when he holds out his pack of cigarettes and offers me one, I decide that he couldn't be too bad. I take a smoke, and he holds up his lighter, a small flame appearing in my face with the flick of a finger. I lean into it and inhale deeply before blowing out a cloud of smoke.

I shrug my shoulders and look out at the party. "I don't know. I haven't had a chance to count yet."

Knox purses his lips and looks over me, slowly nodding as though he's impressed. "Why?"

"Why what?"

He steps a little closer, still trying to figure me out, but he never will. I'm a mystery to myself; not even I can figure this shit out. "Why do you have to steal? I saw that bike you've been riding around town, and that shit ain't cheap. Clearly, you don't need the money."

I raise a brow. "On the contrary," I say. "I won that bike in a bet and did everything I could just to keep it running. I'm not from around here. If I don't steal cash, I don't eat."

He grins as though my struggles are amusing to him. "Ever heard of a job?"

I shake my head. "Ever heard of a foster kid? I'll be shipped away and lost in the system before I'm able to even complete an application. There's no point. Sometimes you gotta do what you gotta do, even if it means lifting a hundred-dollar bill off an unsuspecting rich kid like yourself."

Knox laughs, and a sparkle hits his eyes as though he's just decided that he's about to spend the rest of his night trying to figure me out. "Okay, I guess I judged you too soon," he tells me. "Just do yourself a favor and don't steal from Carver and his boys. They'll tear you a new one, and when I say they're not so forgiving, I really mean it. Be careful."

I glance up at him, my brows furrowed as I'm pretty damn sure that I just hit everyone here, though I have a feeling I know who he's referring to. "Who?" I question, just as my stomach growls, demanding attention. My hand falls to my stomach as it starts to hurt.

"Dude, what the fuck was that?" Knox laughs, his eyes wide as he looks at me in horror. "Was that your stomach? Holy shit, girl. When was the last time you ate?"

I shrug my shoulders, my mind trying to take me back over my day. "I don't know. I think I had half an apple at lunch."

He shakes his head and pulls out his phone before pressing a few buttons. "What's your go-to pizza order?"

"Huh? Why?"

"Why," he scoffs. "Why do you think? I'm ordering you a pizza. Why the fuck aren't you eating properly?"

I shake my head and start backing away from him. "No," I say. "Don't bother. I don't let random guys at parties do me favors because nine out of ten times, what they want in return is something I'm not willing to give."

"Chill out, babe. I'm ordering you a fucking pizza, and that's the end of it. Besides, you've already stolen my cash. You can pretend the pizza is for me and steal that too if it makes you happy, but either way, you're eating before you leave here tonight."

I let out a sigh and give in. My stomach is hurting far too much to keep up this bullshit game of denial. I should just take the handout and be done with it. Besides, with Irene and Kurt keeping me from their kitchen, who knows when I'll be eating properly next.

"Fine," I tell him as he finishes with his phone and slips it back into his pocket. "My name is Winter, by the way, not babe, and I can't have you buy me a pizza and still hold onto your money. That just feels … wrong."

He shakes his head as a puff of smoke blows out toward my face. "It's nice to meet you, Winter. Your pizza will be here in ten," he tells me. "Trust me, I won't miss the cash. Just keep it, but you have to promise that you'll spend it the way that I would spend it. It's only fair."

He nods back to the party, indicating for me to join him and for some unknown reason, I find myself following along. "Oh, yeah?" I question. "And how's that?"

Knox grins and looks back at me with a cheesy-as-fuck grin. "Drugs, alcohol, and sex."

I roll my eyes, wondering if I've found my first friend in this shitty over-the-top town. "You're such a guy," I tell him as we fall into the crowd.

"There's no other way to be," he tells me before grabbing my hand and dragging me toward a bunch of drunk guys who look like trouble. "Now, we've got ten minutes to waste, teach me how to lift the way you did."

I can't help but laugh. "Okay, but I'm warning you. It's a fine art, and if you get caught, I had nothing to do with it."

Knox looks back at me with a wide smile. "Deal."

I can't help but laugh at the excitement in his eyes, and for the second time tonight, I find myself thinking that maybe this godforsaken town has more to offer than I realized.

3

Pushing myself up on my elbows, regret pounds through my head instantly. What the hell was I thinking staying out at that party all night?

I got back home at three in the morning and set off three car alarms on my way, making sure that the neighborhood hated me even more than they already did.

After scarfing down the pizza that Knox so kindly bought me last night, I was going to hit it and quit it. I had a whole plan to get the hell out of there and stock up on food I can hide in my room. Then I was going to crash for the rest of the night.

That didn't happen because, damn, these Ravenwood Heights kids can party. My throat burns from chain-smoking, or maybe it's from the constant laughing with Knox. We fucked around all night, and hell, I might even have the courage to say that I made a friend. We didn't talk to anyone else, just hung out as he told me about the ins and outs of Ravenwood Heights. He warned me not to steal from Carver and his friends, but that was the last he mentioned of them. It killed me all night not to ask, but I have a feeling those are questions I don't want answered.

I'm sure we would have stayed out longer had the cops not broken up the party, and to be honest, I'm surprised it took so long. We weren't exactly quiet, and it makes me wonder if bullshit like this happens on the regular. One thing is for sure, knowing that the cops around here are pretty laid back is always a bonus for me. I have a little issue with ending up on the bad side of the police in every single town I've stayed in. Hell, it's part of the reason I've been shipped away sometimes.

I clench my eyes, willing the throbbing to ease from my mind, but I'm sure after a hot shower, I'll be fine. Not wanting to leave my bike behind, I was smart enough to not drink, but the noise and atmosphere have me regretting my choices this morning.

I pull myself out of bed and reach over to silence my old phone. It's only seven in the morning, but with school starting in less than two hours and having shit to do, I need to get going.

A loud banging on my door rattles the whole frame, and I whip my head around to watch as the door shakes. "Get up," Irene's deep tone rumbles through the room. "You have twenty minutes to be out of here. I'm not waiting around for you."

Fuck.

Her fist bangs against the door, and I groan, wishing for the opportunity to introduce her face to my brass knuckles. "Alright," I yell back. "I'm coming."

"Don't you use that tone with me, young lady. I promise you'll regret it."

Yeah, right. I'm sure there's nothing she could do to me at this point that would really make me regret anything. I've already suffered through a million kinds of hell, and this cow has got nothing on the last bitch I was dumped with. Though, to be fair, I really made her earn her check every month.

Irene gives in and leaves me to get ready, and I don't hesitate to do just that. Besides, the quicker I'm out of this house, the better.

I peel myself out of bed and instantly pull the blanket back. I have a feeling that Irene isn't going to give a shit if I make my bed or not. However, after staying with people who were anal about it, I learned very quickly that it's always best to do the little things.

I grab an unfolded towel off my shelf and have to do a sniff test just to make sure that it has been cleaned before being shoved in here. Satisfied that it's not about to give me some sort of disease, I venture across the hallway and dump it on the vanity before locking the door and double checking it. The last thing I need is to have Kurt barging in here and getting more than he bargained for.

I rush through the quickest shower of my life, and although my hair needs to be washed, I don't bother. I won't risk being naked in this house for a second longer than I need to. Perhaps I can wait until I have PE at school and can take a proper shower afterward. Hell, I don't even care if the girls at school are mean and try to embarrass me by stealing my clothes. I'll take that a million times over it happening here.

As I step out of the shower and wrap my towel around me, I scan the sink and countertops frantically. My stomach drops as I realize that I left all of my clothes in my room. How can I be so fucking stupid?

I cringe and stand before the door, working up the courage to dart across the hall in nothing but a towel. But still, I can't deny that if Kurt tried anything, I won't have an issue breaking his nose just like I broke that dickhead's last night.

The reminder of my epic ass-kicking makes me feel a million times better about my situation, and I take a deep breath. I unlock the latch and pull the door open before flying faster than I've ever flown before. I barge into my room, ignoring the low, sleazy whistle that comes from Kurt at the other end of the hall.

I slam my bedroom door and quickly flick the lock in place. The old canvas bag that Karleigh had given me at thirteen still holds all of my clothes, so I practically dive across the room to get dressed.

I scan through the bag, wishing it was easier to find the things I wanted, but I refuse to hang my clothes in the closet. There's no point; I won't be here long.

I eventually find what I'm looking for and get dressed as quickly as possible, not trusting that these guys don't have a key to my room.

I pull on my black high-waisted ripped jeans and my boots before finding a cropped lace cami and finish off my look with my favorite leather jacket. I start working on everything else, and within moments,

I'm pulling my long, brunette hair up into my signature high pony.

Checking over my reflection in the cracked mirror, I raise my chin and remind myself that if I've already made it this far, I can always keep going.

I step into the mirror while grabbing my black choker and fastening it around my neck. Moving quickly, I find my favorite plum lipstick and drag it across my lips, adding a bit of black liner and a thick layer of mascara. This is the best it's going to get. I'm just lucky that Ravenwood Heights Academy is one of the few private schools in the country that doesn't force students to wear ugly uniforms. I can't even begin to describe how many awful uniforms I've been forced to wear over the years.

I'm not stupid. I know guys like the way I look, and without sounding like a complete asshole, I like it too. I have a sexy, dark barbie vibe that I absolutely love. I like feeling desired; I like the looks of appreciation I get from the opposite sex, and sometimes even the girls. I love that it makes my confidence soar, and I won't ever apologize for it.

I'm not going to lie, along with my looks, always comes the negative. Girls can be bitches when they see me as a threat. As if I have any desire to steal their pre-pubescent boyfriends; no thanks, I'll pass. It's the guys who concern me. I can handle the bitches, but dudes … their comments can be lethal. Nine out of ten times, the words just bounce off me, but that one time, something will be said that cuts me deeper than a knife.

Checking the door is still closed and firmly locked, I peel back the bedside table from the wall and grab the stack of cash that Knox and I made off with last night. I couldn't believe my luck. Knox really had no skill when it came to stealing from people he knew. They'd catch him before he had a chance to do anything and strike up some bullshit conversation that he was itching to get away from. Me though, I had no issues at all. Though, I was smart enough to keep away from the guy I assumed was Carver. Fuck, I wasn't going to risk that again.

In the end, Knox and I walked away with three grand, and while I felt like the biggest asshole taking off with that kind of money, I also knew that it came down to my survival. I offered half to Knox, but he laughed and told me that he shits that kind of money. I realized that the whole exercise for him was all about having a little fun and maybe being nice to the pathetic, new chick.

Not wanting to leave the whole stack of cash here when Kurt is bound to be home all day, I shove the whole lot of it into my backpack before slipping straight out the bedroom window. Screw sticking around to say goodbye. They'll know I'm gone when my bike rumbles through their house.

As my boots hit the ground, I pull my backpack over both arms and avoid the little yappy dog on my way to my bike. I smile at her as she comes into sight, the flare of the sunlight against her shiny chrome sending waves of excitement through me. God, I'll never get over how lucky I am to have this bike. She's so damn pretty. I'm just thankful that the drunken prick who I won it off was nice enough to give me a crash course on how to ride it before taking off with his equally drunk friend.

I bet he woke up the next morning and regretted ever going out that night, but screw it, he's never come looking for it and I've never asked questions.

After climbing onto my bike and feeling the familiar rumble of the engine beneath me, I take off, leaving another thick, black line on the driveway.

I have a bit of time to waste, so I head to the grocery store to grab a few things I can hide in my room. With my backpack full of easy snacks, I stop by the local cafe to order a decent breakfast. It's not often that I get to eat a good meal before school, but if I can make a habit of it, I'll be one hell of a lucky girl.

After wasting just enough time, I get back on my bike and head to school. As I'm sliding into the back of the student parking lot of Ravenwood Heights Academy, it's 8:50 on the dot, and the bell is a distant echo.

I sit back on my bike, watching the students around me, every single one of them just standing there, ignoring the bell, and staring at me as though I was lost. In reality, maybe I am. I really don't belong in a school like this.

I let out a sigh and reach forward, cutting the engine of my bike. Without the familiar rumble, the silence of the crowd seems so much louder. If I hadn't done this a million times before, I'm sure I'd be anxious as shit, but as it is, I just don't care anymore. Though, a part of me is secretly hoping that this is the last 'first day' that I'll ever have to suffer through.

After climbing off my bike and removing my helmet, the girls around me seem to hiss as a slew of whispers begin, just as I knew they would. I groan to myself. Whatever happened to girls supporting girls? When will they all realize that I'm not here to steal their boyfriends?

Just one time it'd be nice to have a girl approach me and genuinely want to be a friend. I don't have many girlfriends. In fact, I don't really have any friends. There's no point. I'm never around long enough to form real attachments, but there have been a handful of girls over the years who have stayed in my heart.

I tuck my helmet under my arm while keeping the impressive skull fully on display and start making my way toward the front gates. Every eye in the school follows my movements, not one person with the balls to actually approach me, and honestly, it's a bit disappointing. Being such an elite school, I figured that there'd be at least a few kids around here who were brave enough to take a risk.

Just before I walk through the front gates, I look back at my bike to find a group of guys hovering around it and checking it out. Not one of them is touching it, which makes me wonder if they're being respectful or if they're scared shitless of me.

I go to turn back when the same black Escalade from last night comes tearing into the lot and aims straight for my bike. Gasps are heard around me as the Escalade comes to a screeching halt before squeezing right in beside my bike on an angle, making it impossible for me to get around it. I'll be stuck here until that dickhead decides to move his car, but I don't worry about it, seeing as though he doesn't strike me as the type to hang around after school.

The four guys get out of the Escalade, and just like last night, people flock to them like celebrities. The four guys ignore the crowd as if everyone here is below them.

The driver, who I'm guessing is this mystical Carver guy, raises his head, and as if sensing my stare, his gaze locks onto mine. I suck in a breath, not ready to go through that same bullshit from last night, so without sparing him and his friends another glance, I turn on my heel and stalk into the school. I know without a doubt, these guys are going to be major pains in my ass.

With the bell ringing the second I showed up, I'm well and truly late for my first day, but it doesn't seem to be an issue around here as students still linger in the hallway.

Not having time to check-in at the student office, I grab the handbook out of my backpack that I'd found in my room, quickly scanning through it to find my class schedule and homeroom.

Mr. Bennett, room eighteen, Block C. I gape at it for a moment. Well, shit. Are there seriously that many classrooms that they had to be broken up into blocks?

Not having the slightest clue where Block C is, I stop by a timid girl who stands outside her locker, collecting her things. "Hey," I say. She instantly whips her head in my direction, her eyes going wide, and within seconds, she's shrinking back from me as though just talking to me is going to send her straight to hell. Ignoring her silent pleas to be left in peace, I show her the map of the school that's on the very next page. "Can you show me where Block C is, room eighteen?"

"Oh, umm … yeah," she murmurs, her voice low as she visibly seems to relax, realizing that I'm not about to steal her lunch money, though there's a possibility I stole it last night. She points out the room and shows me the quickest way to get there, and the second she's finished explaining, she disappears right out of sight, desperate to get away from the troubled girl.

I take my time getting to homeroom and walk through the door of Mr. Bennett's room with every eye on me, but what's new? "And you are?" the old, stubborn teacher at the front of the class demands, looking at me as though he'd happily assign me to a different classroom.

"I'm Winter," I tell him.

He scans through his class roll, his brows creasing the further down the list he gets. He shakes his head, clearly unable to see my name. "Winter who? Your surname isn't listed."

"It's just Winter."

Mr. Bennett's head snaps up with rage shining in his eyes, the whole class watching on as though this is the biggest motion picture of the year. "When you walk through my classroom door, all games are to be left behind. I do not appreciate your attitude. When I ask for your full name, I will receive your full name, and I will not tolerate anything less. Is that understood?"

I raise my brow, dropping my backpack on the table of the kid sitting by the door. "Crystal clear," I tell him, not in the mood for his bullshit. "And as I stated, my name is Winter. Just Winter. I do not know my surname, nor was I given another by the state. My home was burned to a crisp in a fire that killed both of my parents, taking my birth certificate right along with it. After the state lost track of who I was, so did I."

I was only a baby. I had no idea what my name was until I was three years old. That's when my foster mother started calling me Winter because she didn't think Jane Doe suited my personality. Winter, however, suited my cold demeanor just fine. "Now if you don't mind, I would very much like to take my seat. Or would you prefer to dive further into my personal life and dig up more irrelevant information? I could tell you all about how it's impossible for me to get a driver's license, apply for any kind of loan, or get anywhere in life because I don't have a proper name."

Mr. Bennett clenches his jaw as the students seem to watch me with a closer eye. "Take your seat, Winter," he says, almost spitting my name.

I give him a sickly-sweet smile and grab my backpack off the other kid's desk before trudging through the room and taking a seat at the only available desk.

The room is deadly quiet, and I use the last five minutes to relax, taking slow, deep breaths to prepare myself for the next few hours. That little story about my dead parents and not having a proper name is bound to spread like wildfire, and by the time I step out of this classroom to face the rest of the student body, there are going to be stares of pity coming from every direction.

Being orphaned as a baby wasn't exactly something I wanted the world to know. I usually keep these secrets close to my chest, but for some reason, the words just came pouring out of me. After having no sleep and dealing with the foster parents from hell, I don't think I can handle all the bullshit—at least, not today.

4

The cigarette sits between my lips as I hold the lighter in front of my face, inhaling deeply and sucking in my first deep breath of nicotine for the day. I instantly regret it as it burns down my throat, reminding me that I smoked way too much last night. I should probably be drinking water instead of adding to the problem, but hey, I don't think I'll make it through the day without it.

I stand outside of the school gates, looking over the student parking lot during the first break. It's been a shitty day just as I expected it to be, but honestly, it could be worse, so I should consider it a win.

I stare down at my Ducati, wishing so desperately that I could climb onto it and ride off into the sunset. If it wasn't so brutally blocked in by that stupid Escalade, I'm sure I'd already be gone.

I grumble to myself and take another drag, needing the small hit to bring me back to reality. As Taylor Swift once told me, I need to calm down. I can't keep getting so worked up over such little things. It's going to kill me one day.

Flopping back against the wall, I tear my gaze away from the Ducati and Escalade and focus on the students coming and going. I watch with interest. They're just walking straight off the school grounds as though they're allowed to. I've never been to a school that's allowed that before. It's pretty freaking awesome if you ask me. Though right now, it only serves to remind me that my ride out of here is trapped between someone's daddy's mid-life crisis and a stupid SUV.

I drop my cigarette to the concrete and stub my toe over it, putting it out with a little extra effort. I should be going inside and getting familiar with the school. Yet, I find myself leaning against the wall and letting the few minutes of my break tick by.

"Rough day?" A feminine voice says, creeping up beside me.

I glance over to find a short, slim girl with deep brunette hair, so dark that if we weren't standing out in the sun, I would have mistaken it for black. "You could say that," I tell her, watching as she moves in beside me to lean against the wall.

She pulls out a packet of cigarettes before holding it out to me. "Want one?"

I shake my head. "Nah, I'm good," I tell her. "After smoking a whole pack last night, I could use a break from the stuff."

"No shit. Were you at the party last night? I think I saw you hanging out with Knox."

"Yeah, that was me. Are you friends with him?"

She shakes her head. "Not really," she says. "I haven't got anything against the guy, just haven't really had a chance to spend any time with him. My friend is close to him though, and she thinks pretty highly of him, so I'm assuming he's alright."

I nod. "I guess that's good to know."

She gives me a warm smile, and I instantly decide that I like her. "I'm Ember by the way. You're Winter, right? Winter with no last name?"

I groan. "So, the rumors are spreading. That's nice."

"Nah, not really," she laughs, pushing her hair back over her shoulder. "Well, maybe. Who knows? I was in your homeroom listening to you put that old dick in his place. I don't think I've ever seen anyone shut him down like that. It was fucking awesome, and I decided right then and there that I had to meet you properly."

"Oh, yeah?"

"Uh-huh. From now on, I'm your go-to girl. Whatever you need, just hit me up. I'll teach you everything you need to know about this place."

I push off the wall and study the girl. No one has ever been this keen to be my friend. "I don't know," I tell her. "You look like drama."

Ember laughs—a real belly type of laugh—before giving me a wide smile. "Oh, trust me, I'm definitely drama, but only the good kind. But, tough shit. I'm here now, and you're not going to get rid of me that easily. I'll grow on you, I promise. It might seem like hard work now, but one day you'll find yourself sitting in an empty room wishing that I was there to chat your ear off."

I watch her a second longer, and as her smile seems to stretch wider and wider across her face, I realize that she's truly genuine. Where the hell could I go wrong with that? "Fine," I say. "But there's only ten minutes left before third period, and I still know nothing about this school."

Ember beams at me, putting her cigarette out against the brick wall before looping her arms around mine and dragging me back through the school gate. "Just as well, I'm a fast talker," she tells me, more than up for the challenge. "I hope you can keep up, though. I'm not one for repeating myself."

Damn. She sounds like my kind of girl. "Hit me with it."

She drags me through the school, pulling at my arm, and forcing me to keep up with her. "So, I'm sure by now you've already figured out that there's a hierarchy around here?"

I shake my head. "Nope. I've been more interested in hiding out than actually noticing anything that's been going on around me."

She rolls her eyes. "Jesus, I'm going to have to start right from the beginning then." She pulls me into the cafeteria where the majority of the senior students are loitering. The second the door closes behind us, their stares hit me like a freight train. "Ignore them," Embers says. "They're just jealous that you're smoking hot and they can't pull off a look like yours to save their lives."

I smile, appreciating that one little comment more than she could ever know. She keeps pulling me through the crowded bodies, not seeming to care that being with me means that the curious stares are now on her too. "So, let's begin with the bottom, shall we," she tells me, indicating to a group of people sitting around a table, some standing, some resting across the table like it's a freaking living room. "This is the stoner group. They're usually too fucked up to notice anything that's going on around here," she explains before glancing across the cafeteria. "We have the hippy group over here. If you ever get confused, you can generally find them at lunchtime because they'll be the people meditating right in the middle of the football field."

I laugh, a grin pulling at my lips. "I'm sure the football team hates that."

"Fuck me, understatement of the year. They've been at war over it for years, and no matter how many times Principal Turner asks them to meditate somewhere else, they always end up right back in the middle of the field, only with more people."

"They sound like my kind of people," I murmur. "You know, apart from the meditating part."

"Right?" Ember laughs. "Though, speaking of the football team. You'll find those assholes sitting in the back. They're the noisy turds who can't keep their comments or hands to themselves, but for the most part, their attention is usually aimed at the cheerleaders who sit right across from them. But if you ask me, the cheerleaders are practically begging for their attention, and it doesn't matter how they get it as long as it's theirs."

"Ugh," I grumble, spying the cheerleaders at the back of the cafeteria, knowing that, without a doubt, they're not the kind of girls

I'll be hanging out with. Don't get me wrong, I'm sure a few of them are really sweet and awesome chicks, but the way Ember has described them as a whole, they reek of desperation. "So, who's next?"

She stops in the middle of the cafeteria and starts slowly scanning the room, walking in a circle as she does it. "Let's see," she says, pointing out groups as she goes. "There's the mean girls, the really mean girls, the douchebags, the computer nerds—though half of the computer nerds are also part of the science geeks—but they're all super cool if you ask me. Umm, over here we have the Satan worshippers, the dudes who are going to fuck you up, and of course, the guys who are probably going to try and drop a pill into your drink at a party."

I make a note of that, scanning over that last group and memorizing their faces to be sure that I don't get caught out with any of them. I circle around, trying to remember it all when I realize that there are a few faces in here that I haven't seen. "What about Knox and those guys who rocked up in the Escalade? Where do they belong in all of this?"

A smile cracks across her face. "Oh, girl. Has Carver already caught your attention?"

I shrug my shoulders. "Depends on which one is Carver," I tell her. "But don't get excited, if he's the guy I think he is, then he's a complete asshole."

"You've got that right," she says, hooking her arm through mine again and dragging me out of the cafeteria. "The cool kids don't like to hang out in the cafeteria; it cramps their style. They usually just chill out in the quad where they can watch over everything, but by the end of lunch, all the desperados are out here doing everything they can to get noticed."

"And what about you?" I ask as we walk out to the quad. "Where do you fit in?"

She shrugs her shoulders. "I don't know. I guess I'm a free spirit. I jump around to all of the groups, but before that, I'm not going to lie, I was one of those desperados wanting to get noticed by Carver and his friends."

I shake my head, letting out a deep sigh. "What's so special about them? Everyone seems to be either terrified of them or wishing they'd be fucked and then fucked over by them."

"Trust me, wait till you meet them properly and you'll just get it. I can't even describe them to you. They just have this air about them that draws people in. You have an air like that too."

I scoff, looking at her as though she's lost her mind. "You're crazy," I laugh. "I'm the furthest thing away from that."

She shakes her head. "I think you're wrong. You're intriguing; people want to know more about you. They're curious, but you have this solid wall that makes them too scared to approach you. It's kinda like you're off-limits."

My brows furrow, but as we make it out to the quad, all train of thought fades away.

There they are; the four celebrities of Ravenwood Heights.

My gaze begins sweeping over them, starting with the guy who I'd pissed off at the party last night, the one I assume to be the all-famous Carver. He's tall, and as the sun shines down upon him, he almost seems larger than life, and without question, I know that Ember was right. This guy really does have an air about him that draws people in. Hell, I experienced it first-hand last night. He's the tallest of the four, dark hair and a stare that I wish was on me.

"That guy in the middle," Ember starts. "That's Dante Carver, the one you've been hearing about and the dick who blocked your bike in this morning. He's the leader of the pack. Fuck, the leader of the whole damn school. But if I were you, I'd stay away. Stay away from all of them. They're trouble, and not the good kind, but the dangerous kind. They'll screw you over in all the worst kinds of ways."

I narrow my gaze on the guy in question, unsure why I want him to screw me over so badly, but before I start drooling, I cut my gaze to the next guy.

"Who's that?" I murmur, unsure why I'm keeping my voice so low while there's no one around to overhear our conversation.

Ember follows my gaze to the guy who looks like he belongs locked up for all the right reasons. His dark floppy hair sits in his eyes, and even from a distance, they look like the kind of eyes that could have girls dropping their pants in a heartbeat. "Ahhh," Ember says slowly. "That's Hunter King, though he just goes by King. He's almost the worst of them all. If the devil was in human form, that's who he'd be. He's got the whole dark, dangerous, and deadly thing going for him, and if guys like him didn't scare the shit out of me, I'd be on my knees begging for it."

I raise a brow, looking back at Ember with a grin. "Wow, looks like we've got a wild one over here," I laugh, making her roll her eyes before we both cut our gazes to the third guy, the one with the mousy brown hair, the wide chest, and the eyes that seem to sparkle like diamonds. "Him?" I ask, my gaze sweeping right over his body like a hungry lioness ready to pounce.

A softness comes over her stare. "Cruz Danforth," she says with a dreamy sigh. "He's the flirt, which almost makes him the scariest of them all. He could work his way into any girl's heart, but for the most part, he's kinda sweet. Well, at least the sweetest out of that group. He's the least likely to tear you a new asshole if you get in their way."

Mmmm, Carver, King, and Cruz. Why am I so desperate to know the fourth guy?

The more she says, the more intrigued I seem to get. "And the last guy?" I ask, cutting my gaze to the guy who's sitting by himself while still seeming to be a part of the group. He's all kinds of delicious, and the way he stares and silently takes note of what's going on around him almost makes him appear lethal, and fuck me, it's the sexiest thing I've ever seen.

"That's Grayson Beckett," she explains. "He's the silent brooding one. He doesn't say much, but when he talks, bitch, you better listen. All four of them are a bit like that. It's like they're living in a different universe than the rest of us, but I don't know. They're just so compelling. You should see them in action, though. They're like brothers. They always have each other's backs and it makes them impenetrable."

I scoff. "You're talking about these guys like they're gods, or something. Like they're larger than life."

Her brows raise with a knowing smirk cutting across her face.

"That's because they are," she explains, her shoulder bumping into mine. I look her way to find a cheesy as fuck grin across her face. "You know, apparently they're a part of some bullshit secret society."

I stare blankly. "What?" I say, a laugh bubbling up my chest. "Are you kidding? Who the hell does that?"

She shrugs her shoulders. "I don't know. I don't even know if it's true. It's just some stupid rumor that's been going around since they were kids. They've never confirmed or denied it, so it just kinda kept circling."

"What kind of secret society?"

She shrugs again. "Beats me, but judging by their sheer level of badassery, I'd dare say it's something epic."

I roll my eyes. "Twenty dollars says there is no secret club."

"Bet," she says, holding out her hand. "I think there is, and I bet they even have a secret handshake too."

I laugh as we watch a blonde cut across the quad and throw herself at Carver. "I seriously doubt that guys like that are living by the honor code of a secret handshake," I say, watching the blonde with a fierce, heated stare.

"Ugh. Watch out for that bitch," she tells me, pointing out the chick who all but hangs off Carver's arm. "That's Sara Benson, and she'll cut any bitch who gets too close to her man."

"Her man?"

"Yeah, Carver. They're not actually together though, and Carver would shut her down if he knew that she was going around claiming that he was hers, but in her eyes, it's practically a done deal. She wants him. Actually, I'm pretty sure she'll take any of them. She seems desperate like that, but Carver is the main prize, and a girl like Sara, she'll stop at nothing to get what she wants."

For some unknown reason, a fierce jealousy tears through me as I watch Sara doting on a less than interested man. My claws instantly come out. Why do I feel the need to tear her away from him? My hand balls into a fist, my brass knuckles tightening around my fingers.

What the hell is wrong with me? I need to chill the fuck out.

I try to shrug it off. I shouldn't feel threatened by this girl. I don't even know these guys. They're just douchebags who blocked my Ducati in and who have issues when it comes to staring—but like I can talk. I've been staring at them every chance I get.

What will be, will be. If this Sara chick wants to start shit with me, then that's on her. I can handle her. I've handled girls like her at every school I've ever been to. The only difference is that this time, I'm actually interested in the guys she's trying to keep me from. Though, I don't know why. I'd definitely like to get under each of them, maybe on top of them too. But I'm certainly not interested in dating them. They all seem like full-on alpha dickheads, the overprotective type that I'm so not down for.

As hard as it may be, I tear my gaze away from them and let Ember pull me down to the concrete. She leans back onto a palm and raises her chin to the sun, soaking up the last few minutes of our break before we have to head back to class. "You know," she grumbles. "They all fight."

My brows rise in interest, and I can't help but slice my gaze back to the four boys only to find Cruz's curious stare already on me. "What do you mean?" I murmur, hoping the guy can't lip-read. "Like MMA or something?"

"Nah," she says. "None of that professional shit. I mean like, down and dirty kind of fighting. They've never been in fights at school, but I was out at the club with my friends one night and the four of them were there. We watched them take on this massive group of guys. There must have been ten of them, and they fucked them right up. It was amazing. I had to go home and take care of business that night if you know what I mean."

Cruz refuses to look away, and not being able to handle the intensity of his stare, I look back at Ember. "I know what you mean," I laugh, positive that after having these guys in my head for the rest of the day, I'm going to have to do exactly the same thing.

The bell sounds through the Academy, and just like that, my moment of staring at the chiseled gods across the quad comes to an end. But something tells me that I haven't seen the last of these guys. Not even close.

5

I step through the door of my advanced math class and instantly glance around. It's the last class of the day and I'm exhausted. I'm not usually so tired, but after the party last night and having Ember filling me in on every little detail of the school throughout the day, it's been a lot to take in.

I start making my way deeper into the class when a voice cuts through the soft chatter of the room. "Hey, if it isn't the local thief. Come to steal some hearts, or just cold, hard, cash?"

My head snaps up and I follow the voice across the room to find Knox sitting alone at a double table, indicating for me to come and join him. I give him a beaming smile and make my way across the class. "I don't do hearts. I'll take the cash," I tell him, more than aware of every student in the room listening in on our conversation.

I drop my things on the table and plonk my ass down onto the chair before resting back and feeling the need to sleep rushing over me. "What's going on?" he asks, glancing at me with a cocky grin. "I haven't seen you around school today."

"Then you're as blind as a bat," I tell him. "I've been the topic of conversation since I rocked up here first thing this morning. I've hardly had a chance to relax."

"No shit," he laughs. "But come on, you can't act like you didn't expect it, especially at a school like this. You stand out like dog's balls."

"I know," I groan. "That's the problem. For once it'd be nice just to fade into the background."

Knox leans back into his chair, shaking his head. "I don't believe that for one second," he tells me, as charming as ever. "Look at yourself. You don't strike me as a girl who wants to fade into the background."

I roll my eyes and just as the teacher stands to take his class, the door opens and every eye in the room falls toward the two guys who step through it, demanding attention and oozing sex appeal.

I suck in a breath.

Grayson Beckett and Cruz Danforth.

Both of their gazes sweep through the room and as they fall on me, that's exactly where they remain. I look between the two as they slowly move across the classroom, their stares full of an intensity that has me crippled to my seat.

How are two guys capable of making me feel this way?

Grayson and Cruz come straight up beside me, and I'm hit with a heavenly, manly scent that comes with them. Grayson walks past me, keeping as close as possible so that the hem of his shirt drags over my arm, making me squirm in my seat while Cruz doesn't hold back. His fingers trail across the edge of the desk, over my hand, and right up my arm to my shoulder.

I can't help but look up as he passes, and the wicked grin that lifts the corner of his lips has me drowning in a sea of green intoxication.

Excitement bubbles within me.

The second he passes, I let out a breath and force my stare to the front of the classroom, more than aware of the two guys who take up the seats behind me. The minutes tick by and the more time that passes, the more their whispered conversation that's aimed at the back of my head begins to bother me.

I'm more than used to dickheads talking about me behind my back, but when it comes from these guys ... I don't know, it just hits differently.

Without taking a second to think about what I'm doing, I raise my chin and stand from my seat before turning around and throwing my leg back over my chair so that I'm straddling it, just facing the back of the classroom and the two dickheads who sit back here.

A grin stretches across my face and I can't help but take in their relaxed posture as they lean back in their seats, completely oblivious to the rest of the class around them.

Cruz meets my stare, a cocky grin of his own stretched wide across his face as though I just became the most interesting game he's ever played. Grayson though, he stares at me with nothing but disdain. Clearly, he's not a fan of mine.

My eyes dart between the two before settling on Cruz, because let's face it, he's given me a whole lot more to work with than the statue beside him. I raise a brow, my smug grin still stretching from ear to ear. "Can I help you?" I ask, watching the way Cruz's eyes narrow, intrigued by the girl who dares call them out on their shit.

His eyes drop over my body, roaming over my chest and the long ponytail that sits over my shoulder. "Depends," he murmurs, his chin raising in a slight nod. "Are you down to fuck around, because if you are, there's a whole list of shit that you can help me with."

My eyes become hooded as I watch the excitement bubbling up in his eyes, making them sparkle with danger. The teacher ignores us, and I wonder if he hasn't noticed or just knows better than to tell these guys where to go. "That's cute."

"What's cute?" Cruz murmurs, his tongue slowly running across his bottom lip, making me wish that I could suck it into my mouth and bite down hard.

I lean forward, almost as though I have a secret, and the intrigue in both their eyes seems to grow. "That you think that you could handle me," I whisper. "Trust me, you couldn't even come close to satisfying a girl like me."

Cruz leans over the front of his desk and I suck in a breath as his fingers trail down the side of my face. He takes my chin, gripping it between his thumb and forefinger before bringing his face right in front of mine, his lips so close that I could finally bite it if I had the nerve. "Wanna make a bet?"

His voice is a whisper that brushes across my face, and for a second, I'm left completely speechless. Most guys would have given up. They would have floundered under the pressure and run away with their tails between their legs, but not this guy. Cruz is the kind to meet my challenge with another of his own, and I wasn't ready.

His hand moves from my chin as he brushes his knuckles over my cheek. "That's what I thought," he murmurs before releasing his hold on me and sitting back in his chair. "All talk, no play."

I watch him for a second longer, damn sure that he's got me wrong, but if that's the girl he wants to make me out to be, then that's on him. "Go ahead," I tell them both. "Underestimate me. It'll be the most fun I've ever had."

And with that, I turn back around, leaving them behind me, staring at the back of my head in complete silence, knowing damn well that I just threw down one hell of a challenge, but then, so did he. All that matters is that the two assholes behind me are more than aware that I'm not going to sit back and take their bullshit lightly. I fight back, and when I do, I fight till the death.

I focus on my work, at least, I try to until Knox's elbow comes ramming across the table and slams into mine. "What the fuck was that?" he whispers with a shocked and nervous laugh. "Do you have a death wish? You can't go around challenging those guys to pissing contests because, fuck babe, you might be hot, but you're way out of your league. They will crush you without a second thought."

I look back over my shoulder, knowing damn well that they're both listening in on Knox's warning, and as I meet Cruz's curious, cocky stare, my bottom lip gets caught between my teeth. Heat floods through me and maybe … just maybe being crushed by a guy like Cruz Danforth is exactly what I need.

The minutes tick by and as they go, I do everything in my power to try and concentrate on the work before me, but achieving that is like achieving the impossible. Knowing these two guys are sitting right behind me and trying to figure me out is like some sort of challenge that I feel like I'm failing.

I ignore everyone and everything around me, and do nothing but focus on my work, and after a long, painful hour, the two assholes stand and step around their tables. My whole body tenses.

The guys slowly walk back around, passing close to me just as they had earlier, only this time, they're a little more obvious about their bullshit intimidation tactics. Grayson passes first and as I glance up, I find his heated stare already on me. His eyes narrow, and for some reason, he looks as though I just climbed into his car, dropped my pants, and pissed all through it. There's no love here, and for a brief moment, I wonder what the hell I did to get on his bad side.

The thoughts are gone a second later when Cruz passes and he stops by my side. His hands come down on my desk as he leans over me, his face coming way too close for comfort. I feel his breath on my skin, and in an instant, goosebumps begin tingling their way over my body.

My head tilts, and as I bite my bottom lip and meet his gaze, I know that Knox was right. This guy will crush me like a piece of trash beneath his shoe, but fuck me, I'm going to let him. Cruz doesn't say a word, just allows his eyes to roam over my face, taking in every little curve.

I watch, completely mesmerized as his tongue slowly rolls over his lips, and then without warning, the side of his lip pulls up into a lopsided grin that has everything inside of me clenching. A scoff comes shooting from deep within him, and just like that, he's gone.

I stare after them as they walk out of the classroom, the teacher not saying a damn word about it.

It takes me a moment to catch my breath, and I'm left wondering what the fuck just happened. How do these guys already have this effect over me? It's insane. They draw me in like no one has ever done before, and while bullshit like this would usually terrify me and have my hands curling into fists just to feel my brass knuckles tightening around my fingers, I find it exciting. I find Cruz exciting, while Grayson screams of a dark mystery that I want nothing more than to uncover. I should be taking Knox and Ember's warnings and running for the hills.

The door slams behind them and as my gaze slices back down to my work, the bell sounds through the school, putting an end to the day. My things are packed up within seconds and I'm out the door in a flash while Knox's voice rings out behind me. "Babe, where are you going? Wait up. I thought we could chill."

I don't stop. I can chill with him tomorrow, right now, I'm far too interested in these guys. I need to know more.

I hurry out to my locker and watch in amazement as the school empties around me. No one stands around to talk shit. They all throw their things into their lockers, get what they need, and get the fuck out of here.

I grin to myself. Now, that's the kind of shit I can get down with.

I grab my helmet and my backpack out of my locker before slamming the door and making my way out of the school. The bodies quickly fade to nothing, and before I know it, I'm the only person left in the halls.

I break through the doors to find cars spilling out of the student parking lot, but what I don't expect is to find four delicious men hovering around my bike. The sight brings me to a standstill, and for just a moment, all I can do is stare because it's not my bike they're looking at—it's me.

I let out a shaky breath before pulling on my award-winning bitch face. I've got this. I can handle a bunch of dickheads intent on intimidating me. This is the kind of shit I live for.

Tucking my helmet under my arm, I start making my way toward the student parking lot, and with every step I take, their eyes narrow further.

Excitement bubbles within me until I can hardly control myself. Why does the idea of getting under their skin thrill me so much?

The lingering students stop to stare, and the more audience I seem to have, the braver I begin to feel. Whatever they want to throw down, I'm ready to pick right up and destroy.

I reach the parking lot and walk straight up to them, my bike still blocked in by Carver's Escalade. All four of them continue to stare, and as I scan my gaze over them, I realize just how much fun this is going to be.

King watches me as though he's trying to work out just how sweet I'll taste, while Cruz looks as though he's trying to figure out just how many different positions he could bend my body into. Carver and Grayson—they're different. They look at me as though just my existence is offensive to them, and that very thought is what drives me forward.

I step into the ridiculous little circle they've formed around my bike and drop my backpack onto the seat. "Hey boys," I say, glancing around at them as I hang my helmet over the handlebar of my Ducati. "Are you lost? I might be new here, but I'm pretty sure I can handle giving directions to the Escalade right behind you."

A smirk cuts across Cruz's lips as his gaze drops over my body. "I could be wrong boys, but I think this pretty little thing was just telling us to fuck off."

"No, no," I say, studying his body in the same way that he's doing mine. "When I tell you to fuck off, you'll know it."

King scoffs, and I don't bother looking his way as I dive through my backpack and pull out my pack of cigarettes and lighter that I'd bought at the store this morning. "You've got balls."

At that, a laugh bubbles out of me and I can't help but look up into his blue, tortured eyes. I pull out a cigarette and step around my bike, putting me directly in front of King as I size him up. "Well," I murmur, my voice a low, seductive whisper. "Someone has to."

His stare hardens and I spin around to face the other three. "What's your big plan here?" I ask before King gets a chance to throw some more of his douchey bullshit at me. I light my cigarette and take a quick drag before blowing the smoke out around us. "Corner the new chick, try to intimidate her before she finds the nerve to fuck up the hierarchy that you've somehow managed to put in place around here?" I look at each of them, studying their blank expressions, not one of them giving away a single thought. "I've got news for you, boys, I'm not interested. Your intimidation tactics won't work. I've dealt with far worse than a bunch of over-privileged high-school douchebags. You can't touch me, but from the way you're all crowding around my bike and showing your hand, you're making it more than obvious that I can touch you, and you know what? Maybe that's exactly what I'll do."

I take another drag as all eyes seem to focus on Carver, looking at him to deliver some kind of alpha fuckery to mess me up. He takes a step forward, towering over me, his large frame nearly twice the size of mine.

The smoke blows out of my mouth just as he grips my chin and forces my gaze up to his. Carver pinches the cigarette out of my mouth and drops it between us. "Make no mistake, Winter," he says, his voice wrapping right around me and forcing me to focus every ounce of my attention on him, making it impossible to pull away. "You have no idea who you're fucking with."

"Then enlighten me, Carver," I murmur, purring his name and refusing to give in. "What could you possibly do to me that hasn't already been done? You can't fuck with someone who has nothing to lose, but a guy like you who holds the whole world in the palm of his hands, yeah, a guy like that might just crumble."

His eyes narrow on mine. "You couldn't touch us even if you tried," he tells me, his eyes dropping down my body, slowly taking it in with a disinterested leer. "You look like a smart girl, and I'm sure that wherever the fuck you came from, you were the baddest bitch around, but here, you're nothing. So, believe me when I say that this warning is for your own good; stay out of our fucking way. Don't go around trying to cause shit, and don't even think about trying to make a stand." Carver leans in, his face impossibly close to mine so that I feel his breath brushing across my lips. "You will lose every fucking time."

I pull my chin free of his tight grip and push my knee between his legs, moving my foot forward until my boot is pressing down over the lit cigarette and the top of my thigh is rubbing against his junk. My toes squish the cigarette as my eyes meet Carver's fiery ones, my hand sliding up his strong chest and feeling the sharp thumping of his heart beating beneath. "Like I said," I whisper, raising my chin just an inch to feel my lips gliding over his. "Your bullshit isn't going to work on me because I'm not scared of you, Dante Carver. In fact, quite the opposite. I don't know you, and I don't want to know you, but your little game looks like fun. Just a warning, though, you're wrong about me. I never lose."

Carver's jaw clenches as I feel his friends' eyes darting between us. "Don't be stupid," he says, almost with a growl. "You're punching way above your weight class in a game that you couldn't even begin to understand. Back off before you get yourself in the kind of trouble you won't be able to fight your way out of."

I bite down on my lip and pull away from him, my eyes narrowing as I feel my fingertips roaming over my brass knuckles. How does he know that I fight? Despite the brave words that spill from my lips, I've never met such intimidating guys. They ooze power and it has me desperate to shrink under the weight of their stares, but I won't dare. I'll die before ever caving like that. Sometimes girls like me, all we have is our pride.

Trying to keep my cool, I walk back over to my bike and pull my backpack on before throwing my leg over my only form of freedom and straddling it. All four guys continue staring, and I do my best not to break under the pressure. I nod my chin toward the Escalade. "I'm sure assholes like you have somewhere better to be than hanging around school and measuring the size of your dicks, so why don't you go ahead and do it?" I turn to Cruz. "For the record," I say with a seductive wink. "In case your small brains can't work it out, now I'm telling you to fuck off."

Cruz's eyes seem to sparkle with amusement while Carver's seem to get impossibly darker. Grayson scoffs and is the first to turn away, more than done with the conversation. He stalks toward the Escalade, practically tearing the door open before sliding into the front passenger seat. My attention flies off him when Cruz laughs. I slice my gaze across to his and can't help the smirk that settles over my lips as his heated stare bores into mine.

Fuck me, this guy. He's got it all. *He's* going to be the one to get me in trouble.

Cruz shakes his head, not wanting to laugh too hard and piss off his friends, and without warning, turns and stalks back to the Escalade just as Grayson had done, only he looks back at me as he goes, his lips pulling into an intrigued, flirtatious grin that speaks right to my pussy.

"So, then there were two," I comment, raising a brow as I reach for my helmet, preparing to pull it over my head.

King just keeps staring as Carver puts on a show of being the big guy in charge, refusing to be the one to break, but little does he know that despite his capabilities to intimidate me, I'll still happily do this all day long. There's something about his stare that pulls me in, and damn it, it's the most thrilling thing I've ever experienced.

King, on the other hand, doesn't have time for games, and while his interested gaze is still heavily on me, he's more than ready to give it up. He rolls his tongue over his lips and turns away. "Come on, bro," he calls to Carver. "Let's get out of here. We've got shit to do."

Carver doesn't move, holding my gaze for a moment longer until Grayson's frustrated scoffs fill the nearly empty parking lot before he leans over to the driver's side and lays on the horn. Carver's gaze narrows further and a silent message passes between us, telling me to watch my back while I remind him that I'm not the bitch to be messed with.

After kicking up the stand on my Ducati and balancing the bike, Carver turns on his heel and makes his way to the Escalade. He climbs in, and I can't help but watch as all four stormy eyes are set on me one last time, the tension thickening by the second. Our eyes finally break as Carver hits the gas and takes off like a rocket, leaving me behind in a cloud of smoke, wondering what the fuck just happened.

I pull on my helmet and flick down the visor, bringing my bike roaring to life. As I give the school one last glance, I notice Sara Benson standing with her hands on her hips and a furious scowl across her face. It's damn clear that she just witnessed whatever bullshit just went down between the boys and me. For some reason, knowing that it gets under her skin is just the icing on top of one hell of a delicious cake. Though as it is, I don't know what kind of cake it is yet, but it screams of danger, and that's just my kind of treat.

I can't help but laugh, and although Sara can't see my face beneath my helmet, I get the feeling that she knows I'm laughing at her. So just to rub salt in the wound, I rev my engine as loud as it can go before peeling out of the parking lot, intent on having a good afternoon.

6

"Where the hell have you been?" Kurt slurs, giving me just enough warning to duck out of the way before the empty bottle of whiskey comes hurtling toward my head. "You should have been home hours ago. Look at this mess. Clean it up."

The bottle smashes behind my head, and the pieces ricochet all over the living room. I close the front door just in time before the dog comes running in and cuts his feet all over the broken glass.

My glare snaps up, and I meet Kurt's furious stare. "Excuse me?" I demand, dealing with Carver and the boys giving me way too much confidence. "I didn't make this mess. You're a grown-ass man. Clean up after yourself, and if that's too hard, then get your wife to do it. I'm not your little bitch."

"What did you just say?" Kurt questions, struggling to get to his feet. He stumbles across the living room, having to catch himself against the wall to avoid crashing into the side of the lounge. "You sure have a little mouth on you, don't you? You're a disgrace. No wonder nobody wanted you. You're lucky that me and Irene took pity on you and took you into our home, and this is how you repay us? Show us some fucking respect."

I can't help the way my face pulls up into a disgusted sneer. "Ugh," I groan, watching the show before me. "You're one to be preaching about respect? Tell me, when was the last time you got off your drunk ass and went to work? Ever heard of helping your wife with the bills? No wonder the cow stays out all night gambling every cent she makes."

Kurt's hand flies out, and I pull back, watching almost in slow motion as the momentum from his swing has him spinning around and losing his balance. His head slams into the wall, and he crumbles to the ground, his face sliding down the wall and making his top lip catch against the drywall, pulling up as he falls.

He grumbles in pain on the ground, and I watch in horror. No matter what happens in my life, I know I have to do better than this.

I step over his fallen body and make my way to my room, making sure to close the door behind me and lock it, despite Kurt already being well and truly knocked out.

It's only two months; I can do it. I'll keep myself distracted with Ember and Knox. They seem like cool people, and I'm sure once I get to know Ember, I'll even take a chance on her, maybe spend time with her after school, but until I can trust them, I'm stuck on my own. In the meantime, I have four boys who I'm sure will hold my attention, though right now, it's impossible to tell what kind of attention that will be.

I drop down onto my bed and instantly empty my backpack, letting the food I'd bought this morning spill out onto my bed. My stomach instantly growls, and as I stare at the crisps and health bars before me, I wonder just how long I can keep living off this stuff. Maybe I can order UberEATS tonight and sneak out the window. I'll have the guy meet me up at the top of the hill, then eat on my way back and hope that all evidence of my meal is gone before getting back and risking Kurt taking it for himself.

That prick, I don't doubt that he'd do it. If he found my cash stash, it'd be gone and spent in seconds.

I hate it here. Irene and Kurt are such douches. I've never met anyone like them. Usually, the foster parents give at least a little bit of a shit about the kids they take on, but these assholes … nope. Nothing. They're money-hungry grubs, and the day I can finally get out of here, I'm going to stick it to them.

Out of habit, I leave my boots on. Actually, I rarely take them off, and by this point in my life, I don't know if it's a foster kid thing or just a Winter thing. When my boots are on, it's one less step I need to take before I can escape, just the same as keeping my bike keys shoved down my bra and my brass knuckles always wrapped securely around my fingers. I keep my vices close, never allowing them to get away from me because, in my world, I never know when I'll need to run.

The afternoon slowly ticks by, and after going over the math work that I failed to do during class, I put my order through with UberEATS and get myself sorted out for the night. By nine o'clock, my whole body is agitated, and the need to fly is pulsing through me.

I hate being holed up in a shitty room. There are blank walls, boring sheets, no pictures to make it feel like home. Just a blank canvas with my old torn bag of things thrown in the corner to remind me that this place is definitely not somewhere I will ever call home.

I don't think I've ever been so bored in my life. When this feeling pulses through me, this is usually the time when I start craving blood. My body itches with the need to start trouble, to find an outlet for all the anger that courses through my body.

I can't even remember when this started. All I remember is over the past few years, I've become angry. A permanent chip has sat on my shoulder with no signs of leaving. Maybe it's the life in the foster system, or maybe it's just the bullshit hand I've been dealt that brought it on. Who the hell knows?

After double-checking the door and jamming an old chair under the handle, I finally pull off my boots and lose my ripped jeans. I get dressed into a worn tank, and after not being able to find my pajama shorts, I scoot down in bed and pull the old blankets up to my chest. I must have left my shorts in the bathroom this morning when I ran out of there, intent on avoiding Kurt.

After tossing and turning for way too long, a nightmare-filled sleep finally takes over me. But when a chilled breeze sweeps over my skin, my eyes fly open, and the feeling that someone is watching me slams through my chest.

Panic takes over, and I sit up in bed, staring around my dark room. My heart races in my chest as the first thing I find is the open window and the sound of the stupid dog yapping out in the yard. My fingers curl into a fist.

Someone is in here.

My head whips around the room, staring into the dark corners until a shadow moves just enough to tell me that my instincts were right.

It's not the first time someone has snuck into my room, but it sure as hell is the first time I've been caught off guard by it.

I fly out of my bed, not prepared to hang around and allow this dirty fucker to get his hands on my body and have his wicked way with me. A low growl comes tearing out of me.

I have two choices. I can run, or I can beat the ever-loving shit out of this motherfucker.

Yeah, option two sounds fucking delicious to me.

I run at him, my brass knuckles firmly in place, and my wild spirit desperate to prove herself. "Not today, fuckface," I growl, my fist rearing back.

The shadow moves like lightning, stepping out of the darkness and moving into the little moonlight streaming in through my bedroom window. His hand shoots up, and before I can nail him in the face, King catches my fist in his large hand and squeezes it tight. "Calm down," he orders, his tone coming out as a sharp bark that demands my absolute attention. He slams his hand down over my mouth to keep me quiet. "I'm not going to hurt you, not unless you tell me to."

I suck in a gasp, and for some stupid reason, I completely believe him. He meets my eyes as a brief moment passes between us before he slowly peels his hand away from my mouth.

"Fuck," I grunt, pulling back and ripping my fist out of his strong grip, only to attempt to smack it over his wide chest. "What the hell do you think you're doing in my room? I thought you were Kurt trying to get his dick wet. I was ready to tear you to pieces."

King scoffs, pushing me away as though just the idea of me tearing him to pieces is absurd. He forces me backward until the backs of my legs are pushed against my bed and I fall into the mess of sheets. I scramble to my feet on top of the bed, standing eye to eye with his impressive height. I shove my hands against his shoulders and push him away from me. "Are you fucking kidding me right now? Do you make it a habit of sneaking into girls' bedrooms in the middle of the night, or am I just lucky?"

King's gaze drops to my body, his eyes roaming over my subtle curves with that same interest that he had in the student parking lot, and it takes me a moment to remember that I'm wearing nothing but a flimsy tank and a pair of black panties. "Trust me," he rumbles, his voice low and filled with desire, instantly making something come alive within me, something that takes me completely by surprise. "You're far from lucky."

My eyes narrow, that quick flare of desire instantly bubbling away and morphing into a strange mix of confusion and annoyance. "What the fuck is that supposed to mean?" I demand, hissing through my teeth and trying to keep my voice down. The last thing I want is to wake Irene and Kurt and have their asses in here too.

King slowly walks around my bed, his eyes never moving from mine. "Why did you jam the chair under the door?"

My brows pull down; the confusion this man is making me feel is beginning to infuriate me. "That's none of your goddamn business," I snap before repeating for what feels like the millionth time. "Why are you in my room?"

"You need to watch yourself," he tells me, his warning coming off less than genuine. "Starting shit with my boys … that's not a smart idea. Cruz will fuck with you, but Carver and Gray, they'll fucking destroy you."

I roll my eyes, a soft scoff shooting through my lips. I jump down from my bed and put myself right in front of him, the dark shadows of the night making his hair seem impossibly darker. I stand before him, much like I'd done with Carver this afternoon. "Let them try," I murmur, tilting my head to meet his hard stare. "Carver and Grayson think they're pretty tough, huh? But what about you? Why are you really here? Because I don't buy it for one fucking second. You're not here to warn me away from your friends." I slowly begin circling him just as he'd done to me on my bed, my finger trailing over his warm skin as I go. "You want me all to yourself. I saw the way you were watching me at school, so what's the deal? Trying to get a taste before Carver lays down the law and tells you who you can and cannot fuck with. Because he will, right? And you'll nod your handsome face like a good little boy. How does it feel being his 'yes' man?"

I watch King's face in the moonlight, taking in his clenched jaw, not appreciating the way I challenge his friendship. "You don't know what the fuck you're talking about."

"Oh, no?" I question, putting myself in front of him once again and raising a questioning brow, the excitement pulsing through my veins like a raging fire.

"No," he says firmly, stopping me short. The fuck does he mean no? I was so sure. I know I didn't read his signals wrong. Maybe I crossed a line, but I haven't said anything that should set him off yet, especially considering that these guys are supposed to be able to handle it all. A comment like that should have just been shrugged off.

King takes my finger that still rests against his chest and throws me across the room, coming right along with me until my back slams up against my closet doors, his large body pressing up against mine. "I didn't come here to fuck you, but if the offer of your sweet pussy is on the table, I'm not going to say no."

I meet his eyes, my breath coming in hard, fast pants. "Then why the fuck are you here?"

He pulls back just an inch, his tongue rolling over his lip. "I came to warn you."

I shake my head and let out a soft, disappointed sigh. "Well, there was no need. I got Carver's warning loud and clear in the parking lot, but too bad for you, I haven't changed my mind. If he's going to insist on fucking with me, then I'll be right there, ready to throw it straight back at him."

He shakes his head. "Good, I hope you do. It's been a while since Carver's met his match, but just so you know, Carver doesn't lose. None of us do, and we will end you if you push us to it." King leans into me, his lips roaming over my skin. "That's not the warning I'm here to give you though."

"And what is, dare I ask?"

"Knox," he says flatly. "Keep the fuck away from him. It's one thing fucking with us, but screwing around with that prick is only going to get you into the kind of trouble a girl like you couldn't handle."

My brows furrow as I stare at him in shock. He's got to be kidding me. My hands press against his chest and I push him away from me. "Okay," I say with a roll of my eyes, stepping out from his hold. "This little game of yours just got old really fast." I point toward the window as I cross my room and find my pack of cigarettes. "Get out of here. It's one thing breaking into my room in the middle of the night and throwing yourself at me, but telling me who I can and cannot hang out with, that's crossing a line. That's some next-level Carver bullshit right there, and I'm so not down for it. I've got myself this far in life, I don't need some douchebag coming and telling me what's best for me."

I pull a cigarette out of the pack and grab the lighter before slipping straight out of the bedroom window, sensing King following behind. I walk around the side of the house and light my cigarette before taking a deep drag. "What's it to you anyway?" I ask, regretting not finding a pair of pants before coming out into the fresh air. Hell, even a pair of shoes would have been nice.

King grabs the cigarette and throws it to the ground before putting it out under his boot. He shrugs his shoulders, backing me into the wall once again. "It doesn't mean shit to me," he tells me, and from the harshness in his eyes, I'm inclined to believe his every word. "Hang out with the fucker if you want. It makes no difference to me if you get screwed over. That's your business, but let it be known that I did my part. I warned you, and when it all goes to hell, no guilt will come down on me."

His eyes bore into mine and the intensity instantly spikes between us. I study his stare for a moment, the silence growing between us, neither of us ready to say a word, but with each passing second, the desire pools within me.

I raise my chin, knowing that there has to be something more here. How could there not be? I know I only met the guy today, and so far, he really hasn't said a single kind thing to me, but what does it matter? The sexual tension is off the charts, and if I don't take him now, I fear that I'll regret it for the rest of my life.

"You don't scare me," I murmur into the night, hearing nothing but the sound of an owl hooting in the distance.

King nods, taking my word as gospel. "Good," he whispers, his lips gently brushing over my skin with his words. "I never intended you to be scared of me, but I'm not a good guy. I'm not the guy you want to be with."

"Who said anything about being with you?" I question, pushing up to my tippy-toes so that my lips hover right in front of his, enticing him with silent promises. "I want to feel you."

A low growl pulls from the back of King's throat, and not a second later, his hands are at my waist, the electricity instantly pulsing between us. The tension circles us, drawing us closer and closer, making him impossible to resist.

I have to have him, and right now, I don't care how.

Without warning, the gap is closed between us, our lips crushing down on one another's with a wild intensity. Desire flares, and as our teeth clash together, I remember that I don't even like this guy. Sure, he's fine as hell with intense dark blue eyes and the kind of hair that could get any girl wet, but personality-wise? So far, he's been nothing but a dick. So, why can't I pull myself away?

He draws me in. He's like the best kind of curse. So dangerous and filled with dirty little promises of a good time, a good time that I might just die without.

King's hands grip my waist tighter, and just as my hands roam over his chest and to his shoulders, he lifts me, and my back instantly scrapes against the brick wall of the house. Yet, I don't care; the burn only makes me need him more.

My legs wind around his waist, and I can feel his erection through his sweatpants. There's no doubt that he can feel how wet I am, even through my panties. King's lips fall to the sensitive skin of my neck, and I groan deep from within, wishing he would just tear my panties straight from my body and slam that big cock right through me.

What the hell has come over me today? The second I laid my eyes on these four guys, I turned into this needy bitch with more than just one itch to scratch. This isn't me, but damn it, it feels so good. I should stop. I should pull myself away and have a little class, but something tells me that things with these boys will get really messy really fast, and this might be my only chance to reap the rewards.

What can I say? I'm not the kind of girl to skip out on an opportunity when it's looking me right in the eye. I'm going to grab it with both hands and let it take me for the ride of my life.

"We shouldn't," King pants, not for a second relenting as he tortures my neck with the sweet workings of his warm and skilled tongue. "This is just going to complicate things."

"What's complicated?" I moan as he grinds his hard cock against my pussy and makes everything clench within me. "I hate you now, and I'm sure as hell that I'll hate you after. It's just sex, and something tells me it's going to be fucking awesome."

His lips pause on my neck and I sense him trying to talk himself out of it, probably because boss man wouldn't approve of it, but fuck Carver. This is too good to stop now. "Are you sure?"

"Hell, yes," I groan low. "I need you to fuck me and I need you to do it now. So, either you can make me come, or I will. Take your pick?"

"Fuck," he growls, the curse pulling from somewhere deep inside of him, making every little nerve ending in my body stand at attention. The growl of his voice is driving me wild, speaking right to the vixen within me. King adjusts his hold on me, pressing my body harder into the side of the house to free his hands. He reaches down between us, and just as I had hoped, grabs two handfuls of my panties and tears the fabric apart.

I instantly feel the cool breeze against my pussy and it only serves to excite me more. I'm dripping wet, desperate to feel him inside of me. I watch with hungry eyes as he dives down and frees his heavy erection. It sits against my stomach, and I lick my lips, taking in the thick, angry veins working their way from the base of his cock right up to the tip.

King smirks, watching the desire on my face and then without warning, he pulls back and instantly thrusts forward, effortlessly slamming deep inside of me. I cry out, adjusting to his sheer size, my eyes roll back as my teeth sink into the skin of his shoulder. "Fuck, that's a sweet, tight little pussy," he growls through his teeth, slowly drawing back out, only to slam into me again.

"Holy shit, King. Again," I pant, knowing deep in my gut that this isn't just going to be a one-time thing. This is too much, too good, and I'll be his little whore begging for more if that's what it's going to take.

Okay, maybe not a whore. I might be acting like one now, but for the majority of the time, I can control myself. There's just something about this guy that has me acting like a complete fool. I just hope this doesn't come back to bite me on the ass. But I don't see how, not when we're both getting exactly what we want out of it.

King obliges to my every need like the good little 'yes man' I know him to be.

He winds up my body, bringing me right to the edge, playing with me, teasing me with the hopes of an earth-shattering finish before starting the process all over again. He's keeping me wound tight until I just can't take it anymore.

His thrusts are forceful, his hands on my body are strong and confident, giving me exactly what I'm wanting. He takes from me over and over again, but it's nothing that I'm not taking right back. It's like a secret sexual language that comes so damn naturally that it couldn't possibly be real. I've never been so compatible with someone before, and if I'm honest, it kinda scares the crap out of me, but either way, I'm not stopping.

I feel that familiar burn building within me, and King reads my body like a pro. He brings his hand down between my legs and presses against my clit to rub slow but forced circles over it; I fucking lose it. My orgasm tears through me and I clench down on his hard cock. "KING," I cry before biting down on my lip, distantly remembering that we're up against the side of the house and that there's a whole street filled with sleeping bodies. All of whom probably don't want to know what I sound like when I come.

King comes hard, and I feel his hot seed shooting deep inside of me, and it's moments like this that I'm thankful for the contraceptive rod that I had inserted into my arm last year. I've been caught in a position where condoms were forgotten before, and a month later, the pregnancy scare was enough to have me running straight for my doctor. Though, I'm not going to lie, letting King fuck me without a rubber is still stupid as shit. I should know better, but I'm not going to deny how good it felt.

He slowly pulls out of me and I feel his warm cum beginning to slide down my leg. Usually, I'd be running for a bathroom, yet having him there is only making me want to start all over again. King pulls back, meeting my eyes as he tucks himself back inside of his pants. His eyes widen. "Condom. Fuck. That was stupid."

"Yeah," I breathe, still unable to believe that we just did that, and how fucking good it was. "You're good. I'm on birth control."

Relief takes over him and as he looks back to me, he raises a brow. "Do you still hate me?"

I grin wide, unable to stop the laugh from bubbling up my throat. "You fucking bet I do."

"Good." King leans in and kisses me deeply before pulling back once again. "I fucking hate you too." Then just like that, he winks, making everything twist inside of me before disappearing into the dark night and leaving me panting against the side of the house with cum dripping down the inside of my leg. I wonder when the hell we'll get to do that again.

7

My Ducati roars through the streets of Ravenwood Heights before coming to a stop in the student parking lot. I'm earlier than yesterday, and there's no sign of a black Escalade or anyone who I need to avoid, making my morning that much better.

"WINTER." My name is screeched from across the lot and I glance up to find Ember stepping out of her shiny convertible. A wide smile stretches across my face, and as I kick down the stand of my bike, I watch as she scrambles across the lot, struggling to keep her books from falling right out of her hands.

"What's going on?" I ask, hooking my arm through the open visor of my helmet and grabbing half the books out of her hands before she eats dirt and completely embarrasses herself in front of hundreds of our peers.

"Shit, thanks, girl," she says, finally getting herself under control. "Has anybody ever told you how fucking hot you look riding that bike? I swear, you would have straight girls all over the world questioning if they're actually bi. If I didn't like dick so much, I'd probably hand over my straight card and already have my les application signed and dated."

I can't help but laugh as I knock her shoulder with my own. "You're such an idiot," I say as we start making the walk up to the school gates.

"It's true," she insists. "I just followed you in the lot and the way your ass just claims the seat of your bike in these dope leather pants … damn. I wish my ass looked like that."

I stop walking and let her go ahead before dropping my gaze over her ass and instantly shaking my head. I hurry to catch up with her. "What the hell are you talking about? You have the tightest ass I've ever seen. I bet bikini season is your favorite time of the year."

A smug smile stretches across her face as she peers over at me. "I'm not going to lie; I am fond of a good bikini."

I roll my eyes. "Why am I not surprised?"

The people around us start slowing and looking back at the student parking lot and out of curiosity, I find myself doing the same. I regret it instantly.

Carver's black Escalade pulls into the lot, and just like every other time I've seen the guys, people start flocking toward them. I can't help but groan. I don't get it … okay, I kinda get it. The guys are freaking hot. The girls want to be the closest thing to them when they're ready to fuck, while guys all over are wanting to be the one who they draw into their inner circle.

No one has a chance in hell. Though somehow, King was more than willing to throw me up against the side of a house and screw me until we couldn't breathe.

A fond grin stretches across my face as we watch the Escalade come to a stop right beside my Ducati, just as it had done yesterday, only this time, Carver was smart enough not to block my bike in. Though I have to admit, I made it a little harder this time. If he wanted to block my bike again, he would have had to block the whole road, and while he's definitely a douche, he doesn't strike me as stupid.

The guys climb out of the Escalade, and I don't miss the way Carver's sharp gaze travels over my bike, but my attention is quickly stolen when King walks around the back of the Escalade to meet his friends. He instantly raises his head as if he can sense me watching, and as his deep blue eyes pierce through mine, I'm hit with the memory of his cock sinking deep inside of me as I screamed out his name.

A thrill pulses through me and I'm forced to clench my thighs to relieve the ache rapidly building between them.

I don't know how, but looking at the way he's watching me now, it's clear as day that he's thinking about exactly the same thing. He winks and my fucking cheeks flame bright red. Red? Me? What the fuck? I'm not that chick who blushes over a guy. What's gotten into me?

Carver looks up at King before following his gaze to me with a strange confusion in his eyes and judging by the way King instantly looks away, it's clear that he hasn't told his friends what went down between us last night, only making the grin on my face stretch wider.

I wonder what would happen if the oh-so-ever disapproving Carver knew that one of his best friends, one of the very people who are supposed to have his back, snuck through my bedroom window to fuck the absolute shit out of me until we were completely spent?

Interesting. I wonder what he'd think if we did it again?

Carver's stare narrows and I raise my chin, more than ready to throw down the challenge and walk my ass down there, only to screw King on the hood of Carver's precious Escalade. Now, that sounds like the best idea I've had in ages.

"Dude," Ember says, clicking in front of my face to get my attention, instantly robbing me of my plan to seduce King, though if I'm honest, I don't think it would take much convincing. King and I were like two flames coming together to create an inferno of all things sexy as hell. I'd pay just to experience that again. "What the fuck is going on with you? Have you even heard a word that I've been saying?"

Whoops.

"Umm … no. Sorry," I laugh. "I was distracted."

"Yeah," she scoffs. "Clearly. What's your deal with Carver and those guys? You know everyone has been talking about your little showdown with them yesterday after school. I got like fifty texts all through the night, asking me if I knew what was going down."

"Oh, it's nothing," I say, turning back to face the school and picking up my pace once again. "Carver was just trying to make a point that he's the boss around here, and I just kindly let him know that I didn't give a shit."

Ember's eyes go wide. "Oh, no, no, no, no. Tell me you didn't?" she begs of me. "Please, tell me that this is just some bullshit mix up and you didn't just declare some ridiculous war against the guys who could destroy me just for being nice to you?"

My face twists into a guilty cringe. "Well, I certainly declared something."

"Fuck."

"Chill out, it's fine," I tell her, briefly wondering if I should let her in on the finer details of my night before deciding better of it and keeping my late-night workout to myself. For some reason, I feel like that little snippet of information would fly around this school in a matter of seconds, and right now, I don't know if it's something that I want to use against Carver or just something that I don't want to fuck up in case I plan on doing it again, which is more than likely. "Carver and I definitely have our differences, but it's not as though I told him I was going to destroy him, just fuck with him a little."

"You're asking for trouble," she tells me as we reach the front doors of the massive school. "He's going to take that as the worst kind of threat and come at you hard."

I can't help the wicked smile that pulls at my lips. "I hope he does."

Ember shakes her head as we make our way down to her locker. "You, Miss Winter with No Last Name are the most confusing creature I've ever met."

"You're damn right," I laugh as she dumps the rest of her books into my hands so she can hash in the code for her locker.

She gets the door open and grabs them all before shoving them to the very back and closing the door once again. "So, tell me this," she says, looking back at me, hooking her arm through mine and leading me over to my own locker. "Why do I get the feeling that being your friend is going to be the stupidest, but most exciting ride of my life?"

I shrug my shoulders, unable to tell why I like this girl so much. Maybe it's her raw honesty or the way that she doesn't hold back with what she needs to say. She doesn't sugarcoat, just says exactly what's on her mind, and for some reason, when I look at her, I see nothing but loyalty. "Who knows?" I tell her. "But I hope you're right. We all need a little stupidity in our lives. Otherwise, we'd all be bored."

"I've never heard truer words."

We stop at my locker, shove my helmet in, and am just sorting out which books I need when a body slams heavily into the lockers beside us. "Hey, Winter," Knox says with a cheesy grin. "Where'd you disappear to yesterday? I thought we could have chilled out for a bit, but one second you were sitting beside me in math class, and the next you were gone."

"Yeah, sorry. I kinda ran out of there like my ass was on fire," I tell him, glancing over at him and instantly deciding that King was wrong. There's nothing bad about this guy to watch out for. He's just that goofy friend who secretly wants to fuck, but doesn't have the balls to admit it. Every school has one. Maybe King was just jealous.

"You good?" he asks, feigning concern when it's obvious he's just digging for information, making me wish that I wasn't so good at reading people. "Did Cruz say something when he was leaving? I can say something if they're bothering you. Make them back off."

Ember scoffs beside me and throws her arm out, gently knocking Knox's shoulder. "Oh, yeah right," she laughs. "Stop trying to act all tough. Even if they were bothering her, you know just as well as everyone else around here that you can't do shit. If Winter has an issue with them, then it's up to her to solve it. That's just the way those guys are, and you know it. Besides, I get the feeling that Winter isn't the kind of chick who's going to allow some random guy to fight her battles for her. She's the kind who will go out for blood and make sure she looks good doing it."

A proud smile rests on my lips as I look at my new friend. I don't think I've ever heard anything so sweet. I think I'll keep her.

Knox rolls his eyes. "Whatever you say," he tells her, throwing attitude at my new friend and instantly pissing me off. Why does she deserve to get shit for saying it how it is? "But one day all you people are going to realize that Carver and his boys ain't shit. They're just regular people. You all act like they have fucking crowns on their heads, which is the only reason they have such big egos in the first place. If everyone just treated them like nobodies, then that's all they'd be."

I narrow my gaze at Knox, unsure why his judgment of the guys irritates me so much. Don't get me wrong, everyone is certainly entitled to their own opinions, but in this case, he's wrong. Carver, King, Cruz, and Grayson will never be nobodies. It's just like saying the sky is blue or that bunny rabbits are scary as hell. They're cold, hard facts.

The tension between us begins to rise and I laugh it off before it turns into something more. "I think you're underestimating those guys," I tell him, shrugging off his comments. "Don't let Carver catch you calling him a nobody."

"Yeah," he says with a scoff. "You're probably right. Guys like that are assholes. They'd probably try and beat the shit out of me just for thinking less of them. There's no winning there."

I nod, my fingertip roaming over the top of my brass knuckles. "Yeah," I say slowly. Why the hell do I feel as though I'm the only one allowed to hate on them? Hell, why do I feel as though I might be the only one who could possibly get away with it?

"Listen," he says, stepping into me in some half-assed attempt to block out Ember as I feel four lethal stares piercing into my back. "I wanted to chill out with you yesterday because my uncle is having this epic party at one of his clubs on Saturday night, and I wanted to see if you were down. It's going to be fucking awesome, but you're going to need a fake ID."

My brow raises and a slow smile stretches across my face. I glance at Ember, slightly adjusting my stance to make a point that she should be included. "What do you say? You down to party?"

She grins wide. "I'm in if you are."

Irritation crosses over Knox's face, and is gone a second later, leaving me with an odd suspicion that he was going to try and use the party as a way to get me alone, but I'm not that fucking easy. I only lose my pants for guys who can make me feel something, even if it's just confusion while being pressed up against the side of a house.

"Alright," I tell him. "Count us in."

Knox's gaze flicks to Ember before coming back to me, his lazy grin now pulling up as though he has some sort of chance with me, leaving me wondering what the hell happened to the cool guy I met at the cemetery party. "Alright, cool," he says, playing the role of the cool guy who doesn't get affected by a girl agreeing to go out with him, though this is nowhere near a date, just a fun party at what I hope is going to be an incredible club. "Are you right for IDs?"

I glance at Ember who nods before looking back up at Knox. "We're good."

"Cool," he says again before pulling out his phone and handing it to me. "Give me your number and I'll text you the details."

I hesitate for a moment. Handing out my number isn't something I do often, and after the weird vibe he's been giving me this morning, I'm not exactly sure I want to share it with him, but I don't have a good reason to say no.

With the bell due to sound soon, I take his phone and quickly hash in my number before shoving it right back into his hands and turning to my locker. Knox gives me an awkward smile before realizing our conversation is over and subtly backing away, making himself seem like a complete idiot while talking to a girl.

The second he's gone, Ember bursts into laughter. "Are you kidding?" she asks. "Are we seriously going to spend Saturday night hanging out with him? Did that not feel … I don't know … weird?"

"Yeah," I laugh. "It was definitely weird, but I was hanging out with him over the weekend and he seemed cool. Maybe he's just having a weird day. Either way, if he's being weird at the club, we can just ditch him and chill by ourselves. Besides, there's going to be a bar and a dance floor. What else could we need?"

"Good point," she says. "Either way, I'm excited. It's going to be epic."

"Right?"

Ember gets all giddy as I jam my backpack into my locker before grabbing the stack of books that I need for my morning classes. The bell finally sounds and I slam the door before stepping away. Ember ducks into the bathroom so I'm left to walk down the hall by myself, but I really don't mind. It gives me a chance to watch the people around me and try to get a good feel for who I'm spending my days surrounded by.

I walk past Sara Benson and laugh as her shoulder rams into mine, trying to make some kind of point, but she's fucking with the wrong girl. I'm not the bitch she wants to mess with, just as Carver and his boys shouldn't want to mess with me either. But I've said it before and I'll say it a million times over, having those guys all up in my business might just be the best thing that ever happened to me. I don't know why the thrill of screwing with them keeps hitting me so hard, but damn it, I'm excited.

I keep going, not letting Sara's bullshit insecurities mess with my morning. I get halfway to my homeroom when a warm, large hand curls around my elbow, and I'm yanked into a small supply closet, my back slamming up against the packed shelves. "The fuck?" I screech, just as the light is switched on.

King stands before me, baring down as though he has some kind of right to do whatever the fuck he wants to me now. "I thought I told you not to fuck around with Knox."

My brow raises and I stare at him in disbelief. "Are you fucking kidding me? I let you fuck me and all of a sudden you think you can tell me who I can and can't talk to? Fuck off, King. I don't know if you've realized this, but I'm not the kind of girl who takes that shit lightly."

"I'm not warning you again."

I raise my chin, staring right into those dark blue eyes that have the potential to haunt me until my dying days. "I'm a big girl. I can take care of myself. I don't need you throwing this weird protective bullshit my way. I'm not your girl, not even close."

His jaw clenches and the rage comes pouring out of him so strong that if I look closely, I'm sure I'll see steam coming from his ears and nose just like they do in kids' animated movies. "He's bad news."

"And you're not?"

Fucking silence.

"Yeah, that's exactly what I thought." I press my hands to his chest and force him back a step, only I go right with him, letting him know exactly who has control around here. I step in nice and close to his body, my tits grazing over his chest. "Now, is there anything else you'd like to demand from me?" I murmur, my lips brushing over his jaw as my tone drops to an enticing whisper. "Perhaps a quick, hard fuck? God, if only you knew how good it felt having your cum dripping out of me last night. It drove me insane. The second I slipped back between my sheets, I had no choice but to touch myself, thinking of your hands, your tongue, your rock hard cock slamming inside of me over and over again."

King growls deep in his throat before grabbing my waist and shoving me up on the shelf. My pants are gone in two seconds flat and without hesitation, his cock is free and slamming deep inside of me. I have to bite down on my lip to stop from screaming his name and having a faculty member come and bust us.

King's urgent thrusts make it damn clear that I'm not his favorite person, but fuck him, he's far from mine too, but the electricity that pulses between us is undeniable. Why do I have to be so sexually compatible with such an asshole?

He fucks me hard and fast, his fingers rubbing against my clit and giving me exactly what I need until I'm coming undone around him. King climaxes with me, his fingers digging into my waist and bound to leave bruises, but I welcome it.

He stills, catching his breath as he remains seated deep inside of me for a moment longer than necessary. "You good?" he asks, knowing damn well that was a lot harder and faster than last night.

He slowly draws out of me and I groan at the feeling. "I'm good."

King nods before looking down my body and cringing. "Hold still," he says, turning around and scanning the shelves. "Let me find you something to clean yourself up with."

"Wow, what a gentleman," I say, adjusting my tank and making sure my tits aren't falling out. He ignores my comment and I can't help but watch him as he searches. "So, tell me, does boss man know what we've been getting up to?"

"No," he scoffs, finding an open roll of paper towel and tossing it at me, "and he's not going to. He'll have my balls." I raise my brow as I pull off a few sheets. "Don't even think about telling him."

"Never said I would."

"I can see it written all over your face. You're thinking about it."

I shrug my shoulders and jump down from the shelf. "I can't deny that the idea doesn't intrigue me, but I'm also not stupid. If I go and tell Carver about our little extra-curricular activities then there's a good chance that this won't ever happen again, and I don't know about you, but damn, that would be a shame."

King nods and I realize that's all I'm going to get from him so I indicate for him to turn around so I can have a little privacy to fix myself up. I get it done as quickly as possible and am just buttoning my leather pants when he turns back around with his deep eyes sparkling. "So, before we step out of this door and you go back to hating me, were you telling the truth? Did you really rub one out while thinking of me?"

I laugh before reaching for the door. "You'll never know."

The lights are flicked off and as I pull the door open, letting the clinical light from the hallway flood the small supply room, I find Carver standing right outside the door, leaning against the opposite wall. A muffled "fuck," comes from behind me and all I can do is grin.

King instantly walks away and as Carver's sharp glare hits me, I make a show of licking my lips, letting him know exactly what just went down in there, but before he can say a word, I turn and walk away, no doubt leaving a raging storm behind me as I laugh to myself, never so proud of getting under someone's skin.

8

As I pull my thigh-high boots into place, I stare at my reflection, feeling more than ready for a wild night out. The week dragged by just as I knew it would, but knowing that I had a date with my new best friend at one of the best clubs in town really kept me going. Though, the two epic orgasms that I'd gotten from King earlier in the week went a long way in helping too.

I haven't gotten him alone since the supply closet and something tells me that's been intentional. He's been keeping his distance and I can't help but feel that it has everything to do with Carver, that fucking clam-jammer, or whatever the female equivalent of a cock-blocker is.

My lips are painted with my favorite plum lipstick, my eyes are lined, and not a moment later, my hair is thrown up into a high pony. After slipping my brass knuckles back onto my fingers and fastening the thin black choker around my neck, my signature look is complete.

I check my phone to find a text from Ember.

Ember — Leaving now. Meet you there in ten.

Perfect.

Winter — K.

After attempting to slip my phone into my back pocket and failing because the leather is too tight, I shove it into my bra before double-checking that I have enough cash on me to last the night, a pack of cigarettes, my lighter, and my fake ID. The perfect mix to ensure the best kind of night. Though, it'll be better if I can work out where the hell King lives and slip through his window to return the favor.

It's well past ten at night, and with Kurt already passed out on the couch and Irene nowhere to be seen, slipping out of the house is easier than it should ever have to be.

I straddle my bike, and within moments, I'm flying down the road, roaring over the hill at the end of the street. I make it into the city in no time, and after circling the club, I find a safe-ish place to park my bike. I hook my helmet over the handlebar and cut the engine before making my way around the front of the club.

I instantly find Ember standing on the curb, looking out for me in a skin-tight black dress that isn't her usual style at all. I can't help but wonder if she's wearing it just to fit in with me before deciding that I don't really care. If this is what she wants to wear, then so be it. I can lend her my lipstick and find a spare choker if she wants, but I'm drawing the line at my boots. No one gets their hands on these bad boys.

I sneak up behind her before blowing across the back of her neck. She jumps and a loud squeal pierces through the night. I burst into a fit of laughter, which only gets worse as she turns around and gives me the nastiest glare she can possibly come up with, a glare that couldn't even frighten a fly. After a second, her glare turns into an exhausted sigh. "Seriously?"

"What?" I laugh, shrugging my shoulders. "You know me well enough to know that I'm not one to skip out on an opportunity, and you presented me with one. I had no choice. I had to scare you."

"Right," she groans as I hook my arm through hers and start pulling her toward the massive line at the entrance of the club.

"Have you been here before?" I ask, scanning my gaze up and down the building and instantly deciding that I like it.

Ember shakes her head. "Nope, but my cousin came here the night they had a foam party and she said it was ridiculously wild. I can't wait."

A grin stretches across my face as she says the magic words.

My phone buzzes in my bra and I dive in to get it only to find Knox's name flashing on the screen. I hit answer and shove the phone between my ear and shoulder while trying to block out the noise coming from the club to hear him better. "Hey, what's up?"

"Are you guys here yet?" he calls, his voice drowned out by the noise around him.

"Yeah, we're just outside waiting in line."

"Line?" he scoffs. "Fuck that. Give me a second."

The line goes dead and I shove my phone right back into my bra and just as I'm about to start explaining what the phone call was about to Ember, Knox's handsome face appears from the entrance of the club. His lips pull into a dorky grin and he all but skips down to us. "Hey, you ready?" he asks, his gaze sweeping over me in a perverted leer as he completely disregards Ember.

I hold back a groan. After he asked me to come here on Tuesday morning, the creepy factor slipped away and I put it down to him just being nervous about asking me to come, but his creepiness is back in fine form. I don't know how long I'll be able to deal with it until I finally snap and make him regret his choices. Perhaps King was onto something.

"Yeah," I say, grabbing hold of Ember and pulling her out of the line. What can I say? Knox might insist on being creep-tastic, but he's also going to save us thirty minutes of waiting in line, and I can't deny what a bonus that is.

The bouncers check our IDs and despite it being blatantly obvious that they're fake, they let us straight through, leaving me wondering what kind of standards this place works by, but the lower they are, the better for my night. There's nothing better than a messy night, especially when I have nothing exciting to go home to.

We pass through the doors and the second we step inside, the heavy bass from the speaker sinks into my chest. I feel its vibration like a second heartbeat and a wicked smile sets over my face. It really is going to be a good night.

"Drink?" Knox calls, looking back at us.

"Yeah," Ember yells back as I nod my approval.

Knox drags us across the club, pointing out all the different areas before looking up to a mezzanine level that overlooks the massive dancefloor. "That's the VIP area," he explains. "My uncle is up there. He has clubs all over the city. I'll take you up there to meet him later. He could sort you out with a job if you're interested."

My brows instantly raise as I feel the excitement pulsing through my veins, but I know better than to get my hopes up. "Interested? Fuck yeah. I'd love to work in a place like this," I tell him, knowing that if I was to work here, it'd only be a temporary thing. It always is when it comes to me. Permanent isn't a word that fits in my vocabulary.

Knox gives me a proud smile, seeming pleased that he was able to get a good reaction out of me. We reach the bar a second later, and I scan over all the choices, not understanding a single one. In my world, when someone says the word cocktail, that usually means a mix of vodka, Malibu, a splash of pineapple-orange juice, and one of those stupid little umbrellas on top. Though, if they want to get fancy, I might get a pineapple piece wedged on the edge of my glass.

But this shit … this is like studying for finals. I've never been so confused. "What do you want?" Knox asks, leaning around Ember to get my order.

I shake my head, having absolutely no idea. "Fuck it, I'll just get a vodka sunrise," I say, going with what I know.

"Ugh, boring," Ember says before ordering some ridiculous cocktail that I can't even pronounce.

I roll my eyes and she instantly bursts out laughing before Knox gets the bartender's attention and calls him over. Our drinks are ordered, and ten minutes later, I'm standing in the middle of the dancefloor with my drink in hand, staring up at the incredible club.

I never get to experience stuff like this.

We get two drinks in before I learn that Ember is a lightweight and a chatty drunk, which speaks volumes considering that she's already chatty without the liquid courage. I don't know how she does it. The words come flying out of her mouth like vomit, most of them coming so fast that I can't distinguish one word from another, but I smile and nod, and that's all she wants from me. Though with all of the dancing, I can't figure out how she's not gasping for breath. I'm that girl who can't talk while running. I'm more than capable of kicking someone's ass, but if the fight goes on longer than a few minutes, I'm screwed. I should probably start working on my fitness.

Ember's constant chatter keeps any more creepiness from spurting out of Knox's mouth, but as it is, he seems fine just to stand around and pretend to dance while Ember and I have the time of our lives. But if I'm honest, I think after another hour or so, we might ditch Knox and do our own thing. He seems like the type to hover.

"Hey," he calls, cutting off Ember's chatter while we busily work on our third drink of the night. "Do you want to head up to the VIP room and check it out?"

I look at Ember and the matching grins that spread across our faces are almost comical. I've never been considered a VIP before, and I doubt it'll ever happen again. So, with an opportunity like this staring me in the face, I take it with both hands and run with it.

"I take that as a yes," Knox laughs before nodding his head toward a set of stairs with a bouncer standing at the bottom. He starts leading the way, and Ember and I follow behind, the excitement bubbling in my veins and making me furious for allowing myself to get like this. I usually like a little more control on my nights out, especially when I ride my bike. Perhaps I'll have a few glasses of water after this.

We reach the top of the stairs and we walk into a room that's completely decked out with its own bar, everything shines as if it were made from silver and gold.

Knox leads us around the room, taking us to the balcony that overlooks the rest of the club, and I look out, completely amazed by this place. Downstairs, I could hardly see anything that was going on around me with all the bodies crammed in together, but up here, I have a bird's eye view of everything.

The lights shoot across the room, the DJ does his thing, girls dance in cages, putting on a show, and I realize that there are four more bars that I hadn't even noticed when I was down there.

I feel someone's stare on my body, and I spin around to find an older man lounging back on a chair, looking like some kind of mafia pimp with his gold chain and white suit. Knox looks over at me, and seeing that I have the man's attention, he takes my elbow and pulls me along with Ember following closely at my side. "Hey, Uncle Sam," Knox says fondly to the man. "This is the girl I was telling you about who has just moved to town with a new foster family."

I cringe at the way he explains that I'm a foster kid. It's not usually something I go bragging about, especially to people I just met, people who could potentially be my boss one day.

Sam gives me a strange look before forcing a smile across his face. "What's your name?"

"Winter, sir," I say flatly.

He nods before glancing at Ember, his eyes raking over her like a strange evaluation. "And who's this?"

Knox jumps in before Ember gets a chance to answer the question for herself. "This is Ember Michaelson. Just a chick who I go to school with." The dismissal in Knox's tone has something tightening within me, and for a moment, I want to smack him before he continues. "Winter here might be interested in a job—if you've got anything on offer."

"I do," Sam says, his gaze sweeping back to mine, something glistening deep within them that puts me on edge. "How old are you?"

"Umm … technically, I don't exactly know. My parents were killed in a fire when I was a baby and my birth records were destroyed. My guess is nearly eighteen."

Sam's eyes narrow. "So, what you're telling me is that you snuck into my club with a fake ID tonight?"

I shrug my shoulders, not about to fall into his trap. "Well from what I can gather, Knox has already told you about me, meaning you would have already known that I was only a senior in high school, and seeing as though you didn't kick us out of here the second Knox introduced us, I'd dare say that you don't have an issue with it."

"You're a smart girl," he says, considering me for a short moment.

"Do you know how to mix drinks?" His eyes rake over my body, probably checking to see if I'll fit in with the other staff he has working his clubs, no doubt realizing that I'm more than a perfect fit. Though fitting in with them is different than actually knowing what I'm doing, and when it comes to mixing drinks, I haven't got the slightest clue.

"Umm ... no," I tell him honestly. "But I'll learn fast. I don't know, I could come and do a crash course or something if you want me to. I just need some cash to back me up when my foster parents kick me out in two months. I'll even take the shitty shifts that no one wants."

He raises a brow before looking back at Knox with an approving nod. "I like her," he says, giving me that same weird vibe that I get from Knox and leaving me wondering if it's a family trait. He glances back at me. "Why don't you go and enjoy the rest of your night and come see me for an application before you leave?"

Fuck, yeah.

I resist doing a happy dance in the middle of the VIP room and keep my cool before hooking my arm back through Ember's and nodding at Sam. "Thanks, I will," I tell him before letting Knox pull us away.

We get back down to the main floor, and before we've even hit the bottom step, I let out an excited squeal while grabbing Ember's shoulders. "Did you hear that? I'm going to get a job. A FUCKING JOB. I'm going to have my own freaking cash and be able to live. Well, at least a shitload more than what I can now."

"I know," she booms. "We need to celebrate. How about another drink?"

I grin wide. "I've never heard sweeter words."

Ember drags me back toward the bar and as we stand in line, I quickly notice that Knox is nowhere to be seen, but I can't bring myself to care. He probably went back up to the VIP area to see what his uncle thought of me.

Ember gets busy scanning over the impressive lists of cocktails before telling me that she's ordering me the fanciest one that she can find. I roll my eyes and just listen as she orders while telling myself that I should probably start memorizing some of this shit better.

The bartender gets busy and I watch with a keen eye until a body moves in beside me, instantly sending an uneasy feeling shooting down my spine. My whole body stiffens and as I become more aware of the man beside me, I notice my arm pressed up against his wide chest, my skin tingling where it touches him.

My head slowly turns to find Carver hovering over me, his stare boring into mine with a bigger scowl than I've ever seen on his face. My jaw clenches. I don't bother asking what he's doing here because that's like stating the obvious. He's here because of me, and I don't like it because if he's here, then all four of them are, and that could only mean bad news for me. The only question is, how the hell did they know where I was?

I hold his stare, neither of us relenting, neither of us willing to be the first to back down.

Not a damn word gets said between us, but the message is clear. I'm pissed. He's pissed.

Fuck him. I don't care why he's here. All I know is that I came here to have a good time and that's exactly what's going to happen. Maybe I'll find one of his friends and fuck them just to make it even sweeter. Though, the only way it could possibly get better is if I could somehow make him watch. Now that would be hot. I wonder if he'd be jealous or the kind to join in? I bet a guy like Carver has a whole artillery of secrets when it comes to his tricks in the bedroom.

The intensity grows between us by the second and I don't dare look away until Ember makes it physically impossible, pulling at my arm and nearly making me trip over her six-inch black pumps. She pulls me away, completely oblivious to Carver standing right beside me.

The bartender shoves my drink into my hand, and I'm suddenly aware of the stares zoned in on me from every direction of the room. At first, I didn't think anything of it, but now I know better. My whole mood begins to plummet, and within seconds, the fancy cocktail is poured down my throat.

I try to forget about them, focusing on Ember and the party around us. Yet with each passing minute, the vision of Carver's stormy dark eyes only seems to scream louder inside my head, consuming me until I can't possibly take it anymore.

Rage burns through me, sobering me, and killing my vibe.

God, I hate him so much. All of them. They came here to ruin my night, and just like that; mission accomplished.

My hand curls into a fist, feeling my brass knuckles tightening around my fingers as the familiar adrenaline begins to pulse through me. I lean into Ember. "I'll be back in a minute," I tell her, knowing that she isn't one of those girls who like to accompany her friends to the bathroom, though in a place like this, it'd probably be smart to stick together. Ember can handle herself though. She doesn't need me breathing down her neck every five seconds.

She nods, not giving two shits that I'm stepping away from her as she loses herself in the music. If the rest of the night is anything to go by, I'd dare say that by the time I get back, she'll be right here where I left her.

I dart through the bodies as I focus my eyes on the back entrance, knowing damn well that four sets of dreamy eyes are following my every move.

Hitting the door, I barge through them only to break out into a back alley, right where I feel at home.

I stumble up the broken concrete before six or seven shadows move in from the edges, all coming at me with excitement brimming in their eyes.

I come to a stop, a smile spreading across my face.

Fucking perfect.

9

The men start circling me as I come to a complete stop, so I use the few seconds that I have to really take them in, making note of their height, weight, and searching for any weaknesses to use against them.

It's like a drug to me, and tonight is going to be my biggest high yet.

Seven. Wow.

What do guys like this think they're doing? Do they just hang out back here waiting for drunk sorority girls to stumble out before taking advantage of them? Fuck that. Unfortunately for them, tonight is not their lucky night, it's mine. Besides, it's better I deal with them than leave them for the next drunk girl to stumble out the door.

If I'm completely honest, I've never taken on seven before. I handled five men by myself over the weekend, but I basically had two of them out of the way before the other three were even aware of what was going on. This is seven men, all bearing down on me, each of them ready to go, each of them wanting a show.

It'll be tough, and after the few drinks I've had, it's probably not the best idea, but I hold the element of surprise; I fight back, and I don't lose. I also come fully equipped with a brutal rage pulsing through my veins after finding Carver inside the club. Mix that with my need to feel flesh being pummeled beneath my fists, and I feel like the odds may be in my favor.

I guess there's only one way to find out.

Before the perverted men can finish their assessment of me, I launch for the closest one, my hand curling into a fist and nailing him right in the face. He flies back with a surprised roar and as the others all jump into action, I slam my elbow straight back into the center of someone's throat, not needing to look back to know what kind of damage I've done.

With hands coming at me and men scuffling around, I duck and back up a few steps to keep on the outside of the circle, only as I back up, I slam into a hard chest and all my anger comes soaring out at once.

Before I can fly around and tell Carver what the fuck I think of him coming out here, he grips the top of my arm and throws me back into Cruz, who catches me with ease and holds me so tight that I can't even think of getting out of his hold, I can hardly even breathe.

"Motherfuckers," I growl, but without hesitation, Carver, King, and Grayson go for the men, beating the ever-loving shit out of them despite being outnumbered. Though I shouldn't be surprised. I was ready to do exactly the same thing, and if I can handle it, then these guys should be able to take them on with their eyes closed.

With each blow they deliver, completely rendering the men unconscious, I see it as nothing but a missed opportunity for me, which only has my need to fight growing. I have to hit something. I need to let go of control, I need to be free, and find a way to get this rage out. It's times like this that my other vices won't work. I need to hit something and I need to do it now.

My elbow slams back into Cruz's stomach, and the shock of my hit has his grip loosening just enough so that I can slip out of his hold. I race forward, aiming for the closest guy despite him already being out cold on the ground. My hand curls into a fist, but before I can even get close, Cruz is there, pulling me back against his chest with an impenetrable hold, making it impossible to take what I need.

"Get off me," I growl, squirming against his body and doing whatever the fuck I can to try and get free.

"Fucking hell, babe. Don't stop," he taunts with a deep groan, somehow his hold seeming so soft on my skin while gripping me with a bruising strength. "I've been wondering what it'd feel like to have your sweet little body rubbing against mine, and these pants don't leave much to the imagination."

My ass slams back into his groin, my stiletto heels making it possible for my ass to reach exactly the right height. Cruz groans low but he doesn't relent and it makes me wonder if he'd prepared himself for that very moment, though I have to commend him. That particular move has brought every other man who I've tried it on to their knees.

Fuck him though. That was the last trick I had saved up my sleeve. I'm all out of options.

My body sags as I feel the desperate devastation washing over me and Cruz does nothing but hold me up, keeping me safe in his arms as I feel everything falling apart. I have no other choice but to watch as the three guys take on my fight, easily annihilating the seven men with precise, practiced moves as though they were trained to do just this.

It's over within seconds, and as the last man falls, so does my pride. Even more so when Carver turns around with split knuckles and fury rippling across his face. "WHAT THE FUCK WAS THAT?" he roars, the first actual words he's spoken to me since trying his bullshit intimidation tactics in the student parking lot almost a week ago. "ARE YOU FUCKING STUPID?"

With the threat of the men gone, Cruz releases me, and I don't hold back. I aim for Carver's face, and my fist barrels toward him as all of my rage and desperation takes over. Despite knowing he was only out here to save my stupid ass, fuck him. I didn't need saving.

His lightning-fast reflexes kick in, and his hand shoots up and catches my fist with ease, spinning me and pinning my hand to my back. He throws me forward until my body slams against the wall, my breath coming in short, sharp pants. "Let go of me."

"No," he snaps back at me. "You're a fucking mess. Look at yourself. I'll release you when you can get in control of yourself."

"I hate you."

"Yeah," he scoffs in my ear, leaning into me and letting his breath brush over my skin, sending goosebumps soaring over my body. "The feeling is mutual."

His words cut for a reason that I can't work out, one that I don't have the energy to look into right now. I fight against his hold, but he only pushes me harder against the wall, my face squished against the bricks. "Why are you even here? Did you follow me? You knew I was going to be here."

"Of course we fucking knew you were going to be here," he says as though it should have been obvious, and honestly, it was, but I needed him to admit it to make me feel better about myself. "That's why we came. We fucking warned you about Knox, but you didn't listen. You don't listen to shit. It's always the Winter show, whatever the fuck Winter wants to do, she does."

"What the hell is that supposed to mean?" I demand, my eyes flicking up to King to see nothing but a scowl across his face as he glares back at me, not a hint of a fight covering his body. His clothes aren't messed up, his hair is perfectly falling forward into his eyes, and not a single drop of blood covers his knuckles. "You dickheads don't even know me."

Carver sighs before giving in and easing up on his hold, but only enough to spin me around and slam my back against the wall, giving me a perfect view of all four of the guys under the harsh club lights. Carver takes a step back, but the other three move in to block me against the wall, and while I'm not physically restrained, it's still impossible to get out. "What?" I demand, my gaze sweeping past each of them. "What aren't you telling me?"

King's stare is lethal and I know better than to try him right now. There's no point trying to break Carver, and Grayson … that's a mystery that's not meant to be solved today. So, I focus on Cruz, keeping my stare trained on his until he lets out a soft sigh, his shoulders slightly sagging. "Knox's uncle, the guy he had you meet with tonight …"

"Sam," I cut in.

"Yeah, him," he says, spitting the word as though it's poison in his mouth. "He's a sex trafficker. The biggest one in the fucking state, and Knox just lead you straight into his fucking trap."

My brows pull down as I start shaking my head, the night instantly playing on replay as I go over everything that happened inside that club. "No, that's not …"

"Oh, come on," Carver roars in frustration. "What do you think this is? You're a fucking nobody. Knox brought you here to parade the pathetic foster girl around in front of his uncle, hoping to get a cut."

"No," I snap. "He wouldn't have. We were just having a good time. I was going to get a job."

Carver's hand slams down on the wall against my head, making me flinch. "Stop being so fucking naive. You're supposed to be smarter than that. Knox was using you. You're the easiest target that's come through here in years, and with a body like yours, Knox would have cleaned up. Tell me, who's going to miss you when you're gone, huh? Kurt and Irene? Would they even notice that you're gone?"

My head falls back against the brick wall, and for some reason, I look to King for some kind of help, though I doubt he'll give me what I'm really looking for. "Is it true?"

His jaw clenches, too pissed off to actually talk to me, but he still nods, and the second he does, the fear cripples me. I nearly walked straight into a trap, one far worse than the bullshit I've already gone through.

Anger burns within me, and I step right into King's chest, pushing hard against him, desperate to get some kind of reaction out of him. "You should have told me."

He shakes his head. "I gave you two warnings to stay away from that dick, but you had to go and prove some bullshit point that you didn't need some prick telling you who you can and cannot spend your time with. Remember that? You had to go and act like a stubborn little princess. What did I tell you, huh? I said that it wasn't my business if you got screwed over and you laughed it off. You're just lucky that Cruz has a fucking conscience that would have torn him apart if he just sat back and did nothing."

I step closer, trying to push him again. "You. Should. Have. Told. Me."

King pushes me right back. "You should have listened to my warning and kept far away from him when I told you to. You know I'm right, but you're still too busy trying to be this tough bitch that you can't even admit it, not even to yourself."

"Don't act like you know me."

His eyes shine with all sorts of secrets that instantly puts me on edge. "Oh, but I do. I know you better than you know yourself."

Carver's hand shoots up and slams against King's chest as a signal to back the fuck off, and all I can do is glance away, King's words rocking through me like some kind of destructive explosion that I can't even begin to handle. Am I really that stubborn that I can't admit my own fault, not even to myself?

My back falls against the wall and as the four guys watch me, I feel nothing.

Knox tried to have me sold.

I start shaking my head, unable to believe that this bullshit really happens. It's the kind of stuff that you hear horror stories about, but never expect to happen.

Sold.

That fucking prick.

"What is it?" Cruz asks, stepping closer and proving again that he's maybe the only one out of the four who has a kind bone in his body. His fingers raise and brush gently down the side of my arm, his usually flirty grin and wink nowhere to be seen, now replaced with nothing but pure, genuine concern that completely throws me off course.

"I'm …" I have to swallow to collect myself before raising my head. "I'm going to kill him."

Not one of them flinch at my declaration and it forces me to pause as I wonder why the threat of killing a man doesn't have them glancing around nervously. Do they just think I'm being sarcastic and not capable of following through with a threat like that, or is there something more going on here? Something much, much darker?

I take a few calming breaths before pushing off the wall. "I have to go," I say, trying to squeeze past King and Carver's massive shoulders only to get held back.

"You're not going anywhere," Carver says, nodding to King who instantly picks me up and throws me over his shoulder, his hands coming down over my ass.

"What the fuck do you think this is?" I demand as all four of them start walking back out of the alleyway as though they didn't just kidnap me off the street. "Put me down, asshole."

"You see, I would," King says with a hint of wicked sarcasm in his tone. "But apparently you love it when I'm rough."

My fists drum against his back, but he's like a freaking robot, not even flinching at my touch. "I hate you," I remind him, despite being positive that it's already been made perfectly clear.

King's hand slams down over my ass with a sharp slap. "The more you say it, the less I'm starting to believe it," he says just before grabbing me and shoving me through the back door of Carver's Escalade.

"What? No," I rush out, scrambling across the backseat trying to get to the other door only for it to be blocked by Grayson on the other side. "What do you think you're doing? I'm not going anywhere with you assholes, and I'm definitely not leaving Ember or my bike behind. You can all go and get fucked."

Carver glances back at Grayson, and it's almost as though they're having some kind of secret conversation that lasts less than ten seconds before Grayson is gone and all the doors are slammed closed, locking me in with Carver and King, the one place I don't want to be.

I start looking around for Cruz when the familiar sound of my bike roaring to life down the street rumbles through my chest. "No," I breathe as my worst nightmare slams straight through me. "What the fuck is that asshole doing? He's going to ruin my bike."

"Chill out," King murmurs beside me, his hand dropping to the seat and brushing against mine, his silent way of showing me that, for some reason, he actually gives a fuck, maybe two. "Cruz probably rides that thing better than you do. You'll get it back tomorrow."

I meet King's gaze before my brows drip. "How'd he get the key? It was shoved down my bra."

King just looks away, leaving the question floating between us, the answer to that one clear as day.

As we wait for Grayson, and what I'm assuming is his mission to get Ember out of there, Cruz flies past the Escalade, his shirt blowing up in the wind behind him and showing off his perfectly muscled torso. He looks as though he belongs on my Ducati more than I do, and honestly, he probably does. I don't think I've ever seen anything more erotic in my life.

A fierce jealousy cuts through me. I'd do anything to be on that bike and feeling the freedom that Cruz is no doubt experiencing right now.

I stare after him, and once he fades into the distance, I find my gaze shifting to Carver's who watches me through the rearview mirror. I have so many things that I want to say to him, but not a damn one that I'll allow to pass my lips. He's such a mystery to me. They all are, but there's just something about Carver that I can't quite get a grasp on, especially the mystery of why he wanted to come and save my ass tonight.

I'm just about to work up the courage to ask when the side passenger door is opened and Ember practically comes flying through. Grayson slams the door behind her, and not a second later, he's in the front passenger seat and the Escalade is roaring down the street, putting as much distance between us and the club as possible.

Ember finally rights herself, pressing her ass into the seat and grabbing hold of my leg to keep her sitting upright. She glances around, way too late realizing where the fuck she's sitting. Her eyes go wide before she gapes at me, her jaw dropped as the shock radiates out of her. "What the fuck are we doing in Dante Carver's Escalade?"

I shake my head, unable to resist glancing up at him through his mirror. "Trust me," I grumble. "I'm still trying to work that out."

Silence falls around the car, and before I know it, Ember is fast asleep, her head resting against my shoulder as her light snores sound through the car.

I stare out the windshield and as Carver drives, I'm left with nothing but my own thoughts. The guys were right. Tonight could have been avoided if I wasn't being so stubborn and listened to King's warnings to stay away. I really was being stupid, though I firmly stand by my opinion that his warning of 'stay away from Knox' could have been delivered with a little more substance so I knew exactly what I was dealing with.

There's no way I would have ever taken Ember to that club had I know Knox's intentions were to parade me around in front of a sex trafficker. For the most part, I can handle myself but put Ember in my position, and I don't know how she would have survived. She's sweet, and while she can more than stand up for herself, she wouldn't be able to fight someone off. My stupidity put her life at risk, and I'll never forgive myself for that. She deserves better from me as a friend.

The Escalade comes to a stop and my gaze snaps up to find Carver's stare already on mine. "Is this her place?"

My gaze sweeps out the window to find a big home, complete with big white pillars stretching across the front of the property. We're definitely not on my side of Ravenwood Heights anymore. I shrug my shoulders. "How am I supposed to know? I've been here a week."

King groans. "I guess there's only one way to find out." He gets out of the car and walks around to the other side before scooping Ember out and holding her tightly in his arms. "Well," Grayson prompts. "What are you waiting for? Are you staying the night with Ember or going back to your shithole across town?"

Well, shit.

Without another word, I'm out of the Escalade and rushing after King, reaching them just in time to help him unlock Ember's front door. We get in and make our way up the stairs before finding her bedroom. King dumps her on her bed as though she doesn't mean shit to him, and as he turns on his heel and stalks back to the door, I find his disappointed gaze on me, his silence screaming so damn loud.

It cuts right through me and for a moment, I wish there was something I could do to have changed how the night had gone, but in the next second, he's gone, closing the door between us and leaving me behind with nothing but my own traitorous thoughts.

10

"Are you fucking kidding me?" Ember breathes for the twentieth time, still unable to wrap her head around Knox's disgusting little side-hustle. "I can't … really?"

"Right," I say, still in disbelief as I dig into the pancakes Ember's mom made for us, making sure to set out the cream, strawberries, and maple syrup, which naturally she paired with freshly squeezed orange juice. I don't think I've ever had freshly squeezed OJ in my life. It's always the bottled shit that costs way too much to bother. "I couldn't believe it either. At first, he seemed like such a cool guy. No wonder he was so quick to want to know the new chick."

"Fuck," she says, shaking her head, staring down at her pancakes and letting them get cold. "What are you going to do?"

"What do you think I'm going to do?" I question, a sly grin stretching across my lips.

"Please tell me that you're going to teach him a lesson? It makes me sick just thinking about how many girls he's done this to in the past. Not to mention, the ones he's going to go for next."

I let out a breath. "To be honest, I haven't worked out exactly how I want to handle it, but I can assure you, I won't leave him a chance to do it to some other poor girl."

"What about the uncle?"

I shake my head. "I … I don't know. I want so badly to put an end to it, but this is so much bigger than me. What's a seventeen-year-old foster kid going to be able to do? I mean, apart from calling the cops and giving them his name, how else can I help? As much as I want to fuck him up, I think I'm way out of my league."

"What about the guys? How did they even know about this?"

My lips press into a hard line as I meet her questioning stare. "That's the million-dollar question."

Ember lets out a sigh and I get back to shoving my pancakes down my throat. Last night's ordeal left me without an appetite, but when you don't know the next time you might get a hot meal, you make every one of them count.

With Ember's extended family due to come over for lunch, I get out of there as soon as I can. Don't get me wrong, I would have loved to chill out and be anywhere but at Irene and Kurt's place, but seeing a happy family all gathered around a table usually crushes something deep inside of me, so I start walking.

With every passing step, I groan. Ember lives on the opposite side of the city with the rest of the rich kids, and without my bike between my legs, I'm in for a nasty walk.

Ten minutes turn into twenty but I hardly notice it as my mind swarms with every little detail from last night. How did the guys know what Knox and his uncle were up to? But more importantly, why the hell haven't they done something about it? I know I'm new around here, but it's as clear as day that Carver and the boys have a power that normal kids just don't have. Surely they could help in some sort of way. It's not like they're worthless; I've seen the way they fight. If they can't do things the legal way, then I'm sure as hell that they could make a lasting impression by taking matters into their own hands.

The very thought kept me awake all night, and the more I think on it, the more it seems to piss me off. How many innocent lives have been ruined because of Knox's uncle? How many young girls did Knox lure into his trap?

It makes me sick.

I get halfway through the city when the familiar rumble of my Ducati has my back stiffening. I stop walking and spin around to find Cruz roaring down the street, his shirt whipping in the wind, showing off his sculpted body as his mousy brown hair flies around, flicking back and forth and getting in his eyes.

The engine slows as Cruz brings my bike to a stop right beside me, holding out my helmet. "Get on."

He's in-fucking-sane.

"Here's an idea," I say, raising a brow and studying him. I drag my gaze up and down his body and find it impossible to deny just how good he looks straddled over my bike. "Why don't you get off and give my bike back?"

He revs the engine, making it damn clear that he's prepared to ride off without me. "Get. On," he repeats, leaving no room for argument.

Fuck me.

I let out a frustrated sigh and grab the helmet dangling from his fingers. I pull it over my head before stepping up to the side of my bike and laying my hand over Cruz's large shoulder. Using him for balance, I slide my leg over the seat and get comfortable behind him, hating just how close I have to sit to him, but if I'm being honest, a wicked part of me doesn't hate it at all. My hands slide around his tight waist and without warning, he hits the throttle and takes off down the street.

It takes me no time at all to realize that the fucker isn't taking me home.

"Where are you taking me?" I call over the rumble of the bike and am instantly ignored.

I have two choices here. I can either duck and roll off the back of this thing, hoping to whoever exists above that I don't fuck something up and kill myself in the process, or I can wait and see where he's taking me, and for some reason, I'm far too intrigued for my own good.

Cruz flies through the city, showing that he has absolutely no reservations when it comes to his riding abilities. He handles my Ducati like a pro, making me wonder if he has a bike of his own. I wouldn't be surprised.

Within the space of two minutes, Cruz is coming out of the city and heading back toward the richy-rich area that I only just walked out of, rendering my morning walk a complete waste. He rides through the streets, being obnoxiously loud about the engine, but I suppose it doesn't matter seeing as though it's well past the crack of dawn now.

Cruz passes through the streets until he comes to a secluded area, one I haven't ridden past before. There's a private road and I watch with a keen eye as he stops at the top and is made to enter a code to gain access.

"What is this?" I ask, taking note of how the road is positioned so that random people can't just accidentally stumble past and let themselves in. "Some kind of gated community?"

A small scoff bubbles up his throat but he doesn't give me any answers as the gate slides back, allowing us in. Before I can get what I'm looking for, he hits the throttle and sends us soaring down the private road.

The houses down here are immaculate. I've never seen anything like them. The road is long and windy and screams of privilege. These houses aren't just mansions, they're fucking castles fit for royalty.

Okay, so castle is probably stretching it, but what other word is there to describe this monstrosity? I've never seen homes like this before. It's literally like a scene out of a ridiculously expensive movie, one that I most likely have never seen before and probably never will.

Each home has a massive iron gate, and as Cruz rides right down to the bottom of the cul-de-sac, he passes at least twenty houses—

including one with a very familiar black Escalade parked right out front. But it's the house at the end that catches my attention. It's beyond perfect, standing proud and demanding respect.

It's simply beautiful.

"Is this your home?" I ask, looking through the big iron gate at the stunning white pillars that stretch across the front of the property like some kind of manor. There's a huge water fountain in the center of a magnificent circle driveway, and it looks as though this place has been looked after by only the best grounds men that money can buy. It's the kind of property you'd see splashed across the front of a bridal venue magazine.

Cruz's family must have some pretty epic housekeepers and gardeners they keep on staff because even the hedges have been manicured like nobody's business. I can't even begin to fathom the kind of money a property like this would cost to maintain.

Cruz just grunts as the gate opens wide and I resist rolling my eyes. Why is it so hard for males to string one single sentence together? Come on, is it really that hard? I guess no matter where you go, men are always the same.

He revs the engine and we start riding down the massive driveway and I can't help but wonder if he's going slowly out of respect for his home or if he just wants to give me a second to take it all in. Either way, I appreciate it.

We finally reach the top of the driveway, and as he brings the bike to a stop in front of the massive grand entrance of the home, I look up at it in awe. It looks so much bigger from here.

Cruz cuts the engine and slides off the Ducati as though he's done it a million times before. He starts walking toward the staircase and gets at least ten feet before stopping and looking back at me sitting alone on the back of my bike. "Are you coming?" he grumbles as I peel off my helmet.

My lips press into a tight line and I shake my head. "Why'd you bring me here?"

Cruz shrugs his shoulders, his lips twitching right at the sides. "I don't know. I figured you'd be happier scowling at me all day here than spending your Saturday in that shitty house you've been staying at."

Fuck. He has a really good point, one that I can't deny holds every ounce of my interest.

"So," he continues, holding up the keys to my Ducati, a cocky little shimmer lighting his flirty eyes that I can't seem to resist. "What's it going to be? Are you coming in or do you want me to put these keys back where I found them?"

His eyes shine with laughter and I remember that the dickhead had somehow pulled them straight out of my bra, though how and when that happened, I have absolutely no idea.

Without another word, I find myself sliding off my bike and balancing my helmet over the handlebar before following Cruz up the steps. By the time we reach the top, my thighs are burning and I can't help but stop and turn around, taking in the impressive view, one that I'm sure would be even better from the top balcony that sits three floors above my head.

My position from the top of the stairs allows me to see right down the long, private street, overlooking each house, like I'm standing in some kind of boss house.

"Come on," Cruz rumbles from behind me, irritated with how long it's taking me to get from point A to point B.

I glance back to find the massive front door wide open and watch as Cruz walks into his home. I follow behind, gaping and gawking with every step I take. I've never seen anything like it.

The foyer alone is bigger than Irene and Kurt's entire home, and the sound of my heeled boots echoing off the marble floor just tells me how much more of this place I have to explore. Though I can't deny the one thing I notice about it—it's quiet, like deathly quiet.

"Are your parents home?" I ask, following Cruz through to the main part of the house while being equally as blown away.

Cruz scoffs. "I haven't seen those assholes in at least six months."

My eyes bug out of my head, and for some reason, I feel as though maybe I have just one thing in common with this guy. I haven't seen my parents in forever, though that's because they were killed in a fire, not because they chose to be away from me. "That must suck," I comment. "Being away from them for so long … I don't know, if mine were still alive, I'd do everything I could to have them in my life."

He shrugs off my comment and walks deeper into his home. "It really doesn't suck as much as you think it does. Parents like mine … sometimes it's just easier without them."

"So … what? You just live in this big empty house all by yourself?"

He shakes his head. "Nah, most of the time I just crash with the boys. Our parents … they're all … they work together," he states, almost struggling to find the right words to use. "They're all gone, so me and the boys just stick together, but the older we've gotten, the longer they seem to stay away, which is fine. We learned to survive on our own and we like it better this way."

I nod, feeling as though the conversation isn't open for comments, and when he doesn't look back and just keeps walking through the house, that becomes startlingly obvious. I'm left wondering if the absence of his parents is a little touchier than he's letting on, but more so, what the fuck is it that all of their parents are doing to afford properties like this?

I silently follow him, taking in all its glory as I go until he walks into a beautiful sunken living room with the biggest TV I've ever seen. He looks down into the room before nodding to one of the couches. "Here, make yourself at home. All the remotes for the TV are in the drawer of the coffee table and the kitchen is fully stocked, so feel free to rummage through it."

I start walking down the three steps into the sunken living room when I notice he's not coming with me. "You're not staying?"

He shakes his head. "Nah, I have a few things to do, but I'll be around if you need me. Just call out."

"Okay, cool," I say watching as he turns on his heel and stalks out of the room. I flop down onto the massive couch and instantly sink into it. A groan slips from my lips and my eyes roll into the back of my head. "Hooooly fuccccccck," I moan under my breath. I don't think I've ever laid on a couch this comfortable in my life. It's like falling into the softest clouds, clouds that I never want to get out of.

I stare up at the ceiling, listening to the sound of Cruz's footsteps as they fade into the massive house, and while I've never felt so alone, I also feel more at home than I've ever felt in any of the foster homes I've lived in.

Minutes pass before I peel myself off the couch and look through the room. There are no family photos or anything to tell me what kind of people Cruz's parents are. It's almost like they built the house with absolutely no intention of living in it.

I take Cruz's invitation to 'make myself at home' and wander around the mansion, peeking into the empty rooms and taking in the over-the-top finishes and details woven into the design of the house. There's no doubt about it, the house is simply magnificent.

Two hours pass before I wander into the massive sunken living room again to find Cruz lounged back with the TV on and a bowl of popcorn resting on his stomach. Without looking up at me, he pats the space beside him and I find myself moving toward him. I drop down beside him, crossing my legs and taking the bowl of popcorn for myself.

He glances over at me, his eyes shimmering with something I can't quite figure out. "Give yourself the grand tour?" he questions.

Guilt flares through me before remembering that he invited me to, and for that, there's no reason to feel as though I've just been caught out doing something wrong. "Yep," I announce. "I got lost three times, but I just followed your stench and I was able to find my way out."

"Good, I'm glad I was able to help."

An awkward smile twists across my face and I slice my gaze toward the TV to find one of the many *'Fast and Furious'* movies playing, but the sound is down so low that it's nearly impossible to hear, making me wonder if he'd done this on purpose to be able to hear me wandering around his stupid massive house.

A minute ticks by when I feel his heavy gaze resting on the side of my face. I look back at him to find his stare as curious as ever. "What?" I ask, reaching for a handful of popcorn just to have something to do with my hands.

"You caused quite a bit of trouble last night."

I scoff, looking back at the TV, fearing that if I stare at his handsome face for too long that I might just introduce it to my brass knuckles. "I didn't ask you dickheads to come and play the role of the white knights. I had it under control. That was all on you and your stupid friends."

"You had nothing under control."

I turn my body and set a lethal stare upon him. "I don't know if you've noticed this yet, but I'm not the girl who needs some random guys swooping in to save her. I've taken care of myself for the past seventeen years. I don't all of a sudden need you guys looking out for me. So, thanks, but no thanks."

Cruz just stares, a grin slowly spreading across his face. "Baby, I know you don't need a fucking hero, but here I am. Now, I don't know if you've noticed this, but I like playing the role of your white knight, so unfortunately for you, you're stuck with me and because you're stuck with me, you're stuck with the guys. Think of it as a package deal."

I fly to my feet. "You can take your package deal and shove it up your ass. This is not happening. You four need to pull your dicks out of each other's asses and leave me the hell alone. Let's go back to being at war. I liked the idea of tearing you all down and you assholes never gave me a chance to do it. This whole hero complex you've all given yourselves is ridiculous."

With one arm thrown over the back of the couch and his feet hitched up on the edge of the coffee table, he levels me with a stare that would make any girl weak. "There's just something about you, Winter. You have the four of us divided."

Divided? My brows furrow as I watch him closely. "What's that supposed to mean?"

"King and I had to practically beg Carver and Gray to help your dumbass last night, and that's not how we do shit. If just one of us doesn't agree, we let it go, but you've got us fighting for something that not one of us can explain. They were ready to let you figure out that shit on your own just to teach you some kind of lesson while me and King … I don't fucking know, babe. The thought of you ending up under Sam's thumb, I don't like it."

I cross my arms over my chest and focus heavily on his stare, my eyes narrowing further and further by the second. "You're lying."

"What?" he snaps, my brows flying up. "The fuck are you talking about?"

"I don't know about Grayson, but I believe that he was more than willing to throw me to the wolves, but not Carver. I see it in his eyes. He would have been the ringleader of the moronic Winter patrol. I don't know about the dynamics between your little group, but it's clear that Carver calls the shots. He's the reason you guys were there last night, he's the reason that I didn't get my pound of flesh, and he's the reason that you guys haven't done anything about Sam yet."

Cruz's face hardens, clearly not liking my accusations. "What's that supposed to mean?"

"I'm not stupid," I say, distantly noticing that he didn't deny a damn thing. "You four have a certain … pull. You're not scared of dickheads like Sam, like most of the other men around here, and I saw the way you guys fought last night. You're all professionally trained in some sort of martial arts, and clearly have the money to back up whatever the fuck you want to do, so if you already knew what Sam and Knox were doing, why haven't you done anything to stop them?"

Cruz's lips press into a hard line as his feet drop from the coffee table. He stands before me, crowding me, but I don't dare take a step back. "You don't know what you're talking about," he tells me. "This world … it's not as clear cut as you think. We can't just run in there and bust his operation wide open."

Fury ripples through me and I press into him. "Why the hell not? You know the girls he's stealing off the streets are girls just like me, girls who have nothing, have no one looking out for them, girls who won't be missed by anyone. I'm lucky that I have the means to look after myself, but a lot of them don't. If you can do something about it, then you should have already done it before it became a problem. How many girls have you four let slip through the cracks because you refused to do something about it?"

"It's not like that," he snaps back at me.

I shake my head, feeling the disappointment wash through me. "It sure as hell seems like it," I tell him, turning around and walking up the three steps toward the massive entryway of the living room. Once I hit the top, I stop and look back at him. "You know, I'm disappointed," I tell him. "For some stupid reason, I let myself believe that maybe you guys were the heroes around here, but turns out, you're nothing but a bunch of villains playing God."

With that, I walk out of the room and straight for the front door, slamming my hand down on the hallway table and scooping up the keys to my Ducati. I walk straight out the door and fly down the stairs, not sure why the thought of Carver and the boys being assholes bothers me so much. I guess I really did have higher hopes for them.

11

Fuck Mondays. I hate Mondays. Mondays can kiss my sweet, sweet ass.

I peel myself out of my bed before reaching over and hitting the home button on my phone. 8:33 a.m. My eyes bug out of my head. "Oh, shit," I screech into the quiet room before racing through my morning routine. This is exactly why I hate Mondays. There is always something that goes wrong. So, hopefully just being late to homeroom is as bad as it's going to get today, though, we all know it won't be, not after what I have planned for today.

There's a certain someone who needs to make amends for his massive screw-up, and I won't be letting him slip through the cracks.

I get myself dressed and ready, bypassing the whole shower thing because honestly, there's no point. I have a feeling that I'm going to be needing another one later on anyway.

Six minutes later, I'm out the door while still tying my hair up. I hurry over to my bike and throw my leg over it before listening to the sweet, sweet rumble of the engine. My helmet is pulled over my head and within mere seconds, I'm flying down the street toward Ravenwood Heights Academy.

I do my best to focus on the road in front of me, but after spending those few hours at Cruz's mansion yesterday, my head has been a mess. I haven't been able to get him out of it, all four of them for that matter. I want to hate them so bad, but I'm finding it nearly impossible.

The fact is, I was out of my league on Saturday night, no matter how hardcore I think that I am. I'd had one too many drinks, I wasn't thinking straight, and I allowed Knox to take advantage of me. King warned me to stay away, but I was an idiot thinking that I knew best.

It comes down to the fact they protected me when I couldn't protect myself, and for some insane reason, I feel that I can trust them. Though deep down, I know that's the last thing I should ever do.

I pull into the student parking lot and come right into my usual spot, only this time, the black Escalade is already here with all four of the guys standing around the car, all eyes on me. I glance their way, my gaze resting over Cruz's first.

I hate how I walked out of his place yesterday, but I needed space to think and I couldn't do it while those flirty, playful eyes were on me, distracting my every thought. He looks hurt but there's no denying the interest that still shines bright.

My gaze travels to Grayson next, who just stares blankly like he always does, and I can't help but wonder what's going through his mind. Something tells me it won't be long until I find out. He doesn't strike me as the type who can hold his tongue and I can't wait. If he wants to let loose on me about some stupid bullshit, then I'll be ready, and I'll happily give it straight back to him. As I watch him, a scowl pulls at his lips and I roll my eyes before moving on to the next.

I pull my helmet off my head and swing my leg over my bike, getting to my feet as I glance over at King. He still watches me as though we have some kind of secret, and it has me questioning if the rest of them actually know about us or not. Either way, I don't have time for it right now.

I go to move around them when Carver steps directly into my path, bringing me to an abrupt stop. He looks at me with nothing but disdain in his eyes, making his message loud and clear; he doesn't like me, and he sure as hell has a few things to say about it.

Boo-freaking-hoo. I have more important things to do.

Without a word, I slam my helmet into his chest and step around him before storming up toward the school. I feel the four boys fall in behind me but I don't bother looking back. They're only going to slow me down.

I get halfway before peeling my backpack off and dropping it into the manicured grass of the Academy. I hear it hit the ground, and not a second later, it's instantly scooped up by one of the guys.

Dragging one finger across the top of my brass knuckles, I can feel the energy and need pulsing through me. I reach the school gates and fly through them without a second thought.

All eyes are on us, and I can't help but wonder if it's because I'm still the new chick who looks as though she's ready to kick someone's ass, or if it's the sight of the boys at my back. To be honest, I don't give a shit. I have one thing and one thing only occupying my thoughts. I'm just glad that one of the boys hasn't tried to stop me.

I walk through the school, barging my way through the crowded hallway, but after getting halfway, the rest of the students figure out that they better get out of my fucking way.

I find who I'm looking for and grab his shoulder, spinning him around in the same instance.

Knox's eyes widen before taking me in. "Babe, what happened to you on—" he cuts himself off, noticing the four guys standing at my back. His mouth drops, but before he can get another word in, my fist flies free, the skull sitting over my knuckle slamming into his nose with a deafening crack.

Knox is sent flying back against his locker with a loud metallic bang and instantly crumbles to the ground, but I don't dare stop.

I fly at him, grabbing the front of his shirt and slamming him down until he's flat on the ground. I straddle his waist as Carver, King, Grayson, and Cruz form a protective circle around me, letting me go and do what I have to do. No one will dare try to break through their circle, not if they value their life.

I don't hesitate, slamming my fists into Knox's body over and over again, each blow only getting stronger as the rage burns through me, each punch dedicated to the poor girls who fell into his trap before and didn't have someone watching their backs.

"Winter," Knox cries between blows. "What the fuck? Stop. I didn't do anything."

"Are you fucking kidding me?" I roar, my fist slamming up under his ribcage and watching as he's instantly winded. "You don't think I know what the fuck you were doing?" punch. "Trying to parade me in front of your sick fucking uncle," punch. "Hoping he thought I was pathetic enough to be pulled into his twisted little sex trafficking operation? Fuck you." Punch. "I hope you rot in fucking hell."

My knuckles ache and blood drenches my hands from his broken nose, but I'm not nearly through with him. Because of Knox, there are young girls hidden in cells being raped every night. Because of Knox, girls are scared to go out at night. Because of fuckwits like him, the whole female population is terrified of being unprotected, walking the streets, going for runs, even just being home all alone. No, he won't be getting away with anything and I'll see to it.

"What? I ... I'm sorry, Winter. Please, stop. I didn't mean ... please."

"No fucking way. You're a piece of shit, Knox."

I beat the living shit out of him until I physically can't punch anymore, and only then does Cruz step into my side and offer me his hand. I instantly take it, and he helps me to my feet, but seeing Knox lying helpless on the floor with his eyes fearfully on mine, I can't resist kneeling next to him as the rest of the school watches on.

"If you ever hurt another girl again, I swear to you, the next time,

I will not leave you breathing. Is that understood?"

He violently nods his head, only now just realizing what a huge fucking mistake it was to mess with me. "I … I swear," he cries, tears pooling in his eyes.

I raise back to my feet, and as I go to walk away, I'm pulled back. Before I can even let myself think about what I'm doing, my boot slams into the side of his ribcage, and I listen to the sweet sound of his bone cracking beneath my kick.

Knox cries out in pain as the satisfaction tears through me, and knowing that I'm either about to be kicked out of school or suspended, I don't bother hanging around. There's no way I'll be able to ride my bike, so I turn to Cruz and hand him the keys to my Ducati.

Carver's curious stare hits mine for a long second, but as my body starts to ache and the emotions begin to overwhelm me, I grab my backpack from King's hands and shove my way through the guys' large shoulders before getting the fuck out of here.

An insistent knock sounds at the door and my brows instantly pull down. Who the fuck could that be?

"Winter?" Ember's shrill voice calls from the other side of the heavy door, her knuckles still wrapping against it. "Winter, babe? Are you in here?"

I dive for the door, quickly unlocking it and opening it wide to allow her in. "Hey, sorry. I didn't want to just let random people into Cruz's place, but how did you know I was here?"

"Okay," she laughs, walking past me into the massive foyer and looking around in awe. "Do you have any idea how many things are wrong with that sentence? First off, Carver told me you were here. He said something about the security system and told me to come and chill with you, and secondly, what do you mean this is Cruz's place? He lives four doors down. Whose house is this?"

"What do you mean he lives four doors down?" I gasp, staring at her in horror. "No, you've got to be wrong. Cruz brought me here yesterday and I asked him if this was his place. I mean, he didn't exactly come right out and say 'Yes, Winter, this is my house,' but it was implied … I think."

"No," she laughs, pulling me back out the door to stand on the grand entrance, overlooking the rest of the street. "Trust me, I've all but stalked these guys since I was ten years old." She points down the street. "Carver lives just there in the obscenely intimidating house with the stunning bay windows, Grayson is directly across from him in the Hamptons-style home. King lives two doors down from that, the one with all the cars in the drive, and Cruz, bless his sweet cotton socks, lives four down from here on the left, which begs the question, whose house did you just break into?"

I stare at her in horror. "Tell me you're lying," I beg of her. "I swear, Cruz brought me in here just yesterday and told me to make myself at home. I spent two hours snooping around the place. FUCK, if I knew it wasn't his place, I never would have come here."

Ember just shrugs her shoulders and I'm left gaping at her. "Sorry girl, I don't know what to tell you."

"SHIT. Shit, shit, shit." I hurry back through the door, desperately trying to remember where I'd dumped my backpack, more than ready to get out of here. If Carver has seen me on a security camera, then I can guarantee that whoever actually owns this place has seen me too.

To be honest, I don't even know what I'm doing here. One minute, I was racing out of the school, desperate to forget everything that had been going on, and the next thing I knew, I was entering the code I'd watched Cruz hash into the gate yesterday, but damn, it was a long walk.

By the time I got to Cruz's place, or what I assumed was his place, I'd found the gate for his drive already open and was thankful that he'd forgotten to close it yesterday. I broke in through the side window that wasn't closed properly, and there I was, feeling that same comfort that I'd felt yesterday.

Fuck, how stupid. What was I thinking coming here? It's not even his place.

Ember hurries in behind me. "Wait," she calls. "How long have you been here?"

I shrug my shoulder. "I don't know. Maybe an hour."

"Well, then why the hell hasn't the owner sent the cops to get you out of here? Maybe they don't care that you're here."

I look back at her and scoff. "I highly doubt the owner of a house like this wants some troubled teen fucking around in their home."

"True, but like … do we have to go right now? I'm kinda curious to snoop around and I bet this place has a killer pool."

I raise my brow, keeping my gaze locked on hers. "I mean, you have a good point. Surely, if I was being a nuisance, I would have been kicked out of here ages ago, and Carver did tell you to come and find me here. I don't know, maybe all their families own the house or something. After all, Cruz knew the codes to get in and Carver has access to the security system."

She shrugs her shoulders. "It makes sense to me while also making absolutely no sense at all."

As if on cue, a grin stretches across both of our faces. "I mean, this place really does have a killer pool."

Ten minutes later, I'm sitting poolside with an ice pack against my knuckles while Ember tries to feed me a cocktail through a bendy straw. "You really kicked his ass," she tells me. "You should have seen it after you left. The whole school was talking about it. After the boys finished off Knox—"

"Wait. What? What do you mean after they finished him off?"

"Once you left," she clarifies. "I mean, you certainly did a number on him, but he was still left conscious, and that's not how the guys do things around here. Carver beat the shit out of him until he was out cold while the guys stood back, keeping that circle around them so no one could get in, not even the teachers. It was insane. Knox was left unconscious and the boys just walked away from it, no questions asked or anything. It's all anyone could talk about, and you were the highlight of the story."

I shake my head. "I shouldn't be. I was just doing what had to be done. Guys like that don't get to cross me without suffering for it. Besides, I wasn't really doing it for me. I can live with the close call; my whole life has been a close call, but what about all the other girls who couldn't defend themselves? Someone needed to stand up for them."

"Exactly, every girl around school was talking about it. Though to be fair, they only understood bits and pieces of the story, but they got enough to understand what happened, and now they look at you like you are some kind of rockstar. You're their brand new idol. I'm just glad that I get to say that I'm your best friend. But you should be warned, Sara looked pretty pissed that all the attention was on you for a change, but I didn't get to hang around to see her explode because Carver sent me to come here."

"I …" I cut myself off, not really sure what to say. I don't exactly want to be praised for beating someone up, but at least people now know that I'm not someone they want to cross. "What happened to Knox?"

"He was taken away and the school called an ambulance. As far as I can tell, he didn't say anything, but why would he? What's he going to say? 'I got beat up by the chick I paraded in front of a sex trafficker in hopes for a commission.' Get stuffed. Besides, he wouldn't dare say a word, not about you, especially when you have Carver and the boys at your back."

"They're really not at my back," I explain. "To be honest, I have no idea what Saturday night or today was all about, but for some reason, they just happen to be around whenever shit is going down and they like to play the role of white knights."

Ember scoffs before taking another big sip of her cocktail. "You're blind if that's what you think. Given, I don't know them on a personal level, but I've gone to school with them enough years to know that's not how they do things. They never back people in fights, they're more about letting people sort out their own business. They keep to themselves, and the fact that they publicly stood behind you while letting you do your thing shows that you have their protection. You're one of them now."

A burst of laughter shoots out of me and I find it impossible to control myself. "Holy shit, Ember, that's funny," I say, wiping the tears out of my eyes. "Thank you, I really needed that laugh."

"I, uhh … I'm not joking."

I stare at her blankly. Is she insane? "You're kidding, right? You really think that?"

"Yeah, I do. I've been around long enough to know how they work, and you, you big turd, have just been recruited as their fifth member. They fought those guys for you on Saturday night, Cruz watched over you yesterday, and now today they back you in a fight, finish the job, and don't say a word about you chilling out here all day? I don't know what it is, but something has changed. You're one of them and you don't even notice."

I roll my eyes. "You're insane," I tell her, dropping the ice pack onto the sunbed and taking my cocktail out of her hand. "Tell me about them. What else is there to know?"

She shrugs her shoulders. "I don't know. They really do keep to themselves. There's not much to say. I know about the secret society rumor and how all of their families are supposedly involved in it. I know that they all live together because their parents are always gone. It's probably better than being alone in their big ass mansions. They're as tight as brothers, but it's one of those things where their loyalty to each other is thicker than blood."

My brows raise, intrigued by this group of guys. "Shit," I say, still not sure I really want to believe this secret society rumor, but from the sound of it, Ember is a true believer, and she's been around here a lot longer than I have. Not to mention, Cruz did say something about all their parents working together. I wonder if that's what he was referring to?

"Yeah, they're literally an impenetrable force. The four of them together … it's something else. I've never seen anything like it."

"What do you know about this secret society?"

A grin splits across her face. "Not much," she admits, clearly excited by the idea. "But word has it that they're called Dynasty and it's been around for generations. Like, so long that even my parents had heard of the rumors long before I did, even their parents."

"What? Seriously?" I ask, starting to wonder if this rumor has a bit of merit.

She nods her head like one of those bobble-head dolls. "Yeah," she says, taking another quick sip of her drink. "That's all anyone really seems to know about it, so my guess is that it's true, but it's probably just a bunch of old dudes who like to suck each other's dicks to feel important, and when they die, it'll move onto the next generation of dick suckers."

I can't help but laugh, when it comes down to secret societies, most of the time, that's exactly what's going down. It's like a frat house for old guys who didn't want to say goodbye to their college years. "Okay," I tell her. "If all of this is true, then why the hell are they interested in protecting me?"

Ember looks at me, her brow raising in suspicion. "You know what?" she says, taking another long sip. "That's a really good question."

12

Ember was right—the girls at school have suddenly become team Winter and I fucking hate it.

I sit in the middle of the quad, watching the school around me as I eat my lunch and listen to the not-so-soothing babble coming out of Ember's mouth. I don't know how she does it, but she always has something to say. Usually, I'd find a trait like that deathly irritating, but with Ember, it seems to be the one thing that helps keep my mind at ease and not focused on all the things it shouldn't be thinking about.

My fingers curl into a fist, feeling my brass knuckles tighten around my hand as the need to walk out of the school and light up a cigarette fires through me, but I can't. Not with the eyes of everyone on me, it's too risky. Smoking isn't exactly a crime around here, but it's not something I usually do with the eyes of the world on me. It's my vice, my coping mechanism, and I hate when people know when I'm feeling weak.

The very thought of feeling weak has my gaze shifting across the quad to the four boys who hover around a table, all four of their eyes already on mine. No wonder I feel so freaking weak all the time. What girl wouldn't with their intense stares on them like that?

I seek out King, knowing that when I look at him, a sense of power usually shoots through me, and when his stare turns into one of pure desire, I get exactly what I'm looking for. I raise my chin, finally beginning to feel somewhat like myself.

I slept over at the non-Cruz mansion. It was nearly eight last night when Ember finally decided that it was time to go home, and after offering me a lift, I kindly declined and somehow ended up crashing in the massive master bedroom. It was the first good sleep I've had in … shit, I can't even remember how long, but knowing the boys were close by had me feeling safer than any girl in my position ought to feel.

Despite my usual confidence slamming back into me by means of a male's appreciation, I can't help but finally feel good about myself. I spent the night sulking about my situation after drinking way too many cocktails by the pool with Ember, but now I'm ready to get back on track.

I have four random guys wanting to play hero in my life, two of them blatantly hating me, one wishing he could hate me, and the other hoping he could flirt his way into a good time. Though, I bet he could. With eyes like that, mousy brown hair, and a smile that completely knocks me off my feet, all he'd have to do is promise me a good time and I'd be all his. Well, for the night that is. I'm not into the whole boyfriend thing. Being stuck with the same possessive guy night after night isn't my thing. I've tried that too many times to count and every time it's failed so hard that the few days spent together wasn't even worth the struggle.

A grin begins creeping across my face, and as King's eyes bore into mine with the overwhelming reminder of the two times we've been together, everything clenches within. "Hey, do you have King's number by any chance?" I ask Ember, wondering if King would be down for a quick screw behind the bleachers or maybe in the back of Carver's Escalade.

"Umm .... I don't know." Ember's face twists as she tries to remember exactly whose numbers she has stored in her phone when she looks back at me, her brow slowly raising as a smug grin pulls at her lips. "Why?"

I feel my cheeks flame and feel like such a dork. I don't think my cheeks have ever blushed so much in my life. I swear, before I came to Ravenwood Heights, I didn't even think I was capable of blushing, but here I am.

My gaze flicks back to King's and I bet he can tell by the grin on my face exactly what I'm thinking. "Umm, so I can—"

"Umm … hey Winter," a timid voice cuts through my musings and I whip my head back around to find Knox stepping into my side, hovering over me with his arm in a sling, a crutch under his other arm, and his face all different shades of black and blue.

I instantly get to my feet, my sudden need to have King bend me over and fuck me until I cry completely gone from my mind. "What the hell do you think you're doing?" I snap, grabbing Ember who stands beside me and dragging her ass away from this creep. I sense four imposing bodies creeping in behind me, and although they keep far enough away to let me run the show, I still want to throat punch each and every one of them. "I thought the message to stay the fuck away from me was clear."

"Yeah, I ... yeah, it was," Knox stammers out. "I guess I was hoping that we could talk."

A throat clears behind me and I watch as Knox snaps his gaze up to Carver's. His eyes bug out of his head and he starts to back away, but this isn't over yet. For Knox to think that he can come and talk to me the very day after I kicked his ass, then he clearly didn't receive my warning very well. I have absolutely no intention of hearing him out, but if anyone is going to scare him away, it's going to be me, not any of the imposing asshats behind me.

"Say what you need to say," I demand, taking an obvious step to the right and placing me right in front of Carver, making a point that I run this show, not him, which only serves to make something clench deep within me, knowing my move would have Carver raging on the inside.

Knox nervously glances up at the guys behind me before meeting my stare and making me briefly wonder why the hell he isn't wasting away in a hospital bed. Considering that a hospital is going to do nothing but draw attention, I'm assuming that neither the boys or Knox's uncle would be comfortable with him there.

"I came to apologize," he says, his gaze jumping around to the other students that hover closer as they notice what's going on, all of them hoping for something new to paste all over YouTube.

"Do you honestly think some piss-poor apology is going to make up for the fact that you paraded me around in front of your uncle in the hopes that he decided I was worth enough to sell to one of his clients as a sex-slave? Fuck you, Knox. Tell me, how many girls have you personally been responsible for trading to your uncle? No, no. You know what I really want to know? Tell me about the payout you get for bringing girls to his doorstep. Is it worth it? Do you sleep well at night under your piles of dirty cash knowing that you're responsible for those young girls being raped day-in and day-out?"

"No," he spits, wobbling against his crutch. "I never wanted to do it. He ... he made me. Do you have any idea how horrible it is growing up with him as my uncle?"

I can't help but laugh. "Are you serious? You really want to compare war stories about growing up in a shitty situation because I can guarantee that I'll win. So, how about this? Be a fucking man and tell him no. You're almost out of high school and can't stand on your own two feet. Do you have any idea how pathetic you've made yourself look?"

Knox clenches his jaw and takes a step forward, which prompts the line of muscle behind me to do the same, instantly sending Knox flailing back three steps until he's at a comfortable position. He seeks out my stare and gives me puppy dog eyes that make me want to hurl. "Please, Winter. You have to believe me. I never intended to hurt you; I was just doing my job. Please, don't tell anybody about this. You're going to destroy any chance I had of getting into an Ivy League college, and my parents ... if they knew about this, they'd fucking hate me."

I resist laughing, unable to fathom how he can't understand just how serious this shit is. Does he not get how he's destroying these young girls that he's trading to his uncle? Does he not understand what happens to them once they are sold into the hands of these monsters? Fuck me.

I shake my head. "Do yourself a favor—turn around and walk away. You and me; we're never going to be cool. You're a piece of shit, and just know that if someone comes asking questions, yours will be the first name I give. You're dead to me, and I cannot wait to watch you and your uncle crash and burn. Take my word for it, both of you are going to end up in prison or dead, and I want absolutely nothing to do with you. Don't come near me, don't come near Ember, and for the sake of your life, don't go near any other girl, otherwise I will fucking end you, and that's a promise. Got it?"

Knox's eyes widen, and as he holds my stare, I don't doubt that he can see just how serious I am, but he knows just as well as I do that I have absolutely no credibility. Not a damn person is going to believe my story over his. I'm just a nobody from a shitty foster home who's going to have to scream a shitload louder than everybody else just to be heard. Destroying Knox and his uncle will be a fucking marathon, but I'm down for the challenge.

Seeing me as a threat to his bullshit side-hustle, he finally starts to back away, and this time, I think he gets the point. He won't be coming back to fuck with me, but unfortunately for his pea-sized brain, I don't think he understands just how wrong what he's been doing is. Though, perhaps he does understand but just doesn't care.

Once he's finally out of sight, I let out a breath and spin on my heel to find the four boys staring right at me. "Do you guys seriously think that I can't handle myself?" I ask, focusing my stare on Carver before shifting down the line. "Fuck you all. I'm not a damsel in distress."

A smile pulls at the corner of Carver's lips, and for the first time since first meeting him over a week ago, he looks at me as though he sees some kind of potential, but all it makes me want to do is slam my knee up into his junk and call it a day.

Realizing that I'm not about to get anywhere with them, I turn on my heel only to find Sara Bennett standing right in front of me with a smug-as-fuck grin stretched wide across her face. I've been at enough schools and had enough run-ins with the 'popular girls' to know that she thinks she has me backed into a corner, but I still can't work out why. What's her problem with me? Does she think I'm trying to take Carver from her? Because the way I hear it is that she doesn't even have him herself, but what does it matter? Carver can go and fuck a pinecone for all I care.

"Need something?" I question, sensing the guys hanging around.

"Oh, hell no," she laughs. "Not from you. Who knows where you've been? I don't want to catch something."

I can't help but laugh. "That's the best you've got?" I ask, a little disappointed. "I thought you were going to give me something good but you're coming at me with the disease shit? Oh, honey, you're going to have to try a lot harder than that."

She grins, and for a second, I falter. I've never had a run-in with her, but so far, she hasn't flinched. That usually tells me that she's got something hidden up her sleeve, and from experience, it's never anything good.

Her hand twitches and I follow it down to find her phone resting in her palm and my whole body stiffens. "Oh, honey," she mocks in a sing-song tone, attempting to mimic me. "I don't need to fucking try because I have everything I need right here."

"Please, do share with the class," I ask as her friends around her begin to snicker and laugh, pointing at me and calling me a whore.

Sara laughs. "Okay," she says, bringing her phone up in front of her and looking down at the screen as she presses a few buttons. "But just remember that you asked for this."

I roll my eyes but as she turns the phone around and I find my face staring back at me with my lips curled around some guy's cock, everything shatters inside of me.

A video plays and it takes me only a second to realize that this is a video loaded onto Pornhub, a video that was taken without my consent when I was only sixteen.

Humiliation washes through me as I watch myself go to town on someone's dick, knowing damn well that Carver, King, Grayson, and Cruz stand right behind me, with a more than perfect view of Sara's phone. I feel myself beginning to close down but there's no way in hell that I'm about to let this bitch know. "So, you're into statutory rape and kiddy porn, huh?"

"What?" Sara snaps as I desperately hold back tears, only able to do so when Carver steps right into my back with his hand falling to my waist and slowly beginning to circle it, holding me tight.

"That's exactly what you're looking at. I was sixteen when that was recorded by a guy who got me drunk at a party and told me he was a senior in high school. Turns out that he was twenty-two, and he knew damn well that I was a minor. Meaning that video that you've no doubt been distributing around the school to a bunch of other minors is actually child pornography, a criminal offense. I wonder how a jury would feel about you having child pornography saved in your phone." I cringe, before sucking in a horrified gasp. "Oh, no. A criminal record isn't going to look good on your college applications."

Sara's eyes widen in horror, but before she can pull her phone away, Carver's hand snaps out and clenches down around her wrist, his other hand tightening on my waist and getting looks from everyone watching the show. "What are you doing?" she demands, her wide eyes raising to meet Carver's, filled with betrayal, assuming that he was going to stand by her.

Without a word, Carver takes her phone from her hand, locks it, and instantly slides it into the back pocket of his pants.

"What are you—" she cuts herself off, looking in panic up and down the line of muscle behind me before coming back to Carver. "This isn't funny, Carver. Give me my phone."

King scoffs. "What's not funny is trying to humiliate someone by displaying them all over the school in a vulnerable position."

"But I ... I didn't—"

Carver leans in over my shoulder, his face moving in right beside mine as he captures her whole attention. "Run."

And just like that, she's gone.

With one scathing look from Carver, the crowd around us disappears, including Ember, and I'm left with only the guys. Carver spins me around, and without the crowd to hold me accountable, the humiliation takes over and I break.

"Fuck," Cruz grunts, stepping into me and pushing Carver's hold away from my waist. His warm arms wrap around me and he pulls me into his chest. I take a few seconds to find myself, breathing in, breathing out.

"We'll handle it," Grayson's voice comes from behind Cruz.

I raise my head, looking over his shoulder to find Grayson's stormy gaze on mine with nothing but a promise in his eyes, and as I glance back at King and Carver, I find the same thing shining in theirs. I let out another shaky breath before pulling myself together and reluctantly pulling out of Cruz's arms, confused as to why I find him so comforting. "No," I say, glancing around at them all. "I appreciate the offer, but I've got this. It's already been handled, and like I said before, I don't need you guys fighting my battles. Besides, I doubt Sara will be bothering me again."

King shakes his head. "That's not—"

"She said no," Carver rumbles, meeting King's stare with one of his own, a million messages passing between them until King finally nods and turns his gaze back to me.

Unable to handle the weight of their stares while feeling so vulnerable and embarrassed, I quickly nod, silently thanking them for having my back again before slipping away. I walk back through the school, feeling all eyes on me, but this time, also feeling their laughter, jokes, and comments. Despite Sara learning that she can't fuck with me, the damage has already been done.

After stopping by my locker and grabbing my things, I hightail it out of there, wondering when the hell the guys decided that I was worthy of their protection.

13

A sharp knock at my bedroom window has me flying up out of my bed and desperately searching for a weapon. From experience, a knock on my bedroom window either means that someone is coming for me, or an egotistical badass with a big dick is coming to lay down the law, and something tells me that King isn't planning an unexpected visit tonight.

I stare out the window, my heart racing a million miles an hour, only to find Ember staring back at me with a goofy-as-fuck grin plastered across her face.

I hurry to the window and quickly slide it open before her head flies through the opening. "What the fuck, bro?" she demands. "What are you wearing? I told you to be ready by eight and it's already half-past. Hurry up, we've got to go."

"Go where? What the hell are you talking about?"

"The party under the pier," she says, staring at me with a blank expression. "Are you kidding? We've only talked about it a million times this week. I thought you wanted to go."

I cringe. "Sorry," I grumble, keeping my voice low so I don't alert Kurt, who's yelling at the dog to shut up from the other side of the house despite it being impossibly silent at Ember's feet, watching the top half of her body disappear through my open window. "I kinda forgot but I don't know. I'm not really feeling a party tonight. It's been a shitty week. Can't we just chill at your place or something like that?"

"Hell no," she whisper-yells. "My parents are having some hoity-toity dinner party with a bunch of stuck-up assholes from my father's bank. There's no way we're hanging out for that. My mother will have you married off to an investment banker who'll abuse you behind closed doors in no time."

I stare at her in horror. "Please tell me that your mother isn't trying to set you up with old dudes?"

She shrugs her shoulders. "Yeah, but it's no biggie. After the third time, I started showing up to the dinners in my pajamas with blackout stickers over my front teeth and a fart machine hidden under the table. I've been good since then."

I can't help but laugh, and while every time I've been past her house, I felt envious of her family life, moments like this make me thankful that I don't have to suffer through the bullshit of having other peoples' values and rules forced on me.

"So, what's it going to be?" she continues. "Are you coming out with me to get wicked wasted and forget the week from hell, or are you staying here to hide out in your room like a little bitch?"

"Well, shit. When you put it like that …"

A wicked grin stretches across her face. "That's what I thought."

I quickly race around my room, picking out an outfit as Ember silently plays with the dog, and when I start climbing out through the window, I meet Ember's stare. "Kay, I've got everything I need, but I haven't showered and I refuse to do it here before Kurt passes out for the night, so we have to head back to your place."

"Deal."

"Oh," I say, looking over at my Ducati. "I'll also need to stash my bike in your garage. I don't trust Irene and Kurt not to pawn it."

Ember nods. "I figured that was part of the deal."

A wide smile tears across my face, and not a second later, she's climbing into her convertible as I straddle my bike, and as if on cue, the rumble of both our engines echo through the quiet street. We take off and I follow her back to her place before rushing inside and throwing myself into her bathroom.

Ember comes barging in with me and sits on the toilet, chatting away as I strip out of my shitty clothes and step into the shower. The water comes down over me and I moan into the warm stream, completely gob smacked by the fact that I didn't have to wait five minutes for the water to heat before being able to step under it.

I quickly start washing myself, and as my palm roams over my legs,

I realize that it's been way too long since I've shaved and taken care of business.

Hmmm, I wonder if King is going to be there tonight?

My head flies out of the shower and water drips all over the floor as I meet Ember's stare. "Got any razors?"

"Razors?" she questions in disgust. "Who shaves anymore? Don't you get laser?"

I can't stop the scoff from flying out of my mouth and hope to whoever exists above that I don't offend her. "Laser?" I laugh. "Do you honestly think I can afford to get laser treatments? I can't even afford to scratch my own ass most of the time."

Ember rolls her eyes and gets up from the toilet. "Let me have a look."

I finish washing myself as I listen to Ember rummaging around in the bathroom drawers and let out a relieved sigh when she shoves her head into the shower a minute later with a wide grin and a brand new razor held in front of her face. "You can thank me later," she says before glancing down and pulling a face. "Shit, girl, look at those legs. Let me pay for your laser treatment for your birthday."

"Get stuffed," I grumble, pulling the door closed between us. "It's not that bad. Besides, I'm a natural blonde, I just box dye my hair brunette so I don't think laser even works for me."

"Good point," she says, shoving her head back into the shower with a stupid grin. "Are you going to shave your kitty? I bet King likes a nice clean palette to work with, though, I bet King likes a lot of things."

My mouth drops. "King? Who said anything about King?"

"Come on," she groans, falling back onto her toilet. "Don't act like nothing is going on there. You're screwing him, aren't you? Or at least, you want to." I roll my eyes and ignore her questioning, but it turns out that she wasn't after an answer anyway as the words just keep falling from her mouth. "To be honest, I kinda thought you were into Cruz for a hot minute, but I really picture you with Carver. The two of you together would be hot, buuuuuut," she says, drawing it out. "If King is the one wetting your panties, then that's cool too. I bet he's the type to fuck a girl whenever and wherever he likes, you know what I mean?"

I bite my bottom lip to avoid the comments that are desperate to fly out of my mouth and concentrate on the sharp razor traveling up and down my legs.

"You know," she continues, her tone dropping low and filled with dark desire. "I used to fantasize about King stripping me naked in the middle of a classroom and throwing me down on a desk just so he could spread my legs and run his tongue up my cat like his life depended on it."

My brows raise as I work on shaving every inch of my body, and the second the idea of King's tongue roaming over all my lady bits enters my mind, every word Ember says fades into the background.

I finish my shower and before her parents can drag us into their fancy dinner party, we're out the door and racing toward the pier party.

We get there within ten minutes flat only to find the party in full swing. People are spilling out everywhere and I instantly recognize a few people from school, people who've been more than happy to call me a whore over the past few days. The need to retreat to Ember's car is overwhelming. But no, I didn't go to all that effort shaving all my bits for nothing. There's no point peeling a potato if you don't plan on mashing it, and damn it, this potato is going to get mashed.

Ember clings onto my arm, dragging me through the party until we find a table set out with every drink under the sun, but unlike the parties that I usually attend, there's a bartender here who happily makes us whatever bullshit concoction Ember throws at him.

It takes him only a minute, and before I know it, I'm sipping on something fruity with a bright pink straw as my toes sink into the sand beneath the pier.

Lights twinkle and music is blasting, but what really pulls me in is the sound of the waves crashing against the shore. I've never really been to the beach, and honestly, I didn't do enough research about where I was going to know there was even a beach this close to us.

I've only ever been to the beach once before and it was a disaster of a day. I was only thirteen and staying with Karleigh, and while the day itself was incredible, it was also the day I found out that I was being taken from Karleigh and the trip to the beach was just some stupid way to soften the blow.

I put it to the back of my head. I'm here to have a good time, not to dwell on the past. I throw back what's left of my drink when Ember's grip on my arm tightens and she pulls me back with wide eyes. "What's wrong?" I ask, looking back at her and desperately trying to figure out what's caught her eye.

"That's Jacob Scardoni," she hisses, using her chin to indicate across the party to a guy who's standing around a bonfire with a bunch of friends.

I look at him for a moment, not able to recognize his name or face from school, "Umm … who?" I ask. "Am I supposed to remember him from somewhere?"

"No," she says. "I know I talk about Carver, King, Grayson, and Cruz like they're my soulmates, but this guy … he's the one I really like."

My brows rise as I look over the guy again, taking in the dark shaggy hair, the cocky grin, and the body that any girl would be happy to get under. He's not bad at all, but nothing compared to the four assholes of Ravenwood Heights, though considering the dreamy look in Ember's eyes, I'd dare say that for once, she might not agree with me. "How do you know this guy?" I ask, feeling an odd protectiveness for my new friend come over me. "Does he go to our school and I've just been missing him?"

She shakes her head. "No, he goes to school with my cousin across town. I met him last year and instantly fell in love with the guy despite hardly knowing him. I got drunk and he looked after me like a gentleman and I've sort of been obsessed ever since. He was a total sweetheart and now I've sort of gone to every party since just so I can see him."

I stare at her blankly. "Are you kidding me? Go and talk to him if you're crazy about him. What are you waiting for?"

"Don't be stupid," she tells me, shaking off my comments. "He's like the most popular guy at school. He's like the Carver of Castlereagh

Academy. That's the all-boys private school. They are douches over there, but it doesn't matter because there's no way he'd be interested in me, I'm a complete dork. Besides, I doubt he'd even remember me. That party was ages ago and I looked completely different."

I shake my head. "Don't put yourself down like that. You're fucking gorgeous. Any guy would be lucky to have you, now throw back the rest of that liquid courage and go and get yourself a date. Who knows, maybe you two were meant to be together and fate is just waiting for you to pull on your big girl panties."

Ember narrows her eyes at me. "Ha. ha. You're so damn funny. How did I not realize this before?"

"Get lost," I tell her, giving her a shove toward Jacob. "You'll be fine, and if it starts going downhill, you could always flash him your titties and tell him about your lasered pussy."

"Okay," she says, trying to pump herself up. "I can do this. I'm a bad bitch. I can talk to him."

"You're damn straight."

With that, she walks directly toward him, holding her chin high as pride pulses through me, making me feel like a proud momma bear. I watch her for a moment and laugh as she does the accidental knock into him, instantly gaining his attention, and just like that, he has stars in his eyes as she shamelessly flirts with him.

I realize that there's a good possibility that I just got ditched for the rest of the night, but I don't really care. There aren't many people from my school here and it gives me a chance to actually enjoy my night.

I head back over to the bartender and get a refill of whatever the hell I was drinking and walk right down to the water, putting my feet into the shallow waves and feeling as the tide draws in and out of the beach, sinking my feet into the sand.

Why can't every night be like this? Instead, it's full of shit and I have to deal with assholes like Irene and Kurt. At some point, my life is supposed to get easier, right? It's not fair of the world to keep throwing me shitty curveballs.

I stare out at the water, watching the shimmer of the moonlight shining against the horizon, and as peace settles over me for the first time since being in Ravenwood Heights, my mind finally calms, and I can see everything clearly again.

This week has been shit, but I've been stuck on one thing. After Sara showed the video to the world, the boys declared that they were going to handle it, but they saw me hand Sara her ass, so what could they have meant by handling it? What was left to handle? It's not like they have the power to have the video removed off the site, or do they? I'm not going to even pretend that I know how that works but I'm sure one very expensive email from a lawyer might do the trick. Apart from that, the only other participant was the douchebag twenty-two-year-old who tricked me into sucking his dick, but that was years ago.

They couldn't have meant him, could they? But how the hell would they find him? I don't even know his name, though I'm sure I could identify him by his less than impressive ... equipment.

I try to put it to the back of my mind and go back to enjoy the party, but with every passing moment, the thoughts become louder in my head until I find myself back up by the road and hitching a ride with a few girls back into the heart of Ravenwood Heights.

They drop me right at the gate for the private road and I instantly hash in the code I'd remembered from Cruz last weekend. The gate opens and I can't stop the thought that I belong here, which is completely ridiculous.

I start walking down to the guys' homes, and as I go, I realize that I'd completely forgotten to tell Ember that I was leaving. I whip my phone out of my bra and get busy.

Winter - Dude, I'll be back in a bit ... maybe.

Ember - Don't worry about me. I'm good. Soooo freaking good, babe!

I roll my eyes as a grin stretches across my face. That's my girl.

Winter - Wrap it before you tap it, girl, and remember, not all guys like a finger up the ass.

I put my phone away and just as I'm reaching the big iron gate in front of Carver's home, a set of headlights appear over the hill and come straight for me, slowing as they reach Carver's driveway.

I recognize the Escalade as easily as though it's a part of myself, though I should, I spend more time looking out for it than any girl ever should admit to.

Carver pulls right up to the gate, and as his window rolls down and he leans out to hash in the code, I quickly notice that the other guys aren't with him, and I'm momentarily caught off guard. Since when are these guys not tied at the hip? "Get in," he grumbles without bothering to look at me.

I pause for a brief moment before deciding that I have nothing to lose. Besides, the worst that could happen is Carver telling me to get lost when I start demanding answers, and really, does that even matter so much? Probably not.

I hurry around to the passenger side and climb up into the Escalade, feeling awkward as he hits the gas and slowly rolls down the long drive, the gate closing behind us.

The short drive to the front of the house is agonizingly awkward, and I want nothing more than to roll out the door and make a break for it, but when we finally reach his house and Carver swings his door open, the tension seems to fly right out with it.

"Come on," he says when I don't automatically make a move to get out of the Escalade.

I hurry after Carver and circle the front of the car until I meet him at the massive set of stairs. I can't help but look up at the imposing house, and while it's not quite as big as the one at the end of the road, it's definitely still remarkably bigger than anything I ever grew up living in. I wonder if it bothers him that he doesn't have the biggest house on the street? Carver strikes me as the kind of guy to want the biggest and the best and refuses to settle until he has it.

I find it hard to picture the four boys living here together, and while I try to get a sense of what it might be like, I realize Carver didn't bother to wait for my gawking and is already halfway up the stairs.

I skip up the stairs, and by the time I reach him, we're already at the top. Carver enters a code and then swipes something kinda like a key fob and a light turns green right beside the handle of the door, letting him know it's okay to enter.

I gape at him. What the hell happened to having a good old key to get inside your house? Since when did people start having fancy-ass locks like this? At this stage, I wouldn't be surprised if he leaned into the door to have his eyes scanned to confirm his identity before entering.

Carver opens the door wide and I follow him in through the huge foyer and right in through the main part of the house. He stops by the kitchen before turning to me. "Hungry?"

I shake my head and watch as he shrugs his shoulders and continues through his home. He leads me to a grand staircase and starts making his way up, and for a moment, I feel as though I should wait downstairs, but it's not as though he didn't know I've been following him through the whole house. If he didn't want me there, surely he would have said something. Besides, I'm far too curious to wait behind.

Carver leads me right up the stairs into a long hallway and I follow him into a room that I'm assuming is his bedroom. "What are you doing here, Winter?" he asks, grabbing the back of his shirt and shrugging out of it as he walks straight into his massive walk-in closet.

I find myself following him and leaning against the open door frame, my eyes roaming over his naked chest and taking in every little defined line of his abs before following it down to that deep 'V' that demands every bit of my attention.

Carver clears his throat and I realize that he's still waiting for my answer. "Oh, I, umm … I was looking for some answers."

His eyes narrow and I watch as he pulls a white shirt off a shelf before pulling it over his head and getting started on his pants. They drop to the ground and I do everything in my power to look away, but I can't. I'm like a moth to a flame, unable to control myself. "What kind of answers?" he questions as he finds a pair of grey sweatpants and quickly steps into them, leaving absolutely nothing to the imagination.

I swallow back the fear in my throat that's telling me not to push him, but my determination wins out. "What were you guys talking about the other day when you said you'd handle the whole Pornhub thing?"

A smile tears across his face and he walks out of the massive closet, stopping right in front of me as he flicks off the light. "Really? Out of all the things you could have asked me, that's the one you're going to go with?"

"I…" I cut myself off before shrugging my shoulder and realizing what a missed opportunity that was. There are a million things I could have asked him and I chose to go with something that really means nothing at all. Rookie error.

Carver watches me a second before stepping in even closer. "Why'd you come to me and not King or Cruz?"

"I didn't," I tell him honestly. "I figured you all would be here, and I thought that between the four of you, I'd be able to squeeze the answers I'm looking for out of one of you. It didn't occur to me that you wouldn't all be together."

He nods, not giving even the slightest hint if he approves of my response or not. "The guys wanted to party and I wasn't feeling it, so I dropped them off at that pier party, but from the looks of it, you were just there."

I glance down my body to my rolled-up black jeans that got wet at the bottom and the little bits of sand still randomly found over my feet and ankles. "I was," I tell him. "But I left."

"I see that."

I curse myself for saying something so blatantly obvious before raising my chin and getting right back into it so I can get out of here. "So, what's it going to be?" I ask. "Are you going to answer my question or do I need to head back to the pier party and bat my eyelashes at Cruz until he breaks?"

Carver watches me for a long moment before finally letting out a low sigh. "What we meant by handling it was that we had every intention of tracking down the bastard who took advantage of a sixteen-year-old girl and beat his ass to a pulp after getting the video removed."

"I …" I stare up at him, unable to figure out why this means so much to me, especially since I'd already kind of worked it out. "And did you? Find him and beat him to a pulp, I mean?"

Carver holds up his hand to show me his split knuckles, and I instantly take it in my hands, holding it tight as though he holds every last answer to every damn question I've ever asked. "That's where we've been all afternoon," he tells me, looking deep into my eyes as though he can see right through to my soul. "There's something about you, Winter. I don't like seeing you hurt."

Something settles within my chest and I find myself dipping my lips to his hand and pressing a feather-soft kiss to his broken knuckles.

We stand in comfortable silence for a long minute, neither of us willing to move until Carver finally tugs his hand out of my grasp. "Come on," he tells me, walking over to his bed and peeling back the sheets. "Just lie here with me tonight, and I promise, in the morning, everything can go back to how it usually is. I'm not ready to watch you walk out that door."

And with those words, I walk across his room, slip out of my jeans, and slide in between his sheets, allowing him to pull me into his arms and feel his strong body pressed up behind mine until we're both falling into a deep and confused sleep.

14

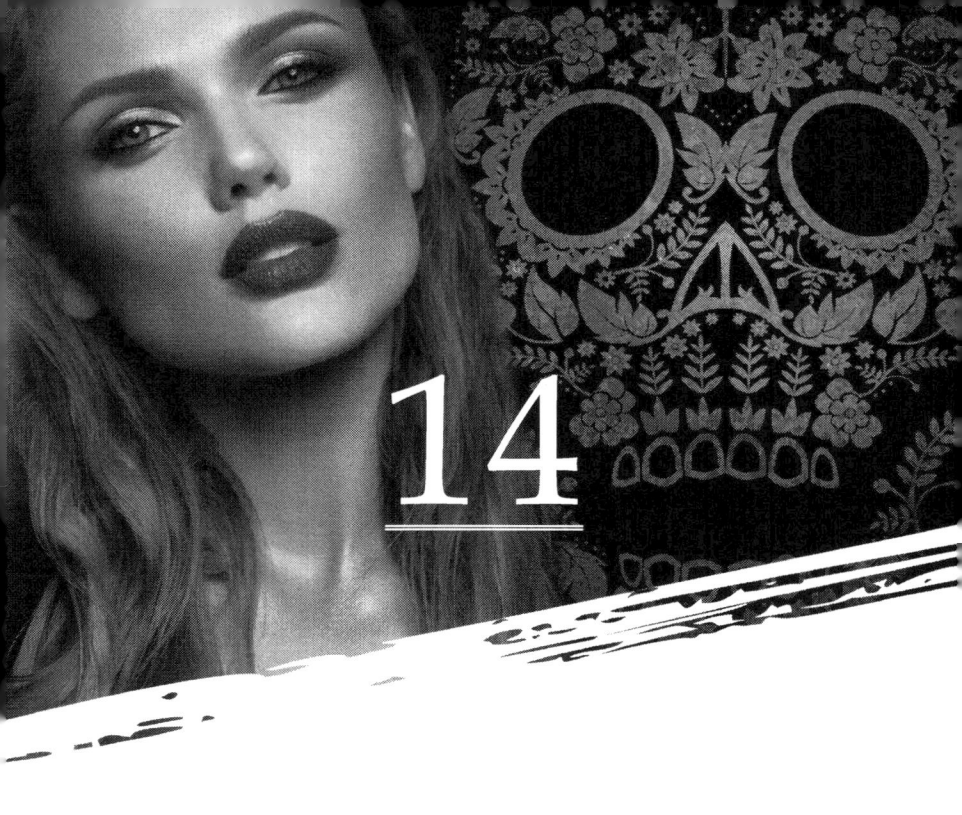

The sound of a door slamming inside the house has my eyes springing open and I realize that I've been asleep in Carver's bed all night.

What the fuck is wrong with me? I'm screwing his friend, flirting with another, and now this? Why do I insist on making things complicated for myself? I shouldn't have stayed tonight. In fact, I shouldn't have come here at all. How stupid could I be? All I've managed to do is ask a question that only made things harder between us, all because now there's no going back. Carver said the one thing he shouldn't have said out loud, making me realize that maybe I don't hate him at all, and now he can't take it back. The words are out there, and now I feel more confused than ever.

Does he hate me, or am I something so much more? Either way, I need to not be here when he wakes up.

His body has been pressed against mine for most of the night, with his arm curled around my waist, his hand securely cupping my left tit, and his cock against my ass. I take hold of his arm and gently raise it before slipping out from under it and all but rolling out of his bed, silently wishing that, come morning, everything that happened here tonight will be forgotten. Or at least we can pretend because the feelings that sat in the air between us tonight were far too strong and intense for me to handle.

Why can't things be easy like it is with King? It's all about sex. It's fun, raw, and exciting, and when we're not screwing, we secretly get to pretend that we hate each other's guts. It's perfect. What more could a woman want? Though with Cruz, I get to bat my eyelashes and make him squirm and I can't deny that the more I see him, the more I'm intrigued about what he'd be like between the sheets. Fuck it, I've thought about all four of them between the sheets, and damn it, I know I'd never be lucky enough to get to experience something like that.

Wanting to get out of here as soon as possible, I pull my jeans straight on, cringing as the bottom of them is still damp against my legs. I can't help but glance back at Carver sound asleep in his bed. I'd give anything to be able to stay here all night and have things be absolutely perfect between us in the morning, but when it comes to Carver, a reality like that isn't possible. That's not who we are, and our relationship is nowhere near being able to withstand something like that. We'd burn it to the ground before we even gave it a chance.

Realizing that the bang that woke me must have been the three guys getting home, I sneak out of Carver's room like a mouse trying to make its way through a hungry lions' den. I make it to the stairs and take a shaky breath realizing that once I hit the stairs, I have to go fast. There's nowhere to hide and if one of the guys sees me, it's game over.

I run.

I nearly fall down the freaking stairs and only just save myself by gripping onto the banister and then easily propelling myself the rest of the way down. I get to the bottom and throw myself behind a massive pillar to give myself a second to calm my racing heart.

I take five slow, deep breaths, and the second I step out from behind the pillar, I crash into a hard body and stare up at Grayson with wide eyes. He studies me for a moment, and it takes him all but two seconds to realize where I've come from.

His gaze narrows and it's clear as day that he doesn't like the thought of me sneaking out of Carver's room in the middle of the night, and I don't doubt that he thinks we fucked.

Just great.

Awkwardness spreads between us, and without a word, I drop my gaze and step around him, heading straight for the door and hoping that I don't go running face-first into Cruz or King.

Finally reaching the door, I pull it open and take a deep breath of fresh air, feeling as though I was never going to make it this far. Still in the danger zone, I sprint down the stairs and get my ass to the bottom before starting on the long driveway, only to feel someone watching me.

I look over my shoulder and there they are; Cruz and King, watching me as though I'm running away from my unfinished business, and I guess on some level, I kinda am, but stuff it. It's the middle of the night and I have absolutely no intentions of handling my unfinished business right now.

Ignoring their lingering, curious stares, I keep my feet moving, one after the other until I finally reach the gate at the top of Carver's driveway. I have no choice but to scale it like I'm some kind of superhero and jump right over the fucker, hoping that I don't set off an alarm.

Once my feet hit the ground, I feel as though I can finally breathe again and start getting myself out of here. The night swarms around me and I soak it up. I've never been one of those girls who are scared of being alone at night, I've always thrived on it, loving the danger, loving the thrill, but tonight, it doesn't seem to feed my adrenaline like it usually does.

With the chill in the air, I keep my pace up and wrap my arms securely around my waist until I'm reaching the gate at the top of the road. I hash in the code, thankful that I don't have to jump this one as well, and after slipping through the opening, I get my ass moving.

It's going to be a long walk through the city and into the shitty areas of Ravenwood Heights, especially as I have nothing but my own fucked-up thoughts to keep me company. God, I'd give anything to have my bike right now, but there's no way in hell that I'm going to wake Ember's whole family just to take my bike out of the garage. Besides, what's a little walking? It's probably good for the soul.

An hour very slowly turns into two before I'm finally sliding open the window of my shitty bedroom. My cold fingers ache against the window frame and I wonder just how much it would piss off Irene and Kurt if I were to run the shower at three in the morning and use up every last ounce of hot water. Though, I wouldn't. Not tonight anyway. I'm too fucking tired that I'd prefer just to shiver in bed.

The dog jumps up against my worn jeans as I slip through the window. As my feet hit the ground, I turn back around to pat her on the head for being a good girl and not waking the entire street with her incessant barking.

I pull back through to my room and close the window behind me before turning around and spying my bed across the room. It calls to me, despite how shitty and uncomfortable it is. After a two hour walk in the middle of a cold night, even the queen would take it. I cross the room, more than ready to drop down between the sheets and finally call it a night.

I start peeling off my jacket, and as I reach for the elastic in my hair, a shadow falls across the room, but as I spin around, I find it far too late. All in one swift motion, a black bag violently crashes over my head, and a rough hand presses against my mouth to muffle my scream.

My heart races as fear rapidly pumps through my veins, every thought in my mind begging me to somehow get out of this. Hands pull at my arms and legs, and the shuffling of feet echo through my shitty room. The hand across my mouth pulls tighter than before, and I fight for the air that won't come.

I try to scream but nothing comes out, and all I see is darkness.

Something is pulled tight around my wrist, so tight it stings, and I fear that my wrists have been sliced open. I pull at my binds, desperately fighting and doing what little I can, knowing that with a limited air supply, I don't have long.

My attackers don't make a single sound, and as my feet are bound, I'm pushed right over, my hip slamming into the ground with a hard thud. While it hurts like a fucking bitch, my fall allowed me just a brief second to pull in a sharp gasp of breath, and with no hands on me, I scream until my lungs give out but not a damn person comes to help me.

I'm on my own.

Tears stream from my eyes, soaking through to the black bag that's shoved over my head, and as the hands start grabbing at me again, I desperately try to squirm away, but in this position, I have no hope at all. It's useless.

I hear the familiar sound of the window being pulled open before the men in my room drag me across the floor, scraping up my arms and stepping on my hair.

My body slams into the wall under my window, and just as someone starts pulling me up, something heavy comes down over my temple and my world falls into unconsciousness.

Cold water is thrown over my body and I gasp as consciousness is violently brought back to me. There's nothing but darkness and my reality instantly comes rushing back. I need to get out of here.

I still have a black bag covering my head, and my wrists and ankles are still bound, leaving me laying on a hard floor like some kind of fish out of water. The floor beneath me is rippled, and judging by the sounds around me, my guess is that I've been tossed into the back of some dirty van and brought to Dodge Alley.

My hip aches as the side of my body screams for relief, but when the van shifts down under someone's weight, all thoughts of aches and pains are gone.

I'm a fighter, always have been, so sitting back and doing nothing is not in my nature. As soon as the hands start pulling at me, I kick up my legs and instantly connect with something. A loud groan tears through the van before a fist slams down against my stomach. "Fucking bitch."

I gasp for air as the blow knocks the wind out of me but I don't dare stop. Like hell I'll be going easy. This is my life and I refuse to live it as someone's pet. I don't know who's behind all of this, but I have a good guess, and there's no way in hell I'm about to go willingly. I'll die before they sell me into sex slavery.

A second set of hands start grabbing at me, and within a moment I'm thrown over some burly guy's shoulder. A thick arm curls over the back of my legs, holding me down, and for a brief moment, I see the sunlight shining through the black bag over my head.

How long was I out? How far have they taken me? And who the hell is going to realize that I'm gone? Irene and Kurt sure as hell won't do anything or raise any alarms, they'll just be pleased to have me out of their house. The guys won't come looking, they'll just assume that I need a bit of space to myself after climbing into bed with Carver, and Ember? I don't know about her. She'll probably think that I'm just chilling out somewhere and hope for the best.

I'm screwed.

The sunlight through the bag disappears as a chill sweeps over my body. The smell of mold hits my nose, and the further the man walks, the darker everything seems to get.

I hear the sound of metal doors clanging, girls whimpering, yelling, crying, screaming. There are scuffles around me, the sound of heavy chains falling against a hard floor, and then the loud screeching of a metal lock sliding out of place with a violent, chilling BANG.

I jump in the guy's arms and instantly start panicking when I hear the metal door dragging open. Fear rattles me and I squirm, desperate to get away but the hands grab at me, and just as the bag is torn off my head, I'm thrown down to the cold ground, my wrists and ankles still bound.

The heavy metal door is slammed shut and I'm locked into darkness with nothing but my senses to guide me.

I curl into a ball on the ground, listening to sounds, screams, and pain coming from the other cells and the insistent drip, drip, drip that slams down onto the cold concrete beside me, each drip somehow getting louder and louder.

I bring my knees into my chest and curl my arms tightly around them, struggling against the bonds that tear into my skin. I duck my head as low as possible and try to become invisible before letting the tears flow heavy and free, and wishing that I could be anywhere but here.

15

Drip. Drip. Drip. Drip.

Violent shivers take over my body as I hold myself close, desperately trying to keep warm. My teeth chatter to the point of pain, and no matter how much I try, I can't make them stop.

My clothes are wet from the ground, my hair is matted with mud, and the chill has more than soaked through to my bones. It's been two nights and I can honestly say that I'd take the lifetime of bullshit in the foster system over the two nights I've spent here.

I haven't slept. Not because sleep is for the weak, but because finding it is impossible.

The heavy banging of metal sounds all through the night, girls screaming and being abused, and then there's the fear that rests heavily against my chest. I just want to go home. I want to sleep in my own shitty bed and see familiar faces.

The darkness is crippling me, and for the first time in my life, I know that if I have to suffer through another night here, I'll be wishing for death.

I can't do it.

All night, I played scenarios over in my head, trying to figure out a way that I could finish myself, but all I have are my own two hands. I've never felt this kind of desperation before, this fear, and agony. I wouldn't wish this upon my worst enemy.

For the hundredth time in two days, the tears begin streaming down my face. I've never felt this low, so alone, and frightened. Every last ounce of energy is drained from my body, but I think that's what they want. They want me complacent, they want me to give in, to cave and allow them to play whatever sick, twisted games they've been dying to play, the kind of games their wives and children would never appreciate or approve of.

Drip. Drip. Drip. Drip.

I'm going to become someone's dirty, secret little whore, and every day for the rest of my life, I'm going to beg for death, but it'll never come. I'll never get out of here, never be free.

I was supposed to be turning eighteen in two months, I was supposed to be given my life back to do whatever I want with it. I was so close.

The sound of the heavy metal lock sliding out of place has become all too familiar over the last two days that my head doesn't even snap up anymore. I've completely given up. My hope is gone and I don't even bother fighting back, or maybe it's just my lack of energy after being bound for two days straight.

My wrists and ankles bleed, and I silently beg that I'll get a nasty infection that might be just enough to do the job.

There's another loud bang before I sense men walking into my dark cell, shining a blinding light in my eyes. The light travels up and down my body before the men come at me. I hear the metallic slide of a switchblade and I try to scream, but I don't have the energy left to make a sound.

The knife slices straight through the bonds at my wrist, cutting up my skin in the process. My arms fall, and my muscles ache from being held so tightly in the same position. A surge of hope fires through me. Are these my rescuers?

"Help. Please help," I whisper, my voice hoarse from screaming.

Not a sound comes from them as the knife slices through the bonds at my ankles. My whole body is sprawled across the floor and it takes me a second to gain control of my tired muscles. I try to move when a hand grips my upper arm and yanks me to my feet.

One man holds me up, and just when I think we're about to get out of here, the light drops over my body, and the other guy begins grabbing my clothes, pulling and tugging them, tearing the fabric until there's not a damn thing left. "No," I scream, fearing this is it. From here on out, I'll forever be ruined, scarred and unable to be the girl that I used to be.

I'm completely stripped naked with not an ounce of energy to do anything about it. My hair is pulled at, my skin bruised and tortured, the jewelry ripped from my body. My brass knuckles are stolen and just when the humiliation sweeps through me, a cold bucket of water is thrown over me and my body is violently scrubbed clean.

"Stop touching me," I sob, the desperate shivers making it nearly impossible to make out a damn word that comes tearing out of my mouth. They grip my hair, rubbing at the matted mud before ripping a comb through it, tearing out chunks as they go. "Stop. Please, stop. Let me go home. I want to go home."

The men ignore every word that comes out of my mouth and continue working on me. I'm dried off and for just a moment, I'm thankful for the damp towel that's thrown over my body, but it doesn't last long until I become their doll to dress up.

Expensive black lace lingerie is pulled from a bag and I watch in confusion as the men force my body into it, strapping me into whorish suspenders and clipping all the little bits together. A pair of sheer thigh-high stockings are drawn up my legs and despite the expensive lace donning my body, I've never felt so cheap.

The men finish dressing me and just when I think they're about to drag me out of here, they release their hold on me and I go crumbling back to the ground. The cramped, dirty cell fades back into darkness, the loud bang of the door is echoed through the cell, and I'm left alone once again.

A blinding light is shone upon my face, startling me awake and I instantly hate myself for falling asleep. I should have been ready. I knew something was coming but with a clean body, my wrists and ankles freed, and my old torn clothes to rest my head against, sleep claimed me just like my captors did.

A man grips my arm tightly as he pulls me to my feet, dragging me from the damp cell. Yet somehow, the persistent drip, drip, drip, sound remains trapped in my mind.

The metal door of my cell slams behind me, and I look around, only now just getting the first look at where I am.

A long hallway looms before me with metal doors lining each side and my gut tells me that every single cell is filled with girls just like me.

Puddles of dirty water line the hallway as I do everything I can to not let the other girls' cries of protest get to me. Their sounds have already crippled me, and if I let them affect me any longer, I won't have what it takes to get myself out of here.

It's darker than normal, so my guess is that I'm on my third night. I must have slept for a while, and because of that, I've found a renewed energy, but I'm not about to waste it here. I need to be careful. I need to play it smart.

Hope is a dangerous thing, but right now, it's all I've got.

The men on either side of me drag me along and I stumble while trying to keep my feet underneath me, but after not eating or drinking in three days, I'm weaker than I've ever been before. Not only does my body hurt, but my mind and heart do too.

We make it to the end of the hallway and the man on the left releases his grip on me and I instantly fall into the other guy who lets me crumble to the ground, scratching up my knees. The guy on the left reaches for a door and unwinds a heavy chain before pushing the door open wide.

The noise hits me first.

I hear a room full of chatter—murmurs, whispers, wolf-whistles. I'm grabbed off the dirty ground, my knees bleeding, and thrown headfirst into the room with a bright spotlight coming down over me, instantly blinding me.

The noises only get louder. Cat-calls and murmurs of appreciation sound all around the room as my aching wrists are gripped and I'm tugged right through the door. It slams with a loud bang behind me, and as the man holding my wrists drags me through the room, I'm put on display.

Random men grab at me, feeling my body, touching what's not theirs to touch, and I can't help but wonder if these are the men who are going to buy me. My fingers curl into fists but the familiar feel of my brass knuckles isn't there. I'm pushed through the crowd, stumbling and running into things as the blinding lights remain on my face, the only bonus being that the chill in the air seems to have vanished in this big room.

I'm put on parade as I'm dragged through the rest of the room, every inch of my body put on show. Men pull at the cups of my lace bra, peeking at what's hidden below as hands slip between my legs, grabbing my pussy, squeezing my thighs and ass.

Running out of Carver's bed three nights ago, I felt like a mouse in a lion's den, but it turns out that I had absolutely no idea what that saying truly meant until this very moment.

"Fuck yeah," a voice murmurs right by my ear, the man's hot breath brushing over my cheek. "You want to come home to daddy? I'll fuck that tight pussy every night, my little whore."

I gag and try to move past him but his arm curls around my waist and he grinds his dirty cock against my ass. A deep growl sounds through the crowded bodies before the man is violently shoved out of the way.

"What have I told you about touching my girls?" A man roars, making me wonder if this is the boss of this whole operation. Maybe Knox's Uncle Sam, but what does it matter? I just want out of here. I'll never be one of his girls.

I'm pulled around a full circle of the room before being dragged up three small steps onto a wide stage. More spotlights fall on me, three on my face, one from each angle of the room, so wherever I look, I'm blinded. Spotlights drag over my body, showing me off as though I'm some kind of prize.

The men at my side push me down into a chair, winding a rope around me to keep me still just as a man in a suit walks out on stage. "Alright," he says, holding his hands out, indicating for the rowdy men in the crowd to shut the fuck up. He looks back at me, his eyes dragging over my body like a leer. His tongue rolls over his lips as interest shines in his filthy eyes. "Look at this beauty," he announces to his captivated audience, drumming them up and stirring the excitement, making it clear as hell that he'll be getting a commission out of each girl he successfully auctions off. "A tight, sweet little body, round perky ass, and a full set of tits that you can sink your teeth into. Who wouldn't want to come home to this sweet little thing? Only fifteen-years-old. I bet a young thing like this could stay wet for hours." Cheers are roared around the crowd before the guy continues. "Let's start at five-hundred-thousand. Who wants her?"

Five-hundred-fucking-thousand? Is he insane? What kind of disgusting rich, entitled men are they to buy girls for half a million dollars?

"Right here," the filthy man who rubbed his dick all over my ass says. I shake my head. No, no, no. I can't go home with him. I'll be raped day-in and day-out. I can't go to anyone. I have to get out of here.

"Five fifty," another calls out.

I start pulling against the rope, desperate to run. "Oh, look at that," the auctioneer rumbles, laughter in his tone. "We have ourselves a fighter. Do I hear six hundred?" Someone raises their hands. "Six fifty?"

It goes up, up, and up.

Seven-hundred-thousand.

Eight hundred.

The men get rowdy as a bidding war starts, the numbers jumping by fifty thousand and the auctioneer enjoying it far more than anyone ever should. It's almost as though dollar signs are shining in his eyes.

It hits a million and then two before the bids begin slowing down, the original dick rubber getting frustrated that his bids are constantly being met and bulldozed.

We get to two and a half million when a new player stands in the far back corner of the room, the blinding lights making it impossible to make out anything but a shadow. "Five million," the man says, drawing the attention of the room.

Gasps are heard all around and the auctioneer stares for a minute too long before remembering that he's supposed to be running the show. He stares out at the man with wide eyes, blinking three times before scanning his gaze over the other bidders. "Do I hear 5.1 million?"

There's nothing but silence around the room, and after a beat, my heart silently racing, the auctioneer slams his hand down over his wrist. "Sold for five million dollars."

Fuck.

16

I'm dragged away, back through the side door and down the long, damp hallway, though now that I'm someone else's property, the hands on my body are gentle, and considering how much that shadow man just paid for me, I'd dare say that these douchebags don't want to risk hurting such a valuable prize.

A migraine settles into the front of my skull from the bright lights, but I try to put it to the back of my mind. I can't crumble yet. I have a feeling this nightmare is only just beginning.

My cell opens wide and I'm thrown back in, my old clothes now gone from the room. Not a word is spoken to me, but why would it be? I'm property, nothing more.

The door slams again with a loud bang, and I'm left all alone with nothing but the torturous thoughts of what's about to happen to me.

Five million fucking dollars. What the actual fuck? I'm a nobody. Who would ever dream of paying that kind of money for me? Sure, if I had four tits, three golden vaginas, and a forked tongue, then yeah, I'd totally get it, but I'm just a nobody foster kid.

The minutes tick by and I lose track of time. Ten minutes could have passed or maybe it's an hour before I hear the heavy metal of my door sliding back. I brace myself, having absolutely no idea who I'm about to come face to face with.

A dull light filters through the room as two men walk through the door, standing over me and studying my body. It's too dark to make out their features; all I can see are the outlines of their bodies as the dull light shines behind them, leaving me to rely on my other senses.

I feel their lingering gazes sweeping over my body like hungry predators. "You've won yourself quite a prize," the shorter of the men says, his voice taking me back to the club last weekend, sitting up in the VIP room and confirming that this is without a doubt Knox's Uncle Sam. I'm sure he's probably come to send me off himself so he can personally thank his new vendor and tell him to come back any time he pleases.

Rage burns through me.

My fingers curl into fists and with the last remaining energy I have, I run at Sam, my fist flying through the air but before I can connect with his face, an impressive tight grip curls around my wrist and forces me back, yet somehow managing not to hurt a single hair on my body in the process.

I go stumbling back a few steps, and my stare flicks to the taller man, my new owner. "Wow," he says. My blood runs cold. "They mentioned that she was a fighter, but I never dreamed that she'd be quite so wild."

Dante. Fucking. Carver.

Betrayal burns through me as Sam looks back at Carver with a wicked grin. "I bet you're going to have your hands full with this one."

"Oh, I hope so," Carver tells him, holding out his hand.

Sam instantly takes it and gives a firm shake. "Excellent. Now, transport? I'm not a holding facility. You have twelve hours to get your girl off my property before she goes back on the market."

Carver nods. "I'm taking her now."

"Like hell you will." A sinister laugh bubbles out of Sam's throat as he looks back at me, his depraved stare soaking up my subtle curves in the disgusting black lingerie. "You'll get your girl once you've paid for her."

Carver looks back at Sam and the stare he gives him almost has Sam shrinking back. "I thought you were the boss around here."

"I am," Sam snaps back at him.

"Then tell me how the hell the boss isn't aware when five million dollars is handed over to his staff?"

"I ... excuse me," Sam says, bowing out of the room to go and check his funds, leaving me alone with Carver and giving me a chance to fucking rage.

He walks toward me and I spit at his feet. "You fucking pig," I seethe, keeping my voice low as to not draw attention to my cell. "How could you? You fucking own me now? What kind of bullshit are you into?"

Carver circles me, stepping into my back and grabbing my waist, his hand flies up over my mouth keeping me quiet. "Keep your fucking mouth shut," he growls, his voice low and threatening. "It was either I fucking bought you or someone else did. Take your pick, because if you're not down, I'm more than happy to rescind my offer and leave you to the fucking rapist who would have bought you instead."

Fuck.

"Yeah," he scoffs. "That's what I fucking thought. Now keep your head down and follow my lead so I can get us the fuck out of here. These pricks won't hesitate to kill us, so don't do anything stupid."

His words are like a ray of sunshine beaming through the darkest night. It gives me the kind of hope that a girl like me should be terrified of, one that I shouldn't allow myself to trust, but what choice do I have? Carver is all the hope I have of getting out of this unscathed.

I allow the hope to fill me and I sink back against him, his tightening hold the greatest comfort I've ever known. It's nearly over. Carver is going to save me.

His head dips and his lips press against my neck. "You're going to be okay," he promises.

I close my eyes, feeling his hands on my body and allowing myself to pretend that we're back in his bed in Ravenwood Heights with his arms securely wrapped around me, back before any of this bullshit happened.

The door rattles and Carver pushes me back to take my own weight, but he doesn't take his hands off me. The door swings open and Sam walks back in with a grim expression. "Forgive me, Sir. You are free to go with what's yours. The funds are paid in full and we welcome you back at any time."

"Good," Carver says, slowly roaming his fingers up the side of my body like he's appreciating what he's about to take home to enjoy.

"I didn't catch your name," Sam says, stepping out of the doorway as Carver's hand falls to my lower back and starts leading me out of the cell.

Carver looks back at him, his brows drawn in confusion. "Because you don't need it."

"Of course," he says, nodding his head. "Then how shall I contact you when I have more … showings?"

Carver releases me and steps up to Sam, towering over him. "You don't," Carver says, leaning in and giving him a stare that suggests he better not even try. "I have what I need, and if my needs happen to change, I'll find you."

Sam hesitates before taking a step back and nodding once again. "Very well," he says. "It was a pleasure doing business with you."

Carver holds his stare for a minute longer before finally stepping away and pressing his hand to my lower back. "Walk," he demands, his voice firm and filled with the type of authority that would have grown men whimpering with fear.

I do as I'm told and walk out through the long hallway, Carver leading me until we break out into the night. With Sam's eye still on us, and probably the rest of his staff, we keep walking until we reach a blacked-out SUV with no registration plates.

The driver's door opens and I recognize Grayson instantly, dressed to the nines in his best black suit, playing the role of Carver's driver. He walks around to the back and opens the backdoor before indicating for me to slide straight in. I don't miss a beat, more than desperate to get the fuck out of here.

Both King and Cruz are already in the car, and the second I can, I scramble across the backseat and fall into Cruz's lap, holding onto him with everything I have. Cruz's arms wrap around me and I bury my face into his shirt as he does everything in his power to soothe me. "You're safe now," he promises. "Always safe with me."

I feel King's stare heavy on my back and I welcome it, wishing that just once he might let me into his arms the same way that Cruz does.

Carver gets in the backseat and Grayson closes the door just as any other professional driver would do. He walks around the front of the car, and the second he gets in the driver's seat, he takes off like a rocket, getting us the fuck out of there.

We get two minutes down the road when I feel a hand gently roaming over my back and I raise my head to find Carver reaching out for me. Without question, I move across the backseat and crumble into his arms, feeling the eyes of all of the boys on me, watching and waiting for me to break.

Carver holds me tight and I don't dare move until the car is parked safely inside Carver's garage with the security system on high alert. He takes my hand and gently helps me out of the back of the car, treating me like a wounded puppy too afraid to take a step.

As soon as I get to my feet, Carver pulls off his suit jacket and drapes it over my shoulders to cover the filthy black lingerie and protect whatever dignity I might have left. He leads me into his massive home and scoops me up before hitting the stairs and leading me into one of the many spare bedrooms, the other guys remaining downstairs to give me what little privacy they can.

Carver places me down on the bed before backing up a few feet. He points to a door behind him. "There's a private bathroom in there if you want to get cleaned up," he says. "I don't exactly have any chick's clothes here, but I can bring you something of mine. They'll be too big but at least you'll be comfortable."

I nod my head, too ashamed to even look up and meet his dark, stormy gaze. "Thanks."

"No problem," he murmurs. "You can stay in here as long as you want. Just come down when you're hungry and I'll make sure there's something for you to eat."

I nod again, and just like that, Carver walks out of the room, gently closing the door behind him and finally leaving me in the safety of his spare bedroom. I stare at a blank wall for far too long before finally getting up and making my way into the massive private bathroom. I close the door and just for my own peace of mind, I flick the lock beneath the handle before turning to take in my reflection.

I'm a complete stranger.

My whole body is either black and blue from bruises or covered in dirt from the filthy cell that I was kept in. Tears well in my eyes and

I hate how weak this whole thing has made me. I was stripped of a piece of myself, and I don't think that I'm ever going to get it back. I was humiliated and made vulnerable, the two things that I've always strived not to be.

Not wanting to dwell on it, I reach behind me and unhook the expensive lace bra and let it fall to the ground only to see the bruises across my breasts, each of them in the shape of a man's finger.

I look away, unable to handle the sight of myself, and step into the shower. The cold water rains down over me and it's like being hit by a wrecking ball, the memories of the cold buckets of water being thrown over me something I will never forget.

The emotions hit me hard and I sink to the floor of the shower, curling into a ball and crying, the sobs pulling violently from deep within my throat. My head drops to my knees and that's exactly where I stay for the next hour until the exhaustion claims me and the sobs finally ease.

I get to my feet and scrub myself until my skin is red and raw, desperately trying to rid myself of the memories. I start on my hair, washing it once, then twice, and go as far as washing it a third time before rinsing the conditioner through it.

By the time I turn off the taps, my eyes are red and puffy, and my body is completely exhausted. It's got to be well past four in the morning but I don't think that sleep will be coming to me for a while.

I grab a towel off the heated towel rack and quickly dry my hair before wrapping the soft material tightly around my body. I find myself stopping to look at my reflection in the mirror, and while the girl looking back at me certainly looks a lot like me, she doesn't feel like me. This girl is weak. This girl allowed hell to be brought down on her and she wasn't strong enough to fight back. That's not the girl I've always prided myself on being. This girl who stares back at me; she's pathetic.

Anger seeps through me and I turn around to exit the bathroom, unable to stand the sight of myself. But as I turn into Carver's spare bedroom and find nothing but darkness, fear begins replacing the anger.

My eyes dart around the room, expecting to find a hidden shadow, ready to jump out at me. I take a few calming breaths before dashing across the room and slamming my hand down over the light switch.

Brightness floods the room, and I flip around, my back pressed up against the door as my sharp gaze sweeps across the room, checking every little corner until I'm satisfied that I'm completely alone.

My heart races and the humiliation hits me like a freight train.

This isn't me.

Letting out a sigh, I try to remember who I really am, and after locking the door, I walk back across the room to find the set of clothes Carver had promised to leave for me, sat right beside a bottle of water. I grab it and instantly take a sip, desperately trying to soothe my sore throat. I get halfway through the bottle before I start to slow down and focus on getting dressed. I take the soft cotton shirt between my fingers and I slip it over my head. I smell Carver all over it and something settles within me, making me wonder when the hell he became my safety net.

The shirt falls to my knees and I tug the towel off from underneath before dragging the grey sweatpants up my bruised legs and pulling the drawstring as tight as it'll go.

Needing to leave the light on, I settle into the soft bed and stare up at the ceiling. Exhaustion rests heavily against my chest, but no matter how hard I try, I can't close my eyes.

Desperately needing sleep, I throw the blankets back and make my way out of the spare bedroom. I walk down the hall, trying to keep quiet, more than aware that the boys are probably sound asleep in the rooms around me while being thankful that the hallway lights are shining brightly.

I find a familiar door and silently push it open to find Carver sitting up in bed, his back resting against the headboard, and from the looks of it, he's been struggling to sleep just as much as I have. Despite knowing that he now owns me, I can't help but need him, which only serves to confuse me more because outside of this room, I don't want a damn thing to do with him.

Carver watches me for a long moment and then without a word, he pulls back the blankets and offers me the space beside him. I look at it longingly, desperately wishing I could be the girl who succumbs to her needs, but then I realize that sometimes taking exactly what you need isn't considered weak, it's called basic human survival. Without another second of hesitation, I cross his room and slip in between the sheets.

Carver scoots down behind me, his warm arm wrapping securely around my body and holding me tight, keeping the monsters at bay, exactly the way I need.

With safety blanketing me, I finally close my eyes and allow myself to drift off into a peaceful sleep. Come tomorrow, it will be time to stand up and face the monsters front on.

17

Sunlight streams through Carver's bedroom and my eyes spring open to find myself alone. I sit up in bed, letting the blankets fall to my waist as my hand rubs over my tired eyes, instantly regretting it as a dull ache settles into my raw skin and I'm reminded that I've spent the last three or four days in tears.

I get up out of bed and cross the room to the massive floor to ceiling window. Looking out over the yard, I find the most luxurious pool I've ever seen with the afternoon sun glistening against the ripples, but all it does is remind me that I shouldn't be here. I don't belong in this world.

I need to wake myself up properly, go and find the boys, thank them profusely for saving my ass last night, and then get out of here, though I don't know what I'm going to do once I get back to my real life. I doubt I would have been able to sleep without Carver last night. He kept the nightmares away, and for that, I'll forever be grateful, but I need to leave this place and learn how to survive on my own again, because in my world, all I have is myself. I can't begin relying on these guys, because one day, they're going to be gone, just like everyone else.

Realizing that I've slept most of the day, I make my way into Carver's personal bathroom and try to fix the train wreck that is otherwise known as me. I pee and after washing my hands, start rummaging through his drawers until I find a spare toothbrush.

Feeling a million times better, I comb my fingers through my hair and bunch up Carver's massive shirt before tying a knot at the side and attempting to look a little more like myself as opposed to the stranger I'd been reduced to.

I roll over the top of Carver's sweatpants and after finally feeling a little more like myself, I make my way out of the bathroom and over to the door of his bedroom. I reach for the handle and as the door begins to open, I find myself hesitating. The second I open this door and walk downstairs to meet with the boys, I won't be able to hide. I'm going to have to face this straight on and there won't be anywhere to run.

I have so many questions and a small part of me is terrified about actually getting the answers I'm looking for.

I take a shaky breath. I'm done being weak. I have to do this now. I'm not a coward.

Pulling the door open, I step out into the hallway and am instantly hit with the smell of food coming from downstairs. My stomach growls, reminding me that I haven't eaten since before the pier party days ago. It's a miracle that I can still stand. I really should have eaten last night but the exhaustion was killing me. I had to sleep.

I hit the stairs and am forced to hold tighter onto the railing to avoid falling to the bottom. I creep through the house, following the sound of the boys murmured conversation. I walk through a maze of formal dining areas, living rooms, an office fit for royalty, before finally coming out to the main living area.

The room is a huge open kitchen with an adjoining living room, and as I walk deeper into it, I find all four of the boys lounging on the massive couches. In an instant, the tension rises in the room. Their conversation comes to an abrupt close as all four of their stormy gazes come sweeping to mine, momentarily knocking the breath right out of me.

"Umm," I start, not knowing who or where I should be looking. "I, umm …"

Shit. Could I sound like any more of a moron? I've never been lost for words like this, especially when facing down a bunch of guys who I've mistakenly been a raging bitch to, but there's just something different about these guys, and I'm finding that where they're concerned, nothing is ever quite so straightforward.

Words fade away into an awkward silence, but Cruz pulls himself up off the couch and walks straight into me, his hands resting at my waist. "Are you hungry?" he asks, his eyes boring down into mine as Carver and King watch on through narrowed, curious eyes.

"Yeah," I say, trying to not let him see just how much his intense stare affects me. "But don't worry about me. You guys have already done more than enough. I'll figure something out when I get out of here."

Grayson's sharp scoff fills the silence, but the guys ignore it as they keep their stares on me. "Don't be ridiculous," Cruz murmurs, leaning in and brushing a soft kiss over my cheek. "There's enough food here to feed a fucking army. Go sit down and I'll get you something."

He releases my waist and walks away before I get the chance to argue, and I'm left with no choice but to walk over to the massive couch and sink into it. "I suppose I owe you all an apology," I say, my eyes slicing up and meeting Carver's before flicking to King's and then leaving Grayson for last, knowing that Cruz is listening to every word from the kitchen. "I may have judged you all too soon and maybe a little too harshly. You literally saved my life last night and I'd done absolutely nothing to deserve that, so thanks."

Carver just nods as Grayson's eyes seem to narrow further, probably assuming my apology isn't genuine, but he should know that apologies don't come naturally to me.

King's arm falls over the back of the massive couch opposite mine. "We weren't about to let you stay there. Who the fuck knows what could have happened to you."

My gaze flicks up to his. "I just ... I don't get it. How did you know where to find me? Hell, how did you even know I was gone?"

King anxiously glances across at Carver and I realize that he's the one running this show, the one with all the answers. "You were gone.

No one could find you, and when Ember explained that you didn't come back to get your bike, we knew something was up. It wasn't hard to connect all the pieces. Once Sam was interested in you, it was like following breadcrumbs."

I look away, unable to handle his stare for too long. "So, what now?" I ask, looking down at my hands, the question swirling around my head but being too afraid to actually voice it. "You just ... own me?"

I can't help but glance back up at him just in time to see him slowly shaking his head. "No, not exactly."

"What's that supposed to mean? *Not exactly?* It's either a yes or a no?"

Carver looks nervously at all the guys who look anywhere but at me. His gaze finally slices back to mine with a defeated expression across his handsome face. "I don't own you," he says slowly. "Dynasty does."

My brows instantly fly up as Cruz comes waltzing back into the room, placing a plate of something down beside me, but Carver's comments have my full attention. I can't even look down to figure out what Cruz gave me. "Umm ... what?" I ask. "I thought that was just some bullshit rumor."

The boys all shake their heads. "Definitely not a rumor," King says, a strange tone in his voice, one that I can't quite decipher.

"Then what? What the fuck is Dynasty?" The guys' sly glances between each other instantly get on my nerves and I snap. "Stop with the fucking bullshit and give it to me straight. Whatever the fuck

Dynasty now owns me and I deserve to know what the fuck it is. So, if you're not going to tell me, then step aside and I'll figure it out on my own."

Carver lets out a sigh as Grayson groans, being the one to find the balls to come out with the information I need. "Dynasty isn't something that we can just go around talking about. We're all bound by secrecy, but what we can tell you is that it's a family business that goes back generations. There isn't one particular thing we do, we're just … everywhere. Always silently working behind the scenes."

I fall back against the chair, slowly scanning my gaze past each of them. "Family business, huh?" I say with a scoff. "So, not just Carver owns me, but you all fucking own me? Great, just fucking great."

"It's not like that," Cruz says, reaching across the couch and pushing the plate of food closer to my leg. "It's more complicated than that. We don't own you; we just footed the bill to get you the fuck out of there. You're completely free to go if that's what you want to do."

I glance at Carver who nods, and for some reason, the thought of him agreeing that I can walk out of here whenever the hell I want cuts deep like a knife. "So, tell me this," I say, finally glancing down at the plate to find it piled high with spaghetti bolognese, my favorite meal. "Does this Dynasty make it their business to be involved in sex trafficking deals?"

Carver shakes his head. "No, but when your name is put on a list that's sent out to purchasers, I fucking made it my business."

"Why me?" I ask. "Do you have any idea how many other girls there were at this place? Why save me? I would have been able to fight them off. Maybe not straight away, but I would have found a way to survive. You could have saved them instead. Why didn't you save them?"

Guilty expressions cross each of their faces but it's Cruz who finally speaks up. "Believe me," he says, inching closer, the guilt in his tone pouring out like it's his biggest regret. "We fucking tried. We've been trying since the day we first found out about it, but Dynasty doesn't get involved. There's a reason no one knows who or what Dynasty is. They have a certain set of … rules that they govern by, and they don't stray, never have since being founded over eighty years ago. They work behind the scenes and keep away from shit like this, and like I told you the other day, things with Sam aren't clean cut. It's complicated."

"No," I say, shaking my head. "That's not good enough. You need to go back there and do something about it. You have the money and the skills to make it happen. Who gives a shit about what Dynasty wants? These girls are going to be sold and raped and they'll never be heard of again."

King leans forward onto his knees. "I'm sorry, Winter, but we fucking tried. We were lucky to even get in there and find you before it was too late. The most we could do is get our hands on Sam and try to locate every single girl he's ever sold, but there's never a paper trail for this shit, never anything to go by. Believe me, babe, if there was something we could have done, we would have done it ages ago."

"No," I say, flying to my feet, nearly knocking the plate off the couch as I go. "What about the cops? Call them. I'll give them a statement if it'll help. Sam can't get away with it. You can't let him get away with it."

"The cops have been on his trail for years, but they can't make a move until they have something solid, but he keeps slipping right through their fingers," Grayson explains. "He's been in this game for a long time and has too many friends in high places."

I collapse down on the couch, feeling completely helpless and desperately wishing that there was something I could do to save all of those girls. I pull the plate of spaghetti bolognese onto my lap and slowly start picking at it, knowing that if I annihilate it like my body is begging me to do, I'm going to end up with an aching stomach.

As I pick at my food, feeling like complete shit for the girls whose lives were stolen out from under them last night, I sense the boys' stares on me. I glance up to find them all watching me closely, but it's Carver who looks like he's thinking the hardest. "What?" I snap at him, unable to control the raging emotions flying around my body.

"There's something we need to tell you," Carver says, glancing away at the last second, making it seem as though this mysterious thing they need to tell me is something that has the potential to break me, but honestly, after what I've already gone through, there's not much that can bring me down.

My brows drop and as I look around at all the guys and sense their hesitance, nerves begin sweeping through me. "What?" I ask, shooting my impatient stare back at Carver, wishing that he'd just get it over and done with, rip it off like a band aid.

Carver lets out a sigh before holding his head high and giving it to me straight, the only way I'd want it. "Your foster father was paid off by Sam. After all that bullshit at his club, Sam still wanted you and Knox gave up every little bit of information he had." I suck in a breath, momentarily cutting off Carver, but he continues. "Kurt knew you were about to be kidnapped from your room, he even let the fuckers in, and in the end, had himself a nice little payday."

My mouth drops, unable to believe what I'm hearing. I know both Kurt and Irene are complete assholes but surely they would not sell their foster child to a sex trafficker. Though, if no one knew I was missing, then nothing would stand in the way of them collecting their check at the end of each month.

I shake my head. "This is unbelievable," I murmur to myself. "Kurt and Irene are literally the two people who are supposed to have my back during all of this and they've done nothing but make my life harder."

Carver stands and takes a step toward me as I slide the half-eaten plate of spaghetti onto the coffee table. He perches his ass right on the table beside the plate and meets my stare. "I know you probably don't want to hear this, but that spare room upstairs is all yours. You can stay there as long as you'd like."

I nod, feeling as though I'm in some kind of daze. "Thanks, I … how … how do you know that?" I ask, my brows furrowed. "There's no way Kurt came right out and admitted to that."

"He didn't," Carver says, something darkening within his stormy gaze, something sinister and downright scary. "We got it out of Knox. After what happened last week, he was more than helpful in handing over the information we needed."

"But he … he told Sam where to find me?" Carver nods and something dies within me. I let out a sigh. "I guess some people never learn. I hope you really beat the shit out of him this time."

A breathy scoff flies from between Grayson's lips and I can't help but look over at him to see a grin pulling at the side of his mouth, his eyes sparkling with a peculiar darkness that has something warming inside of me. How have I never noticed just how fucking handsome Grayson is? Don't get me wrong, he blew me away the second I laid my eyes on him, but when that darkness flashes in his eyes, mixed with that lethal, teasing grin, it just hits right. It's a shame he hates me so much.

I stand up and watch as all four of the guys stand with me. "I just, umm … I think I need a little space to take it all in," I tell them before reaching past Carver and grabbing the spaghetti. I turn on my heel and start stalking out of the room, bypassing the kitchen to dump the plate.

I don't know what the hell I'm supposed to do now. I can't go back to Irene and Kurt's place. If they knew I'd been saved and returned, they'd only try to sell me off again. Besides, what's to stop Sam from trying to get another five million out of me?

I'm screwed. I need to figure out where the hell I go from here because there's no way I'm staying here for much longer. The guys have been amazing, and for some reason they have had my back since the second I came to this godforsaken town, and while I feel that I can start to trust them, I don't trust whatever this Dynasty bullshit is.

I want as far away from it as I can get, only I don't think that's going to be possible, seeing as though Dynasty now owns me. I've suddenly just become one of their interests, and I'm sure after paying so much for me, they're going to want me to pay back my debt sooner or later.

I find my way back to the stairs and am about to start making my way back up to the spare bedroom when Cruz appears from across the foyer. "Hey, wait up," he murmurs, keeping his voice low.

I pause on the bottom step and wait for him to catch up. "What's up?" I ask as he steps into me, his hand on my lower waist.

"I just wanted to check in," he says, keeping a straight face for only a second before his usual flirty grin stretches wide across his face. "That was probably a lot to take in, and just so you know, I'm here if you want to talk, or maybe need something to get your mind off things."

I step back and smirk up at him. "My, oh, my. Cruz Danforth, you wouldn't be trying to get into my pants the day after I was rescued from a sex trafficking ring?"

His eyes bug out of his head. "Oh, fuck. When you put it like that, I sound like a fucking dick."

I can't help but laugh and step up onto the next step to put me eye to eye with Cruz. I lean into him and press a kiss to his cheek, unable to resist him. I don't know what it is about him, but something keeps pulling me in. He's dangerously lethal and intimidating as hell, but there's also an innocence about him that I so badly want to protect.

"Thanks," I whisper, watching as Grayson passes behind us, his stare heavily on the way Cruz's hand lingers at my waist, making me wonder if, to Cruz, this is a little more than just innocent flirting. "Maybe I might take you up on your offer. I always love a good … chat."

A grin stretches across Cruz's face, and before another word can slip from between his lips, I make my way up the stairs and find my way back to the spare bedroom, which has now been declared as mine. I close the door behind me, and as a wave of unwanted and haunting thoughts and memories take over my mind, I crash down onto the soft bed and desperately wish that things could be different.

18

Hands pull at my clothes, tearing and yanking them from my body as I shriek, desperately trying to get away. "NO," I scream with hot tears on my face, trying to free myself from the faceless men.

My clothes fall away, my belongings, my pride, everything stripped from me until I stand naked at the mercy of strange men. I'm thrown down, their grip so tight that it's bound to leave my skin bruised and scarred.

"No, no," I cry, begging the torture to stop, begging to be back home, but where is home? I don't have a home. I have nothing. Nowhere to go, nowhere to be. I'm all alone in this violent, unforgiving world.

The hands pull and push, forcing me down. I beg, scream, and cry for it all to be over, but they don't let up, they don't relent. My body is grabbed, my breasts squeezed, my ass thrust against. When will it stop? Please, someone, make it stop.

The faceless man presses into me, his body heavy against mine, and as a wicked grin stretches wide across his face, my eyes fly open, and I find myself alone in the darkened spare bedroom of Carver's mansion.

"Holy fuck," I breathe, racing out of bed and slamming my hand down over the light, letting the room flood with brightness despite it being the middle of the night.

When the hell did I allow myself to fall asleep? How stupid could I be? I can't sleep alone. I need Carver to keep the monsters away.

After scanning the room for unwelcome shadows, I drop down on the edge of the bed, my head resting heavily in my hands. *It was just a dream. I'm okay. It's over now. I'm safe.*

When the hell am I going to be okay? This can't keep happening. How long am I going to be a prisoner to my own fears, my own nightmares? Sure, Carver took pity on me yesterday and allowed me to spend the night in his arms, but he's not going to do that forever, and I can't ask him too.

Needing a minute to calm down, I climb off my bed and make my way downstairs. I doubt sleep will come for the rest of the night, but I need something to take my mind off it, something to keep me distracted. As I make my way down the stairs, I consider figuring out which one of these doors Mr. Danforth is hiding behind and taking him up on his offer to 'talk.' But with guys like that come feelings, and I'm definitely not the girl he should be falling for.

I make my way into the kitchen and start searching through the cupboards for a glass, then proceed to make as much noise as possible trying to fill it with iced water.

The clock on the wall tells me that it's just after eleven at night and I gape at it for a second. When in the fresh hell did it get so late? After talking to the boys today, I retreated back to my room at about four in the afternoon, then I stared at the ceiling for a few hours, contemplating how my life got so fucked up in such a small amount of time. I don't remember falling asleep but here we are. It must have happened at some point.

I sip on my iced water, standing at the kitchen sink and looking out the massive window into the back yard. It's freaking incredible. The pool is massive and gives me major summer vibes, but I doubt I'll ever get a chance to use it. As soon as I figure myself out, I'll be out of here.

A noise coming from the main living area catches my attention, and I spin around, looking out into the darkness. King sits on one of the massive couches, leaning forward and reading a paper with a set of headphones over his ears, completely oblivious to me standing in the kitchen.

I roam my greedy eyes over him. He's not wearing a shirt, and the top of his headphones rest on the back of his neck. I don't know why—but damn. It's the most attractive thing I've ever seen.

Before I even know what I'm doing, I start making my way to him, my hungry stare eating him up like Christmas pudding, and as I take him in, I realize that he's exactly what I need. King is my lucky ticket to claiming myself back. Only I control my body. Only I get a say in who or what touches it. I don't belong to those faceless monsters; I belong to me.

I'm going to claim myself back, I'm going to steal back the control, and King is going to help me do it.

The closer I get to him, the more liberated I start to feel, and despite the hell I've been through, I know this is right. This is exactly what I have to do.

As if sensing me getting closer, King raises his gaze from the papers in front of him and slowly swivels his heated stare to mine. He reaches up and pulls the headphones down so that they're resting around his neck and I find myself sweeping my stare over his chiseled, sun-kissed chest.

He's perfect, every muscle, every hair. He's every woman's version of a wet dream and I'm about to have him.

The desire flares in my eyes and he reads me like a book, knowing exactly what I've come for, and in an instant, the same desire flashes in his eyes, but unlike me, he has his head screwed on properly.

He shakes his head and I see the regret in his eyes. "No, babe. Not after what happened. Maybe give it a few days and then I'll give you what you need."

I finally reach him and hook my thumbs into the side of my sweatpants before pushing them down over my hips. They're so big for me that they fall effortlessly to the ground and I don't waste a second climbing up onto King's lap and straddling him. My hand presses down over his mouth, feeling his growing erection beneath me. "Shut up and fuck me," I tell him, sensing another argument on his tongue. "I know what I'm doing."

King meets my eyes and holds my stare for a minute too long before a wild growl pulls from deep within his chest. He grabs the hem of my shirt, tears it over my head, then takes my waist, pulling me in.

I arch my back, pressing my chest into him and he wastes no time circling his lips over my nipple and sucking it into his mouth, his tongue teasing me as he flicks it over the sensitive bud.

I grind down against his cock, desperately needing him, and as he goes to reach down between us, I shake my head. "Uh-uh," I groan. "I'm running this show."

Sensing my need to be in control, he backs off and lets me take whatever I need from him, putting his hands back on my waist and roaming them over my heated skin. "Hard and fast," I warn him, meeting his eye, though I don't know why I bother with my warning—hard and fast is the only way King knows how to fuck. If I was after a slow and steady wins the race kind of fuck, I'd be knocking on someone else's door.

I reach down between us and free King's large, veiny cock from his sweatpants, and as I go to line him up with my entrance, King grabs my face, forcing my eyes back to his. "Are you sure?"

I nod, a pant slipping from my lips.

Just like that, he releases his grip on my chin and I sink down over him before fucking him with everything I've got, claiming back that fragile piece of me that was stolen away.

Grabbing hold of his shoulders, I drop down over him again and again, clenching my pussy and squeezing him as I ride up and down his dick, grinding, loving, panting.

He fills me so deeply, his wild growl only pushing me harder as his fingers dig into my skin, silently begging for more.

I don't hold back, letting that animalistic part of me take over and claim his body as my own, free to do whatever the fuck I want with.

King scoots down on the couch until he's lying beneath me. He grips my hips and I instantly take him deeper, moaning his name into the darkened room. "Fuck, King," I groan, leaning into him and burying my face into his neck as his hand lowers to my ass, squeezing it tight before spanking it hard. "I'm going to come."

"Not fucking yet," he growls, his deep tone vibrating right through his chest and making me clench down harder around him.

My ass bounces as my slick pussy glides up and down his hard length, spreading wetness between my legs. King's large hand reaches right around me until he's feeling where his cock slides in and out of me, his fingers instantly becoming soaked in my wetness.

He trails his fingers up to my ass, teasing me there as I continue to fuck him. I press back into his touch, silently telling him that it's okay, and he doesn't skip a beat, pressing his fingers into my ass as I wildly ride his cock.

He pushes harder and my orgasm creeps up on me. "Fuck," I grunt into the darkness, my pants becoming wild and out of control.

"That's right, baby girl. Fuck me," King growls, his deep voice speaking right to me and making me feel like his filthy little whore in all the best kinds of ways. "Take it."

I ride him faster, desperately wanting to take everything he's got, but knowing that with him on top, he'll be able to hit me just right and push me over the edge, I pull back and meet his heated stare. "I need you to fuck me."

He raises a brow, a wickedly excited grin stretching across his face, and within a second, I'm flipped onto my back with my legs up around my head as he slams deep inside me, so much deeper than I would have managed on my own.

I grab a cushion and shove it into my mouth to keep myself from screaming out as I watch his body grind and roll with each thrust, the moonlight shimmering against his side and showing him off like a priceless work of art.

King doesn't look up at me, just keeps his stare on my aching pussy, watching as he rams inside of me and making me feel like the most desirable woman on the planet.

His thumb presses down over my clit and as he rubs tight little circles, my pussy clenches around him, and just like that, my world explodes. I throw the cushion away, not giving a shit if I wake everyone and scream his name. "FUCK YES, KING!"

A deep growl comes tearing out of him as he comes hard, sending hot spurts of deliciousness shooting inside of me, but he doesn't let up, keeping his heavy cock moving in and out as my body convulses beneath him, his thumb still working my clit like a fucking wizard.

As I come down from my high, King releases my legs and scoops his arm around my waist. Keeping his cock buried deep within me, he adjusts us on the couch so that I straddle him once again, and not being able to help myself, I slowly rock my hips back and forth as I desperately try to catch my breath.

King grabs my chin and forces my face to his before crushing his lips to mine in a bruising kiss, something I definitely wasn't expecting from him, but I'm not stupid enough to reject it. I kiss him back, our tongues fighting for dominance, but when it comes to a guy like King, there's only so much control he's willing to give up.

I keep my hips rolling over his, and as he kisses me, his hand slips between us and he rubs lazy circles over my clit, instantly bringing my body back to attention and winding me up all over again. "Did you get what you needed?" he asks, his lips moving down to my neck and roaming over my sensitive skin.

I think about it, wanting to give him an honest answer, and as I do, I can't help but feel as though I completely took my control back. I claimed that part of me that I felt was missing, and the old Winter is right here, ready to pick up where she left off.

"Yeah," I whisper, tilting my head back and loving the feel of his tongue roaming over my neck. "I sure fucking did."

"Good," King murmurs, pressing harder against my clit as I pick up my speed.

My orgasm sneaks up on me, and before I know it, I'm coming on his cock again, my pussy clenching down and convulsing around him. I ride it out, and the second I'm done, I climb off his lap without a word, press a kiss to his cheek, grab my clothes, and walk away as I feel his warm come seeping out of me.

I make my way up to the spare bedroom, no longer desperately needing the lights on, and take a quick shower. Then despite feeling like myself again, I get dressed into Carver's shirt and sweatpants before slipping back out of my room and making my way across the hall.

Carver wakes as the light from the hallway shines upon his face, and just as he had the night before, he pulls back the blankets and I slip right in, feeling like the worst kind of bitch as I still feel the welcome ache of his best friend between my legs.

19

My hand skims over the banister as I make my way down the impressive stairs and hit the bottom feeling like I'm ready to get my life back on track. I just need to find my bike and find a new vice to rely on because those fuckers took my brass knuckles, but I will be getting them back. I don't know how or when, but mark my words, I will.

I make my way into the main living area and my eyes instantly scan over the couch where I'd worked out all my issues on King's cock last night and I struggle to keep the smirk off my face.

Fuck, that was a good night.

I walk deeper into the house and come into the kitchen where

I find both Cruz and Grayson sitting up at the massive dining table, Grayson with a feast before him while Cruz just sips on a coffee. I stop for a second, not having expected to see anyone up at this time.

It's just past six in the morning, and after lying awake for the last hour, I slipped out from under Carver's arm and decided to get a start on my day. After all, I have a life to figure out.

"You're up early," I say to the guys, stopping by the fridge and scanning through it before letting out a sigh and deciding to focus all my attention on the complicated coffee machine sitting on the counter, staring at me as though it's daring me to try and figure it out.

I start fiddling as Grayson takes a bite of toast. "Got things to do."

"Like what?" I grumble. "It's just after six in the morning. You have hours before you need to be at school. Wait ... what day is it? Wednesday?"

Grayson's stare drops back to his plate, making it clear that his daily routine is absolutely none of my damn business, but did he really have to snub my question? I'm still in the dark on the whole Wednesday thing.

Cruz gets up from the table and steps right into my back, placing his coffee down on the counter beside me and pressing his whole body up against mine, letting me feel everything he has on offer. "Need some help?" he grumbles into my ear, both his hands coming down on the counter on either side of my hips.

A shiver runs down my spine, electricity pulsing through my body, and I can't help but press my ass back into him. Cruz pushes back, his hand falling from the counter and sweeping around my waist. "I think

I can handle it."

"Uh-huh," he whispers, reaching around me with his other hand to press a few buttons on the coffee machine and get the stupid thing running. Silence falls between us as the machine does its thing but he doesn't dare step away from me. He stays exactly where he is, his hand slipping under the hem of my shirt and skirting across my skin, leaving goosebumps in its wake.

My eyes roll back and I thank the heavens above that neither of the boys can see my face right now because it would completely give away the fact that I'm starting to crush on this flirtatious bad boy, which right now, is exactly what I don't need. You know, considering that I've been sleeping in Carver's bed while also screwing King until I scream for mercy.

Shit. How did I get myself in this situation?

The coffee machine beeps and Cruz reaches around me to grab the mug before pressing it into my hands. "Coffee?" he questions.

I do everything I can to wipe the cheesy smile off my face as I take it from him and turn in his arms until his green eyes are staring down into mine. "Thank you," I murmur, holding the mug with both hands to avoid the possibility of my other hand roaming where it shouldn't go.

Cruz leans into me and presses the softest kiss to my cheek, holding his face right by mine for a second longer as the words, "My pleasure," come rushing from between his lips, gently brushing across my skin.

Without another word, Cruz takes a step back before turning away and walking back over to the table. I follow his lead and take a seat opposite the boys, and just as I lift the mug to my lips, King walks through to the kitchen, his hair ruffled from sleep and still wearing the grey sweatpants from last night, his shirt still missing and giving me the perfect view of his strong torso.

King's hand rubs over his chest and the movement has me snapping out of it and realizing that I've been staring, and most likely drooling too. He walks deeper into the kitchen and as my gaze raises to meet his eyes, I find his curious stare already boring into mine.

His eyes shine with our dirty little secret as he cuts across the kitchen and hits the buttons of the coffee machine. I hide a smile, knowing that if anyone was to look my way, our secret would be exposed in a heartbeat, and I'm not exactly down for having to explain what I've been up to. Though Grayson caught me coming out of Carver's room that first time and has been witness to all of Cruz's shameless flirting, so there's a possibility that the cat's already out of the bag.

I force myself to look away from King as he crosses to the pantry for a box of cereal. He starts getting his breakfast sorted out and I focus solely on the mug in my hands while trying to figure out what the fuck is going on between us. We're sleeping together, but do I actually like the guy? I don't know. I guess apart from furious warnings, scowls, and glares, we haven't actually had a proper conversation. Apart from the fact that his cock is fantastically impressive, I really know nothing about him. Fuck, I can't even remember his first name.

I focus harder on the mug, desperately trying to think back to that first day at school, going over Ember's rundown of the guys. She said something about wanting to suck his dick and then told me that King is practically the devil in human form, and if I take the way he fucks into consideration, then yeah, I'd definitely agree with that. Personality-wise? I don't know. Maybe he's misunderstood or just puts on a mask for the outside world.

But what was his first name? Fuck. I'm going to have to check that one with Ember because after fucking the guy three times, perhaps it's rude to admit that I can't remember his damn name.

Once his coffee is ready, King makes his way over to the table with his bowl of cereal and drops down into the seat beside me, his natural musky scent hitting me as he passes and nearly making me come in my pants. He makes himself comfortable, slipping his hand under the table and dropping it high on my thigh, silently teasing me.

I suck in a gasp and as all eyes fall to mine, I pretend to choke on my coffee, making some bullshit lie about it going down the wrong hole. King's eyes sparkle with laughter, but his face remains void of any emotion, making him nearly impossible to read.

Crap. Hunter. That's it. Hunter King. I like it.

Silence falls around us as the boys work on their breakfast, and I can't help but notice the way Cruz's curious gaze flicks between King and me as if he can sense something there. He leans back in his chair and looks as though he's about to start asking questions that I'm not ready to answer when Carver comes striding into the room and steals a piece of toast right off Grayson's plate, while walking into the kitchen for a glass of OJ.

Carver returns to the table a second later, also watching me with a curious stare and I can't help but feel as though he's wanting to ask a few too many questions as well.

I have to get out of here.

All four boys watch me. Grayson with annoyance, Cruz with suspicion, Carver with confusion, and King with one hell of a steamy secret. I finish my coffee as fast as humanly possible.

The second the last drop is gone from the mug, I fly to my feet and rush into the kitchen to rinse it out and drop it into the dishwasher. I turn back to the guys, awkwardly standing before them. "So, umm … I just wanted to say thanks for letting me crash here the last two nights, and you know, saving my ass, but I think I'm going to head back to Irene and Kurt's place to grab my stuff, then head over to Ember's place until I figure out where to go."

"What? No," Cruz demands, flying to his feet. "That's ridiculous. First off, you have a perfectly good place to stay here, and secondly, there's no way in hell I'm about to let you go waltzing back into Kurt's place. I'm sorry, babe, but you're fucking insane if you think you're going back in there. Let me go, I'll get your shit and bring it back here."

I laugh, honestly thinking he's joking but seeing the look on all of their faces I realize that maybe they all feel that way. "Umm … no. That isn't how this is going to happen. You guys don't get a say over how I do things. I'm not your problem. I can work it out for myself."

"I'm with Cruz," King says, getting to his feet and leaning against the back of his chair. "I think you're fucking stupid for going back there."

I gape at him, wondering when the hell he decided that he was entitled to an opinion on my life, all of them for that matter. "It's not like I'm planning on sitting down and telling him all about my adventure with the sex trafficker. I'll sneak through the window and get out of there before he even notices what's up. None of you need to worry, I'll be out of your hair in no time."

Carver scoffs as though I'm missing some big point, but he can go fuck himself. I get exactly what they're trying to say, but the threat has passed. I'm not going back to live with Kurt and Irene, I'll be getting my stuff and flying straight out the door.

Carver goes to get out of his seat and my eyes bug out of my head. That's not good. I can trust Cruz and King to hold their ground, but Carver will insist on locking my ass in his spare bedroom just to keep me here, which I honestly still don't get.

He turns to face me, a challenge in his eyes, but I beat him to the punch, raising my chin in defiance. "You told me yesterday that I was a free agent. I know I'm technically owned by the Dynasty bullshit, but you said that I could leave. So, what is it? Am I a prisoner or am I free to walk out the door?"

Carver's stare hardens before it finally drops and he waves his hand toward the door. "You're not a prisoner here, Winter. You're free to go whenever you want."

I walk over to him before stepping right in front of him and pressing a soft kiss to his cheek. "Thank you," I whisper before meeting the other guys' stares. "You honestly don't need to worry about me. I'll see you guys at school."

With that, I hightail it out of here knowing damn well that every single one of them are frustrating enough to try and stop me.

I break out through the front door and my whole world brightens when I find my Ducati patiently waiting for me at the top of the drive. I hurry down the stairs until I hit the pavement and finally see my bike. I knew it was locked safely in Ember's garage but a weird part of me thought that I might never see it again.

I grab hold of my helmet and find the key hidden safely inside, wondering which of the guys thought to bring this back to me before realizing that the engine is still warm. Considering that Carver and King looked as though they just fell right out of bed, it would have had to be either Grayson or Cruz early this morning, and judging by my few run-ins with Grayson, my guess would be Cruz.

A smile cuts across my face, and just as I go to pull my helmet over my head and get the show on the road, the massive front door peels open and a second later, I'm looking up at Grayson as he hurries down the stairs taking two at a time.

I wait patiently, my gut telling me that I should just get on my bike and leave, but after everything these guys have done for me over the past few days, I owe it to him not to be a raging bitch. "What's up?" I ask, as he hits the pavement and starts making his way to me.

"I don't like you," he tells me, stopping just shy of the Ducati and keeping his harsh stare on me.

"Geez, thanks, but you didn't need to come all the way out here to tell me that. You've made it perfectly clear since day one."

He shakes his head. "No, I haven't," he says. "You confuse me.

You're different from the usual girls we get around here and I've been wary of you. That's what you've been sensing, but over the past few days I've been watching you, and I see you getting closer to each of my friends, and I don't fucking like it. Do you think they're stupid? You're sleeping in Carver's bed, flirting with Cruz, then fucking King last night. They're going to figure it out, and when they do, it's going to end badly, and I can guarantee that it'll be you it ends badly for."

My mouth drops, having absolutely no idea what to say. "I …"

"Don't," he says, cutting me off before I make a dickhead of myself by stumbling over some bullshit explanation. "Either pick one, or don't pick any at all, but if you hurt them … I'll fucking end you. Got it?"

Grayson doesn't wait for a response, just turns on his heel and stalks back up the stairs leaving me gaping after him and feeling like a complete ass. He's right; I've been playing them all, but I don't want to choose. King gives me what I need in a physical sense while Cruz feeds that other part of me, the part that needs a man to tell her how pretty she is and make her feel like the only girl in the world. Carver … Carver is different. He keeps all the monsters away, and for the first time in seventeen years, makes me feel like I don't need to scream.

No, I don't want to choose, but why should I? Why can't a girl have it all?

It doesn't matter anyway, it's not like I'm coming back here and it'll never work anyway. King, Carver, and Cruz all strike me as the alpha male, over-protective, and jealous types. I highly doubt that they're down to share.

I put it to the back of my head and climb onto my bike. I have more important things to worry about this morning. I can deal with the guys later.

My engine roars to life and I fly down Carver's long driveway to find the gate already open, and the second I can, I get the hell out of here, riding awkwardly in Carver's borrowed clothes and no shoes.

My engine roars through the streets, and within the space of twenty minutes, my bike is pulling into the shitty concrete drive of my Ravenwood Heights home, though 'home' really isn't what this place is. Home is the furthest from how I feel when I'm here.

I stare up at Kurt and Irene's house. It's just before seven in the morning and I can guarantee Irene is locked in her room, fast asleep, while Kurt is sprawled out on the couch.

I have two options. I can either sneak through my bedroom window, grab my things, and be out of there in no time, or I can make a fucking scene.

Damn it, what kind of obvious choice is that?

I go for the fucking scene.

I slam my way through the front door, letting the wood splinter and break. The door rebounds off the adjoining wall and I watch in satisfaction as Kurt jumps awake on the couch, more than terrified for his life.

I barge my way through the house, making as much noise as possible. I grab my duffle bag and throw every one of my belongings into it then race back out of the shitty little room, pleased that I'll never have to walk in here again.

By the time I come back out to the living room, Kurt is still trying to peel himself off the couch, and as he looks up at me, he blinks a few times, hardly able to believe I'm here. "Surprised to see me?" I growl as I look down at him with disgust.

He tries to stand but I shove my palm against his shoulder, sending him sprawling back to the couch. I lean into Kurt, dropping my duffle bag to the filthy carpet as I crowd him onto the couch, letting my feelings for him fly free. "Listen here, you dirty, drunk sleaze," I spit, letting him see exactly what I think of him. "I will come back here, and when I do, you better be ready because I am going to slit your throat for what you did to me. You hear me? I'm going to fucking kill you."

Kurt laughs and pushes me back, sending me back a step and surprising me with the strength that he has after spending another night drowning in alcohol. "Don't you come into my house making threats, bitch. You should be grateful that I gave you a place to live."

"You sold me to a fucking sex-trafficker. You should be grateful that I didn't send your ass to prison, but there's no point because you'll be dead before that happens."

"All talk," he laughs. "All fucking talk."

Without a second of hesitation, I rear back and slam my fist right into his nose, feeling the cartilage shatter beneath the force. The satisfying crunch echoes through the room, and I know that one sound will stay with me for the rest of my life.

Kurt falls back into the couch as blood rushes from his nose, and all I can do is laugh as I shake out my hand, desperately wishing that I had my brass knuckles wrapped securely around my fingers. It would have made this moment so damn perfect.

"You fucking bitch," he roars, holding his nose and choking on the blood that pours down the back of his throat.

All I can do is laugh as I scoop up my duffle and turn for the door. "All fucking talk, my ass," I scoff, grinning back at him before walking out the door and leaving the fucker wide open so the rest of the street can watch and see just how damn pathetic he really is.

After pulling my helmet back on and awkwardly climbing onto my bike with my duffle bag pulled over my shoulder, I hit the throttle and fly back through the city until my knuckles are wrapping against a heavy door.

Ember's face appears a second later, and before I can even get a word out, she crashes into me and wraps her warm arms around me, holding me tight. "You're fucking staying here with me, bitch," she tells me, making me wonder if maybe the guys have already gotten to her. "I've already cleared it with my parents, now hurry up and come in, Mom's already cooking us breakfast."

20

The top of my pencil freezes against the desk as I stare at the door of the classroom, watching as Cruz happily welcomes himself in despite not being part of this class.

What the fuck does he think he's doing?

He walks through the rows of students, only stopping when he steps up beside the kid who sits right by me. "Move," he says, making the kid practically shit his pants and fly up out of the chair as the teacher gapes at him, her mouth hanging open, as for the first time all morning, she finds herself lost for words.

Cruz drops down in the now vacant seat beside me and swivels until he's staring right at me with that goofy-as-fuck grin stretched wide across his far too handsome face. I stare at the teacher dumbfounded. Is she planning on doing something about this or just going to keep standing by and let Cruz do whatever the fuck he wants?

I wouldn't be surprised. That seems to be the code this school lives by. Carver, King, Cruz, and Grayson can't seem to do any wrong, despite every move they make being super douchey. How the hell do they get away with this shit? Any other student would have been reprimanded and then crucified the second the door opened.

Realizing that the teacher is just cool to stare at him for the next hour, I turn my gaze back to Cruz's, finding his heavy stare already on mine and his eyes sparkling with laughter. "Can I help you?" I ask, narrowing my eyes and daring him to make a smartass comment just so I can kick his ass.

He shakes his head, making a show of getting comfortable in his seat. "Nope, I'm good," he says, throwing his arm over the back of his seat. "What about you? How was your morning?"

Ahhh, it all makes sense. The boys want to know what happened when I went back to get my stuff this morning, so they sent the one guy who could flash a devastatingly reckless smile and make me cave like a little bitch. Well, I have news for them. They're going to have to try harder than that.

"My morning was great. Though it would have been nicer if I didn't have four guys leering at me."

"Oh yeah?" he questions, playing along. "Sounds like a good time to me."

"It was ... mostly."

"Mostly?"

I nod before scanning my gaze back to the teacher who just ignores the fact that we're having an open conversation in the middle of her class and gets on with her lesson plan. "Yeah, I just feel like it would have been a lot smoother if someone wasn't trying so hard to get into my pants all morning."

Cruz sucks in a sharp gasp, his hand falling to his chest. "What? No. I'm wounded."

"What? You?" I ask, pulling back and feigning confusion. "Why would you be wounded?"

"Wait," he says, his brows dipping as he watches me. "Aren't you talking about me?"

I shrug my shoulders, only now just realizing how much fun it's going to be to fuck with him. "Maybe I am, maybe I'm not."

His eyes widen before he shakes his head and flops back into his seat, a heavy sigh pulling from deep within him and drawing the attention of the students around us. "I fucking knew King was trying to make a move. That motherfucker. I knew it. He was being far too shady at breakfast."

"King?" I ask, my brows furrowed, as I fight a laugh. "Do you think King is into me? Hmm, I didn't get that vibe from him."

"Huh? Then who the fuck are you talking about? Carver?" I shake my head and he scoffs. "No, now I know you're lying. There's no way Grayson was trying to get his dick wet. There's just no way. I'm sorry to break it to you, babe, but you must have been reading that situation wrong. He wasn't trying to get in your pants. Me, however," he says, a wild grin splitting across his face. "That's a different situation."

I can't hold back my laughter any longer, and as he watches me, the pieces of the puzzle fall into place and his face falls. "You were talking about me all along, weren't you?"

I nod. "Yeah," I say, leaning over and nudging his shoulder. "You make it far too easy to fuck with you."

Cruz groans and the look that crosses his face when he realizes that he's been played is honestly the most adorable thing I've ever seen, as just for a split second, he looks like a vulnerable little boy, but his hard lines and cocky demeanor come flying back. "Let's cut to the chase," he finally says. "What happened after you left this morning? I'm assuming that since you're still here in school, you just went straight through your window and out again like you promised. You didn't try to beat the shit out of Kurt?"

I press my lips into a hard line before glancing up at the teacher and then indicating down to my work. "Shhh," I tell him, quickly glancing his way. "I've got work to do."

Cruz lets out a soft, pained groan and leans forward onto his desk before pulling out his phone and busily texting, most likely sharing what he's learned with the guys, despite the fact that I technically didn't confirm nor deny anything.

He gets distracted with his phone and I get busy trying to catch up on the work I missed from the first half of the week, and before I know it, the bell signaling the end of class sounds through the school, and I'm finally able to pack up my shit.

I walk out of class with Cruz right on my heels, silently following me as I make my way to my second class of the day, only Cruz falls away the second I reach the door and find Grayson already sitting in the classroom, his ass perched in the chair right beside the one I usually take.

I spin around to demand answers out of Cruz but he's too far away, so I stalk into the classroom and put myself right in front of Grayson, knowing damn well that he's not about to give me the answers I need. "What the fuck is going on?" I demand, hissing as the students fill the room around us. "Why are you assholes taking over my classes? Don't you have somewhere better to be?"

"Trust me," he grunts, leaning back in his chair and looking up at me with those stormy grey eyes. "I have a million better places to be than sitting in on your American History class."

"Good, then go do them," I tell him, stepping around his single desk and dropping my books onto mine.

"No can do," he says.

Anger pulses through me. Why the hell do I find it cute when Cruz does it, but so irritatingly frustrating when it's Grayson? "Why?" I demand. "What's the purpose of you guys sitting in on my classes? Do you have some bullshit roster? Who am I going to expect to come barging into my chem class? What about English?"

Grayson just stares at me before silently slicing his gaze back to the front of the room and watching as my teacher comes in and starts setting up for his lesson, refusing to answer me. But what's new? I knew that was going to happen.

Grayson has made it obvious since day one that he doesn't like me, so out of all of them, he confuses me the most. Why does he bother? If he doesn't give a shit what happens to me, why is he always there, always protecting me and putting himself at risk to keep my ass safe? It doesn't make sense. The only explanation I have is that the other guys give him no choice, which in the long run, only makes him resent me more.

His little speech by my bike this morning went a long way in proving that. He wants me to stay away. He can sense the dynamics changing, and he doesn't like it one bit. But if I'm completely honest, I don't want anything to do with their dynamics. I want out. I want so far out that they won't even remember me being here, yet for some reason, they're constantly pulling me back in.

My History teacher gets on with his lesson, and with every passing minute, my irritation for the boys only gets stronger, wilder, and grows so much more frustrating. Grayson sits in silence beside me, and it only serves to eat away at my patience.

God, I can't wait till lunch and give them a piece of my mind. This bullshit is not going to fly.

The minutes tick by extra slow, and by the time the bell sounds, giving us a break, I'm ready to start raging. Yet when I make my way out to the quad to find the guys, I come up blank. How is it that they're everywhere I don't want them to be, but when I need them, they're nowhere to be found?

Fucking assholes. They're doing this on purpose.

The rest of my day drags by like a bad smell, each of my classes completely overtaken by assholes. Though I'm just that unlucky to have both Grayson and Cruz already in my Math class, so I guess I can't be angry with them about that. However, my point is still there, and despite not having a valid reason to be pissed, I'm damn furious.

After the end of school bell has rung loudly through the Academy, I find myself flying out of the school gates, intent on beating them at their own game. If they think they can avoid my wrath, they're dead wrong.

Knowing their eyes are on me, I pull my helmet over my head and ride out of the student parking lot like my ass is on fire, glancing in my mirror to watch the four of them come together and start walking down to the black Escalade, looking pretty fucking proud of themselves.

I take off, knowing that once I hit the end of the street, they won't be able to see what direction I turn from the school. Being a sneaky, conniving bitch, I turn right toward the expensive part of Ravenwood Heights and park my bike in the bushes outside of Carver's home, more than ready to bust some balls.

Twenty minutes pass before the Escalade comes tearing down the street and pulls to a stop at the top of the driveway. I hear their chatter inside the car as Carver's window is rolled down and he hashes in the code for the gate.

I push back into the bushes, keeping myself hidden and the second the gate opens and the Escalade disappears down the long drive, I make my break.

I run for the gate, slipping through it just before it closes while having to keep my bike trapped on the outside, but no one drives down here anyway. With the first gate at the top of the private road and my bike hidden in the bushes, it'll be fine. If only for the hour it'll take to bust their asses wide open.

The second I get in through the gate, I dive into the shadows of a tree, keeping myself concealed as I watch the Escalade make its way down the drive. I run from tree to tree, getting closer each time and hoping that the guys haven't spotted me, but they're probably far too busy discussing the size of their dicks to even notice that I've broken onto the property.

It takes me ten minutes to get from the top gate to the actual house, but it's definitely worth it, especially when I sneak up the front stairs and slip straight in through the open front door.

I step behind a vase that is nearly as tall as I am and listen carefully, trying to figure out where in the house the guys are. I hear Carver's booming laughter coming from the kitchen with King but that's all. Cruz and Grayson are a mystery. They could be anywhere, but I need them all together; otherwise, confronting them won't work. I need to back them into a corner and watch each of their expressions carefully.

I head for the stairs, making my way up as quietly as I can to not alert King and Carver before grabbing hold of each door handle and swinging them wide until I find what I'm looking for.

I get halfway down the hallway and after just passing the room that was declared mine, I open the next door and hear a low groan coming from deep within. My attention is instantly piqued, and I find myself stepping into the bedroom.

I quickly glance around and find nothing but an open bathroom door. The shower is running and hot steam is pouring out through the door, fogging up the windows and mirror. I know I should turn around and give him his privacy, whichever him it is in there, but the low moan that comes echoing through the bathroom speaks to the wild vixen within me, and before I even know what I'm doing, my feet are moving me forward.

My shoulder presses against the doorframe of the bathroom, and I instantly find Cruz, butt-naked with the hot water showering over his flawless golden skin. My tongue instantly rolls over my lips, hunger and desire flooding through me like a wave as I follow the strong line down his body to find his palm slowly drawing up and down his thick, veiny cock.

His other hand is propped against the shower tiles, leaning his body into it as he tilts his head down, watching as he pleasures himself.

My bottom lip gets trapped between my lips as everything below the border clenches.

Holy shit. I knew Cruz was going to be something special, but I never expected this. He's simply divine and has desire pulsing through me like a rocket.

His head turns, and for a moment, I freeze, terrified for being caught watching the show, but as his gaze sweeps over me, taking in the need in my eyes, he doesn't dare stop. His palm keeps moving up and down, squeezing his tip and groaning low.

His eyes lock onto mine, and for a hot minute, I absolutely hate myself for being fully dressed.

"What are you waiting for?" his low voice grumbles through the steamed bathroom.

I don't fucking hesitate.

I walk straight for the shower, not bothering to shrug out of any of my clothes, but why would I? I'm here to bust their balls, and while I'm more than down for playing with his, he still needs to be punished, and because of that, I won't dare give him a taste of what he really wants.

The shower door opens and Cruz's heavy stare remains locked on mine. The water instantly drenches me as I step in close to him, the scent of his body wash strong in the air. My fingers slide over his strong arm and over his large shoulders, leaving a trail of goosebumps in their wake.

I put myself right in front of him and Cruz instantly grips my chin before sliding his hand around the back of my neck and using his thumb to force my chin up. He moves in nice and close as my hand falls to his strong chest, his eyes never leaving mine, and without warning, he presses his lips to mine, kissing me deeply.

His hand continues moving up and down his large cock and not being able to help myself, I take over.

As his hand travels down to his thick base, I curl my fingers around his tip, curling my thumb over the top and swallowing his soft moan against my mouth. Cruz releases his hold on his cock and lets me do the work as his lips drop from mine and travel down to my neck.

His hands roam over my body as I work my small fist up and down, listening to the sound of his moans and letting him tell me exactly what he wants, but when his hands start pulling at my wet clothes, I can no longer resist.

He strips me naked, and while I won't completely give in to him … just yet, I don't see why I can't enjoy myself too. After all, I'm the one who's been wronged here. It's only fair that he makes it up to me.

Cruz's hands roam over my body, touching and exploring every inch of me as my hand works his cock. He pinches my nipple, cups my breasts, and strokes his strong fingers over my skin, making me come alive under his touch.

The familiar burn begins building within me, proving that he knows exactly what he's doing. He hasn't even really touched me yet. How does he already have me so on edge?

My pussy aches, desperate for his touch, and as if reading my body, his hand goes to slip down between my legs, but I pull myself away, shaking my head. "Uh-uh," I say, meeting his eyes with a seductive smile pulling at my lips. "Not for you."

"What?" he groans, the devastation clear on his face.

"Not after your bullshit today," I explain, slowly turning and showing off my body as I keep my hand moving against his cock. I look back over my shoulder. "You can look, but you can't touch."

A deep, guttural growl pulls from within him and a satisfied smile tears across my face. Now, why the hell did that feel so good?

Cruz leans into my back, dipping his head over my shoulder and gently biting it as he comes to terms with the fact that he won't get to make me come, but that doesn't mean that I'm a complete monster. He can still enjoy the rest of my body.

His hands roam over me as I grind my ass back into him, loving the feel of his strong body pressed up against mine. His arms circle my waist, his hands teasing my breasts, flicking my nipples until they're tight, pained buds.

Desperately needing a release, my hand trails down my body, skimming over my stomach, and traveling down until my fingers are rubbing over my soaking clit. I groan with instant satisfaction and knowing that Cruz's eyes are on me only makes it better.

My head tilts back and he instantly takes advantage of my neck, kissing it with everything he's got and making me squirm as my name is whispered through his lips.

His hand covers mine over his cock, and he squeezes it tight, kicking up the speed and bringing me even closer. Needing more, I slip two fingers deep inside and fuck myself as his other hand squeezes my breast. "Fuck, Cruz," I pant, wishing that I wasn't so fucking stubborn and would just bend over and let him slam his thick cock deep inside of me.

I rub my thumb over my clit, hitting it just how I like it, only it's so much better with Cruz's hands on my body. My orgasm builds and as Cruz's lips fall back to my neck in the sensitive spot just beneath my ear, I cum on my fingers, clenching down hard and groaning his sweet, sweet name.

"Holy shit," I pant, slowly pulling my fingers out of my soaking pussy as Cruz continues to watch me, both our hands still roaming up and down his long, hard cock. I go to rinse my hand under the stream of water, but Cruz grabs my wrist before I can, spinning me to face him in the process.

His eyes bore into mine, and before I even realize what he's doing, he sucks my fingers into his mouth, licking them clean until there's not a drop of me left. A deep groan travels up his throat and I feel it vibrate against my fingers. "I knew you would be fucking sweet," he murmurs as my fingers slide out of his mouth, making everything clench deep inside of me.

I press up into him. "Do you want to see just how sweet I can be?"

His brows raise and before he even has a chance to respond, I drop to my knees, letting the water slam against my back. I take his thick cock in my hands, needing both because he's just that big. Keeping my hooded gaze on his, I take him deep into my mouth, feeling him slam against the back of my throat. As I take him deeper, circling his tip with my tongue and loving the way he groans with pleasure, his fingers knot into my hair.

My head bobs up and down, and as his hold tightens in my hair, he comes hard with a deep guttural moan. His cum hits the back of my throat and I swallow until there's nothing left for me to take, and then just like that, I get back to my feet, press a kiss to his cheek, and silently step out of his shower.

I steal his warm towel off the heated towel rack, leaving him with nothing, and as I go to walk out of his bathroom, I look back, meeting his confused stare. "Get your ass downstairs, cowboy, because I'm about to bust it wide open."

21

"Alright," I demand, staring down the four assholes who sit before me, three of them wondering why I'm wearing nothing but a towel with my hair still dripping wet while the other holds his tongue. "You have three seconds to explain why the fuck you bitches have followed me around like a bad smell all day, and don't act like you weren't. I know you purposefully avoided me at lunch just to avoid this bullshit now."

The boys share glances between themselves, and I can't help but feel that a million messages are passing between them, messages that I can't even begin to work out. "Umm," King says, drawing my attention his way. "I think the bigger question is why the fuck are you wearing nothing but a towel? Did you just shower?"

"Of course I just showered," I snap, watching the confusion filter over the guys' faces. "Do you think I just like to bust into peoples' homes and walk around in a towel for fun?"

King shrugs his shoulders. "I mean … I don't know you that well. You're not exactly an easy chick to read, but why the fuck did you shower just now? It's a bit of a weird time of the day to shower, don't you think? Do you usually just walk into other people's homes then decide to strip down to your birthday suit, and shower before even telling them you're there?"

I roll my eyes, not wanting to get distracted by this bullshit topic change, while also wishing that I'd used a better excuse like falling in the pool or getting dirty outside. At least that would explain why I don't have any clothes to wear. Had I showered like a regular human being, I'd have dry clothes to put back on, but dickheads like me apparently like to walk straight in fully clothed, allowing a long, hard cock and a stone-hard body to make a fool out of me.

I focus my stare on King. "My shower habits and what I am or am not wearing right now is irrelevant, so don't even bother trying to change the topic again. Why were you all being assholes today?" Grayson just grunts and I amend myself, glancing at the other three. "Okay, why were you three bigger assholes than usual? I thought the asshole role was usually just Grayson's thing."

Cruz chokes back a laugh and slices his stare to Grayson, loving that he was just called out for his usual bullshit. "I don't know about these guys," Cruz says, his sparkling eyes hitting mine as a secretive grin pulls at his lips, telling me that he's currently picturing the sight of me fucking myself and remembering the taste of my cum on his tongue. "But I feel as though I was extra sweet today."

I bite my tongue, resisting the urge to throw a cushion at his face, or possibly my fist. "Stop being a dick," I tell him. "You were being a complete asshole, just like the other guys, and I want to know what's up? Is this some Dynasty bullshit where you need to keep me in check and are going to go about it in all the wrong ways, making me try harder to get away from you?"

Cruz meets my stare, something hardening in his eyes. "You don't like hanging out with us?"

"I ..." I shake my head. "That's not what I said," I tell him. "I don't like my freedom being taken from me, and if it continues in the obviously douchey way that you're all going about it, then yeah, I'm going to start resenting you guys. I know we all started off a bit rocky, but I don't really want to have to hate you guys," I turn my gaze to Grayson, just to throw his usual bullshit back at him. "Except for you, I'd happily hate on you."

Grayson narrows his eyes as his lips twist into a sneer while I grin back at him, feeling like a complete badass, despite not really being sure if I even hate him at all. I mean, can I even hate the guy after he saved my ass? That just seems like a bitch move.

Before I get sidetracked thinking about it too much, I turn back to the others. "I can put up with a lot of bullshit, but I won't put up with that," I tell them. "Be real with me. What the fuck is going on?"

Carver lets out a sigh and scoots up on the couch so that he sits on the armrest. "This is all on you," he explains, giving me the cold, hard facts, and not being shy about it either. "We're not being douchey stalkers because Dynasty is making us, we're keeping close to you because you decided to be a fucking idiot and take yourself back to Kurt and Irene's place against our better judgment."

"What? What has that got to do with anything?"

"Look," Carver says, getting to his feet. "We're not here to tell you what you can and cannot do. If you want to go and put yourself in harm's way to prove some kind of point, then that's your business, but we're also not going to stand back and let Sam get to you again."

"Sam?" I question, keeping my stare on Carver as it seems that he's the only one willing to give me the answers I'm looking for.

"You made it clear to Cruz this morning that you made a scene with Kurt and Irene when you went back there, and you've got to be a fucking moron if you don't think that they're not going to try the same shit on you again. They got away with it once and cleaned up from it. What's to stop them trying again?"

I let out a heavy sigh and drop to the coffee table, being careful not to flash the guys in the process. "You really think that they'll try it again? I thought it might have been a possibility, but … I don't know, I guess I might have thought that I was in the clear."

King shakes his head. "Sorry babe, Sam got five million out of you. One call from Kurt saying that you made it back to him and he'll be all over you. Sam's girls don't make a habit of getting away. He'll want to keep you quiet, and to do that, he'll either try to sell you for another five mil, or he'll put a bullet through your head.

We're not playing games here. You're not safe, and until we know that you are, your ass isn't stepping out of our sight. It's as simple as that."

The heaviness of the situation begins to come down on my shoulders, and I glance up at Cruz, for some reason picking him to take my anger out on. "Why the hell didn't you explain that to me this morning? I never would have gone back there if I knew it would bring Sam back to my doorstep. FUCK." My face falls into my hands and I try to focus on taking slow, deep breaths. "You guys shouldn't have let me go. You should have stopped me. I was just trying to be a stubborn bitch and prove that you guys couldn't boss me around."

Cruz slips off the couch and falls to his knees in front of me, his hands resting against my knees. "You're alright, Winter. We're not about to let that shit happen to you again, we've got this, but at the same time, we're not about to keep you as a prisoner. You're free to live your life, and I think I can speak for all of us here, but we don't want you feeling trapped or being scared that the world is going to cave in on you every time you leave the house."

I raise my head and meet Cruz's stare, feeling like I could break at any moment. He scoops me off the coffee table and takes me back to the couch where he settles me onto his lap, but I find myself looking up at Carver, the problem solver of the bunch. "What do I do?"

He flicks his gaze round to the other guys before coming back to mine with something sinister deep within his stare. "You have to make sure that Kurt doesn't get around to making that call."

"How the fuck am I supposed to do that?"

Carver just stares as the others fall into a strained silence, the answer lingering in the air between us.

I have to kill him. It's as simple as that.

It's either my life or his.

22

I stare at the ceiling of the darkened room, my heart racing with what I have to do. If I was to ask the boys, they'd do it without hesitation, but this is my mess. I have to get myself out of it. I know the boys have been there every step of the way, but I need to be able to rely on myself, even if it means making a hard call.

It's his life … or mine.

Do I have what it takes? I don't know.

I would like to think that I do, but when it comes down to it, will I be able to end someone else's life?

I have no doubt that Kurt is going to call Sam because he's a greedy motherfucker and he's going to do whatever it takes to get another bottle of whisky in his hands. Hell, I wouldn't be surprised if Irene was in on it too.

What if I'm wrong? What if I end his life but he had absolutely no plans on calling Sam? What would that make me? I'd have blood on my hands, and given that blood isn't innocent, but it's still blood. But then I'm taking the risk that he's already called Sam and killing Kurt isn't going to achieve anything but make me feel better about myself. It sure as hell would eliminate Kurt, but it won't eliminate the threat.

Fuck me. What am I supposed to do?

I glance back at the door, knowing that Carver is only two doors away. If I was to crawl into his bed, I'd sleep like the living dead, but I have to stop needing him like this. I have to start relying on myself. The guys are only interested in me because their stupid secret club is enforcing it. I only wish I knew why.

After learning what I had to do, my world crumbled as I tried to come to terms with it. Cruz scooped me up and brought me up here to my room while King texted Ember to let her know not to expect me back at her place. I haven't moved since, but the more I think about it, the clearer it becomes.

I have to do this and the sooner I do it, the higher my chance of survival is.

It's him or it's me, and without a doubt, every time I will pick me.

But how? Do I slit his throat like I told him this morning? Find a gun? Fuck, what weapon do I use to become a murderer? This isn't a job for a cheap set of brass knuckles. I need to step up my game and I need to do it now.

My hands shake as bile rises in my throat. I throw my blankets back and race into the bathroom before slamming my knees down on the hard tiles. I grab the toilet seat and rip it up just moments before my head tips over the bowl and I let loose, hurling my guts up until there's not a damn thing left.

I drop to the tiles, the side of my face basking in their coolness until I find the strength to get to my feet. I make my way over to the sink and splash cold water over my face before rinsing out my mouth and trying to find the courage to do what I have to do.

All I know is that once I get started, I can't stop. If I do this, there's no backing out, no finishing only half the job. I do it, and I do it right. I get in, I get out, and I don't leave a shred of evidence behind.

Fuck.

I raise my head from the sink and meet my reflection in the mirror before letting out one last shaky breath. I see nothing but a bitch-ass pussy staring back at me, and I instantly hate what I see. I'm stronger than this. I can handle my business. I was born to fucking handle my business.

I stand tall. I've been acting like a fucking idiot up until now, but not anymore.

I turn out of the bathroom and flick the light off as I go before walking straight out of my room, down the stairs, and out the front door. There's a chill in the late evening air, but it's not going to slow me down.

I make my way right up the long driveway, keeping up a good pace, knowing that if one of the boys were to catch me out here, they'd try to stop me. One by one, the boys had come into my room to offer to take the task off my hands, but I denied each one of them before listening to their advice on how they thought I should handle this, but truth be told, I don't think I heard a damn word any of them had said.

They don't want me to do this. They all want to be the big hero of the hour and save me, but they should know better. After the bullshit I've gone through, there's absolutely nothing left to save. I should be the one trying to save them from the same fate. Though, from the effortless way they spoke about it this afternoon, it's left me wondering if maybe the topic isn't so new to them.

I reach the top of the driveway and have to scale the gate while hoping that I don't set off an alarm. I drop down to the other side, wishing I had something better than Cruz's old shirt and sweatpants to wear. I can't say that I've ever dreamed about murdering someone before, but if I had, I'm sure that I'd want to look like a complete badass while doing it, not a drowned rat in clothes twelve sizes too big.

I find my bike still hidden deep within the bushes outside Carver's home, and as I straddle her, I feel her power seeping into me. I can do this. I'm not someone's meal ticket, I'm a survivor, and I'm going to thrive.

I put the bike into neutral and push it down the street until I'm far enough away that the roaring engine won't wake the boys, and the second I can, I hit the throttle and get myself back over to the shitty end of Ravenwood Heights.

It's just after ten when I bring my bike to a stop a few houses down from Irene and Kurt's place, and the first thing I find myself doing is scanning the street for one of Sam's vans. I have to play this smart. There's a good possibility that Kurt has already reached out to Sam and there's a strong chance that I'm about to crawl back through that stupid bedroom window to find a black bag pulled over my head again.

With the street empty and Irene's car missing from the driveway, I hide my bike in the shadows of a neighbor's home. I slip into their backyard and steal a large black shirt off the washing line, before hurrying up the road.

I stand before the house that's going to change it all, the nerves sinking heavily into my gut.

I can do this. I *have* to do this.

It's either me or him.

Not one for repeating my mistakes, I slip around the opposite side of the house until I come to the small bathroom window. Taking a breath, I wrap the black shirt around my fist, and mentally prepare myself.

This is it. It's now or fucking never.

As I let out my breath, I slam my fist into the glass and move fast. If he heard me, he'd be off his dirty couch and already coming to investigate. I break the rest of the glass, making sure there's enough space for me to slip through without cutting myself, then the second I can, I lay the shirt over the windowsill and press my hands to it before hauling myself up and over.

I go crashing down into the bathroom, landing on the broken glass, but Cruz's baggy clothes save me from being cut up.

Getting to my feet, I grab the shirt and shake any broken glass out of it while listening for Kurt. There's no sound coming from within the house, and I let out another breath before putting my hand inside the shirt and grabbing the door handle, being extra cautious about my fingerprints.

I get the door open and hold my breath as it squeaks through the quiet house. I pause, my heart racing a million miles an hour, but at this point, I don't know if it's from fear or the adrenaline.

Wanting to get this over with so I can get the fuck out of here, I take the short five steps up the hall, passing the room where I was first abducted, and do my best not to dwell on it. If anything, it only spurs me on, reminding me just how badly I can't go back there.

I make my way out to the kitchen and peer around the corner to find Kurt sitting back in his favorite recliner couch, feet up, watching his brand new big TV in the dark. An almost empty bottle of whisky hangs from between his fingers, with two empty bottles already thrown across the floor, telling me exactly what I'm working with.

He's fucking pathetic. I hope he enjoyed his stupid TV while it lasted because revenge is a dish best served cold. I bet he even paid for the fucker with the payout he got from selling me to Sam.

I silently make my way around the kitchen, knowing that he's got to have the cash hidden around here somewhere. Keeping the shirt wrapped around my hand, I start searching, beginning with the cookie jar and old containers lined up across the kitchen counter.

I move onto the cupboard, silently rifling through before finding an old mug that looks completely out of place. I reach up onto my tippy-toes and grab it, peering in and scoffing under my breath as I find a measly two thousand dollars.

Is that all I'm worth? I'm sure with the TV, Irene's gambling addiction, and the twenty or so bottles of cheap whisky, Kurt was probably only paid five grand to have his foster child abducted from her bedroom. Just fucking great. I bet he'd be pissed if he found out that I sold for five million dollars. He'd probably have asked for more money, though that would have only got him shot. I suppose Sam was being generous with paying him in the first place. I guess his investment was well worth the trouble.

Either way, money is money. I dip my fingers into the mug, claiming every last dollar for myself. Consider it my cut for the trouble I went through.

I slip the cash into the baggy pocket of Cruz's sweatpants before scanning the kitchen once again. There's a plastic bag, an old shoelace from his boots at the back door, and a good old-fashioned knife.

Choices. Choices.

Suffocation or a slit throat?

There's a chance that he could tear through the bag or the shoelace could snap under the pressure, so I guess that leaves the knife.

Using the shirt again, I pull it from the knife block, damn sure that it's probably blunt, but that just means that I'm going to have to work for it, just like I've worked for everything else in my life.

I study my knife, more than aware that this is about to become a murder weapon, and as I study its sleek clinical line, I realize just how dead I feel inside. Where's the emotion, the overwhelming voice inside my head telling me not to do it? It's not there. It's just me alone with the nothingness inside of me.

Not wanting to put this off any longer, I raise my head and start creeping toward the living room, knowing that if he wasn't such a drunken idiot, he probably would be able to see my reflection in his big-ass TV. I get just a few steps from him when a shrill phone rings through the near quiet room.

I drop to the ground, hiding behind his recliner as he scrambles around on his side table, trying to get a grip on his phone. The ringing continues for far too long, making me anxious before he flops back into the seat, rocking the whole couch.

"Sam," he grunts as he answers the call, making me catch my breath. This is the call I've been dreading. "Where the fuck have you been? I've been trying to get a hold of you all fucking day."

Oh, fuck, fuck, fuck. I'm not too late, but if I don't make this quick, I just might be.

"Listen," I hear the familiar voice roaring through the phone, loud enough that even shoved against Kurt's ear, I can still make him out clear as day. "I told you not to fucking call me. We had a deal. Transaction over. Lose my fucking number."

I get straight back to my feet, thankful that the phone call is keeping Kurt distracted. "But I got another deal for you, and this time, you better fucking pay upfront."

No, no, no.

My fist tightens around the handle of the knife, my heart racing so fast that it couldn't be humanly possible. I start shaking, the fear that was completely vacant before now coming crashing into me, slamming through my chest with a savage desperation.

"It better be fucking good," Sam tells him. "Don't waste my time. That last foster kid was a fucking bitch."

"That's just it," Kurt says, the laughter in his tone making my stomach twist with disgust. "That bitch—"

Nope.

Time's up, motherfucker.

I step into the back of the couch, my hips slamming against it in my rush to end this before it's too late. I grab the phone with one hand before launching it across the room. It slams against the front door, shattering into pieces as I grab Kurt's chin and yank it up. Then without hesitation, I take the blunt knife and tear it across his throat, making sure that he will never hurt me again.

23

Blood spurts from Kurt's throat, hitting the walls, spraying the roof, and redecorating the floors. It instantly soaks through his clothes, and I gape in horror as he fights against my hold, hardly able to understand what the fuck is happening, but it takes less than two seconds for his thrashing to ease.

Kurt starts choking on his own blood, and as it pours out of him in waves, I scream, never having seen anything like it, let alone being responsible for such a heinous and violent murder.

Holy fuck, what have I done?

I throw the knife across the room and listen as it clatters against the wall of the kitchen and drops to the tiled floor. I run.

I race out the door, leaving it wide open in my desperation to get out of there. My feet thunder down the broken concrete, my heart beating a million miles an hour as the vision of blood spurting across the room circles my mind.

I've watched more than enough episodes of *'Criminal Minds'* to know that the blood spurts across the room like that, but nothing could possibly prepare me for how it felt. One part of me is grateful that Kurt's threat will never linger over my head again, while the other part is horrified to learn just what I'm capable of.

I'm a murderer. If I was to get caught, I'd be spending the rest of my life behind bars.

Holy fuck. Did I just allow Kurt to take away the rest of my life? I can't fucking win. Let him live and be abducted and sold to a real purchaser, probably raped day after day until I'm killed, or end Kurt and spend the rest of my life behind bars.

Fuck. Either way, I was going to be screwed. At least with Kurt dead, I can run.

I reach my bike hidden in the shadow of the neighbor's home and climb on, not wasting a damn second with my helmet or bothering to be quiet. My bike roars to life, and within the blink of an eye, I take off, my tires skidding against the road and leaving a thick black line along the asphalt.

I head back into the city and onto the other side before racing up Ember's road. I come closer to her house before realizing that I can't bring this down on her. I can't come here and have her and her family hide me from the rest of the world. That would incriminate them, and

I refuse to do that to her. She deserves so much better.

Before my front tire hits her drive, I pull on the throttle and send my bike flying down the other end of the road, but where the hell am I supposed to go? I'm too ashamed of myself to go back to the boys. They knew I had to do it eventually, but there's something so different between talking about it and actually doing it. No, I won't go back there. I have to disappear. I have to get out of Ravenwood Heights for good.

I ride for what seems like hours, heading out of Ravenwood Heights before turning my ass around and flying straight back into town. I go around in circles, not knowing where the fuck to go or what to do until I pull up at a familiar pier and launch myself off the bike.

I run down to the beach, only stopping when the cool tide hits my feet, and I scream into the night. Dropping into the water, I watch it soak into my clothes and instantly turn the water a cloudy red.

I glance down to find my clothes stained in Kurt's blood and dried against my skin. I scream more before panicking and throwing myself further into the water, desperately trying to scrub it from my body.

I dive into the water, letting it completely submerge me while trying to wash the blood from my hair. I furiously scrub at my skin, leaving it red and raw, wishing it would just go away. But the more I scrub, the more I seem to find. It won't go away, it'll never leave me.

Twenty minutes later, I sit under the pier with water dripping from my body. The night has gotten so much colder, and as I sit in a tight ball, my knees pulled up to my chest with my arms wrapped tightly around them, I shiver, wondering if this is some deformed kind of punishment from the skies above. I deserve so much worse.

I ended a life tonight. Who the hell am I to judge if someone deserves to live or die?

I feel sick.

"Found her," a chilling voice says from beside me.

My head snaps up, and I find King staring down at me with a look in his eyes, so full of concern that it has tears springing from mine. He slips his phone back into the pocket of his jeans before crouching down and scanning his intense stare over my body, completely taking in the train wreck before him.

King reaches out and pushes my cold, wet hair back off my face, letting me see the devastation and pain written over his. He gently shakes his head. "I'd take a fucking bullet for you, Winter. I'd do anything to save you from having to go through that, even if it meant doing it myself."

The tears flow from my eyes, and without hesitation, King scoops me up into his warm arms. He holds me close to his chest as he walks back up through the soft sand until he hits the pavement. He walks toward my bike, and as I raise my head off his chest, I notice a familiar Escalade parked right behind it.

Movement across the street catches my attention, and I find Cruz walking toward us. He meets us by my bike and after his eyes travel over my soaking wet body, he silently throws his leg over my bike and lets the engine roar to life.

King takes me to the front passenger seat of the Escalade and puts me in before standing in the open door for a second just watching over me. He waits a beat, his eyes softly roaming over my broken face before grabbing the seatbelt and silently clipping me in.

Cruz takes off down the street, riding my bike like a professional, and not a second later, King drops down into the driver's seat and kicks over the engine. Before taking off after Cruz, King fiddles with the temperature settings, doing his best to heat up the car to gain control of the violent shivers that overwhelm my body.

Silence falls through the car as he starts driving through the streets of Ravenwood Heights. We get halfway back to Carver's place when King turns and looks at me. He doesn't say a damn word, but his concern is clear in his eyes, and for a moment, I can't find the words to say.

King and I have had a strictly sexual relationship, and outside of that, we pretend to hate one another, but right here, I'm seeing another side of him, one that confuses the absolute shit out of me. Maybe there is something more between us than just hot, fast sex. His comment down on the beach about taking a bullet for me and saving me from having to do what I did completely threw me off.

I don't know what this is, or what it means, but I sense things changing, and that scares the crap out of me. If I'm completely honest, I sense things changing with both Cruz and Carver as well, and I'm terrified that if they were to realize just how far I've been allowing it to go, I'm going to lose every single one of them.

Maybe Grayson was right. I need to choose just one, but I don't want to. They all offer me something so different.

King has never been so open about his feelings toward me. He's always kept them under wraps because I needed him to. I needed it to be just sex without the emotion. His body was an escape just as I felt that mine was for him.

Why did he have to choose now to start making things complicated? But then, maybe it doesn't need to be complicated at all. Maybe it'll be as easy as they come and I'm only overthinking things because fear is holding me back.

Fuck. Why am I even thinking about this now? I just killed a man. Killed.

I rest back into my seat, my hair still dripping wet, but the heat is finally starting to do its thing and really beginning to warm me, though it's nothing compared to what a hot shower and a bed could do for me. I bring my cold hands up to my mouth and blow hot air into them, trying to breathe a little life back into me when something occurs to me.

I turn and look at King driving in the darkness, his face barely visible in the moonlight. "How did you know where to find me?" I ask, my voice coming out as barely a whisper.

King glances at me with a strange hesitation in his eyes. His lips press into a hard line before he focuses back on the road. Just when I think he's not about to tell me, he lets out a soft sigh, keeping his stare heavily focused at the road in front of him. "There's a tracker on your bike. We were able to find you the second we realized you were gone. We just had to wait for you to stop so we could come and get you."

My mouth drops but not a word comes out. I just simply nod, not surprised by his admission at all. In fact, I should have figured it out myself.

When I left school this afternoon, the boys didn't come racing after me, and they sure as hell weren't surprised when they found me making my way through Carver's house. They knew exactly where I was the second I left the school. When I was hiding in the bushes outside Carver's gate, they knew, and when the front door was left open making it possible to sneak in, it was done on purpose.

How could I have been so blind to that? I should be hating on them, raging that they dared take away my privacy, but I can't. I can't find it within me to hate them, not even Grayson. Perhaps after coming straight from Kurt's place, hating on the guys for something so minimal, something they did just to keep me safe, seems so petty. I should be grateful that I have four amazing guys in my life who so fearlessly watch over me. Besides, I'm Dynasty property now, it only makes sense for them to want to keep track of me.

Instead of getting upset and having a tantrum like I usually do, I simply just stare out the window, watching as the city lights slowly morph into suburban streets.

I feel King's stare on me the whole way back to Carver's place, and by the time we come to a stop outside the impressive mansion, I find Cruz standing at the bottom of the stairs, patiently waiting to help get me inside. The concern in his eyes is like nothing I've ever seen before.

He walks around to my door to help me out as King comes out of the other side. They fuss over me as though I'm crippled and I instantly push them away. I don't deserve to have them caring for me like this, not after what I've done.

I make my way up the stairs with the guys on either side of me, and as I push through the massive front door, I find both Carver and Grayson standing in the foyer, patiently waiting.

King and Cruz come in behind me, and as soon as the door closes with a soft thud, Carver tilts his head, jerking it to the side and turning away in a silent gesture for us to follow him.

"Do we have to do this now?" Cruz asks, his voice echoing through the foyer and bringing Carver to a stop. "She's fucking soaked. Can we just get her dry and cleaned up before you hit her with an interrogation?"

Carver looks back at me, and I see anger pulsing beneath the surface, and while he and I both know that I had no other choice, he's more than pissed that I slipped out in the middle of the night without saying a damn word. Though that anger can't mask the fact that he's been looking at me with nothing but concern since I walked through the door, showing just like King and Cruz, that maybe there's something more. "No," he says after a tension-filled beat, stealing his intense gaze away from me. "This will only take a second."

Cruz nods, and without a word, our small group walks through the massive house, following Carver's lead. We walk into the living room that has quickly become one of my comforts in this place, and Carver silently indicates to the couch, suggesting that I should take a seat.

As I cut across the room and drop down onto the couch, the boys all fall around me, making me feel like a delinquent child in the principal's office. "Here," King says, grabbing the throw blanket off the back of the couch and tossing it to Cruz who's closest to me. He instantly drapes it over me, but with the chill so deep in my bones and my hair still soaking wet, the blanket doesn't do much. I need to get in a shower and clean myself up properly.

Once the boys feel like they have me sorted out, all eyes fall to Carver. As he looks back at me, I swallow hard, knowing what he's about to ask but not feeling as though I have what it takes to answer him properly.

"What happened, Winter?" he asks, his tone flat and void of all emotion.

My eyes begin to water but I hold back the tears, refusing to cry in front of these guys. "I did it," I tell him. "When I got there, he was on the phone with Sam and was about to strike a new deal, and I just … I had a knife and I just … I can't go back to living in that cold cell."

I cut myself off, not able to actually tell him what I did. As the emotions overwhelm me, Cruz takes my hand in his big ones and holds it tight. "You're going to be okay, Winter," he promises me. "We're not going to let you go back there. Sam will never get his hands on you again."

I glance away, knowing that he means every single word that comes out of his mouth, but I'm not sure if I can trust it. How can he promise me safety like that? For so long, all I've had is me. When I finally decide to trust someone, they always let me down, and this is too important, too big.

I slice my gaze back to Carver's, letting him know that I'm ready for him to hit me with the next part of his interrogation.

"He's definitely dead?" he asks, his eyes boring into mine, and despite how his questions make me flinch, he doesn't hesitate, not afraid to do what needs to be done.

I nod. "Yeah," I whisper. "At least, he has to be. What I did … no one could survive that."

"You didn't wait to see if he was actually dead?" Grayson asks, cutting in.

My gaze sweeps to his as panic starts to overwhelm me once again. "I … I … there was so much blood and I just … I don't know, I panicked. He was choking on it and the blood was just … everywhere and I … I just ran."

Grayson and Carver share a glance as King and Cruz keep their stares locked on me. "How much blood?" Carver finally questions, making my brows dip low in confusion as he and Grayson start to get agitated, their hands pumping into fists as they find it impossible to stand still.

"Why is that important?"

"Answer the question, Winter," Carver prompts, pushing me on.

I think back to Kurt's living room, remembering the blood splattered over the ceiling, across the walls, and pooled on the old, ratty carpets. Enough blood to soak through his clothes and the recliner. "It was a fucking bloodbath," I finally tell him, giving it to him straight just like he's always done for me. "I grabbed his chin and slit his throat with a blunt knife, and I was fucking brutal about it. So, while I didn't hang around to watch his final breath, I can guarantee that he's dead and that it's a fucking mess in there."

"Okay," he finally says, nodding at Grayson who instantly falls in beside him. The two of them share a glance before Carver looks back at Cruz. "Get her cleaned up and in bed. She'll feel better in the morning."

Cruz nods as he squeezes my hand and just like that Grayson and Carver walk out of the room, leaving me sitting here in confusion. I look up at King, who watches me with a grim expression. "Where are they going?"

"They need to check the scene to make sure you left nothing behind to tie you to it and close it off. We don't want to draw any unwanted attention; the longer the cops keep away from this, the better."

"I …" my words fall flat, and I just nod, realizing that once again these guys are saving my ass.

With nothing else that needs to be said, Cruz silently stands and offers me his hand. I take it without hesitation, and as he leads me out of the room, I can't help but look back at King who watches the way his best friend claims my hand. His eyes flick up to mine and where I expect to find jealousy, I see nothing but a fierce curiosity that makes me wonder if maybe having a relationship with both of them is something that he'd be down with.

The thought leaves my mind as Cruz tugs on my hand and pulls me out of the living room. He leads me through the house and up to his room, where less than twelve hours ago, I'd spent one of the best hours of my life. He leads me right through to his bathroom and instantly turns on the heat lights before stripping me out of my damp clothes.

The shower roars to life, and he leads me right into it, letting the warm water calm my shivering. I tilt my head back, needing it like I need air to survive. As my body adjusts to the warmth, I slowly turn the heat up and give myself what I really need, letting the water turn my skin an angry red.

I glance back at Cruz, who stands by the door just watching me, but not in one of those pervy ways like most guys would. He watches me with concern, almost as though he's waiting for me to break, but I've already had my meltdown. Now it's time to get back up and learn how to move on from this.

"Will you join me?" I ask him, unsure why I so desperately need to feel his comfort.

He studies me for a short moment. "Are you sure?"

I nod, and just like that, Cruz removes his clothes and steps into the shower behind me, curling his arms around my waist and holding me close. "Are you okay?" he murmurs into the shower, his voice thick with pain for me, hating that I'm going through this.

I shrug my shoulders. "I really don't know," I whisper, turning in his arms and pressing my head against his chest as the hot water scorches my body and makes me feel warmer than I've ever been before. I raise my head and meet his stare, hating the concern that looks back at me. "How can you all stand to be around me knowing what I just did?"

He watches me for a moment, really considering his answer before pulling me in closer, holding me tighter, and giving me the comfort I need to feel human again. "Because when it comes down to it, we all do what we have to do to survive. You're not a bad person, Winter.

You're incredible. You're beautiful, smart, and the strongest woman I've ever met. You're not afraid to make a stand even though the world has dealt you a shitty hand, and I know right now, you're probably struggling to believe a word I say, but eventually, you'll see that I was right. You're going to get past this, and no matter what, every step of the way, we're all going to be standing right at your back, making sure you don't fall."

I raise my chin, staring deep into his eyes. "You really mean that?"

"I do," he tells me. "You don't know how badly I wish that I could have gone in your place. I think we all feel that way, and I was going to. I had my plan and everything, but when King woke me up and said you weren't here, I knew you'd already gone, and for just a moment, I hated you for putting yourself through that. Taking someone's life …" Cruz trails off, his gaze raising above my head at the tiled wall behind me. "It's not easy," he finally continues. "It'll mess with your head and have you questioning your worth, but you'll make it through it. I'll make sure of it."

My brows furrow as I search his eyes, looking for answers that I know I'm not going to get. "You've …?"

I let my question hang between us, not sure if I want to know exactly what he means, or even if I'm ready to learn that there's a darker side to Cruz that I didn't know about, a darker side to all of them. But when Cruz just stares into my eyes, I see his answer loud and clear. He's killed someone before, just like I did, just like the rest of them have, and for some reason, even though I don't know any of the details, that little piece of knowledge goes a long way in healing something within me.

I'm really not alone in this.

I push up onto my toes and gently brush my lips over his. "Thank you," I whisper as the heated steam from the shower fogs around us. "You have no idea how much I needed that."

"Trust me," he says, holding me impossibly closer, not letting me pull my lips away from his. "I did." And just like that, he kisses me deeper, momentarily making me forget the turmoil that clouds my mind.

24

Cruz's arm wraps around my body, holding me close as he silently sleeps behind me, his body glued to mine as though the thought of being away from me physically pains him.

It's just after one in the morning and I've been struggling to find sleep, so when I hear the soft thud of the door directly across the hallway, I find myself slipping out from under Cruz's arm and wandering out into the hallway.

I silently grab the door handle of Carver's bedroom and push it open to find him pacing his room, stripping out of his clothes. He spies me the second I walk in and ignores me as he steps through to his ginormous closet. He drops his jeans before finding a pair of sweatpants and walking straight back out of the closet, turning off the light as he goes.

He eyes me as he walks through his room, his stare boring into mine as he steps right up in front of me. "What is this?" he asks, his hand falling to my waist. "I know you're fucking King, and you just spent the night in Cruz's arms. Now you think you can come and sleep in mine?"

I raise my chin and meet his stare, wanting more than ever to be honest with him. "I'm not even going to pretend that I know what's going on with Cruz and King because when it comes down to it, I can't even figure myself out, let alone them."

"And me?"

"You keep the monsters away," I murmur, giving it to him straight. "When I know you're there, I can close my eyes. I can't do that with anyone else, not even myself."

Carver studies me for a moment before finally nodding and dropping his hand to mine. He leads me across his room and peels back the blankets. Within seconds, I'm curling into his chest, my leg hitching up over his hip and his hand falling to my thigh to pull me closer.

My heart begins to race. Carver and I have always had a strict big spoon/little spoon relationship. I've never curled into him like this, and I sure as hell haven't been concerned about jumping his bones behind closed doors. Don't get me wrong, I've definitely thought about what Carver would be like between the sheets, but the opportunity has never quite presented itself like this before. When I'm in his bed, it's about finding peace, about having his comfort, and keeping the monsters of my dreams at bay.

But the way he holds me, the way his thumb roams back and forth over my thigh, the way my body presses against his, something is changing—something big, and I don't know if I'm capable of resisting him any longer.

My hand falls to his chest, feeling the strong muscles and rapid beat of his heart beneath, and as I raise my chin, looking up to meet his eyes, his lips come down on mine with the sweetest, fragile kiss known to man. I sink into him, never realizing just how badly I've been craving his touch.

His lips move over mine like a tortured dance, both of us trying to work out exactly what this means as his tongue sweeps into my mouth, instantly claiming me as his own. He grabs my body, pulling me up over him until I'm straddling his hips and can feel him hardening beneath me.

His hand claims my ass, squeezing it and shifting me on top of him so that my aching, needy pussy grinds against his delicious cock. I groan into his mouth, needing him so desperately, and press my body harder against his.

Our lips fight for dominance but he doesn't dare let up, curling his hand around the back of my neck and gripping my hair. He pulls me back, and our eyes meet for just a brief, tension-filled second before he draws me back in and picks up exactly where we left off, silently letting me know exactly who's the boss. Spoiler alert—it's not me.

My hand slips down his body, feeling the tight ridges of his abs and soaking in the warmth of his skin, but as my hand continues down, he captures it in his own, holding it tightly between his strong fingers. "Stop," he grunts, an air of authority in his tone.

Rejection slams through me and I find myself pulling back even more, unable to look away from his heated, intense stare. "What? Did I—"

"Is it not enough that you've had my friends? You have to have me too? Do you think I'm just going to give it up to you because you're in my bed every night?"

It's like having a bucket of ice-cold water thrown over my head.

My eyes narrow as his comment instantly stings. He didn't technically call me a slut, but it sure as hell felt like it. I sit right up, pushing against his chest as I remain straddled over his waist. "You kissed me," I say in a warning, letting him know that I'm not going to hold back if this is the road he wants to travel down. "I didn't ask you for this, you fucking offered it up. What's the point? Why would you do that if you didn't want it to lead anywhere? Or are you just some sick, sadistic asshole who gets hard off toying with my emotions?"

Carver's eyes drop over my body, taking in the way my pussy still presses against his throbbing cock. "Look at you, baby. You're in my bed, lying in my arms, rubbing your sweet pussy all over me and you're trying to tell me that's not what you came here looking for? I can read you, Winter, I have been able to since the second you showed up here. I know what you fucking want."

Yep. He's definitely calling me a slut.

A frustrated groan tears through me and I pull back off him

before scrambling off the end of his bed. I cut across to the door, and as I go, I look back at the guy who does absolutely nothing but confuse the living shit out of me. "Come on, babe," he says, watching me leave. "You don't have to go. Just come back to bed and we'll sleep."

Ugh. Fuck him. I'm not going to stay here and listen to how he thinks I'm whoring myself out then allow him to spend the night with my body pressed up against his. Screw that. I don't need him. I have other ways of keeping the monsters at bay. Besides, if I'm going to be miserable, then I sure as hell won't be doing it with an audience.

I walk out the door and slam it behind me, hating how fucked-up this whole situation is. I'm kinda with Cruz, and kinda with King, but whatever's been growing with Carver seems so much deeper than that. It's private and intimate despite there being nothing sexual up until now. Though after that performance, he can kiss my ass.

The bigger question is, why am I even thinking about this right now? I killed a man less than three hours ago and instead of asking Carver what happened when he went back there, I was too busy rubbing my pussy all over him.

Damn it. Maybe I am a fucking slut.

Screw him. I was so comfortable with who I am, and after one thirty-second-conversation with Dante Carver, I'm here questioning myself.

I fly back down the hall, marching straight past Cruz's door and feeling like a complete bitch. I was happy lying in his arms despite the fact that finding sleep was impossible. I should have just stayed there with him, but now, if I were to walk back in there, Carver would be right. How can I just go jumping around from one bed to another?

I reach my bedroom and storm right through the door, turning on the light as I go. I walk around my room before doing it again and again, my rage making it impossible to stop. I'd give anything to be able to collapse back onto my bed and close my eyes, but wishing for that kind of peace is like wishing for snow in the driest desert.

My hands curl into fists, opening and closing as I desperately try to calm myself, but the longer it goes on, the more that old burn begins to stir within me.

I need to get out of here. I need to release this anger and there's only one way that I know how to do it.

I strip out of Cruz's soft clothes and find the ones that I'd left in the bottom of his shower after breaking in here when school let out. It's hard to believe that was only this afternoon, less than twelve hours ago.

My clothes are sitting on the edge of my bed, folded nicely and smelling cleaner than any of my clothes have ever smelled before, and damn it, they're even soft. Did Cruz do this? I'll have to remember to thank him later. I don't know how much longer I can go on wearing boys' clothes that are a million sizes too big, but there's no doubt about it, I've never been so comfortable in my life. Though, if I'm going to do this, I'm going to do it right.

I get myself dressed, and within no time, I'm flying back out the door, going quietly as to not alert Carver, who I'm sure is probably still wide awake.

I get downstairs and find the keys to my bike on the small table in the foyer. In one swift motion, I scoop them up, and I'm out the front door taking the front steps two at a time until I hit the driveway.

My bike sits patiently waiting for me, and I throw my leg over it, instantly feeling at home. A raw grin cuts across my face as I start the engine and feel it rumbling beneath me, the sound deafening in the quiet night.

I hit the throttle.

As I fly up the drive, I can't help but look down at the small mirror and wonder just how many times I'm going to sneak out of this house tonight. The first time was a disaster, and while I did what I had to do, it didn't leave me feeling great. Hopefully, this time goes a little smoother.

My stomach drops as I approach the gate at the end of the driveway, but relief instantly filters through me when I find it wide open. I fly straight through it, pushing my bike to its limits.

I have to go fast. King admitted that the guys have a tracking device on my bike, and until I have the sun working on my side, there's no way that I'm going to be able to find it and shove it straight back up Carver's ass. So, until then, I need to get this done as quickly as I can because I have absolutely no doubt that at least one of the guys would have heard my bike and is now on their way after me.

I hit the second set of gates and enter the code as quickly as possible before finally making it to the main road and taking off like a rocket.

I scan the streets, searching through the back alleyways, looking for a target. The adrenaline begins pulsing through me as I find it nearly impossible to sit still on my bike. The need to start tearing shit up is far too strong within me.

I glance down at my hand over the handlebar and see my empty knuckles, desperately wishing that I had my weapon of choice, but for tonight, I'm going to have to go without and hit just a little bit harder. After Carver's bullshit tonight, I doubt hitting harder is really going to be an issue.

I pass a sleazy club just on the outskirts of Ravenwood Heights, and my bike slows as I look over it. There's a flashing light above the entrance that lets me know that if you come with the right amount of cash, anything is possible.

A grin stretches across my face. This isn't just a sleazy club, it's a fucking brothel.

Perfect.

I bring my bike to a stop right by the entrance of the alleyway and spy a man right down the side of the building, his face squished up against the window of a private room as he madly jerks off.

I laugh. This is going to be too easy.

The adrenaline pulses through me as I slide off my bike, feeling like myself for the first time in weeks.

Each step I take echoes down the alleyway, and by the time I get halfway, the man's head pulls away from the dirty window. His eyes widen, and afraid that I'm about to bust him for having his dick out in public, he quickly tucks it back into his jeans.

"Looking for a good time, huh?" I purr, slowly creeping in closer to him and rolling my tongue over my lips. "I could finish you off if you want."

The guy looks over me and I see the exact moment that he assumes I'm one of the working girls from inside the club. "Well, hello to you too," he murmurs, pushing off the wall and making his way to me, his eyes roaming over my body and instantly deciding that he likes what he sees.

I let my gaze sweep down his body as I bite my bottom lip. "You got cash?" I ask, lowering my tone. "Nothing comes free."

A wicked grin stretches across his face as he digs into the back pocket of his jeans and pulls out his wallet. He quickly scans through it before whipping his head back up to meet my stare. "I only have a hundred and fifty."

I step into him, trailing my fingers over his chest and slowly circle him. "Sounds like just enough to me."

A breathy, excited laugh bubbles out of his throat as he curls his arm around my waist and makes a show of plucking the cash from his wallet. "Oh, yeah," he murmurs as he reaches for my body, letting his knuckles roam over my curves and being far too bold as he dips his fingers into the top of my tank, pushing the cash inside the cup of my bra. His skin against mine makes me want to hurl, but I'm not about to stop him. Getting paid was never a part of my plan, but now that I am, it's just going to make kicking his ass so much sweeter. "How do you want to do this?"

"You tell me," I say, stepping closer and leaning into him. "But I'm not going to lie, hard and fast is my specialty. Now that really gets me hot."

"Where?"

I press into him, shoving my hands against his chest and slamming him up against the brick wall of the club. "Right here seems just fine to me. There's always something so thrilling about the possibility of getting caught."

A sleazy as fuck grin twists across his face as his eyes become hooded and his hands fall back to my waist. He goes to pull me in, and I prepare myself for a fight, the excitement building within me, knowing that I'm finally going to be able to satisfy that demanding itch within me.

My hand curls into a fist and just as I go to rear back, a strong grip circles my wrist and hauls me away from my target. My back slams against the wooden fencing that lines the alleyway just as I get a quick glimpse of a tall man slamming his fist against the pervert's temple, instantly knocking him out.

The guy crumbles to the ground, and after I right myself, I fly back toward the newcomer. He seems like a much bigger target, but damn it, I know I can handle him.

The man spins around at the very last second and Carver's face flashes before me. "What?" I stumble out, catching myself, but before another word can come flying from my mouth, a furious Carver grips my arm and yanks my sorry ass right out of the alleyway.

I stumble, desperately trying to keep up with his long, fast strides and avoid falling to my ass as he hauls me back toward his Escalade. I fight against his grip, wanting nothing more than to pummel my fists into his perfect face and hate on him for making me question myself.

How dare he? Why won't these fuckers leave me alone?

Carver walks straight past my Ducati and I pull desperately on his hold before he gets tired of my bullshit and curls his strong arm around my waist, lifting me straight off the ground.

I'm shoved right into the back seat of his Escalade and go flailing across it. The second the door is closed; I fly for the handle only to find the fucker trapped me with the kiddy-lock. He gets straight in the driver's seat, and leaving my Ducati behind, he takes off, his tires squealing against the asphalt.

"What the fuck do you think you're doing?" I demand, launching myself right off the backseat and trying to get to him as he drives, but like lightning, he grips my arm and pulls hard, somehow making my ass land right in the front seat beside him.

"Me?" he demands. "I'm not the fucking problem here. You don't like one thing that I say and the way you deal with it is by coming out to some run-down whore house and throwing yourself at some perverted dickhead? Come on, babe," he scoffs. "I know your standards are pretty fucking low, but I thought even you had a little more class than that."

I fly at him, the anger pulsing through me like wildfire. "I HATE YOU," I scream, but his arm snaps out and I'm thrown back into my seat, his strength like nothing I've ever witnessed before. "Do you honestly think that lowly of me that I'd fucking whore myself out to trash like that? Fuck you."

"Then what the fuck were you doing? Because it sure as hell looked like you were about to get on your knees for him."

"What's the matter, asshole? Jealous?"

He scoffs and I try to fight him off again only to be shoved right back into my chair, this time with a little more force to get his point across. I look over at him, my jaw clenched, but the idea of him thinking so lowly of me doesn't sit well in my gut, not that I should give a shit what he thinks.

I let out a heavy sigh, feeling completely exhausted. "I wasn't throwing myself at him. I was looking for a fucking fight. I was going to beat the shit out of him because storming into your room and suffocating you in the middle of the night seemed like a dick move, but maybe I should have reconsidered."

Carver just shakes his head, the scoff that comes tearing out of his mouth making me feel more pathetic than ever before.

Realizing that I have no way out of this, I relax my grip on his arm and he instantly releases his. I can't help but wonder what's going to happen to my bike, but for some reason, where Carver and the boys are concerned, I feel like it's going to be just fine.

We sit in silence as Carver drives us back to his place, and as he brings the Escalade to a stop, he looks back at me, the moonlight barely shining upon his skin. "Come with me."

Without another word, he unlocks the doors and gets out of his car, making his way up the stairs. I stare after him. There's no way I'm going anywhere with him, not after that bullshit he just pulled outside the club. Who does he think he is manhandling me like that? I'm not his little toy to just throw around whenever the fuck he wants.

Carver reaches the top of the stairs before I finally let out a sigh and climb out of his stupid car. I make my way up, assuming that he's given up and left me the hell alone, but as I push through the door, I find him waiting right in the foyer.

His stare filled with authority and promising that if I were to do anything but follow him, I'd quickly regret it. He turns on his heel and I follow his lead, my fists pulsing at my sides as I imagine just how good it'd feel to knock him out. But something tells me that the four guys who live under this roof are the kind of guys who I couldn't even come close to in a fight.

Carver leads me right through his home until he's pushing into a dark room. He steps around the open door and flicks the light, filling the room with clinical brightness. I stare around the home gym, equally as impressed as I am confused. What the hell does he think he's doing bringing me in here? Does he plan on tying me to his stupid weights and closing the door so no one can hear me scream, making it impossible to sneak out again?

I walk deeper into the room, and Carver silently closes the door before walking over to a set of cupboards and rifling through it for a minute. He holds something in his hand as he makes his way back over to me, and when he grabs my wrist, I try to yank my hand free, but he's far too strong.

Carver starts wrapping my hand in tape before moving onto the next and all I can do is stare. He peels off his shirt and stands before me with that lethal stare in his eyes and I can't hold my tongue a second longer. "What the hell do you think you're doing?"

"You wanted a fight, so fight. Hit me."

A blank stare sits over my face. "Are you fucking stupid?"

"No. But you clearly are," he snaps back at me. "Now fucking hit me. Work out all your bullshit anger so I can go to bed without worrying that you're going to sneak out again."

I shake my head. "No. I—"

"You need to hit something to feel better. So, take it. Stop being such a little bitch about it and *take what you need*. HIT ME."

My fist slams against his rock-hard chest and he takes it like a fucking man, but I don't stop, laying into him over and over again until my body starts growing weak. Carver doesn't relent, he doesn't even flinch even as my fists start to turn his chest and stomach an angry shade of red.

Tears fall from my eyes and the anger pulses around me, easing with each blow until I can no longer hold myself up. I crumble, falling to the ground, but before I hit rock bottom, Carver catches me, scooping me into his capable arms.

I curl into his chest, panting, desperately trying to control my wild emotions as he walks us straight out of his home gym and up the stairs. Carver bypasses my room and takes me straight to his, placing me down on his bed and taking off my tight clothes.

He pulls one of his big white shirts over my head, and I go crashing down into his blankets as he moves in behind me, holding me as I quickly fall into an exhausted sleep.

25

"Ohmigod," Ember screeches as she bulldozes her way through the students early on Thursday morning, the high shrill tone of her voice eating right through my skull and instantly reminding me that I spent the majority of my night sneaking out of a mansion, killing an asshole, going down on Cruz, making a dick of myself with Carver, only to then sneak out again, get called a whore, and then attempt to hand the same douchebag his ass and epically fail.

My night sucked. But it's a new day and all my issues are put behind me, at least I hope. Starting from this afternoon, I can go back to Ember's place and try to figure out what the hell to do from there.

I doubt her parents are going to let me crash in their spare room for much longer, not that I'm ever there much. The majority of the time, the boys find a way to make me stay with them.

That's over now. From here on out, I rule my world.

Ember comes crashing into me, misjudging her speed, and nearly knocking us both on our asses. "He asked me out," she squeaks, as I fight to keep us both on our feet.

"I ... huh? Who did?"

"Jacob Scardoni," she insists, looking at me like I'm an idiot for not having put it together in the first place, but I guess I am. After all, I hold this guy solely responsible for what happened to me despite the fact that he literally didn't have a damn thing to do with it. I mean, I kinda have a point ... though, not really.

After the pier party, I was supposed to spend the night at Ember's house, but then she got all wound up with this Jacob guy, and because of that, I took off and ended up back at Kurt's place where I was abducted. If Jacob wasn't at that party, my night would have been very different, but I doubt Sam would have stopped looking for me until he had me right where he wanted me, and because of that, I went through hell.

Revenge is going to be sweet. I just need to figure out how to make it happen. Though while they haven't actually said anything about revenge, I have a feeling that the boys are going to have my back with whatever plan I want. Though, that begs the question. Carver was all for me stepping up and having to make the decision to end Kurt. He said that he wouldn't stand in the way of what I wanted to do, so why the hell did he feel it was his right to come after me last night?

God, that asshole. The more I think about it, the angrier I get, but at least the majority of that anger was worked out last night. I'm just pissed that he's the reason I was angry in the first place, yet he was the one to help me take it all away. Fuck him. He's so hot and cold, sweet and sour.

It takes me a second to realize that Ember has been non-stop talking about her new boyfriend, and while I'm over the moon happy for her, there's just way too much going on in my head to even begin focusing on what she's saying. So I smile and nod until the whole school becomes victim to the four guys making their way through the front doors as though they're God's gift to women.

"Ugh," I sigh trying to figure out how everything seems to slow down wherever they go. It's like some kind of magical force is putting them into slow-motion just to make all the girls around them scream and beg for them to bend them in half.

They make their way through the hallway, conversations dying as they pass, or maybe it's just me zoning out the rest of the world and not being able to focus on anything but them.

As they get closer, I notice Carver's stare first. He's always the first to seek me out, always the first to set the mood, and damn it, the mood isn't great today. He looks pissed, and it's probably because I kept him up for a good portion of the night. He looks away, and the loss of his stare is almost like having a part of my soul ripped right out of my body.

King flicks his stare at me next, and just as I knew it would be, it's short and sweet—a quick check to make sure I still have all four limbs.

There's not a hint of emotion on his face, despite his declaration of doing anything to keep me safe on the beach last night.

King keeps making his way through the hallway, and not needing his constant approval, I turn to Cruz, but instead of the flirty smirk and sexy wink that I've become accustomed to, there's nothing but a narrowed gaze filled with confusion and a deep question—why the hell wasn't I in his bed when he woke up this morning? In fact, I was in none of their beds.

I slipped out early in the morning and showed up at Ember's place at the crack of dawn after only getting three hours of sleep. I walked out of Carver's mansion to find my Ducati waiting for me with the gate still wide open. Though I still haven't worked out who had gotten up to go and get it. For some reason, I'm leaning toward Grayson but I don't know why. He keeps coming off as the silent hero.

Cruz passes, and his confused stare only has me shrinking back under the pressure, not sure if I'm ready to explain just where I was. I feel that while King is cool with the idea of me being shared around his friends, Cruz seems like the type to get hurt. Carver though, he's complicated as fuck, but considering the bullshit that came out of his mouth after kissing me last night, it seems that's not something I have to worry about anymore.

The thought of Grayson being some kind of silent hero has my gaze sweeping his way only to find a dismissive pissed-off stare coming right back at me. I don't know why, but for some reason, it cuts deep, and as the four of them pass by me, I feel completely drained.

I crash against my locker, leaning my shoulder into it and

purposefully facing the opposite direction so none of them can see the torture ripped across my face at having to deal with them this early in the morning.

And to think I haven't even had a coffee yet.

"So, uh… that was intense," Ember notices, her soft murmur coming from beside me, making me realize that she's still here.

My eyes bug out of my head. I must have looked like a love-sick puppy, and she was witness to it all. "Oh, umm … yeah. They—" I cut myself off with a drained sigh, honestly not knowing what to say about our unique little situation.

How the hell am I supposed to begin explaining to this little ray of sunshine that after being abducted by Knox's uncle, the four devils of Ravenwood Heights had their ridiculously suspicious secret society pay five million dollars to save me from being sold to a rapist? Not only that, but they now own me, and stood by as I went out and murdered the man who gave me up.

Yeah … I know I was MIA for a few days, but no one is going to believe that shit. Though I did tell her about Sam over pancakes, and she was completely on board then. She may be a bit on the wild side, but she's also an innocent soul, and I don't want to be responsible for taking the light out of her eyes.

Ember nods, not commenting on my loss of words, but I see the understanding in her eyes. More than that, I see a raging curiosity, and despite her being the only real friend I have in Ravenwood Heights, I find myself biting my tongue, not quite ready to share the ins and outs of my relationship with the boys.

Feeling the exhaustion coming over me, I lean into Ember and take her wrist. "What's the time?" I ask, twisting her arm around to get a better view of her watch. "We got a few minutes before the bell, and I need a cigarette. Are you coming?"

"You said the magical words."

We walk out the front of the school to the very spot we had first met, and she lights up a cigarette before I steal the lighter from her hands and do the same. We lean against the brick wall in silence, watching the students as they walk into the school; the cheerleaders flirting with the football team as they all make complete asses of themselves while trying to play it cool.

We get halfway through our cigarettes when the bell sounds and I let out a sigh. "Damn it," I grumble, dropping the cigarette to the ground and putting it out with my boot, but at least I got halfway through it, more than enough to keep me going through the day, but I'll definitely need one tonight.

Ember goes to link her arm through mine when we see Principal Turner walking out through the front gates, and I come to an immediate standstill. Usually the sight of the principal walking around the school property wouldn't bring me to my knees, but the two cops standing at either side of him are sure as hell doing the trick.

Principal Turner looks my way before pointing me out to the cops, and I instinctively take a step back as Ember looks over at me, meeting my horrified stare. "What are you doing?" she demands. "The bell sounded. We have to get inside."

I shake my head, trying to pull my arm free. "No," I say, watching as she follows my gaze to the cops who are rapidly making their way over here. "Go and get Carver. NOW."

Ember looks between me and the cops three times before finally nodding like a bobble-head and taking off at the speed of light. I look around me for a way out, but I'm trapped in a corner, there's nowhere to go, nowhere to run.

My heart races. They know.

They creep in closer, the one on the right pulling out a pair of handcuffs as the students around us stop and stare while getting their phones out. With each step they take, it becomes clearer that my life is over. They have me; they know I killed him. There's no backing away. I'll be spending the next fifty years behind bars.

"Are you Winter, the foster child of Kurt and Irene Williams?" the burly one on the right asks, purposefully putting himself right in front of me, making it impossible to run.

My hands shake with fear. "Yes, that's me," I say, my nervousness creeping up and making me sick.

He nods as the other moves in closer. "Where were you between the hours of 8 and 11 p.m. last night?"

I shake my head. "I ...I—"

Principal Turner cuts me off before I can say another word. "You're a minor, Winter," he points out, always advocating for his students, even the ones who don't deserve it. "You don't need to say a word."

I meet his eyes, silently begging him to help me, tell me what I'm supposed to do, but before anything can be done or explained, my wrists are grabbed and I'm pressed up against the wall as handcuffs are fastened around my wrists. "You are under arrest for the murder of Kurt Williams," the burly cop says as the other pulls me off the wall. "You have the right to remain silent. Anything you say can and will be used against you in a court of law. You have the right to speak to an attorney, and to have an attorney present during any questioning. Do you understand?"

I nod, frantically searching as the cops start pulling me away. They lead me down to the main entrance where I see their patrol car waiting to take me away.

The students follow us, keeping their phones on me as I make my walk of shame, the whispers already circling.

We reach the patrol car and just as the cop opens the back door and places his hand on my head, I hear Carver's booming voice cut through the school. "Don't say a fucking word, Winter," he yells, making all eyes turn his way.

I meet his stare and see the panic heavy in his eyes but it's nothing compared to what he must see reflected in mine. "What do I do? You have to help me," I beg of him, my voice quiet but knowing that he can hear me perfectly well.

Carver nods as I notice the others storming out behind him, each of them just as worried, even Grayson. "We will," he promises me. "Just whatever you do, don't say a fucking word."

And just like that, I'm pushed down into the patrol car and the door is slammed in my face, cutting me off from the rest of the world and instantly claiming what little future I might have had.

26

I stare up at the ceiling of my cell, my mind taking me back to the cold, concrete dungeon that Sam had me stashed in, the memories haunting me like a bad dream. I have to get out of here.

How are they allowed to hold me like this? I'm a minor.

It's been well over twenty-four hours. Hell, I've lost count. It's got to be well into the afternoon now, and so far, I haven't had a single lawyer walk through my door and tell me what the fuck is going on. That's not right.

I know my rights. Well, actually, I have no idea what my proper legal rights are, but after watching far too many episodes of *'Criminal Minds,'* I know that I should have been visited by a lawyer and been released by now—unless they're ready to officially charge me with murder. But what evidence do they have? I was careful. I didn't leave any fingerprints behind, but what does it matter if I had? I was their foster child; my fingerprints are supposed to be scattered all over the house.

I've had three interviews, one that went for four hours where I was denied any food or water, and also didn't have a legal counsel at my side. I didn't say a word, just as Carver said, but even if I had, it would all have to be dismissed because of my age. At least, that's what my daytime cop shows tell me. When it comes down to it, I really haven't got a clue.

I'm in deep shit here. I need to get out, and it needs to happen soon. Granted this cell isn't anywhere near as bad as Sam's dungeon; it's still horrific. When it all went dark last night, my monsters came out to play in the worst kind of way. I've never needed Carver more. Hell, I would have been happy if he could have just sat in this stupid cell with me, but I have a feeling that this is only the beginning. I'm royally fucked; I'm going to be living with these monsters for the rest of my life.

Noise echoes through the building and I let out a sigh. This isn't exactly the first time my deranged white knights have shown up in some half-assed attempt to get me out of here. I don't know why they keep bothering. It's not like I'm ever going to get out.

The noise gets louder, more persistent, and their voices become clearer. There must be at least four solid walls between my bullshit cell and the foyer area of the precinct, but there's no mistaking Carver's furious growl or King's terrifying demands that make it more than clear that they're done waiting.

I don't know what makes me do it, but some kind of force has me getting to my feet and moving across my cell. I stand just beside the door, curling my hands around the metal bars and trying to determine exactly what's being said. All I know is that something is different.

Maybe it's the determination or no-bullshit tone that comes flying out of King's voice as he demands my release, or maybe it's the way that every word spoken is done with an authority that has even me flinching. Who are these guys, and where the fuck do they get off having that much confidence? Don't get me wrong, I certainly appreciate how they like to run their show, but damn. I've never experienced anything like it before.

King finishes with his little rant, and despite how badly I want to race out there and see their faces, they're just high school students up against the law. They're going to be sent on their way, and that knowledge has the disappointment pulsing heavily through my chest.

The main door to this bullshit holding cell opens, and I raise a brow as I stare back at the burly cop who had picked me up at school. He strides toward me with a pissed-off scowl, every step meant to be intimidating. But if a guy like this approached me on the street without a badge, I'd have him fucked up in two seconds. He doesn't intimidate me, and judging by the way he watches me, he knows it.

He finally reaches my cell, and I watch as he slides a key into the lock and twists until the door finally opens. He reaches in and grabs my wrists, violently spinning me until my back is to him with my wrists open for the taking. He fastens a set of handcuffs around them, far too tight to be legal, and without warning, I'm tugged out of the cell and out through the door into the main part of the precinct.

The cop leads me through the corridors, pushing through doors with an angry grunt before finally coming out into the foyer, where I find all four of the guys staring back at me. A hint of relief travels over Cruz's face, but as for the rest of them, they just look pissed.

I'm kept away for processing, but I don't miss the way that Cruz inches toward me, ready to grab me and run, but I don't get it. Am I being let go? Did the guys finally get through to these cops? No, that's not possible. I did the crime, and the cops are more than aware of it, at least they think they are. I don't know what evidence they think they have to tie me to it, but apparently, they have something; otherwise, I wouldn't be here.

A female cop steps in behind me and releases my wrists before my fingerprints are taken for what must be the third time. I'm made to sign some paperwork, and then finally, she steps out of my personal space and indicates toward the exit. "You're free to go," she tells me. "But we are watching you, girl. Don't be fooled, we know you did it, and we will be taking you in."

I don't say a word, just silently walk toward the guys. Cruz falls into my side while King steps into my other, twisting his hand around my elbow and pulling me faster toward the door. Grayson and Carver step in behind us and I can't help but feel that the way they crowd around me is like some kind of weird protective formation. It's not normal, not natural.

The second we break out into the fresh air, I all but crumble, sucking in a deep breath of air. "Holy fuck," I sigh, the relief pouring over me like a violent wave.

"Keep moving," Grayson demands from behind me, not giving me even a second to enjoy my freedom as King keeps pulling on my arm.

We walk across the road, and before I know it, King is shoving me through the back door of Carver's Escalade and coming in behind me. All four boys climb into the car, the doors slamming behind them. In an instant, Carver is careening down the road without a word.

Cruz's thigh presses up against mine as King's hand remains wrapped around my arm, but the pressure is gone now, and I can't help but feel that he's leaving it there just to feel my skin on his. The car ride remains silent, and as I look around at the four guys, I realize that not one of them is about to crack.

My frustration gets the best of me and I tear my arm away from King. "Were any of you planning on telling me what the fuck just happened?" I question. "How the hell did you get me out of there?"

All eyes bounce around the car, the four of them trying to figure out who will be the one to break, but when I'm met with more silence, I push harder. "I swear to god, now is not the time for your bullshit. You have two fucking seconds to tell me what the hell just happened, or I will personally make it my mission to make your lives hell."

"Aren't you already?" Grayson grunts from the front seat.

My hand whips out toward him as I feel Carver's eyes on me through his rearview mirror, but I refuse to look up. Cruz's hand snaps out and catches my wrist before I can grab hold of Grayson's head and pull it right off his damn shoulders. "NOW," I demand, more than done with their bullshit.

It's been secret after secret, and every step of the way, I'm being hand-fed just a little bit of information to keep me quiet, but not anymore.

Cruz lets out a sigh, and I can tell that he's going to be the first to break, but when King speaks up, I'm shocked to my core. "It was Dynasty," he explains, making a deep groan come from Carver in the front seat, who clearly doesn't approve of King's admission. "After seeing that the cops were holding you for longer than what's legal, they stepped in and handled it."

"What do you mean they *handled* it? How the fuck could they have anything to do with this?"

Carver slams his hand down over the steering wheel and I glance up to meet his stare in the rearview mirror. "Can't you just say thank you for saving your ass *again* and be done with it?"

"Get fucked," I growl at him. "I don't know what the hell has crawled up your ass today, but this is my life, and if some distorted prestigious group is messing around with it, then I deserve to know exactly what the fuck is going on. Stop being such an asshole and put yourself in my shoes for a change. How would you feel constantly being left out in the dark and not being able to do a damn thing about it? I know I don't know you all that well, but something tells me that you wouldn't be able to handle it at all. You'd be more than a little bitch about it."

Carver's only response is to tighten his jaw as his knuckles turn white around the steering wheel. Not giving me a fight, I turn back to King. "Explain," I say, giving him my best no-bullshit tone.

I watch him for a second as his head falls back against the headrest, and he lets out a sigh, clearly trying to figure out the best way to explain whatever crap is about to come out of his mouth.

"They were trying to hit you as an adult," he explains. "Even though your papers technically don't say your birthday is for another month, but with no official birth certificate, they thought they'd get away with it on a technicality, claiming that you could have already been eighteen."

"That's bullshit. Are you fucking kidding me?"

He doesn't respond, just continues on with his explanation. "They were desperate. They held you for the twenty-four hours that they're legally allowed to keep an adult, but not having sufficient evidence, they exercised their rights to keep you for another twelve, but Dynasty wasn't having it. They wanted you out, and so you got out."

I scoff, glancing around the car to see if anyone else thinks his comment is as ridiculous as I do. "They just wanted me out, huh? It's that easy? Just send your henchmen to go and get the damsel and call it a day. Fuck off. Who do you take me for? I'm not a fucking idiot. They had me on murder charges. Murder charges. They knew I did it. There's no way in hell they just let me walk. I was supposed to be going away for a very long time. It was an open and close case."

Cruz sighs beside me, scooting down on the seat to get comfortable. "They have to let you go when Kurt Williams ceases to exist. You can't murder a man who was never here."

My brows pinch as I turn to look at Cruz. "What?" He just nods, letting his comment sink in as I feel the other guys turning to look at me. "Cease to exist? How the fuck? What does that even mean?"

Cruz meets my stare. "The body they found. Gone. The filed paperwork. Erased. The crime scene photos. Deleted. All that's left are their memories with not a damn thing to back them up. Dynasty completely erased Kurt Williams out of existence, and when someone doesn't exist, how could you have possibly murdered them?"

I slice my gaze up to meet Carver's as he flies through the streets, desperate to get home. "You … Dynasty did that? They have that kind of power?"

He nods, and I feel an intense pressure pushing down on my chest. I lean back against my seat as Cruz places his hand over my knee, trying to be supportive and letting me know that he understands just how fucked up this all must sound. "There's nothing that Dynasty can't do," he murmurs, letting the point truly sink in, letting me know exactly what kind of people I'm dealing with. "They've erased the whole thing. Kurt William's never existed and you never hurt a fly. They made it so that you had no lawyer to come in and create a paper trail, the footage of your stay has already been deleted from files, the footage of your arrest at school doesn't exist, and the paperwork that only just got filled out will also go missing. Dynasty is untouchable. There's nothing they can't do. If they want something, they get it. It's just the way it is."

I stare out the front windshield, desperately trying to make sense of it all, but what I keep coming back to is why Dynasty is so interested in me? First, they paid for my release out of Sam's sex trafficking ring, and now, they got me off murder charges. It doesn't make sense. Why me? I'm just some poor foster kid from … who the hell knows where I'm actually from. I'm a nobody. They should be going after people who could better their cause, make them stronger, not trash like me who gets into more trouble than a horny teenage guy letting loose on a room full of willing chicks.

The five of us are silent until the engine is cut and the garage door securely comes down around us. We all get out of the Escalade and I follow King who opens the door and ushers me in only I come to a startling stop as I find a familiar canvas bag sitting in the foyer of Carver's big-ass house, one that is supposed to be on the floor of Ember's spare bedroom. "What the fuck is this?" I demand, staring at my belongings, which should be nowhere near this place.

Carver walks in through the garage behind King, not bothering to stop as he continues deeper into his house. "Your ass lives here now," he tells me, calling over his shoulder and not even bothering to wait around for an explanation.

"Excuse me?" I grunt, reaching down for my bag. "Are you fucking insane? There's no way in hell I'm about to live under your roof."

"Why not?" Cruz asks, stepping in beside me as King takes one look at the fury on my face and disappears.

"Why not?" I scoff, repeating him with as much sarcasm as I can possibly muster up. "Have you met the guy? He's an A-class asshole."

"Come on, babe," Cruz says, taking the bag out of my hands and heading straight for the steps. "He's really not that bad. You've just caught him at a … bad time. Besides, what's the big deal? It's not like you haven't been sleeping here every night anyway, in his bed for that matter."

"Yeah, but—wait," I say, pausing as I follow him up the stairs and meet his stare. "You know about that?"

He nods and starts walking again. "I'm not a fucking idiot, babe. I know you have nightmares and for some reason, Carver keeps them away. Am I wicked jealous that I can't do that for you? Fuck yeah, but I'm not about to lose sleep over it."

"I—" I cut myself off, not really sure what to say about it all because when it comes down to it, I really have no idea what the hell has been going on between us all. But what I'm getting here is that Cruz really doesn't care whose bed I'm sleeping in as long as he's still reaping the rewards of having me around, and damn it, I think I like that about him. King didn't seem to have an issue with it either, not that I've really talked much about it to him. Carver though—he's different.

I follow Cruz to my bedroom and he stops in front of the door, turning to look back at me as his hand rests against the door knob. "Just stay," he tells me. "Trust me, you're better off here where you have us to look over you, and besides, news of your arrest has been going all around town and I honestly doubt Ember's parents are going to let their daughter crash with a felon."

Cruz opens my bedroom door and dumps my bag just inside before taking off and leaving me in the hallway staring after him. "I'm not technically a felon. I wasn't convicted of anything. Besides, the guy I killed apparently doesn't even exist."

Cruz just laughs as he makes his way back to the stairs. "You did the crime," he tells me, looking back over his shoulder with a sexy as hell smirk that makes me want to tear his clothes right off his body and let him have me right there on the stairs. "Now you've got to do the time."

27

Ice clinks around the bottom of my empty glass as I sit at the lonely dining table. How the hell did I get roped into this? I've gone from living in a shitty foster home, to killing a man, to now living in a fucking mansion with four brooding assholes. This isn't right.

I throw the glass back, letting the lone piece of ice slide down and drop into my mouth before crunching my teeth over it and feeling it melt slowly. I should pack up my things and slip out during the night. I don't know who this Dynasty is, but my gut is telling me to get away, but where? Where can I go that they won't find me? Dynasty can make people invisible, make them cease to exist. I'm sure if they can do that, they can find a runaway.

Screw it. Is living with the guys really that bad? I have Carver saving me from my own subconscious, Cruz giving me all sorts of feels, and King satisfying every wild need within me. It could be worse, so why the fuck am I complaining? Maybe this is an opportunity that I need to take with both hands and never let go.

Getting bored of sitting at this big ass table by myself, I follow the delicious sounds of fists pummeling against flesh down to the home gym. My mind instantly takes me back to a few nights ago, slamming my fists into Carver as he let me work out my frustration on his rock-hard body.

Assuming it's him in the gym, I walk through the open door and come to a stop when I find King attempting to beat the ever-loving shit out of Grayson. Only Grayson is holding his own, and gives it right back to King. I stare in wonder, my lady bits clenching with desire.

Both of their bodies glisten with a sheer layer of sweat and my mouth instantly waters. They're fucking gorgeous. King's fist flies forward with sharp, precise movements, and I watch as Grayson easily blocks it, only to deliver one of his own.

Grayson lands a devastating blow that would have any man down on their knees, but King takes it and fires right back at him, bringing his arm around in a beautiful uppercut that nails Grayson right below his ribs.

Groans and grunts pull from each of them as I become mesmerized, watching it as though I was watching the most intense kind of porn. I wonder how they'd feel if I just took off my pants, perched myself on the ground in front of them, and finger fucked myself until I screamed. I mean, I'm sure they'd happily allow it, even encourage it, but it'd probably mess up their moves, and from my own experience, when someone fucks up one of my fights, I don't get pissed, I get even.

I lean against the open door and the movement catches Grayson's attention, distracting him for a brief moment and allowing King the chance to get through and nail him right in the chest. The blow sends Grayson flying back until he's crashing down onto the sparring mat with a heavy thud. "Fuck," he grunts, holding his hand up to King to indicate that he's done.

King instantly stops and reaches down a hand, helping him up, and the second he can, Grayson shoots a devastating glare my way. I cringe, pushing off the wall. "Sorry, I uh … I didn't mean to distract you."

"Save it," Grayson grumbles, shaking off the blow and striding toward me. "I'm done here."

Whoops.

He walks straight out, narrowly passing me and avoiding slamming me right against the door. I stare after him for a second, watching his fine body as he all but races from the gym. I wonder what I did to piss him off so much—apart from the whole distracting him and causing him to get nailed in the chest thing.

After a short beat, I turn my guilty cringe toward King. "He really doesn't like me, does he?"

King walks across the gym and grabs a small white towel to wipe over his face before dropping it and looking back at me. "It's not that," he tells me, switching the towel for a bottle of water. "If he didn't like you, you wouldn't be here. He just … he doesn't like change, and you, Winter, are a massive fucking change."

"How so?"

"It's been just us four since we were kids. No chicks have ever come in here and had us all in a bind, desperately trying to keep her stupid ass in check."

"Well her stupid ass never asked for it," I point out.

"Trust me," he says with a scoff, throwing his water bottle back down to the ground. "We're more than aware of what you did and didn't ask for."

"Oh, yeah?" I ask, walking deeper into the massive home gym as my eyes rake up and down his impressive body, wondering just how quickly I can get him to fuck me on this sparring mat. "And what exactly do you think I asked for?"

King reaches out, slipping his arm around my waist and yanking me into him until my chest slams against his, and the air is knocked right out of my body. His lips drop to my neck, and he kisses it, his tongue roaming over my skin and making my pussy clench with need. "You may not have asked for it," he murmurs, his breath brushing over my skin and sending goosebumps rising all over it as his knee pushes between my legs and grinds against my aching pussy. "But I sure as fuck know what you want."

I pull back so I can meet his hooded stare, raising my chin so that my mouth hovers just in front of his, and without warning, I bite his bottom lip, pulling at it before gently letting go. "So, what are you waiting for? Give me what I want."

Fire burns in his eyes, and without another word, his hands come to my ass and lift me off the ground. His lips fuse to mine as he walks across the gym and puts me down on a table, keeping us eye to eye.

He tears my cropped tank over my head and drops to the ground as my hands roam over his defined body, taking pleasure in the way his wide chest seems to go on forever. King reaches for the front of my pants, making quick work of the buttons before curling his arm around my waist and lifting me as he tears them down over my ass and past my thighs.

I fall back to the table as my black, ripped jeans are left discarded beside my tank. My bra is forgotten, but neither of us seems to care as all the attention is on the way he tears the flimsy material of my thong and grips my knees.

He spreads them wide, putting me on display as his eyes glisten with a raw heated excitement. He looks down between my legs at my aching pussy, and I watch as the fire burns so much brighter. King licks his lips and everything clenches in anticipation.

If he doesn't fuck me soon …

King drops to his knees in front of the table, and my eyes roll back into my head, knowing this is going to be good. He grabs my legs, hooking my knees over his shoulders and curling his hands around my ass. I'm scooted forward on the table until I'm nearly falling off. My pussy is right in front of him and his warm breath brushes over me, teasing me with what's to come.

I go to lie back on the table when King's hand shoots up, stopping me from moving. "No," he demands. "You're going to watch."

Holy fuck. Yes, sir.

I don't say anything, but I don't need to, my response is loud and clear, and without hesitation, I watch as his thick, warm tongue pushes between my folds and slowly trails up my throbbing cunt, tasting everything I have on offer.

My body burns with desire, and I watch with bated breath as he does it again and again, his eyes focused heavily on mine. King's mouth closes over my clit and I groan as his tongue flicks over the tight bud, tormenting me until I'm moaning his name.

He doesn't let up, and just when I start to need more, two thick fingers push up into me, stretching me as they curl and find my G-spot, making me suck in a sharp, loud gasp. "Fuck, yes. There," I cry, unable to tear my gaze away from the mesmerizing sight.

His tongue doesn't dare stop working my clit as his fingers become drenched in my wetness. My fingers tangle into his dark hair, curling into a tight fist and holding him there as I moan out his name.

King stands and with my knees over his shoulders, my back is slammed down against the wooden table, but even with the movement, he still doesn't ease up on my throbbing clit, his tongue circling, flicking, rubbing.

He pushes down on my thighs, spreading them wider and I groan, feeling the way he draws his thick fingers out of me and spreads my wetness around. His fingers drop to my ass and I suck in a breath as he slowly pushes against my hole, already knowing just how much I like it. "I want to fuck this sweet ass," he grumbles against my clit.

I try to push back into him, taking his fingers deeper but with his hold on my body, moving is near impossible. "Not before I get to taste my come on your tongue."

His eyes flick up to mine and he takes it like a challenge. Not one to miss out on a sweet reward, he gets right back to work, teasing my hole as he fucks me with his tongue. He sucks my clit into his mouth, and as I feel that burn growing deep inside of me, I know it won't be long. "YES, KING," I cry. "Make me come."

King pushes me deeper, moves his tongue faster, sucks, licks, and torments harder, and just when his fingers push deeper inside of me, I come hard, shattering around his tongue as my pussy violently convulses. He doesn't ease up until my body finally stops shaking, and just as I wanted, he releases his hold on my legs and reaches for me. "You have the sweetest pussy I've ever tasted," he murmurs before bringing his lips down over mine.

King's tongue pushes inside of my mouth and I instantly taste myself, groaning with pleasure. He's right, just as Cruz was the other day. I am sweet.

I curl my legs around King, holding him to me as he grinds his cock against my pussy. "You held up your end of the bargain," I whisper as he pulls back, dropping his lips to my neck.

He raises his head and I watch as his brow arches. "Yeah?" he questions, his hand roaming down my thigh and squeezing my ass. "Have you ever done it before?"

I nod. "Once."

A grin splits across his face. "I'll be gentle."

"Really now?" I tease. "And here I was thinking that you weren't capable of being gentle."

King laughs as he pulls back off me. His hands fall to my waist and he lifts me off the table, keeping me in his arms. I curl my legs around him as he walks back across the gym to the sparring mats. As he stops, I uncurl my legs and drop back to my feet. "Where do you want me?"

He spins me around until my back is glued to his wide chest. "Hands and knees," he grumbles, his voice thick with desire as his breath tickles my neck. I bite down on my lip, the anticipation almost too much to bear.

I drop to my knees in front of him and slowly lean forward onto my hands, but it's not enough. I want to give him everything, I want him to see me as the sexiest woman he's ever laid his eyes on. Looking back over my shoulder, I drop to my elbows and then lower myself to my chest, my ass high in the air with my legs wide, offering him absolutely everything I've got.

King groans, and I watch as his loose training pants are pushed down, freeing his large, thick cock.

My mouth waters.

King drops down behind me, one hand on his dick, the other slowly trailing over my back, teasing me with what's to come. "Are you sure about this?" he murmurs, his deep voice drenching my pussy all over again.

I wave my ass in the air, letting him know just how down I am as the anticipation builds inside of me. "Try and stop me."

A cocky smirk crosses his handsome face and I groan as his fingers trail down over my hole and between my legs. He circles my clit and I suck in a breath before he mixes his fingers in my wetness and begins to spread it around.

I can't help but watch as his hand roams up and down his firm cock, only getting myself more excited as he prepares my body. Then finally, he adjusts himself between my legs and I groan as the tip of his cock teases my opening, his precum mixing with my wetness.

"Fuck," I whisper, feeling a slight pressure as he begins to push into me, the pressure slowly turning into a welcomed, thrilling burn.

"You okay?" he asks, his voice deep with pleasure.

"More."

His hands fall to my ass, squeezing each cheek as he pushes deeper inside. "Holy fuck," I moan, slipping my hand between my legs and gently massaging my clit, needing just a second to get used to his size.

I take a few slow breaths before nodding. "Okay," I tell him, letting him know it's okay to start moving.

He doesn't hesitate, slowly drawing back and making a deep groan pull from both of us. I press my ass back, the burn starting to ease as my pussy clenches with desire. King starts to fuck me, taking his time, keeping it slow, and allowing me to really get used to it before starting to pick up his pace. "Oh, fuck," I pant, squishing my face into the mat as his fingers dig down into my ass cheeks, his grunts only spurring me on.

"Yo, King. What's up Gray's ass?" Cruz's familiar voice says, walking into the gym and making King pause deep inside of me. I suck in a gasp, my head whipping to the door as Cruz's head lifts, his eyes widening with shock, clearly not having expected to walk in here to find us fucking on the floor, in my ass for that matter. "Oh, fuck."

Everything clenches and King grunts behind me as I squeeze down around his cock. I can't help but laugh, but when hurt crosses Cruz's face and he hastily starts to back out of the room, I can't help myself from calling out. "Hey Cruz," I murmur in a breathy tone, a devilish grin spreading across my face. "Stay."

Cruz pauses in the doorway, his brows shooting up in interest as he lets his eyes roam over my body with his best friend's cock buried deep inside of me. "Uhh—"

I raise up onto my elbows and look back at King, licking my lips with excitement as I slowly start to move and wait patiently for his reaction.

Heat flares in his eyes as he looks out across the gym and meets Cruz's stare. His hands clench down on my hips, slowly moving back and forth, unable to help himself. Though I know had this interruption not come right now, he'd be fucking me hard, slamming deep inside of me and cursing my name as he came.

A wicked grin stretches across King's face as he lifts his chin and that one small movement has fire burning deep inside of me as he silently invites Cruz to join us.

"Are you sure?" Cruz asks, that same wickedness and excitement reflected in his own eyes as he looks back at me

And just as I said to King, I bite down on my lip and watch how his cock hardens within his sweatpants. "Try and stop me."

A smile kicks up the side of Cruz's mouth and he nudges the door closed behind him before flicking the lock. His eyes become dark and heated, and as he crosses to the sparring mats, King picks up his pace once again.

I groan as I watch Cruz strip out of his clothes, showing me that big, thick cock again. He walks right over to me and drops down to his knees, instantly curling my long hair around his wrist. I meet the raw excitement in his eyes with my own before putting on a show of licking my lips and slowly lowering them to his cock.

I take him deep in my mouth, swirling over his tip with my tongue and tasting that sweet drop of pre-cum. King groans, no doubt watching the show as he fucks my ass, his fingers curling around my body until they find my clit, giving me exactly what I need.

I push back against him as I take Cruz deeper, loving the sound of his deep groan.

King's hand smacks down over my ass, and I instinctively clench around him, making him groan before I feel my orgasm building. He starts working my clit harder and faster and I push back further while moving my lips up and down Cruz's cock, keeping up with King's relentless rhythm.

"Fuck," King grunts, close to the edge as Cruz moans my name.

King spanks my ass again and pulls out as he comes over my back, but a second later, Cruz releases himself from my mouth and grabs me, adjusting us until I'm straddled over his hips. He tears my bra off and as he slams up into my aching, desperate pussy, he watches as my tits bounce.

I groan his name as he fucks me harder, bringing us both to the edge.

My orgasm tears through me, and I come hard, clenching around him, spasming and holding onto his shoulders as hot spurts of cum shoot up into me, all while King watches the pleasure written across my face.

As my body comes down from its high, I remain seated over Cruz, him holding me as we catch our breath. "Fuck," he grunts, looking up and meeting my eyes. "I can't say I was expecting that when I came down here."

I can't help but laugh. "Me neither."

Cruz stands, keeping hold of me, and walks through to the gym's private bathroom. Before I know it, the three of us are in a warm shower, the boys soaping me up and cleaning me off. They get me heated all over again, but before I do anything, I need to know exactly what the fuck this is.

"So," I look up at the two guys who have done nothing but catch my attention over and over again since the very beginning. "Can I be straight with you both?"

King nods as Cruz leans back against the shower tiles, his stare on my body as he grumbles out a raw, "Yeah."

A wave of nervousness comes over me and I look up at them, fearing what they're going to think of what I'm about to say, but knowing that if I don't go for it now, I may never find the nerve to ask for what I really want. "So ... ummm. I think it's obvious that I like you both," I tell them, watching their faces very closely, trying to decipher their thoughts. "You're both so different and offer me different things.

I'm not interested in going behind anyone's back and I'm definitely not interested in stopping whatever … whatever this is with either of you. So, I'm offering you up a deal."

"A deal?" King asks, raising his gaze to Cruz's with suspicion before coming back to mine and narrowing with curiosity.

I suck in a nervous breath, my fingers twitching at my side as my stomach swirls with butterflies. "Yes, a deal," I tell him, momentarily finding it hard to meet either of their stares.

"Go on …" Cruz mumbles, his voice low as he leans back and watches me closely, probably just as curious as King. Either that or they're both anxious about what kind of ridiculous bullshit is about to come flying out of my mouth.

"Okay, so I want to be straight with you both," I start, raising my chin and going for it. "I think it's pretty damn clear that I've been messing around with you both and I don't want to stop being with either of you. You're both …" I roll my eyes, hating to have to admit it out loud, "Well you're both kinda awesome."

"Just figuring this out now?" Cruz smirks.

I can't help but laugh, his comment helping to ease the burning nerves deep inside of me. "Shut up," I groan, swatting at his strong chest. "If I don't get this out now, I don't think I'll ever find the nerve."

"Nerve?" King questions. "Why do you need nerve? How fucking bad is it?"

"Oh, it's bad," I say with a cringe. "Especially if you guys aren't on board, then all I've done is make myself sound like a desperate, cheap whore."

Cruz's fingers tighten on my waist as a smile kicks up the side of his mouth. "But I like it when you're being a desperate whore."

I let out an irritated huff and King instantly gets me back on track. "Hit us with it," he says. "You're a fucking queen, Winter. After what you just let me do to your tight ass, there's nothing you could do or say that would make me think less of you."

My cheeks flame with the memory and I realize that if I can offer myself up to them like that, then there's no good reason why I should be nervous about this. "Okay," I say, meeting their curious stares. "So, here's the thing; I'm not down to be someone's girlfriend and something tells me that neither of you are looking for that anyway."

King shakes his head, agreeing with my assumptions as Cruz's lips pull into a tight line, making me question if that's really what he wants.

I watch their faces closely and continue. "I don't want to hurt anyone or put any sort of strain on your friendship. So, please, only agree to this if you think it could work, but if you're not down, I'll back off, and you'll never hear about it again."

King straightens, his eyes narrowing further by the second. "Spit it out, Winter. What's your deal?" he says, his tone suggesting that if I don't get on with it, he'll happily force it out.

I swallow back the lump that threatens to rise in my throat, the nerves instantly pulsing through my body again. "I was toying with the idea of …" Fuck me. "Sharing?"

"Sharing?" Cruz questions, his eyes narrowing in confusion as he glances at his friend for a long moment. His gaze slowly scans back to mine, his face completely blank, making it nearly impossible to get a read on him. "What exactly does sharing mean?"

"Well, I … uhh … I don't exactly know," I admit, the dread heavily sinking into my stomach. "I can't say that I've ever done this before, but I mean … how would you feel about the idea of me being with both of you?"

"How do you mean?" Cruz asks. "One night you're with me and the next you're in his bed?"

I meet his stare, nervously biting down on my bottom lip. "I mean … is that going to be a problem?" I ask. "We'll be free to fuck whenever we're down, but no jealousy or hating on each other, otherwise it won't work."

Cruz lets out a breath, looking out over my shoulder at King, both of them deep in thought despite the easy, supportive smile that pulls at the corners of his mouth. "I feel so used."

My eyes widen and I suck in a gasp as I press into him. "I'm sorry, I didn't mean to make you feel like that, I just—"

"Chill out, babe," he laughs, taking my waist and pulling me in as King steps in behind me. "I'm fucking with you. I think I like the idea. I see the way you look at us, Carver too," he tells me. "I'm not going to lie, I'd love to have you all to myself, but I can't deny just how intriguing this whole sharing thing sounds. If we all make you happy in some sort of way, then who the fuck am I to say no?"

I beam up at him, feeling the nervousness fading away. "Are you sure? You're really down?"

Cruz nods. "It'll be an adjustment," he laughs. "I've never really liked sharing my toys, but I'm not about to cock block King."

King grinds his cock against my ass, making the point clear as day. "And you?" I ask, letting my hope rise, as I look back over my shoulder and meet his heated stare.

"I'm down," he grumbles, surprising me. "But only if you can guarantee that this won't come between any of us. If things start heading south, I'm out. I'm not looking to fuck up my friendship with Cruz."

"I get it," I tell him, curling my arm up and around his neck as his hands slide up my body and cup my tits. "The last thing I want is to come between you guys."

"Then I'm down," he says. "We share."

Holy fuck. Is this actually happening?

"If feelings start to change," I say, looking up at Cruz. "I'll tell you guys straight away, but you need to do the same with me. It won't work if we're not honest with each other."

Cruz nods. "Promise," he grumbles, as I feel King's nod against my neck.

"Another thing though," I say, pausing for a beat and feeling both of their hands freeze on my body, their curiosity getting the better of them. "I know I'm asking you to share, but is it too much for me to ask that while I'm with you guys, that you're not with anyone else? Call me greedy, but I want you both to myself."

Cruz laughs as King murmurs against my neck. "I have a feeling that you'll be more than enough for the both of us."

"I freaking hope so."

A grin splits across my face as I catch Cruz's curious stare, and I furrow my brows, waiting to hear what's on his mind. "Speaking of feelings," he murmurs, his voice low and filled with lust as his hand slips between my legs and slowly massages my clit. I can't help but arch back, pressing against King. "How does Carver fit into all of this?"

I shake my head as I shrug my shoulders. "I honestly don't know," I tell them, wanting to be perfectly clear with them. King's hands pause on my body, making it clear that he's just as curious about my response as Cruz is. "I'm not going to lie, there is something between us, just as there is with the two of you, but apart from one weirdly twisted moment, nothing has happened, and I'm kinda doubting that it will. Though, if he wanted in on this thing we've got going here, I don't think I want to say no."

The boys meet each other's stare above my head before nodding and bringing their attention back to me. "You're not secretly fucking around with Grayson too, are you?" Cruz laughs.

I shake my head, unable to control the thrill that pulses through me at the idea of all four of them at once. I don't even know how or where I'd put things, but I don't think I'd say no to that either. The four of them ... fuck me. That'd be an interesting night. I can't even begin to imagine the way that Grayson would fuck, but something tells me that he knows *exactly* what he's doing.

"So, we have a deal then?" Cruz questions as I slip my hand down between us and take his rock-hard cock in my hands. "We're sharing you? No jealousy, no arguments, just the perks of a relationship but without the bullshit?"

"Sounds fucking perfect to me," I tell them.

King's lips come down on my neck and a soft moan slips from between my lips. "We have a deal," he says, and just like that, Cruz finds my lips and we seal the deal the best way we know how.

28

My fingers drum against my knee as I sit in my dark bedroom, telling myself over and over again that I don't need Carver to sleep. The last thing I want to do is invite myself into his room with my tail between my legs and seek out his help.

No, I can do this. It's simple, just close my eyes and let sleep claim me. Besides, after the afternoon I just spent with Cruz and King, sleep should be able to come effortlessly. I'm sure with this little arrangement we have, they'd be more than happy for me to sleep in their beds, but then, doing that would mean admitting that I have a problem, and while the guys already know, I don't think I'm down for explaining it.

Carver just gets it.

Trying to find the balls of steel that I must have dropped along the way, I scoot down in my bed and take a few calming deep breaths. It's been a while since I've had a good night's sleep, and with the way things are going, I'll be needing every minute of sleep that I can get my hands on.

Maybe it's a dark thing. Perhaps I should consider becoming nocturnal, that way I'll never have to fear the monsters coming out at night.

My eyes flutter closed, and I stare up at the backs of my eyelids, feeling like a complete idiot, but as the memories of hands on my body begin assaulting my mind, my eyes fly back open. I'm not an idiot; I'm a pathetic loser who can't seem to put the past behind her.

I always thought I was stronger than this. I've trolled streets and allowed random men to touch me just to get close enough to kick their asses. So, why does this bother me so much? Probably because they didn't have my consent. I wasn't open to being touched, and I sure as hell wasn't the one in control.

Fuck me. I need therapy.

Getting frustrated with myself, I fly back out of bed and make my way downstairs. Perhaps I'll watch a movie or three and fall asleep out of pure exhaustion in front of Carver's ridiculously big theater screen. At least the couches are comfortable.

I trudge down the stairs, cringing with every step as I feel the welcome ache reminding me exactly where the boys had been this afternoon. I stop by the kitchen for a glass of water and am halfway through plonking a few ice cubes in when the glass is ripped right out of my hand and slammed down on the kitchen counter, the final ice cube dropping straight to the ground. "Where the fuck do you think you're going?"

I stare back at Carver, taking in the fury pulsing out of his eyes and hoping he slips on the stupid ice cube. "The fuck is wrong with you? I'm not going anywhere," I snap back at him, my eyes dropping to notice he's wearing nothing but a pair of sweatpants that show me everything he's got working for him.

He scoffs, his eyes raking up and down my body. "I'm not falling for your bullshit. You're not sneaking out of here again, and I'm not spending another night running all over fucking town trying to save your ass from getting beat. It ain't happening."

"Screw you," I say, reaching past him for my glass of water and briefly considering throwing it all over him. "Look at me, I'm in my fucking pajamas. Besides, I don't owe you an explanation, especially considering that you're too much of an asshole to even ask nicely, but if you must know, I came down here to watch a movie."

Carver watches me closely, and a few seconds pass before understanding dawns in his eyes. He steps in closer, putting his hand at my waist as though he has any right to touch me. "You couldn't sleep." I look away, not able to meet his eye and confess again that I can't be without him. "Why didn't you come to my room? You could have slept with me. You know I don't care that you're there."

I shake my head, slowly bringing my gaze back to his. "And sleep in the arms of a man who can't be real with me? No thanks."

"What the fuck is that supposed to mean?" he demands, his hand falling from my waist.

"You know exactly what it means. There's so much left that I need to know about Dynasty, and you're the one keeping it from me. Cruz and King … they don't give a shit if I know, I can see it in their eyes. Grayson probably wants me to know just so I'll fuck off and shut up about it, but you. You're the one pulling the strings. You're the one not letting me in, and for that, I can't trust you."

Anger burns in his eyes. "After everything I've done for you, you still can't trust me?"

"Not if you're intentionally keeping something from me. I don't come from a world where I have the luxury to trust. If you want my trust, then you need to earn it, and hope to whoever the hell you believe in that you don't fuck it up once it's there."

Carver watches me for a minute, his eyes not leaving mine for a second, and when the tension grows too high, I turn and start walking away, only he catches my wrist, forcing me to look back and see the conflict shining in his eyes. "Fine," he finally says. "I'll tell you as much as I can without pushing it, but it's not going to leave you feeling all warm and fuzzy. It's going to leave you empty, and with even more questions, most of which I won't answer."

He gives me a second to think about what he's offering me, and knowing this isn't going to be easy sends me spiraling into the same confusion I've felt since I first came here. So, I do what any other person in my position would do and give a sharp nod. "Okay."

Carver watches me a second longer before finally letting out a breath and indicating with a nod of his head to follow. "Come," he says, his tone filled with authority. He starts walking away, and I quickly follow him, keeping close behind him as he slowly walks through the house.

For a brief moment, I wonder if he's taking me to some secret room that holds all the answers. Maybe I'm going to get a full rundown of everything Dynasty, complete with a slideshow presentation. But when he reaches the front foyer and curls his fingers around the handle, I pause. Where the fuck is he taking me?

"Are you coming?" Carver asks, looking back at me when I don't walk through the door.

"Where are we going?"

He doesn't respond, just simply walks out the door, leaving it wide open and making it clear as day that I can either go with him now and find out what I've been dying to know, or I can run back up to my room where I can sleep with my monsters in the dark.

I hurry out the door.

I catch up to him on the stairs and ignore the smug expression that crosses his handsome face when the cool night breeze hits my skin. Instantly I regret racing out of my room in nothing but a loose crop, a pair of cotton booty shorts, and bare feet.

We get to the bottom of the stairs and I fold my arms over my chest, trying to keep warm. I glance at Carver, assuming that he's about to give me some kind of instructions, or at least a hint of what the hell is going on, but after meeting his hard stare, he just keeps walking.

I let out a sigh and follow him in silence, the tension growing between us with each step, or maybe it's just because with each step I take, my feet only seem to freeze just a little bit more.

We reach the top of his driveway and I watch closely as he enters the code 0225, instantly committing it to memory. The gate slowly slides open, and as I stand on the spot waiting for the fucker, my feet seem to scream against the cold driveway. When I look at Carver, I realize that he's also barefoot and probably suffering just as much as I am.

We finally get through the gate and I follow his lead as he turns to the right and starts walking down the long path. I glance back over my shoulder, having expected to turn the other way toward the main road, but I keep quiet and let him lead, hoping that he's not about to lead me into a trap and regret my decision to give him a chance.

The further we walk, the louder the silence gets, and as the tension grows, I find myself forgetting about the cold and thinking about that number—0225. Is it just a number, or is there some kind of significance? Maybe a date? The 25th of February. I wonder if that's his birthday, maybe his parents' anniversary or something like that. Either way, the number is now etched into my brain like a cheesy song from the nineties.

My mind wanders with endless possibilities. By the time we reach the massive house at the end of the road, I'm convinced that 0225 is the date that Carver lost his virginity. Possibly to a thirty-three-year-old sugar baby who was looking for a good screw before going home to pretend her sixty-year-old husband can satisfy her in bed.

"What are we doing here?" I ask as Carver enters the code for the massive gates out front, again entering the same numbers—0225—and really messing with my head. I could have sworn the code that Cruz entered into the gate last week was different. Maybe they've changed it, or perhaps all the boys have separate codes to identify who's entering. That makes more sense.

The gate slides back and Carver makes a ridiculous little gesture, offering for me to go in first. If it were coming from Cruz or King, I'd laugh and skip past them as though I was royalty. But coming from Carver, it seems like a challenge, almost like an insult. So, I keep my head high and walk through to the impressive property at the end of the street.

We make our way to the front door, and just as Cruz had done when we first came here, Carver enters the code for the door and welcomes himself in.

I follow in behind him, instantly letting out a relieved sigh as the warmth of the house immediately begins seeping back into my body. "Okay," I ask Carver as he walks deeper into the grand foyer. "Why the hell do you all have codes for this house when it's obviously not yours, and why the hell do you guys keep making me break in here?"

"Because all of this," Carver says, looking around the massive foyer with a strange fondness, "is yours."

29

What the actual fuck? I knew Carver was fucking insane. I turn on my heel and start walking straight back out the door. If he can't be real with me, then what's the point of even trying? I'm sick of his bullshit. How hard is it to be honest for once?

Carver groans in frustration behind me. "That's right," he calls at my back as I make my way to the massive steps. "Just walk away. Don't bother hearing me out, but remember, you asked for this. I told you that you were going to be left with more questions, so stop being such a scared little bitch and come and hear what you're too afraid to learn."

I stop and spin around, marching straight back to him. "Afraid?" I screech, slamming my fingers against his chest. "I'm not fucking afraid, and I'm sure as hell not some scared little bitch. I asked you to be real with me, give it to me straight, and your opening line is 'this is all yours.' Yeah right! How stupid do you think I am? I'm a nobody, and I'm done letting you try and bullshit your way through things. So, I'm leaving. I'm going to bed and forgetting that I even bothered to give you a chance in the first place."

Carver grabs my hand from his chest and twists it away, but refuses to let go. "First of all, good fucking luck going to bed and making it through the night without me, and second of all, how the hell would you know if I was lying? Do you know who your family was? Do you know where you come from? Because the way I hear it is that you don't even know your real fucking name, but guess what? I do. I've known since the day you were born."

My eyes widen as I tear my hand out of his grip and stare at him in horror. "You're lying."

"Why the fuck would I lie? What do I have to gain by lying to you?"

I shake my head, more than ready to call it quits with this one. I have no idea why he would lie; I just know that he is. How could he possibly be telling the truth? If I don't know who the real me is, then how the hell would anyone else?

Carver lets out a sigh and steps into me, his hand falling to its favorite place on my waist. "Look, I'm sorry. I didn't exactly mean to just blurt it out like that, but just give me a second and I can explain it all. I swear, you might not like it, but you'll understand when I'm done."

"I—"

He cuts me off, seeing the refusal on my lips. "What have you got to lose? Either come with me upstairs and I can show you everything, or walk away and live your life always wondering if what I have to say was worth it or not. What's it going to be? Are you taking a leap and finding the answers that you've always been looking for, or are you done?"

I look up and meet his haunted stare, and just as always, I see something staring back at me, something that tells me that if I don't go with him now, I'm always going to regret it. So, without allowing myself another second to change my mind, I place my hand over his and give it a gentle squeeze. "Okay," I whisper. "Tell me what you think you know."

Carver flips his hand over and weaves his fingers through mine before turning and leading me through the house—which is apparently mine. He walks over to the massive grand staircase and starts leading me up, and with each step I take, I feel more and more like an imposter. It's one thing being inside this house thinking that you're just borrowing it for the day, but having someone tell you that you actually belong there—fuck. That's different. I feel like a fraud, an imposter. Even if he somehow manages to prove that this is all mine, I'd still never feel like I belong.

We reach the top of the stairs and Carver doesn't once release his hold on my hand, and as much as I want to scratch his eyeballs out right now, I can't help but feel comforted by his touch. I follow him down the hallway, glancing around the darkened home and trying to imagine myself here. The first time I'd walked through here, it was some kind of magic. I felt a connection to this home, but with everything weighing down on me, that connection is gone.

Carver stops by a wall that holds a massive floor to ceiling artwork, and I stare at him as though he's lost his mind. "Really?" I grumble. "You want to drop bombs on me and then take a moment to appreciate art?"

Carver just rolls his eyes before stepping into the frame of the massive artwork and gently pressing his fingers to it. A soft beep echoes through the quiet hallway, and I watch in awe as the massive artwork sinks back into the wall before sliding out like a secret door.

"Whaaaaaat," I drawl out, staring in wonder as Carver steps through to the secret room, looking back at me with a cocky smirk. "I didn't think this shit actually happened in real life. Is this real?"

"As real as the one in my place."

"Wait—what? You have a secret room?" I say, stopping halfway to gape at him. I haven't seen anything in his place, but it's not as though I've gone around touching all the walls and searching the bookshelves for a secret opening.

Carver just grins, more than proud of himself. "Just come in. I want to show you this stuff and explain what's really going on."

I nod and walk into the room, following Carver as he leads me over to a shelf. He looks through the books carefully before pulling out one with a leather binding. Silently he scans the cover, then hands it to me. "Here," he says. "Most of the information you're looking for is in this."

My brows furrow and I back up a few steps before dropping into a small armchair and peeling open the book. There's a soft creaking, telling me that this book hasn't been opened in years, but when I look down at the very first page, a soft gasp comes sailing out of my mouth, and everything around me fades to black as I focus on the small family looking back at me.

A man stands proudly with his baby girl in his arms and his wife at his side, beaming up at him with pride. As my eyes travel over her face, I see my own reflection in her features.

No. It couldn't be ...

My head snaps up to Carver and I meet his eyes, tears beginning to fill my own. "Is this my family? My parents?"

He nods. "Yes, they are."

"I ... how do you know this?"

He lets out a sigh and comes to sit on the armrest of the chair, looking over my shoulder at the happy family in the book. "Because your parents were one of the seventeen families that made Dynasty."

My hands pause on the old photograph, my fingers gently brushing over my mother's sweet face as I suck in a breath, fearing what I just heard and what it could possibly mean. "No, they couldn't have been. I ... "

Carver's hand falls to my shoulder as his other reaches down to flip the page to where I find six loose pieces of paper—three birth certificates, a marriage certificate, and two death certificates. I instantly grab them, scanning over the papers. The first is the birth certificate of the man—Andrew Ravenwood.

I suck in a breath as I read over it. "Ravenwood?" I ask, briefly glancing up at Carver. "As in the town name? Ravenwood Heights?"

"The one and only," he confirms with a small nod.

My gaze drops back and I find the marriage certificate, seeing both my parents' names—Andrew Ravenwood and London Moustaff, who married in late September nearly thirty years ago. Andrew and London Ravenwood. My parents.

I can't help but flip back to the first page, now looking at the people staring back at me with names to put to the faces, and as I look at them, a memory pulls at me, but I can't quite figure it out until I look back at the marriage certificate and my gaze drops down, taking in the rest.

I see the names of Andrew's parents—Gerald and Sylvia Ravenwood and then drop further to London's—Janet and Joseph Moustaff.

I suck in a gasp. They were the couple I sat between during the cemetery party after raiding all the rich kids' pockets. The wife had drowned and the husband died shortly after from a lonely heart. I guess twenty or so years later, their daughter and her husband joined them.

I flip to the next piece of paper and scan over it. It's another birth certificate—Elodie Ravenwood, born the same year as me on February 25th.

Elodie.

I slam the papers down. "No," I say, shaking my head as I fly up off the armchair and put the book down as far from me as possible. "No, that's not me. I'm not this Elodie girl, I'm not some fancy rich kid with a mansion and a town named after her parents or grandparents or ... I don't know. This isn't me."

"It is, Winter," Carver says. "You can see your family resemblance just as well as I can. Your parents didn't die in a fire, and your birth certificate clearly didn't get destroyed. They were murdered by members of Dynasty who wanted them out. Your mother, London, died with you cradled in her arms, and you were supposed to die right along with her, but somehow you fought through and survived the impossible."

I just stare at him, not really taking in a word he's saying, or maybe I am and I'm just in too much shock to really hear him. "So, if these people really are my parents, and this is all real, your precious Dynasty were the ones who killed them?"

Carver shakes his head. "No, it's a little more complicated than that."

"Then explain," I snap, being sick of not understanding.

Carver lets out a breath, trying to work out how to best explain something that probably doesn't make sense in the first place. "Like I said," he starts, "your parents were one of the seventeen families that made up Dynasty, just as your father's father was before him and just like my parents and all the boys'. We're all in it, even you. Around the time of your parents' murder, the families were all in disagreement. There was a lot of fighting and nothing was getting done. It was practically good against bad, and eventually, the bad won, resulting in your parents' murder—but that's off the record. A good portion of

Dynasty believes it was an accidental fire that killed them, while the other half ... they know damn well what happened."

I fall back into the armchair feeling an information overload and trying to keep up with everything. "So, these bad families who are a part of Dynasty killed my parents, and then what? I just get shipped off to live in the foster system and forgotten about?"

Carver lets out a sigh and I realize that I'm right on the money. "Dynasty has kept track of you this whole time, followed you from home to home, and we're even responsible for when you had to leave those homes, but most of the time you managed that all on your own. The boys and I have grown up hearing all about you, knowing that once you turned eighteen, they'd bring you back to take your rightful place."

I meet his stare. "Dynasty was responsible for bringing me back here? For putting me with Kurt and Irene?"

Carver's gaze falls to his hands and he slowly nods. "Look," he says slowly. "Dynasty is old money. They're a bunch of old families with too much power and not enough morals. You're the only living survivor of the Ravenwood family and that's all that matters to them, just the name. They don't care who you are as a person or what you stand for, just that you have Ravenwood blood pumping through your veins. That's why they paid five million dollars to keep you out of that sex trafficking ring, not because they care, but purely because they need you alive. Don't be mistaken, Winter, they don't care about you, though they're sure as hell going to pretend."

Not wanting to hear more, I pick up the book and look over the papers once again, coming back to my birth certificate, the one thing I thought I never had but was sitting in this big house all along.

I scan over what must be my real birth date again—February 25th. 0225.

A scoff pulls from deep within me. "Are you kidding?" I ask, ignoring the fact that it's already March, meaning I missed my eighteenth birthday last month. "The code for all these big-ass gates is my birthday."

Carver nods again and I let out a huff. If I have to see his guilty little nod again, I'm going to knock his head right off his shoulders. "Yeah, it was supposed to act as some kind of reminder of when you were being brought back to us. We've been looking forward to your eighteenth birthday for a very long time."

"Wait," I say, looking up and meeting his eyes. "The 25th of February. The day I supposedly turned eighteen; that's the day I first arrived at Kurt and Irene's place."

Carver nods his freaking head again with a stupid smile on his face as though he's proud that I'm starting to put the pieces together.

I fall silent as I flip back to my only family photograph. "So, this really is my house?" I ask, remembering how no one had stopped me from barging in here and how Cruz, the prick, had told me to make myself at home.

"Yeah," he whispers. "You don't have to stay at my place if you don't want to. You'll be just as safe here as you are with me, but I figured because all your parents' things are here ... nothing has changed since the day they died. We've just looked after it for when you came home."

I meet his eyes and nod, not really sure what I want to do. It's a lot to take in and a big house to properly explore. I have a family, at least I had one, but now that I know who they were, I'd like to get some idea of what kind of people they used to be, how they lived their lives, and what made them tick. Were they nice, or horrible people? Were they pushovers, or were they strong like me? More importantly, I want to figure out which of the sixteen remaining families were responsible for taking them away from me, and I want to make them pay.

After scanning over the papers, I get up and start making my way around the secret room, trying to get a grasp on everything I've just been told. I hate how it all makes so much sense. Carver isn't lying at all, but now I so desperately wish he was. No wonder he's been holding back the truth.

As I scan through the shelf and look at all the other books, I see the word Dynasty coming up everywhere, and I pause, looking back at Carver, who watches me closely. "So, this ridiculous group just thinks that they get to claim me, and they expect me to take a seat at some metaphorical table because of the blood that runs through my veins?"

Carver stands and walks toward me and I feel my heart beginning to race. "That's exactly what's going to happen. There's no way around it," he tells me. "And for what it's worth, the metaphorical table isn't metaphorical. It's as real as it gets and it's fucking huge."

Ignoring his comments about the ridiculous table, I let out an irritated sigh. "Why?" I beg, desperately wishing I could get as far away from these people as possible.

"Because your grandfather, Gerald Ravenwood, wasn't just one of the seventeen families, he was the founder of Dynasty, our leader," he tells me. "He built it from the ground up with the vision of greatness, power, and integrity. Dynasty isn't just some legacy passed down through your blood, it's who you are. It's our birthright, and for you, it's your duty. Your grandfather passed his leadership down to his son, just as your father passed it to you. You are the rightful leader of Dynasty, the ruler, the one we've been waiting on for the past eighteen years."

I shake my head. "What if I don't want it?"

"It's not a case of accepting or rejecting. You don't get a choice," he tells me, taking my waist and pulling me close, looking deep in my eyes. "Winter," he says with that authoritative tone that has everything inside of me crumbling. *"You. Are. Dynasty."*

30

The memory of my dead parents surrounds me as I look around the massive living room, probably the space where they spent most of their time. I've been sitting in this same spot since Carver walked out last night and I can't seem to wrap my head around it.

I'm not Winter with no last name whose parents were killed in a fire.

I'm Elodie Ravenwood, daughter of Andrew and London Ravenwood, who were so viciously murdered by the men and women of the prestigious secret society that my grandfather so proudly founded. Murdered by men and women who were disguised as friends. And look at me now.

I wonder if they're watching down over me? I wonder what they think of me? Surely they couldn't be proud of who I am. People like that would have turned their noses up to poor nobodies like me.

Just great. I finally found my parents and already have their disapproval.

I get up from the couch and make my way into the kitchen, shaking my head when I remembered that the last time I came through here, it was fully stocked. The boys must have had it prepared and ready to go the second I hit my eighteenth birthday. Those assholes. The 25th of February was nearly a month ago. I should have been let in on the secret the second I got here. I could have avoided the whole Sam thing, and I sure as hell would have avoided killing a man.

After making something for lunch and hardly eating a bite of it, I find myself upstairs in the master bedroom, sitting on the floor of the massive walk-in closet that's bigger than my bedroom back at Kurt and Irene's shithole. This closet is one of the only places in the whole house that can truly give me a glimpse of the type of people my parents were.

All their clothing is still here, eighteen years later, and I find myself taking it all in—the expensive designer gowns, the impeccable suits, the shoes, Rolexes, the jewelry. It's incredible, it's like nothing I've ever seen before. They must have lived an amazingly glamorous life, one that they didn't get to stick around to share with me. Though one thing is for sure, judging by the clothes they used to wear, I'd dare say that we probably would have clashed heads a few times, and

I can guarantee that they wouldn't have approved of my ...stylistic choices.

Glancing out the door of the closet, I spy their bedroom and the overwhelming emotions begin to creep up on me. This is where they used to rest their heads at night, where they would have shared private conversation, where I … eww, no. I don't want to think about that.

I drag myself up off the floor, and as I make my way out of the master bedroom, I hear the soft thud of the front door closing. I pause, my heart beginning to race. Who the fuck would that be? Realizing that it's most likely one of the four morons from down the street, my wild heart begins to ease and I listen out as I cautiously make my way back to the grand staircase.

"Yo, Winter?" Cruz hollers through the house with a flirtatious invitation drumming through his tone. "Where is that sweet ass of yours?"

A grin stretches across my face, remembering the afternoon we shared with King and the agreement we made to allow this thing to work.

"Upstairs," I call back, listening to his soft footsteps as he makes his way through the house.

I reach the stairs and instantly make my way down them, stopping halfway when I find Cruz approaching, taking in all the handsomeness of his fine body. He really is a work of art, all four of them are. "Can I help you?" I ask, slowly picking up my pace again and walking down the stairs at a snail's pace.

Cruz raises an intrigued brow, watching my every step. "You can hurry up and get your ass down here so I can make sure you're alright."

"Alright?" I question. "Why the hell wouldn't I be alright?"

Cruz's stare tightens and a flicker of worry appears in his eyes before it's instantly dismissed. "Carver told us about your night, and you know ..." he says, indicating around the massive foyer. "I'm sure it was a lot to take in."

"Understatement of the year," I grumble, reaching the bottom step and walking right into his arms. His hands fall to my waist as he looks down and meets my eyes. "You should have told me the second I got here. No—" I cut myself off. "You should have told me years ago instead of letting me get swept up in the foster system. I've always felt lost, never knowing who I was. You guys could have done something about that."

"Believe me, I know," he tells me, his thumbs moving back and forth over my skin. "I'm not thrilled about the whole situation either. I wanted to tell you, but it wasn't my place, it wasn't even Carver's to share this with you last night, and I don't doubt that he's going to get his ass handed to him for coming clean."

My lips pull into a tight line. "What is this? Are you hoping that I get down on my hands and knees and kiss Carver's feet for stretching the rules for me? Get stuffed. I'm not going to worship him for telling me something that you all should have been honest about from the very start. Sure, I'm grateful that I finally know, but I'm kinda pissed."

"I know, babe, and no. No one expects you to go and kiss his ass for telling you. You're completely right. Dynasty never should have put you in the foster system. You should have been here all along, right here with me. You're one of us."

I let out a heavy sigh and drop my ass to the bottom step. "It's just … I don't know. It's a lot to take in. Twelve hours ago, I was the poor orphan girl with a shitty life, and all of a sudden, I have this whole world that I never knew existed, and I finally belong somewhere. I've never belonged anywhere."

Cruz drops down beside me and instantly pulls me into his lap. "You've always belonged here," he murmurs, his hand curling around my neck as his eyes bore into mine. "You just never knew it."

He pulls me in until my forehead is resting against his. A beat passes before he raises his chin and softly brushes his lips over mine. "You never did tell me if you were alright."

"I think I was avoiding the question."

Cruz just nods, reading me like a book and sensing that I'm not ready to talk it through "What do you need from me?" he murmurs, his gaze boring into mine, filled with an intensity that I can't quite handle.

"I just need you to help me forget."

"Consider it done."

And just like that, his lips press firmer against mine, swallowing any further conversation and wiping every last thought from my mind. All that exists in this world is him and the way he touches my body.

Cruz's hands roam over my back, sinking down to my ass and squeezing it tight as I grind down on his lap. He pushes my hair over my shoulder, freeing my neck for his lips to travel down and claim it for himself.

I feel his cock hardening beneath me, and I groan as he grinds it up against my pussy, my head tipping back as my eyes close with overwhelming pleasure.

Cruz reads me and slips his fingers under the soft material of my cropped tank, effortlessly raising it up over my head to find my naked chest below. His lips travel down my shoulder, past my collar bone, and over the curve of my breast until my nipple is sucked into his mouth. His left hand firmly cups my other breast as his right slips into the waistband of my cotton pajama shorts, going further until his hand is resting against my bare ass. He squeezes it and I all but scream as the need becomes too much.

Needing to feel his warm skin against mine, I tear his shirt over his head and throw it behind me, not giving a shit where it lands. My hands wrap around him and my nails instantly dig into the tight, strong muscles beneath his skin.

Cruz grabs my chin and forces my lips back to his as my hips rock back and forth over his hard length. A rumble sounds through his chest and it speaks right to the savage part of my soul, tempting, teasing, tormenting.

I have to have him.

Scooting back on his lap, I grab the front of his sweatpants and free his heavy cock from the confines of his boxers, groaning as my fingers barely wrap around him. This is going to be good, and fuck me, I hope it's going to be fast.

My fist roams up and down, feeling the thick, angry veins under my fingers as my thumb circles over his tip, spreading the warm bead of moisture that appears beneath my thumb. "Fuck, Winter. I need to feel that tight pussy around my cock."

I lean into him and press my lips to his neck, teasing him just as he does to me. I drop my voice to a breathy whisper, tormenting him as I push forward and grind my clit against his cock, wishing desperately that there wasn't a pair of cotton booty shorts between us. "How bad do you want me?"

"Bad enough to take your control and throw your ass down," he says, his hand on my ass, lowering and curling under me until he finds my dripping core and pushes two thick fingers deep inside of me. I push back into him, taking all I can get. "I'm not above begging," he growls, the sound coming from deep within his chest. "Let me bend you over and fuck you the way you need."

Holy shit.

I shake my head, propping my feet on the step and pushing up until I'm standing over him. My eyes burn into his hooded ones and I gently sway my hips as he looks up at me. "You wait your turn."

His responsive growl speaks right to my aching pussy, and as he hooks his fingers into my shorts and begins drawing them down my legs, I watch the hunger grow in his eyes.

I step out of my shorts, but before I can lower myself down over his cock and ride him until I scream, his hand curls around my thigh, his touch so soft yet somehow filled with all the strength in the world. He moves my foot up a few steps until my legs are spread with his face right at my weeping pussy.

I grin down at him. This boy is just like me. When an opportunity presents itself, he grabs it with both hands, and being the stubborn bastard that he is, refuses to let go.

Cruz's hands curl around me, grabbing my hips and bringing me closer until his mouth closes down over my clit. My eyes roll back into my head as my fingers knot into his hair, keeping me from falling. His tongue flicks over my clit, applying pressure before taking it away and building me up until I can't take it anymore.

Desperation courses through me, and I scream out as he dips his head lower and fucks me with his tongue, bringing his hand up and teasing my clit, exactly the way I like. "FUCK, CRUZ," I cry, my fingers tightening in his hair. "I'm going to come."

Cruz shifts his tongue back to my clit, and with a brutal force, slams his fingers deep inside my aching cunt. I scream and he does it again as my pussy clenches down around his fingers, but he doesn't stop. He's relentless, his tongue a force to be reckoned with, and as his fingers work over that one spot deep inside of me, I come hard, my orgasm ripping through me like an explosion.

"HELL YES," I hiss, clenching my eyes as Cruz laps up every bit of my excitement.

His fingers move within me, not stopping until my body finishes convulsing, and the second I can, I drop down over him, guiding his hard cock into my dripping pussy.

"Holy fuck," I murmur, catching my breath as I slowly rock my hips back and forth over his cock. "You guys have to stop surprising me like that. I don't think I can handle it."

Cruz grins and presses his lips to mine, his skilled tongue dipping inside my mouth and driving me wild with need. "I've been dreaming about making you come on my tongue ever since you sucked my cock and swallowed every last drop."

His words speak right to me and have my pussy clenching, ready to go again, and he doesn't miss a thing. "Do you like that?" he questions, curling his arm around my waist and lifting me off him until I'm on my knees beside him. "You like it when I talk like that?"

I bite down on my lip and groan as I nod, not capable of finding the words to describe just how hot it makes me. Cruz gets up and positions himself right behind me, on a lower step, until his cock is level with my ass.

I lean forward, offering myself up like a Thanksgiving turkey and as he pulls my hips back, he pushes deep inside of me, instantly hitting the spot. Cruz growls and my pussy clenches around him, needing so much more. I push back against the step and as he slams into me again, I take him so much deeper.

His pace picks up, and just when I think I can't take it anymore, Cruz pushes my knees wider apart and hits me at a new angle.

Sweat begins to coat our bodies as he fucks me hard, giving me exactly what I need. "Rub that clit, baby. I want to see you touch yourself."

Not one to disappoint, my hand slips between my legs and I

furiously work my clit as he slams into me. My body is on edge, quickly building like a raging fire. I won't last much longer.

Cruz's fingers dig into my hips and I push back even further, listening to his growl of appreciation, and just as he grunts a loud "OH, FUCK," and I feel his hot seed spurting deep inside of me, I come around him, clenching down on his hard cock and collapsing down onto the stairs.

Cruz comes down with me, pulling me back onto his lap to avoid squishing me into the hard stairs as I desperately try to catch my breath. "Holy shit, Cruz," I pant, dropping my hand onto his chest and spreading my fingers to claim as much skin as possible. I feel the rapid beat of his heart beneath my hand and feel myself pressing harder into him, somehow not feeling nearly close enough.

His hand rests against my lower back, his other on my thigh. "That was …"

"Yeah," I laugh, unable to stop the satisfied grin from stretching across my face.

He meets my eyes, his face all kinds of soft and sweet and I watch as something changes in his gaze, something a little more serious than I was ready for. "Listen, I wanted to talk to you," he murmurs, his hand on my thigh gently rubbing up and down. "You know, about us."

My eyes narrow. "I thought we talked about us yesterday?"

"We did," he says. "But that was with King, and now that I've got you all alone, I want to talk … just us."

"Oh yeah?" I question, pressing into him and gently brushing my lips over his. "Why do I feel like I'm about to get in trouble?"

A smirk settles across his lips. "You're not, but I can treat you like a bad girl if that's what you want."

I lick my lips, more than onboard with the idea. "Oh, yeah?"

"Mmhmm," he grumbles. "But let me get this out first." My brows furrow and I pull back just a bit to see his face better, watching as a strange nervousness flickers through his eyes. "I want you to know that I'm in," he finally tells me. "I like you, Winter, and I know you've got a lot going on and that you're not really sure about what you want, but I'm here and I'm fucking sure. I don't care how many of my friends I have to share you with, just one little piece of you is enough."

I stare at him a moment. "I ... are you sure?" I question, wondering what the hell is so special about me to deserve such a declaration.

"I'm sure," he tells me. "A girl like you is rare, and I'm not the only one who sees it. Carver and Gray both see it, but are too fucking stubborn to admit it. King, that lucky bastard, he was smart enough to see it before anyone. I just wish that maybe I'd seen it first and then I could have had you all to myself."

I can't help but laugh as I slide my arm around his neck and pull him in. "Don't you think sharing is a little exciting? Just imagine all the things we get to do."

A grin stretches across his face. "Oh, I know," he says. "Don't get me wrong here. I know that despite how weird and fucked-up this little deal is, that we're all in for an exciting ride. I just wanted to let you know that I'm not going to force you to choose, but if King does, I'm going to kick his ass and take you for myself."

I laugh and lean into him, kissing him again. "Good," I murmur. "And for the record. I kinda can't get enough of you too."

31

My tongue rolls over my black-painted lips as a smug grin stretches across my face. I don't know how the fuck I got myself into this situation, but damn it, I think I like it.

The second Cruz piped up with that gorgeous little face of his and suggested a party, I was all in. Though those four giant assholes forgot to mention that the party was the grand eighteenth that I'd missed out on last month, and the idea of telling me that the party was themed just happened to slip their minds.

Fucking twat-monsters. I should have known when they failed to mention it all week that it was going to bite me in the ass. How the hell was I supposed to know that I was about to be the host of a BDSM themed birthday party?

Fuck me. Tonight is going to be all sorts of interesting.

My gaze sweeps over my black latex bodysuit that cuts in under my tits and pushes them up, making them look at least three sizes bigger than what they are. There are leather straps and buckles all over my body, and I have to admit, the whole BDSM thing is starting to intrigue me. I get why they do it now. These outfits are fucking hot. The only downfall is that it just took me nearly an hour to get into it. Though, I don't think I could ever get down with ball gags and shit like that. There's nothing better than being able to scream out your man's name and let him know just how much you're loving what he's putting down.

I make my way across my room and drop down on the edge of my bed before groaning as I lean forward to pull on my thigh-high black stiletto boots. They go perfectly with my outfit, but actually reaching my legs to pull my boots up, is so much harder than I ever expected it to be. I'm glad I decided to get ready early. Otherwise, I would have had King and Cruz up here trying to get me into the damn thing. Though hopefully when it comes down to taking it off, I'll have one of them by my side, or hopefully both.

I get to my feet, grinning at my reflection and how my boots perfectly complete my outfit. I look like one of those badass assassin bitches on the cover of a killer urban fantasy book, but nothing compares to when I grab the whip off my dresser and slip it through one of the straps by my hip. I mean, if I'm going to go to this party, then I'm going to do it right. What sexy BDSM chick wouldn't come fully equipped with accessories? I just hope I don't feel the urge to pee halfway through this party. Otherwise, I'm fucked.

My hair is up in its signature high pony and my lips are jet black, add the mascara, eye shadow, and liner, and I think I'm just about ready.

"Winter?" I hear hollered through the big house. "Are you fucking ready yet or what?"

I groan, rolling my eyes at Carver's insistent hollering. It's been going on for the past ten minutes. If the boys weren't down there with him, I'm sure he'd already be up here, dragging me down by one of my straps. "It's my party and I'll be fucking late if I want."

I hear his irritated grunt as Cruz tries to coax him to relax, and just for being an ass, I pick up my black lipstick and go for another unnecessary touch-up. Once I've thoroughly irritated Carver, I grab the kitty-cat ears off my dresser and slip them over my head. You know, just to tone down the level of skanky-whore that's exuding out of me.

Deciding that I'm finally ready, I grab my phone, keys, and cigarettes before realizing that I have absolutely nowhere to put them.

I groan and throw them back down. I guess tonight I'm without my vices. I make my way out of my room, my stiletto boots clicking against the marble floors and letting the boys know that I'm on my way, but the thought of my vices has my hand instinctively curling into a fist, only to remember that my brass knuckles are still not there.

Hitting the top stair, I put it to the back of my mind and focus on not falling to my death. How is it that I can usually kick ass in these shoes, but tonight, I feel like a kid trying on her first pair of heels?

What the hell is wrong with me?

I grip the railing and as I start making my way down the stairs, I hear a soft gasp and glance up to find the four boys standing in the foyer, watching me make my way down like a scene out of a fairy-princess movie, only instead of glitter and a gown, I have whips and latex.

All four of them gape, and hell, even Grayson momentarily looks impressed, but as I rake my eyes over their bodies, I have to stop walking and grip the railing tighter as a roaring laugh is torn out of me.

The boys have gone all out for the party, their outfits spot on. They all wear different variations of fetish harnesses with chains and black leather. Carver, King, and Grayson are all shirtless with long black pants, looking like a scene out of a dream I never knew I had. King looks smug, proud of his outfit, while Carver just looks pissed. Though what's new?

My stare lingers on Grayson a few extra moments. He acts as casually as though he's wearing nothing but a pair of jeans and an old shirt, but I can't seem to tear my gaze away from his strong torso as I find it covered in tatts. How the fuck did I not know that? He's simply stunning. I'm going to have to make an excuse to get close to him tonight just so I can take a better look.

Not wanting to get caught staring, I turn my gaze to the fourth member of the Winter patrol and struggle to hold back my comments. My sweet, sweet Cruz has upped his game and stands before me in a pair of latex knickers with his monster of a dick on full display, his grin somehow even bigger. He does a slow circle and I get the full view of the back, only there's no material back there and I get an eyeful of his perfectly toned ass cheeks. Absolutely no shame, but what's a life to live if you're getting around too embarrassed to make a dick of yourself? The best times are had when you decided that you no longer give a fuck about what other people think.

I finish making my way down the stairs, and as I hit the bottom, King steps into me. "Wrists," he demands, a dark sparkle hitting his eye and making me wish it wasn't so hard to get out of this costume.

I wonder just how late we are to this party. Maybe Carver wouldn't mind waiting a few more minutes for King and Cruz to fuck the blinding need out of me first. Yeah … doubt it. Though maybe in these costumes, he might be down to watch. Who knows? Maybe even Grayson too.

I raise my brow and hold up my wrists then watch as King straps a pair of leather cuffs around each of them. "Holy … fuck me in the ass," I grumble under my breath, this whole night already more than I can handle.

"Already done that," King says with a cocky smirk. "Give me a new challenge."

I roll my eyes and raise my chin, meeting his cocky stare with one of my own. "As if you would deny me if I asked you to do it again."

King winks and the grin that stretches across his face tells me to prepare for whatever bullshit response is about to come flying out of his mouth. "Maybe," he teases, his eyes sparkling like Christmas morning. "But only if you begged."

Carver groans. "What is this? Some twisted version of a corsage?

Let's get the fuck out of here already."

I narrow my gaze at Carver and flip him off before walking straight through the guys and heading for my front door, ignoring the hint of jealousy that flashes in his eyes. I moved into this place the second I could. There was no way I was going to spend my nights under Carver's roof, though that doesn't mean that he hasn't been secretly sneaking through my door every night and slipping into my bed just so I can sleep. It truly is a weird little relationship we have going on. I guess it's a weird relationship that I have with all the guys—except for Grayson, of course. His glares and snide remarks seem to be the only normal thing around here.

We break out through the door and King puts in the code to lock the big fucker up as Cruz slides into my side and offers me his hand to help me down the stairs. I take it gingerly and give him a warm smile, and before I know it, we're at the bottom staring at Carver's Escalade. "Seriously? We're driving? Isn't this party only like four houses down the road?"

Grayson grumbles something under his breath and walks around to the front passenger's seat as Carver grunts back at me. "The party's not at my place."

My brows furrow as Cruz opens the back door for me and ushers me in. "Then where the hell is it?" I ask, trying to slide across the backseat. But in all this latex, it's not an easy task.

"King's family owns a cabin in the woods just on the outskirts of town," Cruz explains as he climbs in behind me. "We didn't want to risk having everyone come out here."

"Risk?" I question, meeting his stare. "Why would a party here be a risk? What could possibly happen? Someone forgets it's a costume party and not a real BDSM lounge and ends up fucking on the dining table?"

Cruz averts his eyes and laughs at my comment. "First off, if anyone is fucking on the dining table, it's us," he laughs. "I just meant that we don't usually like letting people into our homes. Most of the time they've heard whispers about Dynasty and are just there to dig into our business or are trying to get fucked."

I scoff. I briefly touched on the exclusivity chat with Cruz or King, but I can guarantee only one hoe is getting fucked tonight, and bitch, it's me. Though I guess Carver and Grayson are fair game.

King finally gets in and Carver hits the accelerator with a fierceness that sends me slamming back into my seat, and I watch as a proud smirk cuts across his stupidly handsome face. "Asshole."

My comment only seems to make him smile wider and I curse myself for letting him win. I just don't get it. How can our relationship be so fucked up? He's my saving grace, but also the thorn in my side. I hate him, but for some reason can't survive without him. Screw him—no, screw me. I should be stronger than that, but a part of me doesn't want to be.

For a nice change, I sit in silence and watch out the front windshield as Carver drives through the town, and it's only a short fifteen-minute drive until we're turning down a long dirt road. Carver turns on his high-beam headlights and we drive for a good ten minutes, deep into the woods until we pull up at a large, luxury cabin that has students from school spilling out of it.

I stare for a moment, unable to believe the sight. It's stunning here, the perfect secluded area to commit every crime under the sun. I love it. The fact the everyone is getting around looking like sex slaves is just an added bonus.

"Time to partaaaayyyyyy," Cruz cheers, swinging his door wide and jumping out before turning and offering me his hand. I take it willingly and jump out behind him, letting him drag me away, knowing that without a doubt, tonight is going to be a great night. Despite not wanting to make a big deal about my birthday with a bunch of strangers, I've been needing a night to let go and unwind after the shitty few weeks I've had in this place.

As Cruz drags me away, I look back over my shoulder and find the three others staring at me as I go but it's King who really catches my eyes, with his panty-melting wink that promises if I'm a good girl, he might just treat me like a bad one tonight. And damn it, I'll hold him accountable for that.

Cruz leads me inside the cabin and quickly shows me around, but the second we find the guy the boys hired to work the bar, the remainder of the tour is forgotten and replaced by a competition of who can down the most shots in the space of ten seconds. Spoiler alert; I kicked his ass.

He tells the guy that I'm the birthday girl and to give me whatever the fuck I want all night. We finish with a fruity cocktail that Cruz pretends to like for my sake before dragging me onto the dancefloor. I find Ember already there in a black leather bikini, a thin chain harness draped over her, and her boyfriend's tongue halfway down her throat.

Cruz keeps going to say hey to a few friends, and with my buzz well and truly hitting me, I barge Ember's boyfriend out of the way so I can party with my girl. She goes to nail me for touching what's hers when she realizes that it's just me, and a second later, her mouth drops as her gaze sweeps down my body. "What the ever-loving fuck? Holy shit! Have you seen yourself? Fuck me. That's it," she says, glancing at her boyfriend. "We're done. I'm into pussy now."

Jacob rolls his eyes and moves in behind her, curling his arm around her waist and grinding into her ass, and I swear, I know I haven't known her for very long, but I've never seen her happier. He leans into her and murmurs something into her ear that has her cheeks flushing bright red, but with the music pumping so loud, I can't even begin to hear what he's saying.

Jacob glances up at me with a curious stare in his eye, but before I have a chance to ask him what's up, Cruz curls his arms around my waist and grinds into me. My head instantly tips back and his lips crush down on mine before I remember where the fuck we are.

Cruz kisses me deeply, dominantly and forceful, almost as though he's claiming me for the world to see, and I don't care one fucking bit. He can have me as long as I can have his friends. When he pulls away, he meets my eyes with a heated stare, and I wonder again how my night is going to end.

He winks and just like that, he sinks back into the crowded bodies and I turn back to face Ember only to find her mouth hanging wide open. "Umm …. WHAT THE FUCK WAS THAT?" she demands, making me realize that over the past week, I've failed to mention that I've been screwing two of the hottest guys in town.

A wicked grin stretches across my face. "Uhh ... a birthday kiss."

"That was more than a birthday kiss," she reprimands, forgetting about her grinding boyfriend behind her. "Have you been hooking up with Cruz Danforth?"

I shrug my shoulders. "I mean ... define hooking up?"

Ember's jaw drops to the ground. "Holy fuck. You have been, you filthy little whore. Tell me all about it. He fucks like a damn king, doesn't he? Oh, shit. I need to hear every last detail."

I shake my head. "Not yet, girl. You're going to have to get me wicked drunk before I start spilling that shit."

Ember nods as though I just set the biggest challenge of her life, and within the blink of an eye, she grabs my hand and drags me back to the bar.

The bartender instantly recognizes me, and seeing the determination on Ember's face, begins lining up more shots. I groan, realizing that tonight is going to be one of the messiest nights of my life, but I can't freaking wait.

32

The heel of my black thigh-high boot trips over someone's discarded shoe and I go tumbling to the ground until a pair of strong hands grip my arms and yank me back to my feet. Glancing up, ready to thank my strong savior, I meet Grayson's stormy glare instead, and the words are instantly swallowed back down.

"Watch it," he snaps at me. "Are you fucking drunk?"

I roll my eyes. "Ahhh, duh. It's my party after all. It wouldn't be any fun if I was being the sober dick hiding in the shadows—like you are. Tell me, have you ever heard of having fun? You know, I bet you'd be a lot happier if you took that stick out of your ass. It's gotta hurt being wedged so far up there."

Grayson just shakes his head and starts dragging me through the crowd. He cuts through the hundreds of bodies before coming to the edge of the room and slamming his shoulder into a door. It opens through to a massive kitchen that's as empty as they come, and just when I think he's brought me in here to kill me, he makes his way over to the cupboard and grabs a glass.

I watch in confusion as he fills the glass with filtered water and drops a few ice cubes in, giving me a quick second to scan my gaze over the tattoos of his back, but before I can really appreciate them or even figure out what half of it is, he turns back around. "Here," he says with a pissed-off scowl, as though catering to me is the most irritating thing he has ever suffered through. Though he should be reminded from time to time that I've never asked for his help. Never have and never will. "Drink this."

Not one to pass up a free hand out, I take the water, and the second I bring it to my lips, I tilt my head back and finish the whole glass. "Holy crap. Thanks," I say, needing to catch my breath after drinking too fast. "I didn't realize how thirsty I was."

Grayson nods and silently takes the glass out of my hand before refilling it and bringing it back to me. He places it down on the counter in front of me, and my finger instantly catches the drop of water that glides down the outside of the glass. "Why are you being nice all of a sudden?" I ask, struggling to raise my eyes to meet his as they get stuck on the tattoos that cover his wide chest, taking in the haunting skull design that travels over his peck and up to his shoulder.

Grayson shrugs and hoists himself up onto the counter and as he does, my eyes glide over the wings that frame the skull, and while I can't be completely sure, my gut is telling me that these are the wings of a raven.

"There's a difference between being a decent person and a nice one," Grayson tells me, stealing my attention away from his ink. "Getting a drunk chick a glass of water to help sober her up so she doesn't end up date raped is just being a decent human being. Don't get your wires crossed here. Besides, the way you're dressed, you're bound to have the wrong attention come at you at some point." I groan, ready to cut him off as anger begins to surge through me, but he's on a roll. "Honestly, after the bullshit that happened to you the other week, anyone would think that you'd make smarter choices."

"Smarter choices?" I snap, grabbing the glass of water and tossing it right at his face and stepping in close, letting him see exactly what I think of his rambling comments. "First of all, this party was all of your idea. You and your friends wanted me to come out to some abandoned cabin and party like a fucking rockstar, so don't get your panties in a twist because I'm doing exactly what you guys had intended me to do. You, Carver, Cruz, and King are the ones who should be making smarter choices. And secondly, fuck you. What did you think was going to happen when all of your dumbasses decided on a BDSM theme around a bunch of horny teenage dudes? If any of the girls at this party get hurt, I'm holding the four of you responsible."

Grayson rolls his eyes. "You don't think we have security here? Do you honestly think that lowly of us that we wouldn't try to protect the people who come to party on our property?"

I step closer into him. "Tell me, what exactly have you done to make me think differently? You groan and grunt with every little thing I say. How am I supposed to know if you're a decent guy?"

Grayson pushes me back and jumps down from the counter, the water from my glass spilling all over the ground. He grabs the glass from the counter and instantly refills it before coming back to me, grabbing my hand and shoving the glass into it once again. "That's what you honestly think of me?" he questions. "That I'm not a decent guy after I've been there to save your ass time and time again?"

I raise my chin. "I don't know. From my understanding, you're only saving my ass because Dynasty needs me still breathing, and if I'm not, I have a feeling it's you four it will come down on."

Grayson shakes his head. "Don't talk shit that you don't understand."

I find myself sipping the water, and as I do, the anger starts simmering out of my body and I take a step back from him. "Why do you hate me so much?" I ask, not sure where that question had even come from. But suddenly, whatever we were just discussing doesn't seem so important.

His brows furrow as he watches me for a moment before grabbing the glass of water from my hands and taking a sip of his own. "I don't hate you, Elodie," he tells me, catching me off guard at his casual use of my real name. "I just don't … get you."

"What's that supposed to mean?"

"You mean change," he explains. "You've been here a month and already everything is different, and I don't know what the boys have told you, but I don't like different. I can't handle different."

"So, you choose to be an ass instead? Because I'm not sure if you've realized this, but I can't exactly help who I am. It's not like I'm intentionally coming in here and changing up your world. I know nothing about Dynasty and suddenly this weird-ass group is claiming that I'm about to be their new leader. So, you're not the only one whose world is being flipped upside down. I guess you should consider yourself lucky that you've had eighteen years to prepare for this change. Me? This bullshit just got dropped on me like a bomb, and I'm still scrambling to catch all the pieces."

He leans back against the counter again, not seeming to care about the water dripping off him as he silently watches me, his gaze filled with a strange curiosity. "I guess I didn't think of it that way, but nonetheless, that wasn't the change I was referring to."

"And dare I ask what is, oh broody one?"

"King, Cruz, and Carver," he states flatly. "They're all falling head over heels like fucking idiots for you, and eventually, there's going to be a fallout, because unfortunately for them, there's only one of you."

My stare lingers on his face, considering how much I should share with him, but after having far too many shots, I throw caution to the wind and hope for the best. I step in closer to him, my chest lightly brushing against his and inhaling the deep manly smell that radiates off him. "What if I told you that I've already spoken to King and Cruz. They're both down to share."

His brow arches, and for a minute, I mentally applaud myself for rendering the broody asshole silent, but it doesn't last long. "What does that exactly mean? Sharing?"

"I can be with them both without jealousy. One night Cruz might sneak into my bed, and the next I might fuck King until I can't breathe." I step in even closer, raising my chin so that my mouth hovers just below his ear. "Hell, sometimes they might take me together."

He gently pushes me back to see my face. "And where does Carver fit in all of this?"

I shrug my shoulders. "He doesn't. He's my security blanket, but he could have me if he wanted to, all he'd have to do is say please," I murmur, letting my hand fall against his wide chest. "You could get in on the action too if you wanted. There's something about a brooding, silent man that intrigues me," I tell him, raising my chin and meeting his heated gaze only to see something there that I've never quite seen before that has me wondering if maybe there's a little something here to be discovered.

I push up to my tippy toes and murmur in his ear, pressing my body flush against his and getting sweet chills as his hand involuntarily falls to my waist. "You know, there's a good chance that tonight will end with King sinking deep inside my ass as Cruz slams into my pussy? I'd hate for you to miss out."

Grayson's eyes bore into mine before dropping to my body. His fingers tighten on my waist as his other hand finds my chin. He gently raises it and just when I think he's about to close the gap and kiss me, he pulls back. "It sounds like you've already got your hands full."

A breathy laugh slips through my lips as a grin pulls at the corner of my mouth. "Two hands, two holes, and a mouth," I tell him with a seductive wink that has his tongue discreetly slipping out and rolling over his bottom lip. "Trust me, I can handle it."

Desire pools in his eyes, and before I get a chance to entice him further, Grayson steals the glass of water from the counter, throws back what's left before looking down and meeting my hooded stare. "You're drunk, Elodie."

He passes by me and all I can do is gape at him as he walks past and disappears back through the kitchen door into the crowded party, my bravado completely fading away and allowing me for a second time to let Grayson get away with calling me Elodie.

That can't become a thing. Elodie is the ghost of a girl that I never got a chance to be, but Winter, that's the real me. Winter is the girl who holds all the scars, and has learned to not only survive, but to thrive in this broken world. Elodie was just a baby when she disappeared. We may bear the same body and the same blood, but we are definitely not the same girl, and as soon as I can, I'll be making sure that name doesn't accidentally slip from between Grayson's lips ever again.

I fill up the glass of water again before having a few sips and stepping into Grayson's vacated spot. I lean back against the counter and find myself wondering about everything else that just went down in this deserted kitchen. Grayson didn't exactly agree to my offer, but he also didn't reject it either. Is he interested in getting in on this little deal I have with the boys? I mean, I wasn't lying, I'm so down, but he caught me off guard. Sure, I thought maybe there was a slim chance with Carver, but Grayson? No, he was always a definite no in my mind.

Damn, just the thought of all four of them. Holy shit. Maybe I have had too much to drink.

Feeling my frustration rise up within me, I finish the glass of water and let out a deep sigh before turning around and placing the empty glass in the sink. I should go back out to my party and enjoy myself, only after Grayson's confusing lecture … or was it a lecture? I don't even know. Either way, my mood is quickly plummeting and I want nothing more than to go back to being oblivious in that happy place I used to live in.

I stare out the kitchen window at the people gathered around, drinking and partying when a smoker catches my eyes.

Perfect.

I push my way out the side door and walk around to the front of the cabin, going slowly in the grass, knowing that just one slip is going to see my ass landing on the floor with a devastating thump that couldn't be good for anyone. Though, maybe good for Sara Bennett. I'm sure that bitch would love to see me go down. If only she knew what else I've been going down on.

I keep the smoking guy in sight, desperate to get to him and steal a cigarette. I'm sure if I just took a few hits, all my troubles will fade away and then I can walk back into that party with my head held high and enjoy the rest of my night. Besides, Ember is still impatiently waiting to know why the hell Cruz's tongue was shoved so far down my throat, and after all the drinks I've had tonight, I might actually consider telling her.

I'm only a few awkward steps from the smoker when he senses me coming. His eyes travel up and down my body with interest before they come back to my eyes. "Hey, baby. What can I do for you?"

I nod toward his cigarette. "Got another one of those?"

He digs into his pocket and pulls out his pack of cigarettes as his eyes heat with intrigue, probably assuming that he's going to get lucky. Now, I know Cruz and King are happy to share, but something tells me that invitation doesn't extend to random guys at parties. "Coming right up," he says, flipping open the top and reaching for one. "I heard you're the birthday girl."

I nod, reaching for the cigarette, getting it just between my fingers when a vice-like grip circles my arm, and I'm tugged hard. I scramble to keep my feet under myself as a high-pitched squeal tears from my throat. My gaze snaps up to find Carver and a beat of relief pulses through me for only a second until I realize that he's not just pulling me away from this smoking stranger, but dragging me toward the woods.

"What are you doing?" I screech, trying to pull back against his hold but it's far too tight, making my attempts seem somewhat pathetic.

He keeps dragging me, not saying a word, but as we reach the edge of the woods, he slows his pace and I finally feel as though I can walk like a normal human being. His grip loosens on my arms, but not enough to get away.

If he were someone else, I'd be screaming, desperately seeking a way out, yet when it comes to Carver, there's something about him that eases the fear with me. Without a doubt, I know that I'm safe with him. Always.

We walk far into the darkened woods until the lights from the party are just a dull glow, but still allows for us to see where we're going. A ferocious growl tears from deep within him, and within the blink of an eye, my back is pressed up against one of the many trees with Carver bearing down on me.

His body presses into mine and my hands instinctively fall to his chest. The tension pulses between us, and I can tell that he has something on his mind, something deep that's been bothering him, but he's not quite ready to let the words fly.

I feel the rapid beat of his heart beneath my hand, and with every passing second, the tension intensifies between us. "What …" I let my sentence trail off, not really sure what I should be saying, but before I have a chance to figure it out, he closes the distance.

Then finally, *finally,* Carver's warm lips press down on mine as his big hand finds my waist, his other curling around the back of my neck and holding me tight. My lips instantly move against his, a soft moan slipping from between them.

How is it so good with him?

Carver's tongue sweeps into my mouth, brushing against mine with an erotic rhythm that makes me need so much more of him. We fight for control, me needing to be the one running the show, while Carver is the one refusing to hand it over.

My chest presses up against his and his hand at my waist curls right around. I'm lifted off the ground and I wrap my legs around his waist as he presses me back against the tree, keeping me pinned against his strong body.

My hands roam over his warm skin, taking in every inch of the body that usually holds me close at night, but it's never like this. I never get to relish in his body, feeling it, claiming it as my own. My nails sink into the strong muscles of his arms and he groans, spurring me on.

I've got to have him.

My body heats, my pussy flooding with need as our kiss grows wild with desperation. I thought for sure I was going to end up with Cruz or King tonight, but damn, if Carver is on the menu too, I guess I'll be ordering dinner, dessert, and a show.

Running out of breath, Carver's lips drop to my neck and I hold him there as he grinds into me, teasing me with just how good it's going to be. My nails draw up his back, over his strong muscles and into the back of his hair. My fingers curl into a fist, knotting his hair into my hand and holding him tight. "Carver," I pant, needing so much more.

My voice is like a lightning bolt straight between us and has him tearing back away from me, wide eyed as he stares down at mine. I search his stare. "What?" I pant in confusion as my legs unwind from his waist and I drop back to the uneven ground. "What happened? What's wrong?"

Carver just stares before slowly pressing into me again, both our hearts racing a million miles an hour as our chests rise and fall with rapid movements. His forehead presses against mine as his hand slips up my body and curls around my neck just as it was before.

He holds me there, neither of us saying a word until we catch our breath, then like a slap in the face, he pulls back and meets my eyes with a heavy regret. "I don't share."

Carver drops his hands from my body and pulls himself away, the loss of his strong body against mine almost painful. He starts stalking back through the woods and all I can do is stare after him, pressing my hand against my swollen lips to keep myself from crying out.

Why does his rejection cut so deep?

I sink to the dirty ground, my chest beginning to rise and fall with those same rapid movements, only this time for a completely different reason. Not knowing how to react to his rejection, my head falls into my hands and I will myself not to cry. Why is it stinging like this? He's pushed me away before and I didn't burst into tears then, though I did sneak out and try to beat the shit out of a drunken pervert.

Fuck me. When will I learn? I keep allowing him to draw me into his trap and I go willingly each and every fucking time.

Stupid. I'm so fucking stupid.

I'm not going to sit here and cry about it. I need to shake it off and make him regret it. Good fucking plan. Besides, there's a whole bar down there with my name on it, a best friend ready to help pour it down my throat, and two guys willing to fuck me until I can't remember my own damn name.

I'm good. I don't need Carver.

I go to pull myself up when Carver's loud panicked roar tears through the woods. "WINTER. GET DOWN."

On instinct I drop to the ground just as a loud BANG echoes through the woods and a perfectly round bullet slams into the tree behind me, right where my head used to be.

33

BANG. BANG. BANG.

Bullets fly past my face and I scramble to my feet. Is some motherfucker seriously trying to shoot me right now, just moments after being rejected by a man like Dante Carver? Fuck me, they picked the wrong bitch to mess with right now. Just wait till I get my hands on the asshole.

What the fuck is going on? "CARVER?" I cry. Where the fuck is he?

BANG.

My terrified scream rips from my throat as the bullet grazes past my face, the panic soaring through me as I run through the woods, desperate to get away. My arm scrapes along broken branches as my ankles threaten to twist on the uneven ground. Why the fuck did I wear these boots?

BANG. BANG.

Damn it. If I had a fucking gun right now …

The noise is so loud and it echoes through the darkened woods, making it impossible to figure out which direction it's coming from. I hear the sounds of the bullets sinking into the trees around me, coming way too close for comfort.

My heart races as panic tears through me. I have to get out of here. I run. I run as fast as I fucking can, trying to follow the direction that Carver had just gone, but I've never felt so lost.

Who the hell is after me? I didn't do anything. I swear.

"WINTER?"

Tears stream down my face as I try to run through the woods, my tears only making it that much harder to see where I'm going. "Carver? Where are you?"

"RUN. FUCKING RUN."

Leaves whip past my face, stinging as I focus on putting one foot after another. I'll deal with injuries afterward, that's assuming I get out of this alive. What the hell is this? Is this Dynasty? Did Sam realize I got away and is trying to deal with loose ends?

FUCK.

I race like my life depends on it because it fucking does, darting and twisting past massive trees like some kind of deranged maze. I fly over a fallen branch and my stiletto heel instantly comes down on an angle. I fall to the ground, feeling my arm get cut up as I roll over broken branches. My heart is in my throat and I find it nearly impossible to take a deep breath.

I hear more gunfire and the sound of feet slamming against the hard earth, coming closer, way too close. There's a scuffle and loud grunts then more gunfire, but this one is more like a PEW, PEW, and I pray to whoever lives above that someone is firing back at the asshole trying to shoot me down.

Terror flies through me and I scramble back to my feet, desperately wishing that I could be anywhere but here. I take off at a sprint. "GET DOWN."

My body instantly slams back against the hard ground, and a second later, King's heavy body falls down on top of mine, crushing me into the earth. I cry out in pain, but not even a second later, the loud insistent BANG, BANG, BANG rips through the air.

King fires back and I scream out as a body steps out from behind a large tree, gun aimed right for King's head. I scream in horror, but King aims and shoots, faster than anything I've ever seen before. The bullet lodges right between the asshole's brows and the fucker goes down like a sack of shit.

Thinking it's over, a deranged sob bubbles out of my throat, but King slams his hand down over my mouth. "Shut up," he hisses. "There's more of them."

My eyes widen. What the fuck is this?

Hearing something deeper in the woods, King flies to his feet, dragging me up and pulling us behind a large tree. He pushes me down to the ground, protectively hovering over me with his gun still in his hands.

A gunshot rings out and I jump, desperately wanting to scream again, but I bite down on my lip, not wanting anyone to find us here. Though, judging by the way King steps out from behind the tree and lets off two shots, I'd dare say these motherfuckers know exactly where we are.

Shots are heard from across the woods and I look through the trees to watch as Carver silently sneaks up behind some guy, grabs his head, and gives it one hell of a violent twist. My eyes widen as I watch the man crumble to the ground before Carver sinks back into the woods.

There's a scuffle to my left and I look over to find Grayson fighting with a guy out in the open, putting himself at risk, but he's quick. He steals the guy's gun, turns it on him and shoots, before kneeling over his dead body and letting off three more precise shots out into the woods. I hear three pained grunts before the sound of them falling to the ground.

What the fuck? Are the boys assassins? How can they shoot like this?

I stare up at King, absolutely horrified by what I'm seeing and hearing. It's one thing to go out looking for a fight, but to be the little mouse caught in gunfire in the middle of the lion's den? Yeah, I'm fucking terrified. This is way out of my league and definitely not what I had in mind for my night.

Shots continue to ring through the dark until Carver calls out and King grips my arms. We start racing back through the woods as I hear Carver, Cruz, and Grayson behind us, finishing off the few fuckers left behind.

I see the lights of the cabin up ahead and I keep my eyes on it, racing as fast as I can toward it with King's hand curled tightly around my arm. My heart races, but I push it faster, push myself faster. I can do this. I'm going to get out of this.

The people in the cabin are completely oblivious to the hell going on deep in the woods as they party and drink, celebrating what should have been a good eighteenth birthday.

We finally break out of the woods and King leads me straight to Carver's Escalade and he doesn't hesitate to throw me into it. The engine roars to life, and before my door is even closed, King fishtails around and drives back toward the woods.

I fall back into my seat and hastily grab my seatbelt, watching wide-eyed as the boys come racing out of there, running toward the Escalade.

King meets them in the middle, screeching to a stop. The boys dive into the backseat and Cruz slams his hand on the back of King's headrest. "GO, GO, GO," he roars. "They're down for now, but more will come."

King hits the gas and takes off like a rocket. He switches off the headlights and then races blindly back down the dirt road, knowing the curves and bumps of the road like he knows the back of his own hand, and for a brief moment, I wonder if the security

Grayson had mentioned earlier, were actually just the four boys. How could they possibly need hired help when they can do shit like that?

The boys all squish into the back seat, looking over their shoulders and out every window, waiting for a threat. When we hit the main road without a hint of another gunshot, they finally begin to relax, and all that's left to do is focus on getting the hell out of there as I take a moment to reevaluate what the fuck I'm doing hanging out with a bunch of trained killers.

"Okay," I say, pacing back and forth in front of the guys as we sit in Carver's living room. My hand presses against my temples, gently squeezing and trying to make sense of what the fuck just went down. I turn and face the four guys sitting quietly on Carver's couch, looking as though it's just a normal Saturday night in their fucking BDSM outfits. "Someone tell me right fucking now what the hell just happened back there? WHY WERE THERE DEAD PEOPLE AT MY SEX PARTY?"

"It wasn't a sex party," Grayson grunts, keeping his eyes anywhere but at me, reminding me of the awkward little chat we had in the cabin kitchen, which seems so far away right now.

I grab a vase off the closest table and launch it at his head. He ducks out of the way and I cringe as it shatters against the wall behind him, but I don't fucking care. If these guys can dodge bullets like pros, then they can certainly handle a vase. "ARE YOU FUCKING KIDDING RIGHT NOW?"

Carver sucks in a soft breath between his teeth, and as my ferocious glare snaps in his direction, I see a whole lot of nothing. "Spill," I demand, annoyed that it's already taken this long for them to let me in on the secret. The four of them sat quietly in the car the whole way home while I did nothing but freak out.

Carver drags a hand over his face, and for a split second, all I can seem to think about is the way his lips moved over mine before he completely shattered me by delivering one hell of a rejection. Like what the fuck is his problem anyway? He clearly wants me. Is he too scared? Does he worry about being compared to his friends? Fuck him. Maybe he's just a jealous bastard.

The guys glance at one another, having a secret conversation before King finally lets out a breath. "What just happened back there," he starts, meeting my furious stare, "was that the families who stood against your father, they just made a stand against you."

"What?" I snap, looking around at the four of them. "What does that even mean?"

Carver meets my stare. "I told you that you were the rightful leader," he says as though it should all make perfect sense, and only looks pissed that I'm not following along. "You're an eighteen-year-old girl who's about to rule over all seventeen families, and for the past eighteen years, they've run free, doing whatever the fuck they want. The fact that you're barely even an adult, and a female at that

... it doesn't sit well with them. That's the reason they went after your parents in the first place."

My back stiffens as Cruz lets out a grunt. "Excuse me?" I say, walking straight up to Carver and meeting his stare. "Are you trying to tell me that I'm the reason that my parents are dead?"

His face falls, and for just a second, I see regret shining in his eyes, but it's gone a second later. "Honestly," he says as Cruz continues to grunt and groan, not so discreetly trying to tell his friend to shut his fucking mouth. "Yeah. Since your grandfather founded Dynasty, it was always said that the leadership would be handed from father to son, but when your father's first born popped out as a girl, things changed. They weren't happy. At first, they were happy to wait until your father eventually had a son, but it quickly became clear that your parents weren't interested in having more children."

Carver sits back, clearly having said what he wanted to say, so I turn to Cruz. "Explain."

He lets out a sigh. Usually, he loves the spotlight on him, but right now, he's never looked so uncomfortable. "Sixteen families," he starts, "equally divided with the seventeenth family, the ruling family, having the final unbiased say over everything. It worked for years … until things became hostile. The best way to think about it is good versus bad. Eight families are always rooting for you while eight will always stand against you."

Cruz gives me a second, letting it all sink in before continuing. "As leader, your father was supposed to be the voice of reason between the sixteen families, until he wasn't. He had good values and was called weak for not making harsh judgments that his father before him would have made. Then he had a baby girl and it became clear that she would inherit the leadership and mess with their traditions. So, those eight families who stood against him, who now stand against you, took matters into their own hands. Without a ruling family, the remaining sixteen could stand equally, but when there's good versus bad, and no one to keep them in line …" He lets out a breath. "It's been a shitstorm for eighteen years."

I nod, following along. "So, let me get this straight. Those eight families, the side who stood against my father, planned to have my family massacred just so they didn't have someone telling them what they could and couldn't do?"

King nods. "In a nutshell. Though, while Dynasty mourned your parents' deaths, the evidence was destroyed, and it was made to look like a house fire that wiped out your family."

"But they missed one," Cruz says, raising his chin as though my very being is something to be proud of. "You're the heir of Dynasty, and once you go through your initiation, you can make it right again. They will have no choice but to kneel down to you."

I shake my head, nowhere near inclined to be the ruler of some weird secret society, the very society that had my parents murdered and covered it up, meaning that the bastards haven't even been punished for it. "And if I don't want it?"

Carver shakes his head. "I told you, Winter. It doesn't work like that. This isn't a job offer that you can accept or deny, this is your blood. It's who you are, and until the day you die, Dynasty will always be there looming over you. Seventeen families, seventeen seats at the table. No one in, and no one out."

"But those men tonight," I say, looking around them again. "Who were they?"

Carver sighs. "Most likely the same hitmen who were responsible for taking out your parents eighteen years ago."

Fuck. I gape at him, slightly hysterical. "And you expect me to go willingly to stand before these assholes and be their ruler? Fuck no. These people killed my family, and now they want to kill me. I don't want anything to do with them. Fuck it all to hell. I'm out."

I start walking for the door but Grayson reaches out. His fingers curl around my wrist, and with one quick move, he throws me back across the room until my ass is slamming down on the coffee table. "I don't think you're hearing us," he growls. "You're the sole remaining Ravenwood, the one person standing between them and their reckless need to rule over governments and take judgments into their own hands. This is people's lives at stake, not just some bullshit game. You don't have a choice, just as your future child won't have a choice. It's who you are, and you're in this position whether you like it or not, so stop bitching about it, stand the fuck up, and own who you are. You're Elodie Ravenwood, the heir of Dynasty, not some bitch-ass nobody with low morals, a bad attitude, and a fucking chip on her shoulder."

I stand, bearing down on Grayson before grabbing the front of his shirt and letting him have it. "Call me Elodie Ravenwood one more fucking time and I will introduce your face to my fist. Elodie is the daughter of money, she stands against everything that I believe in.

She's a complete stranger to the person I am now. She died when my parents did. My name is Winter and you better start using it."

Grayson doesn't back down and we remain locked in each other's stare until Cruz stands and physically pulls me away. "Look, babe," he tells me. "Whether you like it or not, you're the heir of Dynasty. That means that you've got a target on your back. Those eight families won't stop. They don't want you in leadership, and they'll try and try again until they can be stopped."

I stare at him for a moment before slowly looking around at the rest of the guys. "That's why the party was at King's cabin, wasn't it? You knew they were looking for a chance to get at me and you drew them out." Guilty expressions twist across the guys' faces and I want nothing more than to smack each and every one of them. "It's why you sit in my classes, why you moved me out of Ember's place, and why Carver has been sneaking into my bed this past week even though I've not been living here anymore. You've known all along that there was a target on my back, and not one of you thought to say anything."

"It's true," King declares. "We've known since the beginning that this was coming, but we didn't know where or when they would try to hit you, so that's why we've stayed close. But you must know that you're safe with us. We'd never let anything happen to you. We need you."

I scoff, unable to believe a word I'm hearing. "You're all fucking assholes," I say, turning my stare on Carver. "But you're the worst. You should have told me when you told me about my parents. You had every opportunity to come clean and you never did."

Carver's gaze drops. He knows I'm right. They all do.

The silence in the room couldn't be louder as we all take a moment to calm down. I find myself looking at the guys, while also realizing that no matter how angry I am with them, it doesn't take away the threat. Whether or not I'm the heir of Dynasty, I'm still going to have a target on my back. "So, what now?" I ask. "Am I supposed to just go to school every day, looking over my shoulder, and hoping that I don't get shot up in the process?"

Cruz shakes his head. "We just keep going the way we're going. We'll keep you protected, but now that they've made a move and failed, they'll need some time to regroup and come up with a new plan of attack."

I nod. "And when I'm initiated and officially take my father's place?"

"They'll keep coming for you," Carver says. "They'll just try and be a little more discreet about it, try and make it look like an accident."

Fuck.

I stand and start pacing the room, feeling all of their stares on me, but I don't care, there's far too much going through my head. "So, we take out the threat before the threat gets me," I say. "Take out the head of each family, then their sons or daughters will step up, and we'll have a clean slate."

Silence. Fucking silence.

I turn back and look at them, wondering when in fresh hell did I become so comfortable with the idea of murder? I'm a stranger to myself. "What?" I question, knowing perfectly well that the guys don't have an issue with it either. "It sounds like a reasonable plan of attack to me."

The guys start glancing around at one another before all eyes fall to Carver and he stands. He makes his way over to me but makes a point of not being close enough to touch. "For the most part," he says, "your plan is as solid as any of the ones we've come up with."

"But?"

"But you've got one major problem," he says, pausing and meeting my eyes. His lips press into a hard line, and I wait, fearing that whatever is about to come out of his mouth is going to destroy me. Carver lets out a heavy sigh and the hesitation in his eyes is enough to have my whole body tensing, preparing me for the worst. "The head of a family must advocate for their family's beliefs, not his or her own. So, if the son or daughter inherits the position and stands with you, but the majority of their family is against you, you've achieved nothing."

I shake my head. "Yeah, but at least then those responsible for killing my parents are punished."

Carver sighs. "Let me make this nice and clear for you," he tells me. "Those eight families include the Irvine family, the Montgomerys, the Rhodes, Hardings, Kennedys, and the Scardonis," Carver's gaze sweeps across to Grayson's before coming back to mine. "Then you have the Beckett family and last but not least the Carver family." He pauses for just a moment as I suck in a breath, my eyes widening in horror as I realize the weight of what he's saying.

I glance back at Grayson then focus in on Carver. "Your parents were responsible for killing mine," I growl. "They tried to kill me.

Twice."

Carver nods as though it's just a cold hard fact that he's somehow emotionally separated himself from. "They did," he tells me. "And if I kill my father for you, I'm promoted to the head of my family, which means it's me who'll have to stand against you, not him."

My heart races as I stare up at him in horror, and then without another word, I walk away.

34

My back crashes against the headboard of my bed. What was I doing allowing myself to get close to Carver like that? I guess it doesn't really matter about Grayson, it's not like I'd really let him in, but in case he didn't catch on, the invitation to fuck is now so far off the table, it doesn't even exist. But Carver. Damn it, why does that hurt so bad? His family had a hand in my parents' brutal murder, Grayson's too.

Maybe this is just some sick joke? Maybe it's just Carver's way of trying to push me away because I know he felt it in the woods tonight, the connection between us is so damn real. Though, maybe that's why he keeps pushing me away. He knows that when his father dies—from either natural or other causes—he's going to have to stand against me, and when that day comes, it's going to hurt. I guess this is why Grayson has kept himself at a distance.

Well played, Mr. Beckett. Well played.

I hear the soft thud from the front door and I pull my blanket right over my head. I hear King and Cruz's soft conversation as they make their way through the home that I still struggle to believe is mine. Maybe if I hide well enough, they'll just go away. Yeah, doubt it. Though now that I know Carver and Grayson are double agents, maybe I should figure out how to change the security codes for the gate and the house.

A knock sounds at my bedroom door before I hear King's muffled voice. "Babe, are you in here?"

"No."

The door swings open and I find both Cruz and King staring at me. "Go away," I grumble, pulling the blanket right over my head. "Let me sulk in peace."

"No can do," Cruz declares, welcoming himself into my room. "We need to make sure that you're not about to do something stupid, and figured that you might have a whole bunch of questions now that you know what's going on."

I groan and sink further into my bed when I feel a weight dip beside me. "Seriously?" I grumble, throwing the blanket back to find Cruz lying beside me on my bed while King makes himself comfortable at the end. "Do you guys make a habit of welcoming yourselves into girls' beds or am I just lucky?"

"Trust me," Cruz says, grabbing me and hauling me up until I'm curled in his arms. "You're definitely lucky."

I scoff. "Right, because lucky girls have their sex parties crashed by hitmen and spend the night dodging bullets."

"Speaking of that," King says, leaning across the bed and looking at the cuts and bruises over my skin. "How are you feeling? That cut on your arm could use a little attention."

I shrug my shoulders. "Yeah, maybe," I say, looking down at my arm to see it covered in dried blood.

"Come on." King holds out a hand and I reach for it. He pulls me right off the bed and leads me into the bathroom as Cruz groans behind us, complaining about only just getting me in his arms.

I step into the bathroom and suck in a gasp as I meet my reflection in the mirror. Cuts and scrapes cover my body from the delightful little jog I took through the woods, and after leaving them for the last hour, they're not looking too good.

Cruz joins us in the bathroom as I start pulling at my ridiculous latex bodysuit. King steps in behind me, helping me out of it as Cruz watches the show with an amused smirk across his face. I let out a sigh as I unfasten the many leather straps around my body. "I guess wishes really do come true," I grumble.

I watch King through the mirror as he glances up, his brows furrowed with confusion as Cruz grunts. "Huh?"

A stupid little grin pulls at the corner of my lips. "When I squeezed into this ridiculous outfit, I'd hoped that you two would be here at the end of the night helping me out of it, only I had something a little different in mind."

King chuckles, gently rubbing his fingers over my skin as the bodysuit is finally tugged off me. I lean into the shower and turn on the taps before getting in and letting the warm water rush over my body. King and Cruz silently watch me as I shower, and while I'm not intending to put on a show, I can't seem to help myself.

I grab the body wash and the loofah and rub it all over my sore skin, laughing at the way the boys become mesmerized by my movements. "So," I say, forcing their heated stares back to mine as I dip low to drag the loofah over my legs. "Are you guys assassins or something like that?"

King laughs, the amusement twinkling in his eyes. "No. We were just trained to do what needed to be done," he explains. "Just think about it, had your parents still been alive, you would have grown up right alongside us, training with us day in and day out."

I can't help but remember walking in to see King and Grayson in the gym and take in just how powerful they were. I could have been like that. I could have had a family, and loyalty, and grown up right beside them, with friends that I'd never have to say goodbye to, or a home that I could actually unpack my things in. I put the thought to the back of my mind. It never gets me anywhere thinking about what I could have had. "So, if all the families are enemies, how come you all grew up together?"

Cruz shakes his head. "You can't think about it like that. For the most part, the sixteen families all work together like a well-oiled machine. They balance each other out. All the children grow up together, we're like one big family—"

"More like a cult," I scoff, cutting him off.

Cruz rolls his eyes and continues. "We're a family, and in every family, you get the good and the bad. Siblings feud just like the sixteen families have for the past eighteen years. There are rotten eggs, but they all thrive under the Dynasty name."

I nod, feeling like I understand everything so much more when it comes from Cruz's calm explanations, rather than Carver's ranting. "So that's why none of you flinched when I killed Kurt?"

Cruz nods, grabbing my towel off the heated rack and stepping toward the shower door as I begin rinsing off the bubbles. "That's exactly what we've been trained for," he explains. "We all grew up in this lifestyle, where instead of speaking to the police or hiring some bullshit lawyer, we handle our problems quietly, knowing Dynasty is always there to protect us."

"I guess it wasn't so quiet when I was arrested in the middle of the school."

"No," King says. "It certainly wasn't."

I let out a breath and turn off the taps before stepping out of the shower and right into Cruz's arms. He wraps the warm towel around me, and I cringe as his hands roam up and down my body, over my scrapes and cuts while helping to dry me off. "So, what now?" I ask, walking across the bathroom and back to the mirror where I can see myself properly.

I adjust my towel and wrap it around myself as King steps into my side and takes my arm. His gaze sweeps over my injuries. "Now I bandage you up and put you to bed."

"I meant with Dynasty," I tell him as he releases my arm and begins searching through the cupboards for the first aid kit. "How am I supposed to face Carver and Grayson knowing that their families were responsible for killing my parents?"

Cruz grips my waist and steps in behind me, meeting my gaze through the mirror. "They would never hurt you," he insists, his fingers tightening on my waist. "They want to protect you just as we do. They don't hold the same values as their fathers."

"But if and when their fathers are dead, they'll be the head of their families and made to stand against me?"

"Mostly," King says as he starts working on my arm. "We're hoping that when that happens, they can sway their own families and the other six families to stand with you, but you've got to remember that it's good versus bad, and you are neither. You're Switzerland standing in the middle. You're the deciding factor, and while I shouldn't be encouraging this, if you showed favor to them, they'll be more inclined to accept your rule."

"Show favor to the people who sent hitmen after me? Yeah, right."

"That's what I thought," King scoffs.

Silence falls around us as King bandages me up and makes me comfortable, and before I know it, Cruz is slipping his hand into mine and pulling me out of the bathroom. "Come on," he murmurs. "It's late. Let me take you to bed and then we can talk it all through properly with the boys in the morning. I'm sure after sleeping on it, Carver and Grayson will have plenty to say."

I groan and listen to King's soft chuckle as he follows us out of the bathroom, switching off the light as he goes. "They're really not that bad," he tells me. "They're just—"

"Assholes?"

"Yeah," he laughs, not able to deny it.

We reach my bed and Cruz pulls the blankets back then indicates for me to get in, and feeling the weight of the day resting on my shoulders, I don't hesitate. There's nothing I'd like more than to fall into a deep sleep and put the day behind me. Perhaps we can try another birthday party next year, though that's assuming I'm still breathing this time next year.

I scoot down between the sheets, and the second my head hits the pillow, a yawn tears through me. Cruz dips down and gently brushes his lips over mine. "I'll see you in the morning," he says before swiftly disappearing and making his way out of my room to make space for King, who just gives me an awkward smile before turning and walking away.

I can't help but laugh. He's so damn stubborn, but I kinda love that about him. He hates showing that he cares, but he does it in so many other ways that it's impossible for him to deny. His fingers brush over the light switch, and my room instantly drowns into darkness, and as he goes to close my bedroom door, I realize that there's a good possibility that Carver won't be showing up tonight. With the fresh memory of hitmen chasing me through the woods, alone is something I definitely don't want to be.

"Wait," I call, watching as both of their handsome faces appear back in my doorway.

"What's wrong?" King demands, his eyes alert as though he's searching for some kind of threat.

"I …" Shit. *Suck it up and admit your fears, Winter.* "I don't want to be alone tonight. Would you guys stay for a while?"

Not another word needs to be said before Cruz is pushing back through the door and kicking off his shoes. He slips into the bed beside me, instantly pulling me into his arms as King walks around the other side, laying down behind me.

With my body curled into Cruz's side, King rests his hand against my thigh and presses his body up against my back. "We've got you," he murmurs into the dark room. "You can sleep." His hand soothingly moves up and down my thigh, traveling right up to my hip and then back down to my knee, and while his movements are meant to help me sleep, all they do is remind me that I'm as naked as the day I was born between two of the most gorgeous men I have ever had the pleasure of meeting.

My hand shifts from Cruz's chest and I slide it up around the back of King's neck, bringing his face closer to mine. I look back over my shoulder, and just as I had hoped, his lips come down on mine. He kisses me softly, but his touch is so full of desire, so powerful, and desperate.

He kisses me deeper, and as he does, his hand slips over my hips and pushes down between my legs. I groan into him, and as I pull my lips from his and look up at Cruz, King's lips immediately drop to my neck.

My head tilts back, needing more, and Cruz doesn't dare let the opportunity pass. He kisses me, matching King's gentle touch, and while I'm usually the girl who likes things rough, their soft fingers drawing over my skin and sending heated tingles coursing through my body is like nothing I've ever felt before.

They brush soft kisses over my skin as their hands roam over me, gently exploring every inch of my body. I squirm under their touch, so filled with desire and need. It's electrifying. I don't think I've ever experienced a sensual touch before. I never thought I needed it, but I was so wrong. I've never felt so alive.

Cruz grips his cock, slowly rubbing up and down as King's hard length presses against my ass, grinding and teasing me with just how powerful he can be. I adjust myself between them and reach out, wanting to make them feel just as good as they're doing to me.

I brush my fingers down their bodies as King works my clit and Cruz cups my tits, gently squeezing and pinching my pebbled nipples. My hands curl around both of their cocks and I work them just the same, slowly drawing up and circling my finger over the tips, teasing them before going back down.

Cruz groans as King responds by kissing my neck with a new desperation, his tongue roaming over the sensitive spot under my ear. Cruz doesn't let up, his lips moving against mine in an erotic dance.

My back arches off the bed, my head thrown back as I press my tits harder into Cruz's hand. "Oh God," I moan. "You're going to make me come."

Neither of them eases up, they just keep pushing my body, teasing it with their soft caresses, their skilled fingers, mouths, and tongues. My orgasm builds rapidly within me, burning like an inferno and demanding release. My hands move faster over their cocks and they each respond by picking up their pace.

I cry out, the intensity almost too much. My body squirms and bucks under their touch, but they're relentless. "Fuck, yes," I cry out as my orgasm tears through me like an explosion, my body quivering under their hold. Cruz's mouth drops to my nipple, his tongue flicking over it and sending a jolt of electricity coursing right through to my pussy making me jump and gasp, my orgasm somehow even more electrifying.

"Kiss me," I pant with desperation. "Someone fucking kiss me."

King's lips slam down over mine, swallowing my demands, his tongue instantly sweeping into my mouth as I feel Cruz's smile against my tits.

My body finally begins to calm down, but I don't dare stop my hands from gliding up and down their hard cocks, feeling the thick, angry veins and circling their tips as I go.

Wanting to see their pleasure, I crawl up onto my knees and lean over King before closing my lips around his thick cock. I travel down as far as I can go and feel him right at the back of my throat. Cruz groans with desire, watching the show as he adjusts himself behind me.

With my ass up in the air, Cruz sinks two thick fingers deep inside of my soaking pussy, and a soft moan travels up my throat, prompting King to twist his fingers into my hair. Cruz pushes deeper before pulling his fingers out and spreading my wetness.

Cruz moves his cock up and down my pussy, his tip brushing over my clit and making me jump. He grabs my ass, squeezing my cheeks before slowly pushing his cock deep inside of me, filling me to the brim, stretching my walls and hitting places deep inside of me that I didn't know existed.

He slowly drags out of me and I push back, wanting more as my head continues to bob up and down over King's impressive cock. Cruz's arm twists around my body until I feel his fingers against my clit, and he works it just as slowly as he's working my pussy.

It's pure torture, but I wouldn't have it any other way.

He starts to pick up his pace and I do the same for King as I taste a bit of pre-cum on the tip of his cock. He grips my hair tighter and eases me off his cock, and as I meet his eyes, the desperation and need deep within his own is almost enough to make me lose it. "I need to fill that sweet pussy," he begs of me.

A smile spreads across my face as I lick my lips, but a second later, Cruz pulls out of me and I feel my world crashing until King grabs me and pulls me on top of him. I lower down on his cock and the satisfaction instantly fills me again.

I start riding King and as I lean over to kiss his sweet, sweet lips, Cruz moves in behind me once again. His thumb travels over my ass, testing the waters and gently teasing my hole. I push back with a needy groan, more than ready for a little more, and he instantly picks up what I'm throwing down.

I slow my movements and focus on King's lips as I feel the tip of

Cruz's cock at my entrance. He reaches around and gently massages my clit and as I suck in a breath, he presses into me, filling me until I'm completely stretched.

King groans and as Cruz stills, King slowly begins to move, allowing me a chance to get used to their delicious intrusions.

I can't say that I've ever ridden two dicks before, but fuck me, I don't think this is going to be a last.

"Are you okay?" Cruz asks. "Am I hurting you?"

I push back against him and both the guys groan. "You're hurting me in all the right ways. I need you to move."

King's grip on my hips tighten as Cruz starts to move, and within a second, we each find a rhythm that has us all in euphoria. I drop my lips to King's neck which only pushes my ass higher, and as the boys sensually fuck me, I find another orgasm building deep within me.

Cruz doesn't let up on my clit as King's hands roam over my body. "I'm going to come," I tell them, burying my face right into King's neck as the feel of them completely filling me is almost too much.

"I'm right there with you," Cruz says with a grunt, moving faster as his other hand grips my ass cheek and squeezes it hard. "I can't wait to come in your tight little ass."

His words are like taking a shot that leads straight to my cunt. "Hold onto that thought," King tells me, feeling me beginning to clench around him. He raises my hips just a little and fucks me hard, slamming up into me as Cruz does the same to my ass. The boys fuck me within an inch of my life and I scream out. "FUCK, YES. FUCK ME."

They give it to me hard and brutal, every nerve ending standing on edge, and not a second later, an intense orgasm rocks through my body. I clench down around them both, and just like that, they both come, shooting their hot seed deep within me.

My pussy convulses around King and I crash down into him, his arms instantly circling my body as Cruz collapses to the bed beside us with his hand still claiming my ass. We all take a second, catching our breaths, and as I raise my head to tell them just how fucking amazing that was, I find their irresistible smirks cutting across their faces as they meet each other's eyes, mentally high-fiving each other for a job well done.

"You're both idiots," I laugh, rolling off King's chest and falling into the space between them. Exhaustion crashes through me and just when I'm ready to close my eyes and fall into a deep, blissful sleep, I feel their combined cum spreading between my legs.

I climb over Cruz and slip off the edge of the bed. "Where are you going?" King murmurs, his voice thick with satisfaction.

I look back over my shoulder and meet their lingering stares on my ass as I walk away. "I can feel you both between my legs," I tell them. "I need to shower. Are you coming?"

And just like that, the boys scramble off the bed and race toward the bathroom, more than ready for round two.

35

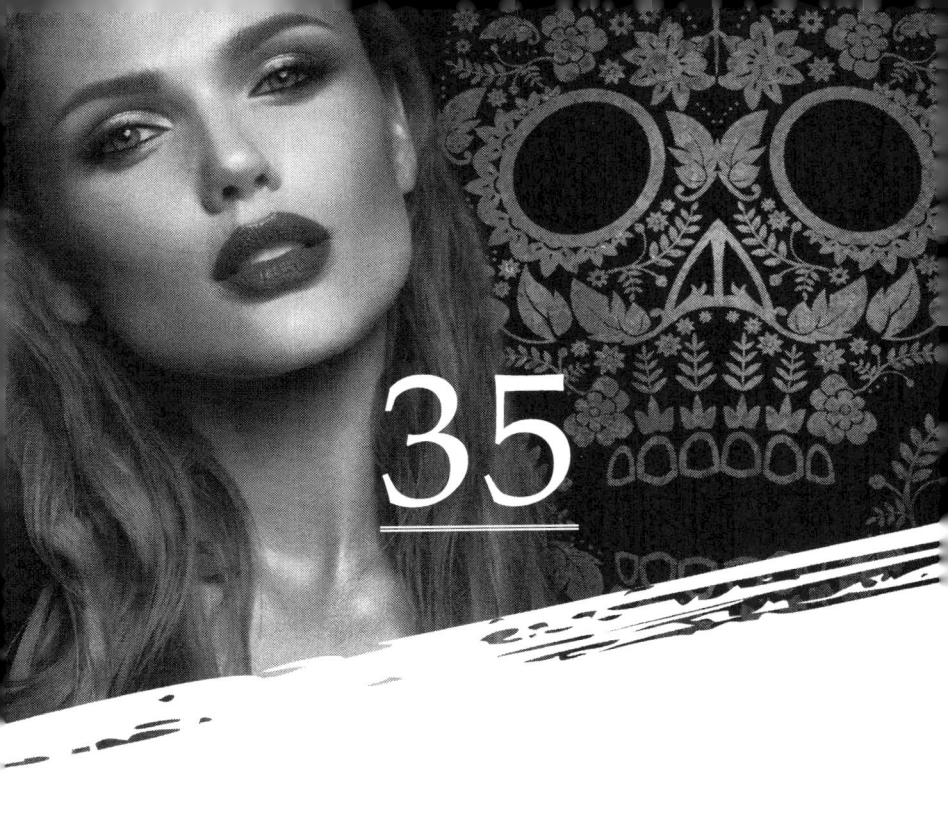

My back arches off my bed as a warm tongue slides from my pussy up to my clit, circling it and traveling back down. A soft moan slips between my lips, and just when I need more, another warm mouth closes down over my nipple, a heated tongue flicking and teasing the tight bud.

My eyes open, and for a minute, I want to kick myself for letting this erotic dream come to an end. But when two thick fingers sink into my pussy, I realize it's not a dream at all, but the best wakeup call a girl could ever need.

I bite down on my lip as my fingers twist into the blankets, scrunching them into my fists. "Good morning," Cruz grumbles, kissing his way up from my breast until his lips are enclosing over the sensitive part of my neck.

"Good morning to you too," I moan as King's tongue flicks over my clit, sending a bolt of electricity pulsing through me. My hand twists into his hair and I instantly feel his wild smile cutting across his face and just when a smile goes to cross my own, he slams his fingers deep inside me and a loud guttural groan is pulled from within. "Oh, fuck. King, yes."

I slip my hand under the blankets and reach for Cruz, and just as my fingers are curling around his thick, veiny cock, my bedroom door flies open and I find Carver looming in the doorway, staring at us with a deep jealousy pulsing in his eyes.

I suck in a gasp as the boys' heads whip around to Carver. My natural reaction is to grab the blanket and cover up, but I don't. I just lie there with my body on display and the pleasure all over my face, letting him see exactly what he's missing out on, and damn it, the longer he gapes at my body, the deeper his jealousy runs.

My fingers brush over my skin and I watch the way he tracks my movements. "Can I help you?" I murmur, my voice low and teasing as my fingers trail down my body, over the curve of my breast, and down between my ribs. "...or do you just like to watch?"

His eyes follow my fingers as they trail down, down, until they find the promised land. I slip two fingers between my folds and slowly circle my clit, making sure to let the softest moan slip between my lips.

Desire pools in his eyes, and just for a second, I think I have him until his eyes harden like stones and he looks at King and then Cruz.

"Get dressed. The sixteen families are here. News of what happened last night has spread and they're demanding an explanation."

Then just like that, he's gone.

My heart instantly kicks into gear and I meet King's stare only to see his own eyes hardening. "Come on," he says, climbing off my bed and finding his clothes as Cruz does the same, neither of them meeting my eyes. "You don't want to keep them waiting."

Fuck.

Realizing I'm not about to wake up to a screaming orgasm, I climb out of bed and quickly get myself dressed into my favorite pair of leather pants, my thigh-high boots, and a black crop, then go just a step further and do my hair and makeup. If I'm about to meet the sixteen heads of the Dynasty families, then I can guarantee I'm going to look like their worst nightmare warmed up when I do.

After painting my lips with my best deep plum lipstick, I fasten the leather choker around my neck and storm through my bedroom door without hesitation. I can't pause for even a second. If I stop to think about what's about to happen, I know I'll lose every bit of my nerve and crumble.

I don't see the guys anywhere downstairs, so I head straight for the door to find it wide open and hear their soft murmured conversation coming from the bottom of the stairs. I walk out to find all four of them standing in a circle, and the second I appear in the doorway, all eyes turn to me, each of them grim except for one.

Usually, I can zone out their stares, but Carver's has me stopping. He's fucking pissed and I don't blame him. Actually, I do blame him a bit. He could have had me just like Cruz and King, but his need to be a cocky dictator stood in the way. If only he was willing to share. It could have been so good.

I tear my gaze away from his jealousy and focus on getting down the stairs without making an ass of myself.

I meet the boys at the bottom, and without a word, they turn and climb into the Escalade. I follow and end up sitting between Cruz and King in the backseat, and when I expect Cruz to grab my thigh or put his arm around me, he keeps perfectly still, keeping his hands to himself.

I don't let it bother me and put it down to the fact that he's about to see his parents for the first time in whoever knows how long. I focus on the drive instead of the screaming silence inside the car. Carver creeps out through my front gate and onto a private road as I suck in a breath.

The otherwise empty road is filled with activity. There are cars parked in nearly every driveway, young children playing in yards, dogs barking, and sprinklers watering the front gardens. "What the hell is this?" I ask, scanning my gaze over the houses as we pass each one.

"I told you," Carver grunts from the driver's seat, refusing to meet my stare. "The families are back in town."

"Yeah, but ..." I let my words trail off as pieces of the puzzle begin falling into place. "Do they all ...?"

"Live here?" Grayson finishes for me. "Yes. There are seventeen homes on this street for the seventeen families of Dynasty."

"But ... how? How do you all live by one another while you're all trying to kill each other?"

"It never used to be like that," King explains. "Before it all became hostile, it was more like one big family, at least, that's how my mom described it. There were apparently grand balls and parties. Now, everyone lives in private, and only returns for council meetings."

Well, shit. It actually sounds like Dynasty might have been kind of cool back in the day, before my family was murdered and the dickhead half of the group decided that they wanted to rule the world and take over governments.

Carver continues down the road, and just before he reaches the main gate, he takes a sharp turn to the right and follows a small road around the first property. I stare in wonder. I don't know if I'm imagining things or just unobservant, but I have never even noticed this road down here before. I figured it was just the one road.

The road is small and I realize that I never noticed it before because the majority of it is hidden behind the first property. My brows drop as I find a building at the end of the road that looks like a small warehouse.

Carver drives right up to it, and I watch as he rolls his window down, leaning out to enter a code. The warehouse door automatically rises, and Carver gently hits the gas and drives in.

I look around, but as it is, there's really not much to look at. It's just an empty warehouse. The automatic door starts closing, blocking out the sunlight as it goes, and making my heart race with anticipation. "Okay," I say, glancing around at each of the guys. "What the hell is this?"

Not one of the assholes responds, and judging by the way they quickly glance at one another, I'd dare say that they're nervous about this too.

The automatic door locks us into darkness, and without warning, the whole car jumps. My hands fly out and I grip Cruz and King on either side of me. "WHY THE FUCK IS THE CAR MOVING?"

Fucking silence.

The whole car starts sinking into the ground and it takes me far too long to realize that we're on some kind of car elevator. It starts spinning us until we're facing the direction we'd come in, and before I know it, we're under the ground and the elevator is coming to a stop.

"What the ever-loving fuck is this?" I breathe in astonishment as I look out at the underground parking garage that lives just beneath our homes. Carver hits the gas and pulls into a spot. As he does, I realize that there are exactly sixteen other cars. Sixteen ridiculously expensive, once in a lifetime, fancy car show kinds of cars. Regular people like me can't even afford to look at cars like these. Though, I guess I'm not as regular as I'd always thought.

We all pile out, and as we walk to the exit of the parking garage, I notice the boys fall into formation around me, and we all walk in a diamond shape, the boys protecting me from whatever bullshit we're about to find in there.

We make our way toward a door and I can't help but look up at Cruz. "What is this?" I ask, knowing damn well that he's not about to answer.

"You'll see," he tells me.

I resist rolling my eyes but my train of thought leaves me as we finally reach the door and Carver curls his fingers around the handle. He looks back at me with a knowing grin before slowly opening the door and letting the private parking garage flood with the clinical light from within. "Winter, this is Dynasty," he says, waving his hand through the open door to invite me in. "Welcome home."

I step through the door in silence, my eyes widening as I take in the impressive reception area with the word 'DYNASTY' in massive block letters across the wall. The room must be the size of just one of the properties above and something tells me that the hallways and doors leading off from here span the entire way back to my place, and probably lead halfway through the city.

I look around the reception area and note that it kinda looks like the lobby area of one of those huge skyrise buildings, just without the hundreds of busy nine-to-fivers rushing around. There's a long desk with absolutely no one sitting behind it, and as we approach it, I notice a Dynasty Directory and scoff under my breath.

"What's wrong?" King grumbles beside me.

I just shake my head. "Is this place seriously that big that you need a directory to figure out where you're going?"

Grayson looks back at me. "That entrance we just came through is one of ten. Dynasty is a whole underground world that spans the length of Ravenwood Heights. It's why we didn't just walk down here. Sometimes, you need to drive."

I raise my brow as I take it all in. "So where are we going now?"

"Council chambers," Carver says, walking in front of me and not looking back. "It's where official meetings take place, and it's situated directly under your home, which is the heart of Ravenwood Heights."

"I'm sorry?" I question, glancing around the guys for clarification.

Cruz takes pity on me. "If you were to pinpoint your home on a map of Ravenwood Heights, you'll find it's directly in the very center of town; hence your home and the council chambers below it, are the very heart of Ravenwood Heights."

"That's kinda cheesy," I tell him, realizing that Ravenwood Heights must be much bigger than I'd realized. I'd always thought that our private little road was on the outskirts of town. Though, it wouldn't be the first thing I've been wrong about.

Cruz shrugs his shoulders. "Don't shoot the messenger. It's your grandfather who built it that way."

That tiny bit of information is enough to warm the cold seeping into my heart and keep my head held high.

We walk for ten minutes, the boys remaining in a diamond formation around me which only serves to remind me just how deadly they can be. After last night, I'll never question their ability to protect me, even though the families of two of these guys want me dead. These four guys put their lives at risk for me, and judging by the way they look around each corner, I'd dare say they might be doing it again.

My legs begin to burn, and I'm just about ready to make my first declaration. That as the new leader of this strange institution, I'll be getting those mall cop hoverboards to get around.

I file that thought away for later because I'm damn sure that it's a good one. I don't know about the big guys, but I'm sure to win over the little ones with a move like that.

Carver comes to a stop and turns to look at me, and for the first time since meeting him, I see a hint of fear in his eyes. "There's going to be a big table with all sixteen families, each of the family heads sitting with their wife and any children of age directly behind them. You're to silently walk in and take your position at the head of the table. You're not expected to say anything, but when directly spoken to, it will be wise to answer with your head held high. Do not give them a chance to question who you are. You need to prove that you can do this. Do not even give a hint of weakness. You are your father's daughter."

I nod and Grayson steps directly into my line of sight. "We cannot stand with you, Elodie. We are here as representatives of our individual families, and as the men who witnessed and dealt with last night's crimes. But if it comes down to it, you know that we have your back," he tells me, momentarily shocking the absolute shit out of me. "We are not to talk or speak up for you unless directly asked, so for the most part, you are alone in this. Don't blow it."

Nerves begin pulsing through me and I just nod, not knowing what the hell to really expect despite their explanations. Carver meets my stare and nods. "Are you ready for this?"

"No," I tell him honestly. "But from the sound of it, I don't really have a choice."

36

The door opens to a dark room, and I see a massive round table, spotlights shining down on the seventeen seats around it. Each chair is taken and I keep my head held high as my gaze swiftly scans around the room.

The men on the right-hand side of the table look pleased to see me, while the other half on the left wear heavy scowls stretched far across their faces. It's easy to see who the head of each family is, and who I need to watch out for.

There is one chair at the very top of the room left vacant and has been that way for the past eighteen years, at least I'm assuming, but today, I'll take it, and somehow, I have to be proud of that.

Carver moves back, allowing me to step into the room first, just how any leader should make an entrance. I keep my chin raised with a blank expression, fighting the need to lash out at the eight men who watch me from across the room. Each of them should be held personally responsible for the murder of my parents and the attempted murder of me.

My boots click against the expensive flooring and I watch out of the corner of my eye as the four boys enter the room and discreetly make their way to their families, standing behind them with their mothers and presenting a united front, but something tells me it's anything but, especially when it comes to Grayson and Carver.

I place myself at the top of the table, and keeping my chin held high, I look over my people, feeling more out of place than ever before. How am I supposed to rule this group of hateful men? Despite my bloodline, I'm still just a nobody foster kid at heart.

From the top of the table, I get a better view of the sixteen families staring back at me, and I take my time, slowly scanning each face and committing it to memory, especially the faces of my enemies. I find Carver's father instantly. He's the spitting image of his son, give or take forty years or so. I can't help but lift my gaze to Carver's, and without a word spoken between us, it's clear that he doesn't want anything to do with the man he stands behind.

I move on, finding Grayson's father next. He looks nothing like his father, but I see the similarities in his mother, who from a distance looks like the sweetest woman I'll ever meet. But I won't be fooled, especially from a woman who sits on the left-hand side of the table.

As I continue around the room, a face stands out to me. Jacob Scardoni—Ember's boyfriend. I suck in a small gasp, but for the most part, keep my expression neutral. Jacob's eyes meet mine across the grand table, and I hold his stare, silently telling him just how badly he fucked up. I feel like a bomb has just been dropped on me, but when I mentally go over the list of names Carver had given me last night, Scardoni was one of them, but I didn't put two and two together, and that's on me. I was too focused on two other names that were mentioned.

Jacob's gaze drops, not able to handle the pressure that comes from my stare, and I clench my jaw, suddenly not so approving of Ember's choice of men. I will deal with him in time. If I had known he was a part of Dynasty, a part of the families that sent a group of hitmen to kill me, I never would have encouraged her relationship with him. But for the most part, I can't help the feeling that he's getting close to her just to get information on me.

I shake off the surprise and move across to the opposite side of the table, the side that's bound to give me the courage to stand up here and say what needs to be said.

I look straight to Cruz before glancing over his family and finding his mother. She's beautiful and the way her eyes shine just like her son's makes me long for my own mother. I quickly look to his father and find a strong, confident man who looks like a complete hard-ass, but the fact that he's sitting on the right side of the table speaks volumes.

King's family is next, and just like Carver and his dad, King and his father are like carbon copies of each other, only King senior puts a little more effort into his dark hair, not allowing his unruly locks to fall into his eyes.

Feeling my confidence beginning to soar, I finally take my seat, sliding into the chair that has remained vacant for far too long. Every eye in the room remains on me, and while I'm not about to give some heartwarming speech, I'm sure as hell about to get this shit over and done with. "Let's get this started, shall we?" I say, keeping my head raised just as Carver had said to. "Now, I'm not going to stand before you and make a mockery of your rules and policies. I know nothing of them, so I'm going to call it like I see it and deal with the fallout later. There are a few topics that must be discussed; some more important than others."

"Yes," the man directly to my right responds while giving me an encouraging smile and making me wish they all had name tags. "Let me start by saying how wonderful it is to see you, Miss Ravenwood. Your parents were such generous people, your father especially. It was a sad day when they were taken from this world. It's been a long time coming, but we are all thrilled to see you finally coming of age and taking your role as the head of Dynasty."

Geez. What a suck-up. I give the man beside me a warm smile. "Your name, sir?"

"Earnest Brooks," he tells me.

"Thank you, Earnest," I say. "While your words certainly are kind, they are not reassuring considering that I spent my night racing through the dark woods of the King property while being chased by no less than ten hitmen. Mark my words, I will find the families responsible for last night's attack, and I will deal with them accordingly."

"Of course," Earnest says. "We were appalled to hear of the attack taken against you last night and we stand with you. There were twelve bodies found on the property, all hired hitmen. However, we are lucky that we have such skilled young men who so willingly protected and served you as our leader. Rest assured, Miss Ravenwood, Dynasty will not let this go unpunished."

Twelve? Shit. Though I can't say that I'm not impressed. I guessed there were ten hitmen in the woods last night and that was a wild guess, but twelve? Wow. The boys certainly are skilled. They're more than that, they're incredible, and I was extremely lucky to have them by my side. I wouldn't have stood a chance without them.

"Laying it on a bit thick there, Earnest," comes a booming voice from across the table. I follow the insulting tone and meet Jacob's father. "Who's to say this had anything to do with Dynasty? She comes waltzing in here and instantly starts blaming the very families of our beloved organization. The girl has been a foster kid for the past eighteen years. We've all heard the stories of random attacks outside of clubs and bars. She has a history of violence. Who knows how many enemies she's made over the years? Enemies who are now our own. Perhaps she brought this on herself and is now using her situation to tarnish our great name."

Gasps come from the other side of the table. "How dare you speak ill of Miss Ravenwood like that." King's father demands.

Before some teenage back and forth bullshit can start, I stand and make my way around the table, keeping my eyes on Jacob's father.

"Your name?" I demand, spitting the words with irritation as I pass Carver, who somehow gives me the courage to stand taller, the pride in his eyes telling me that despite me stepping way out of line, that I'm heading down the right path.

"Preston Scardoni," his name is all but growled as though offering it up to a nobody like me is beneath him.

"Well, well, Preston," I say, stepping in right behind him, no doubt making him nervous as I make up the rules as I go, but fuck it, if I'm the leader, I shouldn't have to be held to rules that are over eighteen years old. I'll run this show exactly how I see fit. "You sound pretty fucking defensive here. Who's to say that you're not the culprit behind this attack? After all, your son was in attendance of my party last night. He could have easily given up my location."

Preston scoffs as the occupants on the other side of the table seem to sit a little straighter. "You have no proof that my son was at that party. It was on King property; therefore, responsibility should fall on Tobias. He should be punished accordingly. Besides, you are our leader, and I would be a fool to step out against you."

"That's fucking bullshit and you know it," I snap, accidentally letting the real Winter show as protests come from King's father.

I make my way back to the head of the table and look at the people around me. "You know what I think?" I say. "I think that there are a select group of men who are threatened by an eighteen-year-old girl taking over leadership, which only goes to prove that their loyalties lie with themselves and not to their cause. I also think that the same group of men responsible for trying to kill me last night are the very men responsible for the murder of Andrew and London Ravenwood."

"That's ridiculous," Carver's father announces, cautiously looking to the other side of the table, his defense instantly putting him on my radar. "Your parents were killed in a house fire out of town, one you were lucky to survive yourself. Don't be stupid, girl. Don't try and dig up old scars. We all mourn your parents."

"You think I'm stupid for challenging your lies, where I think you're a fool for not realizing how easily I see through them."

More gasps are heard around the table, some of outrage while others are filled with laughter. I get the impression that these men are rarely challenged and the thought sends a thrill shooting through me.

Carver's father stands. "My lies?" he demands in an outrage. "I had nothing to do with the Ravenwood deaths. I will not be made a mockery. I am the head of the Carver family. I demand your respect."

"You do not deserve my respect," I spit at him. "Let's cut the crap, yeah? There are eight families all lining the left side of this very table who conspired against my family and murdered my parents, each of you as guilty as the next, and I can assure you that those plans were not discussed or ever brought forward to the gentlemen who sit on the opposite side of the table. I have been hidden away for eighteen years because of the disgraceful men sitting before me, eighteen years of hell, eighteen years of having absolutely no idea who I am or where I belong. The fact that I was hidden away only goes to prove their suspicions against you. You took my world away from me when you murdered my parents, and I will not rest until I have taken everything that you hold dear. Where is my justice? You may have ended my parents, but I will not sit back and allow you to do the same to me."

I take a breath, trying to calm myself before continuing. "I heard that Dynasty once used to be an organization to be proud of, but what I see is an embarrassment of old men who have been let loose for far too long, an organization full of corruption and lies. And while I never met Gerald Ravenwood, I can guarantee that he would be ashamed of what has become of Dynasty, ashamed of the eight men sitting to my left." I focus my stare back on Carver's father. "So, while I would love to stand here and make a mockery of you, I do not need to because it seems that you, along with the other seven men sitting around you, have already achieved that task on your own."

I hold his stare as his face burns a bright red. I can feel Carver's less than impressed stare on me, and I don't doubt that we're going to have a few words of our own, but right now, that's the least of my problems.

Carver's father doesn't respond, so I give him one last chance to stake his claim in front of the whole organization. "So, what's it going to be, Mr. Carver? Are you publicly declaring that your loyalties lie to yourself or to the greater good of Dynasty?"

He huffs, only proving how much of an ass he is, and I hold his stare even longer, relentless in my attack against him. He finally bows his head, not willing to publicly stand against me and bring eighteen years of suspicion to his doorstep. "Of course, Miss Ravenwood. You have my loyalty and my full cooperation."

"You will not stand in my way as I investigate my parents' murders and the attack brought on me last night?"

"No," he growls, averting his eyes. "I will not stand in your way."

"Good." I finally take my seat again, and glance around the room, feeling my nerves beginning to creep up on me again. I didn't know how that was going to go. I had absolutely no plan of attack, but I think it went well. At last, I hope it went well. The fire burning in Carver's eyes suggests that maybe it didn't, while the nervous energy pouring out of King and Cruz only makes me feel sick. Maybe I fucked up.

I glance back at Earnest, having absolutely no idea where to go from here, but he thankfully picks up on my silent cry for help, picking up where I left off. "There is the matter of your initiation, Miss Ravenwood," he tells me. "It is a matter of great urgency."

"Initiation?" I question.

"Yes, ma'am," he says with pride. "Every child born into the Dynasty family is initiated into our ranks on their eighteenth birthday, and unfortunately, at the time of your eighteenth birthday, you were otherwise ... unavailable."

"How urgent is this exactly?"

"We have the ceremony scheduled for this afternoon followed by a grand celebration for our lost heir."

My eyes flick up to Cruz who discreetly nods, and just like that, I give Earnest a forced smile. "Of course. Is there anything else that needs to be discussed?"

"There is a brief induction that we will need to take you through to show you the role that you will be taking on. Usually, this is a tradition passed from a father to his heir after their initiation. However, we find ourselves in a unique situation. Tobias King was your father's closest friend and has personally offered to take you through your induction over the following weeks."

I sit up straighter looking over at King's father in a new light to see a fondness shining in his eyes. He nods, and just like that, I feel like I finally have a connection to my father. I nod back as a mutual respect forms between us. "Thank you," I tell him. "I appreciate that."

"It's the least I could do for Andrew. He would have done the same had the tables been turned," he explains. "Though I do warn you, the position that you are inheriting should not be taken lightly. There is much to learn, and what comes with great power also comes with great burden. I will do my best to guide you through it."

"Thank you," I whisper again before glancing up at the proud man who stands tall behind him. King meets my eye and winks, and for the first time this morning, I feel as though I just did something right.

I glance around the room. "Is that it or can we wrap this thing up?"

The gentleman who sits directly between Tobias King and Mr. Danforth stands. "Sebastian Whitman, Miss Ravenwood," he says, introducing himself. "There is the matter of your wellbeing over the past few weeks."

"I'm sorry?" I ask, watching both Cruz and King flinch and tense at his words.

"The sons of my fellow families were tasked with your protection on your arrival in Ravenwood Heights. I would like to call on Dante Carver, Grayson Beckett, Hunter King, and Cruz Danforth to find out exactly what has been going on. It has come to my attention that not only did you fall into the hands of Sam Delacorte and were put to auction, but you were arrested on murder charges, and have been involved in many violent altercations."

I raise my brows as I see the four guys shifting in their spots ready to stand front and center to explain themselves, but I hold up a hand, stopping them. "You can call on them all you like, but this is on me. They are not at fault. They kept me safe when it mattered. Yes, I fell into the hands of Sam Delacorte after I went against Kin—Hunter's warnings to stay away. I was arrested on murder charges because I killed the man who offered me up to Sam. And as for the altercations ... what can I say? When someone tries to fuck with me or put their hands on my body, I simply handle my business, just as you've all taught your own sons and daughters to do. But when twelve hitmen were sent after me, those four boys were exactly where I needed them, and for that, you cannot fault them. They have done everything in their power to keep me safe despite the shots that continuously keep coming our way. So, you can punish them, but you will be punishing me right along with them."

Sebastian looks across the table at Carver and Grayson before looking around the table. "All in favor to excuse these four men of their reckless endangerment of our leader, Miss Elodie Ravenwood, raise your right hand."

I look around the table and see every hand risen and realize that all eyes are on me. "How do you vote?" Earnest asks from beside me.

"Oh, um ..." I raise my right hand. "They shall be excused."

"Very well," Sebastian says, taking his seat. "Unless anyone else has anything to add ..." He lets his sentence trail off, and as silence falls through the room, the meeting is classified as done.

Without another word, the gentlemen around the table stand and begin excusing themselves from the room with their families on their heels, but I remain in my seat, watching each of them closely, especially the eight who stand to my left. Gazes shift across the room, and before they even walk through the door, I know without a doubt that they're already conspiring against me.

Each of the guys walk out with their families and I'm left alone in the big room. It's stupid. I shouldn't remain here and put myself at risk like this but something keeps me seated.

A war is brewing.

I slowly stand, looking out over the empty table, realizing just how toxic Dynasty really is. It's an organization that may have once stood proud, built on the foundation of loyalty, but now it is anything but. It's family against family, it's secrets, lies, and cover-ups. It's brutal murders, it's devastation, it's a complete disgrace, and I refuse to be the leader of it.

Carver has made it clear that it's not something I can just walk away from. It's in my blood and I am the only heir, so I will do what I have to do.

I will stand tall and accept my position. I will gain their trust and be their leader. I will govern their practices and guide their hearts, and just when I can finally stand proudly before them as the woman my father and grandfather always wanted me to be …

I'm going to burn it all to hell—the boys be damned.

37

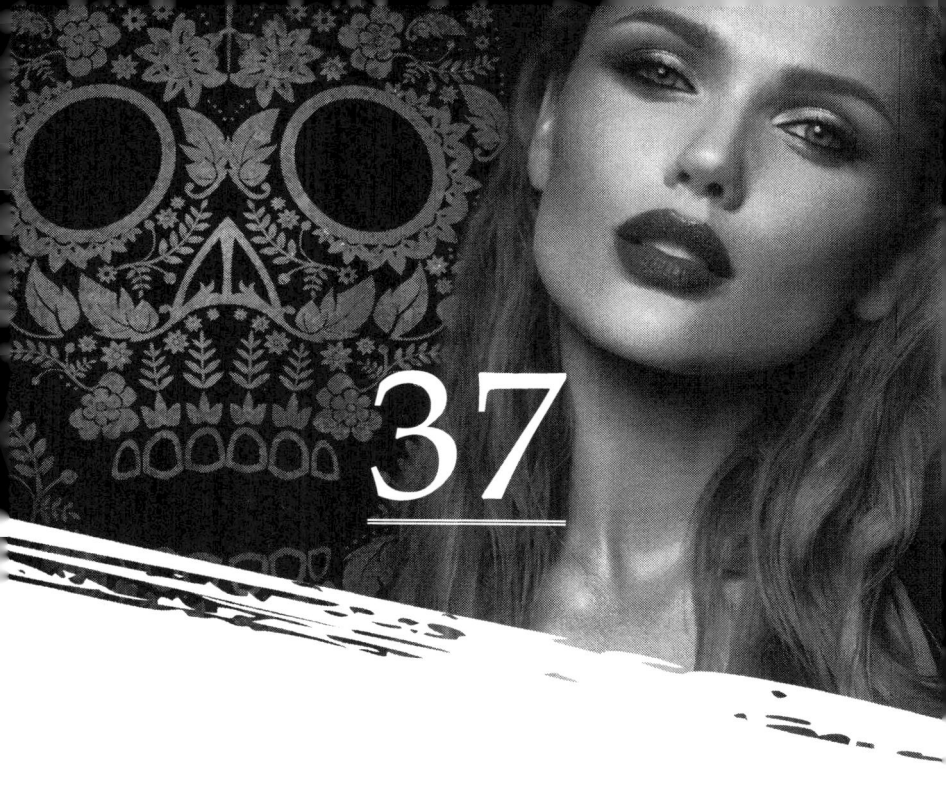

The black silk gown wraps around my body like a second skin, and I slap on a fake smile as I make my way down the grand staircase that leads into the most stunning ballroom I've ever seen, or perhaps the only ballroom I've ever seen.

People must have been working on this all day. The room is perfect and has been decorated exactly to my liking. Black drapes, black carpet runners, black decorations, and even a black chandelier. I can't believe it. When a woman approached me and asked about decorations, I figured she'd shrug me off when I said that I wanted everything black. I mean, where did they even find a black chandelier? It's like a twisted Halloween ball in here just without the fake spider webs, pumpkins, and skeletons. Though, if I was to start opening closets, I'm sure I'll find plenty of skeletons hiding in them.

I focus on the stairs in front of me, one stiletto heel in front of another. After all, all eyes are on me, the good, the bad, and the ugly. I want nothing more than to turn around and race back out of here before I make a complete ass of myself, but I know that's not an option.

I've never felt so lost. When I walked out of the Council Chamber, I was expecting to find the four boys waiting for me. Instead, I was formally met by the heads of the families, each of them giving me some sob story about my parents, putting their hand on my shoulder, and calling me Elodie. Not one of the boys were to be seen until I found Cruz lurking in my mother's closet less than twenty minutes ago, holding the gown and demanding my stupid ass put it on. I had to find my own way out of the underground world, and when I say it wasn't fun, I mean it.

I haven't seen the other guys, but I can't help but feel a strain between us, which is ridiculous, seeing as though I haven't actually seen them yet. Maybe it's because I'm officially their leader, or perhaps because I had to save their asses in that meeting. Maybe they're embarrassed about the whole thing, but something tells me that they're not the type to care about shit like that. Maybe they're just pissed that my declaration to find the culprit who ordered my parents' deaths will surely cause a little trouble. But I'm sure they can handle it. If they can fend off twelve hitmen at a time, they can handle a bunch of pissed off old guys.

A hand is presented as I reach the final step of the grand staircase and I meet Cruz's heated stare, the desire in his eyes instantly speaking to that wild, animalistic part of myself that tends to come out whenever he's around. "You look fucking delic—"

"Don't even think about finishing that sentence," I murmur, keeping my voice low as my eyes skim across the room to find King and Grayson huddled by the bar, their mouths dropped as they stare at me like they're seeing a stranger.

Carver stands by his father's side, his face a hard mask, his thoughts impossible to read. "I feel like a goth barbie in this ridiculous dress. The only good thing about it is that it's got hidden pockets and I don't need to hide shit in my bra. Why couldn't I just wear what I usually wear?"

"Because it's a formal initiation and wearing anything less than a gown would be seen as you shitting all over our traditions."

"Your traditions suck. What if I am shitting all over them?"

"Then I'd kindly request that you do it with a proud smile so that these fuckers don't pick up on it," he grumbles, leading me through the crowd that instantly parts to make way, making me feel so much more important than I really am.

I look up at Cruz's beautiful green eyes and give him a wide, proud smile that nearly knocks him off his feet. "How's that for bullshit?" I grumble through my smile.

"Fucking perfect," he laughs to himself. "You're a natural-born deceiver."

My smile falls from my face, and for a brief second, I wonder if he knows what I'm up to. The thought fades away as we reach the small staircase that leads up onto a stage at the far side of the room, presumably where the initiation is going to happen.

"Do you remember what to do?" Cruz asks, leading me up the stairs as everyone begins to gather around.

"It's not rocket science," I tell him. "Pretty sure that I can handle it."

"Very well. Just don't fuck it up. They don't take lightly to that shit, especially from you."

"Sounds like you're talking from experience."

His lips press into a hard line and I want nothing more than to kiss them deeply when a man steps into my side and offers me his elbow. I glance up to find King's father, Tobias King. "Miss Ravenwood, please allow me to escort you to the dais for your initiation and vow of allegiance."

I drop my hand from Cruz's before taking Tobias' and allowing him to lead me across the stage with the eyes of the whole organization on me. Cruz disappears and goes to stand with Grayson and King, and for just a brief moment, I want nothing more than for Carver to go and join them. Why is he being so weird? Does his father have some kind of hold over him?

Tobias brings me to a stop in the very center of the stage to where a small dais is set with two objects—a fancy as fuck diamond-encrusted dagger that looks like it belongs in a museum, and a plaque with seventeen inscriptions, every family name of Dynasty with Ravenwood the biggest, top and center.

A flare of pride shoots through me until Tobias spreads his arms wide and looks out at his members. "My Dynasty family, I stand before you with the news we have always prayed for. Let me officially introduce you to our lost heir—Miss Elodie Ravenwood, daughter of the late Andrew and London Ravenwood."

Gasps are heard all over the room and it takes me a moment to work out that only the members who are of age would have known that I was alive. As for everyone else, they're only just now discovering my existence. The gasps quickly turn to applause, which morphs into full blown cheers that have me seeking out the boys. I can't say that I've ever been on the other end of an adoring crowd, but I'm sure they experience it every day.

King and Cruz wear proud smiles across their faces as Grayson raises his chin, silently telling me to put on a show, so I do just that and plaster my fake smile across my face and look out at my new adoring fans. I feel Carver's heated stare from across the room, and I can't help but turn his way, seeking out the confidence and the approval that he's always there to give me, but all I get in return is his unnerving glare that tears at something within me.

I long for him, desperate to have things go back to how they were before I found out who his family was, before he pressed me up against that stupid tree, kissed me like he'd never kiss a woman again, and then rejected me. I missed him in my bed last night. I've become way too reliant on his comfort, and that's a mistake that I'm going to have to suffer with because something tells me that I've seen the end of the nights where he would hold me tight and keep the monsters at bay.

Now I have a whole new set of monsters to fight, only this time, the monsters aren't in my head. They're as real as can be, and despite the stupid smile I wear across my face, I've never been so terrified. But I will defeat them. I will annihilate them until there's not a damn thing left.

"So, let us not waste another second and initiate young Elodie into our Dynasty family and finally bring her home."

Cheers are heard all around, and for a moment, I'm left wondering if this is how it always is or if tonight is just extra special.

Tobias waves and asks me to step up to the dais and I do just that. As the crowd begins to settle down, Tobias collects the dagger and presents it to me. "Are you ready for this?" he questions, keeping his tone low.

I nod as I accept the dagger in my hands. "Yes. I know what to do."

Tobias gives me a warm smile, one that I'd expect a father to give a daughter, and for a moment, I feel that connection to my father again. "Okay," he tells me. "Let's get started."

I smile back at him. It's showtime.

"Elodie Ravenwood," he says, his voice loud, somehow bouncing off every wall of the ballroom. "Dynasty welcomes you with open arms into our family and into our home. You are of our being, of our blood, and no longer a child, but an adult coming home to join our ranks, not only as our equal, but as our rightful leader, our heir, and ruler. It is my pleasure to initiate you into our family, and bring our lost daughter home."

There is a booming applause from the crowd, and for a brief

second, I think that it's over until I remember there's a whole question and answers portion of the night.

"Please make your eternal, sacred vows," Tobias continues. "Will you, Elodie Ravenwood, bleed for your people?"

"Yes," I declare, pressing the tip of the knife into my palm and slicing through my flesh until blood pools in my hand. "I will bleed for my people."

"Will you protect them with all that you are?"

I tip my hand over, allowing my blood to cover the plaque and run over the seventeen family names. "Yes. I will protect them."

"Will you stand against all evil and fight for the good of our cause?"

I resist rolling my eyes as I take the plaque and hold it above my head as a declaration that I will hold Dynasty and the families that it was built upon above everything, including myself. "I will stand against evil and fight for the good of our cause."

And then finally, he wraps it up with his final question. "Will you always uphold your values put in play by the great Gerald Ravenwood, and remain loyal to all that is Dynasty?"

Placing the plaque back down and turning to face every man, woman, and child who stands within the walls of the ballroom, I drop to my knee, placing my hand over my heart. "I will forever remain loyal to all that is Dynasty."

"All hail Dynasty."

And just like a broken record, every voice in the ballroom repeats their declaration, mine included as I remain on my knee. "All hail

Dynasty."

The crowd cheers, and I watch over them, feeling like a complete imposter. What the hell was my grand-daddy drinking when he founded this bullshit? It's a fucking cult, not a prestigious organization. A blood vow? That's fucking insane, but it's done now, and I won't have to worry about it again. I just have to make these fuckers think they can trust me so I can destroy everything they believe in because this version of Dynasty is not what it was intended to be. I know I never knew my grandfather, or my own father for that matter, but I believe in them, I share their blood, and this couldn't be what they were trying to build.

As I raise from my knee, Tobias meets me with a bandage for my hand and instantly presses it to my wound. I suck in a breath before he works quickly, and before I know it, King is standing behind me on the little stage and offering me his hand. "It's customary to dance."

My brows crease. "Seriously?"

"Sorry."

I take his hand with a groan and allow him to lead me back down the stairs, being careful with my wounded hand. "So, did you draw the short straw?"

King leads me onto the dance floor and swings me around until I'm facing him with his hand on my lower back and mine resting against his chest. "Rock, paper, scissors," he tells me with a groan. "I don't know how he does it, but I swear Cruz cheats."

I can't help but laugh, imagining these beyond serious guys in their fancy-ass suits fighting over who has to dance with the girl. "I don't think it's possible to cheat during rock, paper, scissors, but let me apologize for how awful the idea of dancing with me must be."

King's arm tightens around my waist and he pulls me in while trying his hardest not to show his emotions as the whole room watches us. "You're an idiot," he tells me. "I'm honored to dance with you, fucking thrilled actually, but we all know exactly what you're going to think of this and neither of us wanted to suffer through the punishment of having been the one to force you into it."

"Good point."

"And for the record," he adds. "I like getting my dick wet, and if that gets withheld, I'm going to be fucking devastated."

A real, deep belly laugh pulls from within me, and before I know it, I'm losing myself to the music and to the feel of King's arms around me as the other couples do the same. He spins me around, and for a quick minute, I'm pretty damn impressed with his skills. Apparently, he can do a lot more than screw and kill. I wonder what other secrets he's been hiding from me.

I'm just about to suggest that we sneak away so that he can show me all the other ways he knows how to move his body when the sound of a throat clearing beside us has me pausing and tearing my gaze away from the handsome man in my arms.

I come to a stop as I find the older version of Carver bearing down on me, his hand outstretched and the eyes of the room still watching my every move. "May I have this dance?" he says, though his tone suggests that I better not argue.

King's grip tightens on my body but not being in a position to argue, he reluctantly takes a step back and offers Carver's father my hand. "Sir," King says out of duty, certainly not respect.

Carver senior's eyes swing to mine and he instantly grips my wounded hand, holding it far too tight as he pulls me in. "Smile," he murmurs in my ear. "We wouldn't want anyone to assume their new leader is less than thrilled with her new position."

Feeling backed into a corner, I force a smile across my lips and find myself staring across the room to where Carver stands, watching us with concern in his eyes. "You have real nerve to approach me like this," I spit, while desperately trying to keep my voice down, though the hatred is clear in not only my tone but my eyes as well. "I know you had something to do with the attack on me last night and played a role in my parents' death."

"Let it go," he laughs. "You're such a girl and only a child at that. You're not capable of handling the pressures of leadership. So, this is what we're going to do. You're going to be the face of the organization but you will answer to me."

"You're fucking insane."

"Watch your tone," he growls back at me, his act slipping for just a second before he pulls himself back together. He tightens his hold on my sore hand and I feel the blood beginning to seep through the bandage. "Let me put this in terms you may better understand. Either you answer to me, or I will continue with my endeavor to end your life."

I gasp and stare in horror while trying to pull out of his arms, but he holds me tighter while the rest of the room continues to spin around us, completely oblivious to the tension rising in the center of the room. It's one thing thinking you know something, but having it confirmed is a completely different kind of shot to the gut. "I knew it," I spit. "You were responsible for killing my parents."

His eyes sparkle with laughter. "Surprise! You caught me," he says. "Your father was weak, just as you are. He wasn't capable of running an organization like this. Dynasty is bigger than him. It has such great potential but needs a true leader to guide her in the right direction. Dynasty could rule the world. We've already infiltrated governments and taken control of the stocks. We need to strike, and when we do it, it will be under my rule, and the world will know my name."

"I will never answer to you," I demand. "You're a piece of shit. You have absolutely nothing to offer the world except your shitty bullying tactics and your bad breath. You're a murderer and I will have nothing to do with you."

He just laughs, a sick sound that makes my ears want to bleed. He pulls me in close until my body is pressed right up against his, his hand against the soft silk of my dress. "Stop acting like you care, princess. I've watched you grow up. You don't care about your parents. You have no real affection toward them. They're just the people who share your blood, but for what it's worth, your mother screamed as I stood above her bed and made her watch the sharp blade of my knife slice across her husband's throat. Blood soaked the bed, but once I slit hers, it pooled. It was quite a remarkable sight."

My whole body shakes with anger, tears threatening to spill from my eyes, but he forces me to stay, forces me to keep up appearances.

"You, Miss Elodie," he continues, proudly telling me of his

betrayal, certain that he's untouchable. "You proved to be harder than I thought. You were only two months old. I should have suffocated you. I should have gone through with it, but I had a son of my own and couldn't bring myself to do it, so I lit the fire. At least they got that part of the story right, those stupid fools. If I had known that you had made it out of that fire, I would have taken your life then and there, but imagine my surprise years later when a rumor of the lost heir hit my doorstep. I tried to find you time and time again, but you always slipped away, always one step ahead of me."

I suck in a breath. "You're the reason I jumped from home to home."

"Not anymore, Elodie," he tells me. "You and I are going to be partners. Now, smile for your audience."

My mind races with fear, with thoughts, and untold horrors of a future living with this man in my life. He's worse than Kurt. He's an absolute monster. I can't do it.

I shake my head, seeking out Carver's stare but it's not there, none of them are. They promised to always protect me, and here we are, right when I need them most and they're nowhere to be found.

This man murdered my family. He set my home on fire. He took away my future. Because of him, I lived with eighteen different families, some so much worse than the other. Because of him, I had to learn how to fight. Because of him, my life was a nightmare.

He slit their throats; he took their lives, and now he stands before me laughing.

No, he will not get away with this. I promised to seek justice and deliver punishment accordingly, but when it comes to my parents, nothing is quite as just as an eye for an eye. The music begins to fade at the end of the song, and I know I only have a few seconds before he walks away.

My hand slips into the hidden pockets of my mother's silk gown and my fingers curl around the hilt of the old diamond-encrusted dagger that I'd stolen from the dais. I yank it out of my pocket and without a second of hesitation, I slam the sharp blade up through Mr. Carver's stomach with every ounce of my strength, pushing it up between his ribs, and knowing without a doubt that I've pierced his lung.

His eyes widen as he lets out a deep groan, his hand falling to his stomach. "Wha—"

"I hope you rot in the deepest pits of hell," I tell him, yanking out the dagger and letting the blood pour from his wound.

The dagger falls to the marble floor, clattering almost in slow motion, and gaining the attention of everybody in the room.

The people around me begin screaming as I stand still, not able to move, needing to watch every last second of his downfall. Mr. Carver begins to crumble, the blood pouring out of him in waves.

A trickle comes from the corner of his mouth, and as he meets my eyes, he drops to the ground and I find Carver standing right behind him, his eyes wide and glued to mine, having watched every last second.

I suck in a gasp, realizing what the fuck I've just done.

Rage burns within Carver's deadly stare, and I see the exact same resolve that I had—an eye for an eye. My heart races as fear begins to rock through me, then in a flash of murderous fury, Carver comes for me as a terrified squeal tears from between my lips.

Dynasty

Boys of Winter Series Playlist

Blood // Water - Grandson
Evil - 8 Graves
11 Minutes - Yungblud Ft. Halsey & Travis Barker
Hate The Way - G-Eazy Feat Blackbear
Control - Halsey
Play With Fire - Sam Tinnesz
You Should See Me In A Crown - Billie Eilish
Everybody Wants To Rule The World - Lorde
Courage To Change - Sia
You Broke Me First - Tate McRae
Yellow Flicker Beat - Lorde
Sweet Dreams - Marilyn Manson
Wicked Game - Daisy Gray
Nobody's Home - Avril Lavigne
Stand By Me - Ki: Theory
Paparazzi - Kim Dracula
Bringing Me Down - Ki: Theory (feat. Ruelle)
Therefore I am - Billie Eilish
I see Red - Everybody Love An Outlaw
In The Air Tonight - Nonpoint
Tainted Love - Marilyn Manson
Saviour - Daisy Gray
I Put A Spell On You - Annie Lennox
Heaven Julia Michaels
Heart Attack - Demi Lovato
Dynasty - Mia
Weak - AJR
Redemption - Besomorph & Coopex & RIELL
Legends Never Die - League of Legends & Against the Current
Time - NF
Rumors - NEFFEX

Thanks for reading!
If you enjoyed reading this book as much as I enjoyed writing it, please leave an Amazon review to let me know.
https://www.amazon.com/gp/product/B08QTYTXBW

For more information on Boys of Winter, stalk me online –

Facebook Page - www.facebook.com/SheridanAnneAuthor
Facebook Reader Group – www.facebook.com/SheridansBookishBabes
Instagram – www.instagram.com/Sheridan.Anne.Author

Other Series by Sheridan Anne

www.amazon.com/Sheridan-Anne/e/B079TLXN6K

YOUNG ADULT / NEW ADULT DARK ROMANCE
The Broken Hill High Series (5 Book Series + Novella)
Haven Falls (7 Book Series + Novella)
Broken Hill Boys (5 Book Novella Series)
Aston Creek High (4 Book Series)
Rejects Paradise (4 Book Series)
Black Widow (A Rejects Paradise Novella)
Boys of Winter (4 Book Series)

NEW ADULT SPORTS ROMANCE
Kings of Denver (4 Book Series)
Denver Royalty (3 Book Series)
Rebels Advocate (4 Book Series)

CONTEMPORARY ROMANCE
Men of Fire Rescue One (4 Book Series)
Until Autumn – Happily Eva Alpha World

URBAN FANTASY - PEN NAME: CASSIDY SUMMERS
Slayer Academy (3 Book Series)